A NARROW ESCAPE

Sofie heard roars in the house, roars up the stairs. She stooped and grabbed the bags and hurried to the balcony, where St. Maur leapt into space even as he was shifting shapes.

He leapt from the balcony railing and, for a second, she thought they'd both imagined it. That he wasn't going to change shapes, couldn't change shapes. That he was, in fact, just a man like other men. That he would now dash his brains out on that neat cobbled path they'd passed while entering the house.

It was easier to believe that she'd imagined his previous transformation than to see what was taking place before her very eyes—that smooth golden body twisting and writhing in midair; a sound like a strangled scream escaping his lips; a tail, wings, paws, scales extruding themselves from that mass that seemed much too small to contain them. And then the wings spreading...

The beast took to the air with a grace that denoted this was its natural environment. The wings of fire spread between her and the sky, and the dragon described a broad circle over the gardens before coming back to her.

Sofie resumed breathing, not aware she'd stopped for a moment. And then she realized that the loud roar behind her was closer, just a tiger's leap away. She looked over her shoulder and caught a glimpse of a tawny, sleek hide, and the vague impression of lifted hindquarters and lowered front as the creature prepared to jump.

There was a sound from the other side of the balcony that might have been a sneeze or a dragon-size exclamation of alarm. Forcing herself not to panic, she turned to see the dragon just by the balcony. Dropping the bags, she jumped onto the broad green back.

The dragon grabbed all the bags at the same time she saw the tiger leap. But it had come too late and could only roar in frustration as the dragon took wing....

SOUL
of
FIRE

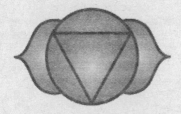

Sarah A. Hoyt

BANTAM BOOKS

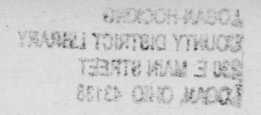

SOUL OF FIRE

A Bantam Spectra Book / August 2008

Published by
Bantam Dell
A Division of Random House, Inc.
New York, New York

ISBN 978-0-553-58967-2

Printed in the United States of America
Published simultaneously in Canada

www.bantamdell.com

OPM 10 9 8 7 6 5 4 3 2 1

To Dave Freer, a good friend
and one of the best writers at work today

SOUL OF FIRE

MAIDEN IN PERIL

"Mama, don't make me marry him," Miss Sofie Warington said.

Seventeen years old, clad in a white dressing gown and clutching a blue muslin dress to her ample bosom—with her hair quite untamed and her expression wild—Miss Warington should not have looked ravishing. But the way her dark hair fell in tumultuous waves to the bottom of her spine, the way tears trembled at the end of the long eyelashes surrounding her dark blue eyes, the way her lips opened to let through her impetuous words would have brought strong men to their knees.

They had less effect on her mother, Lavinia Warington. "Don't be foolish, girl," she said, her voice severe. "What are you doing out of your room? And why are you not dressed?" As she spoke, she skillfully shepherded her daughter up the spacious stairs, carpeted in expensive red velvet that showed wear in discolored, threadbare patches.

Sofie resisted, but it was useless. She felt out of step and like a stranger in this house. She'd been born into it seventeen years ago, and she'd spent her first ten years in its vast, resounding, sun-washed rooms, attended by a native ayah and adored and indulged by her parents' various servants. But at ten, she'd been put aboard a carpetship to London, where for seven years she'd been a pupil in Lady Lodkin's Academy for Young Lady Magic Users.

The summons to return home two weeks ago had overjoyed her. London had never felt like home to her. Too dark, too dank, and people were too ready to sneer at her honey-colored skin—the result of one of her ancestresses' being the Indian mistress of an English officer. She'd felt like a wayfarer in London. And yet, now home proved no home at all.

She'd found her mother and father to be far from the mythical, godlike figures who had watched over her childhood with pride and care. Her mother had grown bitter and her father . . . Her father didn't bear thinking about. She knew nothing of magical maladies, but she knew enough to guess when someone had been using dark magic, and using it far too extensively. And she knew it was an illness that could hardly be cured.

And then there was the reason they'd summoned her back home a year before her education was completed. It wasn't a longing for her company, as she'd hoped. And it wasn't even that they'd missed her. "Lalita told me that the man visiting tonight is a rich native raj from a distant kingdom," she accused her mother. "That he offered for me several months ago, and you . . . you accepted! Before I even returned."

"And how would she know this, since she has been in London as your attendant till just two weeks ago?"

"She says the kitchen servants talked about it. They said that's why you sent for me."

Sofie's mother's lips closed tightly, until they seemed to be but a single red line. "Lalita talks too much."

Sofie turned around fully, still clutching her dress, anxious fingers digging deeply into the folds of the material. "But is it true, Mama? Did she tell me the truth? How can you agree to give me away to a man I haven't even met? A man who..." Oh, if it was true, she had to run—somewhere, somehow—and find or make her own fortune.

"Child, you're being foolish. We are not giving you away to anyone. We found you a most advantageous marriage, one that most women in your position would give their eyeteeth for. The Raj Ajith is a powerful man, the ruler of a vast kingdom as native domains go, and he's agreed to make you his only wife. You will live covered in jewels and surrounded by servants. Trust me, Sofie, your lot could be worse."

As she spoke, Madame Warington propelled her daughter up the steep staircase, till, at the top landing, she could put her arm around the girl's small shoulders and shepherd her gently through the open doorway of her room.

The room, if not her parents, exactly matched Sofie's memories of childhood. It was, by far, vaster than anything she'd seen in England—almost as large as the dormitory that at the academy she'd shared with twenty other girls. The walls were whitewashed, since to wallpaper walls in India's hot and humid climate was quite futile. Even magically applied wallpaper started mildewing from the moisture within days of being put up, and peeled altogether from the humidity and heat within months. But the whitewash was fresh, and if the occasional lizard wandered in through the open balcony door and climbed the wall, it looked like a planned ornament.

The bed was piled high with lace and silk pillows, and covered in an intricate, colorful bedspread. The tightly woven lace netting draped over it lent it an air of romance. At least, it would if you didn't know how necessary it was to keep out the noxious flying insects that flourished in this climate. And all the silk and lace might give the impression of riches, if one didn't know how cheap they were. Why, even the servants wore silken saris and gaudy gold jewels on ears and nostrils.

Still clutching her dress, Sofie allowed herself to be pushed all the way to the vanity in the far corner. The mirror—showing dark spots in its silver backing—gave her back her own image, with high color on both cheeks and moisture in her eyes, and she wondered how her mother could distress her so and not care.

Meanwhile, her mother had removed the dress from Sofie's clutching fingers and clucked at the wrinkles marring the fine blue fabric. "Why, you absurd creature. You nearly ruined this. Lalita!"

Sofie's maid and the constant companion of her adolescence emerged from the balcony, where doubtless she'd run at their approach, trying to evade Mrs. Warington's wrath. But Mrs. Warington was more preoccupied with her daughter's attire right now than with punishing her garrulous maid.

Lalita, whose name meant playful and who looked it, wore a bright sky-blue sari, and large, golden hoop earrings through her ears. Her hair was caught into a heavy braid at her back. Not for the first time, Sofie found herself envying her maid's vitality, her beauty and, most of all, her unrepentant certainty about who she was. Not for Lalita to wonder if she was Indian or English, and which one she might be more. Lalita, born and raised in Calcutta—the daughter of people born and raised there for generations uncountable—might have gone to London with Sofie for seven long years, but she had never had any reason to consider herself anything but Indian.

She walked into the room with an expression of repentance that was no more believable than an expression of humility upon a cat's face. Bobbing a hasty curtsey, she took the dress and fairly ran with it out the door, presumably to do whatever it was one did to a dress to remove wrinkles.

Sofie, who didn't know nor care what that might be, allowed her mother to fuss over her hair. "I can't believe you'd go out there like this, Sofie," Mrs. Warington said. "What if anyone had seen you?"

"Lalita said *he* was with Papa in the veranda off the parlor, and she said he is quite gross. And, Mama, she was right." She shuddered at the memory of the enormous native grandee, his shapeless form covered in bright silks that would have done better service as sofa- or bed-coverings. But it was not his repulsive physique that had disgusted her. No. What made her tremble and swallow hard in fear were his features.

A native he might be, but Sofie, raised by natives, didn't consider that a problem. However, she'd never seen anyone who looked like him. His face was broad and oddly arranged, with a very low nose and cruel lips. Between the scars crisscrossing his features, and the intricate tattoos marking his forehead and cheeks, he looked . . . not quite human.

And then there were his eyes, slitlike and quite

yellow. The pupils were yellow-gold, but the sclera, too, had a yellowish tint, like aged porcelain or the teeth of a heavy smoker. Sofie shuddered at the memory.

"Mama, I—"

"Hush, girl," Mrs. Warington said, pulling hard on the heavy tresses she was plating into braids on either side of her daughter's face. "Don't make this into a melodrama. No one is going to force you to marry anyone you don't wish to. All I ask is that you look at Raj Ajith and think whether you could not stand to marry him."

"I've looked at him," Sofie said, as she remembered the man's smile, and the large sharp fanglike teeth that protruded from his thin lips. "There is nothing that could prevail upon me to consider marriage to—"

With a clatter Mrs. Warington set Sofie's silver-handled brush upon the polished mahogany dressing table. "Sofie, listen. You are old enough to know the truth. And the truth is that the chances of us finding you a respectable marriage with an Englishman in either England or India are next to none."

"I know you're going to say this is because I have Indian blood, but . . . Mother! Plenty of girls with more Indian blood than I have married exceedingly well. And besides—"

"Yes, doubtless," Mrs. Warington said. "Your father's grandmother married very well, but she brought with her an immense dowry accumulated by her nabob father. Enough so no one could say anything about her blood, or about the fact her parents never married and her mother was nothing but her father's native *bibi*. Yes, Sofie, money covers a multitude of sins, but that's where we fail, for we have none."

"No money?" Sofie asked, somewhat shocked.

A shadow crossed her mother's features. For a moment, the greenish eyes meeting hers in the mirror looked away.

"But you sent me to England!" Sofie protested. After all, only a small minority of girls were sent to England for their education, and certainly not those born to the very impecunious. Officers' brats, as a rule, stayed in India. As did almost any girl with any Indian blood. "And Papa inherited his mother's money, and—"

"We spent all our money sending you to England," her mother said, looking down, seemingly wholly absorbed in arranging Sofie's hair. Sofie wished she would look up and meet Sofie's eyes. Then she might judge the truth of her mother's words. Unnatural or not, she didn't feel as though she could trust her. "There is none left for your dowry. But surely you must understand what you owe your father and me. We ruined ourselves for your education. The least you can do is consider the marriage we arranged for you."

Sofie was stunned into silence by this consideration—a silence that subsisted till she was mostly dressed and her mother left to allow Lalita to drape a shawl artistically around her. Oh, she knew her family was not wealthy. But they had sent her to England and she thought there would be at least enough money for a modest dowry.

As soon as the door closed behind Mrs. Warington, Lalita looked at her mistress and said, with remarkable understatement, "You don't like him?"

"Like him? How could I? Lalita, he's the most despicable—" She didn't notice her own voice rising until Lalita put her finger to her lips.

"The other servants say he's not ... not what he

seems," Lalita said, in an urgent murmur. "His kingdom is very distant, but there are rumors..." She made a gesture, midair, as of someone averting a curse. "They call it the Kingdom of the Tigers, and it is said all English who go there disappear."

"But... what could he want with me?" Sofie asked, bewildered. It all came down to that one question. Granted, this man was a local ruler of some distant domain. But why would he want her? What could he possibly see in an English miss raised in Britain that would justify a promise to make her his only wife? "I don't think he's ever even glimpsed me."

Lalita looked grave, an expression ill-suited to her normally smiling countenance. "He told your father he saw your face and heard your name in a seeing. That you were the only one for him."

"He told my father..." Sofie repeated, as she absentmindedly arranged the folds of the shawl. "But you don't think it's true?"

"I... don't know. I think... I mean, I know he was very interested in your dowry."

"My dowry?" Sofie asked, shocked. "I have a dowry? But my mother said—"

"The ruby," Lalita said.

Sofie stared, astonished. "The ruby?" It wasn't that she didn't know what Lalita was talking about. She knew well enough. The jewel was all that remained of her father's half-breed grandmother's dowry. The money had been spent, and the other jewels sold for more money and also used up. All except the ruby.

The only reason it had been preserved was that though it was deep bloodred and of exceptional size, it was also flawed. A dark crack at its center marred not only its aesthetics but its magical properties as well. You could feel power flowing off the jewel, but it was erratic—now starting, now stopping, as unpredictable as the lightning that crossed the sky during monsoon season. And as likely to be harnessed for anything useful. Why, then, would the raj want that? Surely he was neither crazy nor stupid.

It had to be an excuse, and the excuse had to mean that he wanted *her*. But *why*?

"I don't understand it either, miss," Lalita said, and shrugged. "Only, all the talk in the servants' hall is that he insisted on the ruby for your dowry."

Sofie shook her head. From the middle of her room, she could see her reflection in the mirror without turning her head fully. Half-glimpsed out of the corner of her eye, she looked to herself like a comely woman, and shapely enough. Shapely enough to command love where her dowry could not demand respect.

She didn't think much of her dark locks, or the fact that her skin always had a slight honey tinge to it. But she had to admit she looked well enough.

Desperately, she thought of her days in London, and the carefully chaperoned balls she'd attended. There had been several men who had tried to fix their favor with her—though she supposed that her mother would say they did it in the belief her father had made his fortune in India. Perhaps they did. Sofie had always been a little suspicious of those men who declared they'd fallen in love with her after one look, or that one glance from her was enough to sustain them for days. She was doubtful of the ones who sent her roses and flowers and danced attendance to her night and day, with no encouragement and very little sustenance.

But one man hadn't been like that. In her mind rose the image of Captain William Blacklock. He had smoky-gray eyes, and was slim, dark-haired and ravishing in his red regimentals. He had told her he would marry her had circumstances been different. By which she was sure he meant he was afraid her parents would think him a disgraceful fortune hunter. Well, they couldn't think that now.

Her mind brought her, unbidden, the image of the man her parents had chosen for her. Beside Captain Blacklock, he didn't even seem the same species. And Sofie had no doubt whom she preferred.

Captain Blacklock had shipped to India three months before she did. She was sure of it. He'd told her he was being sent to Meerut with his regiment to put down some disturbance related to weres. Sofie hadn't heard about were unrest in India right now, and she'd have thought her parents would have told her. So she wasn't sure she'd heard Captain Blacklock right.

She remembered Meerut, though. She had no idea where it was, but she knew it was somewhere in India. Surely she could make it there. She must run away from home anyway. She had decided that as soon as she'd looked at the cruel, inhuman face of the unknown raj.

In his last words to her, William Blacklock had said he would gladly marry her if their circumstances permitted. Surely if she could make it to his side, he would not refuse her now.

Without a fortune, surely she was not beyond his reach.

DISPOSSESSED

Peter Farewell stumbled down the streets of Calcutta, looking like a drunken man but feeling all too starkly sober.

A tall Englishman with dark curls, his classical features—whose symmetry could have shamed the marbled perfection of ancient statues—were marred only by a black leather eye patch hiding his left eye. The right one, as though to compensate, shone brightly, and often sparkled with irony.

Many a woman had gazed into that eye and been captivated by the verdant depths that seemed to hide all promises and sparkle with possible romance. Peter Farewell knew his gaze's power and had consciously avoided capturing any hearts when he could not offer his own in return. For the last ten years, he'd known he wouldn't make anyone a good husband. Once, he'd dreamed of a world where he could live like anyone else—a world where he loved and could be loved. Now he did not know what dreams he had, if any. All he had was a mission. One at which he was failing miserably.

He walked blindly through Calcutta. He'd arrived here six months ago, and was staying in one of the

palatial mansions of Garden Reach—the place inhabited by East India Company employees and their families. The vast houses would make most noble families
in England blush with envy, and it put Peter's own inherited estate, the rambling Summercourt, to shame.

Summercourt... As his mind dwelt on his ancestral
house, his hand plunged into the pocket of his exquis-
itely tailored suit to feel a bundle of papers. He did not
need to take it from his pocket to see its text floating
before his gaze as vividly as if he were reading. The top
line said: *To Peter Farewell. Lord Saint Maur.*

He hadn't needed to read the next lines—though he
had—nor the twelve pages following to know what his
estate manager was telling him. That Peter's father was
dead. That Peter was now the only heir to that ancient
and noble family name descended from Charlemagne.

The manager's faithful account of Peter's inheritance made Peter groan. He'd received the letter—by
bearer—just before dinner, and how he'd gotten through
dinner he'd never know. He'd left immediately after.
He'd gone, without quite knowing how, all the way to
Esplanade Row, where he now stared at the impressive facade of Government House. Like his estate
manager's letter, it resonated with the power of the expected and the prearranged. The manager never said
it, but it was clear in his every word that he expected
Peter—who for the last ten years had been abroad and
had sown his wild oats, such as they were—to return
and shoulder the name of Farewell, the title of Saint
Maur and the responsibilities and needs of his house
and retainers.

Not that there was much. At least, there hadn't
been when Peter had last seen it. A large, rambling

farm, and an assortment of smaller farms, let to various tenant families. Enough for a shabby gentility of the kind that supported a living similar to a wealthy farmer's, with pretensions that would make the royal family's seem small.

But compared to the way he had been living, it would be paradise. He couldn't think of his north-country domains without longing for the smells of the fields around his house. He craved the twang of local speech; the Sunday afternoons in semi-deserted streets; the parks visited by serene families, the children named for kings and queens; the museums; the lending libraries; the places that had sheltered his childhood when he was, in fact, still full of illusions. When he still thought that he might grow up to be Peter Farewell, Earl of Saint Maur, scion of a noble family.

Only it couldn't be. Oh, England had shape-shifters aplenty among its noble families. Despite the law's command that they all be killed upon discovery, it was an open secret that several noble families threw out weres now and then.

But all known noble weres were foxes or dogs or—at worse—wolves.

There was even a charming story of a Scottish nobleman who turned into a seal at the waxing of the moon. But Peter didn't have that innocuous a form. His other shape was a dragon. An eater of humans. A killer.

It was beyond the pale to even think of such a dangerous beast being tolerated. Witness the story of Richard Lionheart, trudging his weary way home from the Crusades, only to be put to death because more of him was a lion than his heart.

The laws that had allowed John Lackland to execute his older brother and lawful sovereign were still extant. And still enforced.

Tomorrow morning, early, he'd pen a letter for his manager, apprising him of his intent to never return. The man would be disappointed. He would possibly be crushed, destroyed by such a complete break with the past and by his internal certainty that Peter did not care about house or family. Let him think it. If that kept Peter's secret—and if it kept Peter safe—it was enough.

Peter would stay in India and try to fulfill his mission here. He'd find Soul of Fire, the ruby once used to bind all the magic of Europe to Charlemagne. Six months ago, on the highlands near Darjeeling, he'd separated from Nigel, who might be his last friend in the world, and he'd promised Nigel that he'd find the ruby. And then he'd reunite with Nigel—who held the ruby's twin, Heart of Light, which would attract Soul of Fire like a beacon—so Nigel could return both stones to the temple at the heart of Africa, the oldest temple of mankind.

Neither man knew what would happen once the jewels were returned to the temple. They'd been convinced that such an act was necessary to prevent a horrible catastrophe, which would bring them as close to the end of the world as bore no distinction. But Peter didn't think it would in any way improve his life or his material circumstances. He presumed he would still be followed by his curse, still separated from normal men and limited in how close to them he could live. Yet, for the last six months, since his visit to the temple, the curse had been so slight and so easily controlled that he'd dared to dream. Perhaps once the rubies were returned he would be free. . . .

But now, after six months of following a long-dead trail for the ruby that Charlemagne had used to bind magical power to him and his descendants, and then abandoned, he'd grown to believe the jewel had been cut up or destroyed, and no longer existed. His scrying instruments and all his attempts at divination showed him nothing. They had led him here, to Calcutta. For a brief, shining moment, he had been sure the jewel was here. Right in this city. And then, before he could pinpoint its location, the trail had vanished. His scrying instruments had been unable to find it again.

Meaning he'd live out his days in India, futilely trying to find an artifact that couldn't be found.

He'd already broken his father's heart, through no design of his own, on that cold morning so many years ago, when his father had discovered Peter's secret. He had packed his son up and told him to get out—and stay out. Money would find him, but he must not—he must never—make his way to Summercourt again. He remembered his father's dour face and the instruction: "Seek some form of employment that will not disgrace you. And strive not to commit more sins than needed."

Did his father know then that it would be the last time they'd see each other? He had to, didn't he? He'd told Peter to stay away and never let their paths cross again.

Something caught at the back of Peter's throat, something that might have been laughter or tears, he wasn't sure which. He looked up, trying to find something to fix his eyes upon, something that would take his mind off his own misery and the final renunciation of his inheritance, his birthplace—his own being—that he must perform in the morning. And he saw the girl creeping along the outside of a veranda's railing.

"Good God," he said to himself. "What can she be about?"

Then his body contorted in cough, as fear for the stranger's circumstances disturbed the balance of his mind, and allowed the beast within to take control. . . .

DESPERATE GAMBLE

"How far away is Meerut?" Sofie asked.

"I'm sure I don't know, miss," Lalita answered, primly, with just that hint of panic in her eyes. After all, she'd known her mistress since they were both young girls and she'd been party to a thousand of Sofie's plans. She was doubtless thinking of the unfortunate incident with the cat and the bread pudding. "But I'm sure it would be very far away."

Sofie was aware that many of her more elaborate schemes had failed to come off, but this time she had no room for doubt, and no room for fear. Fear was that thing in the veranda with Papa—the unknown raj who coveted her for who knew what dark reasons.

"Yes, I suppose it would," she told Lalita, reasonably. Then, quickly, "Find me one of my carpetbags, the sort I brought back with me. We'll put into it as many outfits as will fit. They will have to do, I suppose."

Lalita hesitated, her lively face showing something very much like a doubt. "Miss, only . . ."

"Only what?" Sofie asked.

"Only . . . shouldn't you dress yourself as a boy,

perhaps, and cut your hair?" Lalita said, as she got the carpetbag from the wardrobe.

"No time for that," Sofie said. The thought had crossed her mind, though. After all, it was what girls did when preparing to run away from home in all the novels that she and Lalita had read while in England. But then, she wasn't running away from home, or not exactly. She was going to find her fiancé. Or at least the man who would be her fiancé as soon as he knew he would be permitted to claim her. As such, it was the height of folly to dress as a boy. William wouldn't like that. Besides, finding male clothes—they would have to be her father's, or else servant attire, and she wasn't sure how that would look since she spoke none of the native dialects and had been away so long that she didn't know any of the customs, either—and cutting her hair would take time. Sofie had none.

"Any moment now, Mama will come back and demand to know why I'm taking so long." While she spoke, she hurried to the large, dilapidated wardrobe that took up a whole wall of her room. Opening it, she reached in, grabbing armfuls of dresses and blouses, skirts, shawls and a sturdy traveling cloak, which she proceeded to try to cram into a large carpetbag.

Lalita made a sound of distress, as any would seeing her own profession so dreadfully misperformed, and took bag and clothes away. Folding the clothing swiftly, she said, "You could wait till after dinner. While the men have port and cigars, you could come upstairs and cut your hair. I'll get a suit of clothes for you while you are gone, and I'll find out the best way for you to take. Perhaps we could take a boat."

"That's quite ridiculous," Sofie said, sternly. "Since

we have no idea if Meerut is near water. As for the rest..." She gave it a moment's thought, then she shook her head. "I don't trust my parents, Lalita. All of this is so strange—their having accepted an offer on my behalf, and such an offer, from a native whose kingdom they haven't bothered to describe to me that..." She shook her head. "They could very well decide to imprison me, or perhaps to give me over to this creature, somehow, during the dinner. I'm sure they will if they sense the slightest reluctance, or even suspect that I have intentions of escaping. No, Lalita, I must leave now."

She could never explain all of it to Lalita. The girl might be her best friend from childhood, but she was also a servant and a native. However, Sofie was thinking of the way her father looked, as though he'd aged thirty years in the seven years she'd been away. That, and the curious darkness around his eyes, spoke of the use of black arts—of employing evil resources such as human sacrifice to augment the natural magical power inherited from his parents. If this was true—if her father had been devoting himself to the unholy—she wasn't even sure that he wouldn't attempt to sacrifice *her*.

She felt unnatural even thinking it, but she had— while in England—read more than fiction. She had read enough of the histories and compendiums in the academy's moldy library to know about dark magic and what it did to people and their morals.

But Lalita looked reluctant and pale. Sofie wasn't sure if she was afraid for her, or simply afraid of the retribution Sofie's parents would visit on Lalita herself, once Sofie's escape became known.

"I'm not sure—" Lalita began.

"I am," Sofie said, firmly.

"Sofie?" Mrs. Warington's voice sounded from down the stairs. "Sofie?"

"I have to go, Lalita." Sofie picked up the valise and ran across the room, then went through the open doors onto the veranda. Behind her, she could hear her room door open and her mother cry, "Where is she, Lalita? Where did she go?"

She couldn't hear Lalita's reply, but she could hear the sound of her mother's hand hitting the maid's face. And then her mother's steps toward the veranda.

Sofie had run around the corner. The house had a veranda on each of the three upper levels—and all completely encircled the house. This one was on the topmost level. From the level below, she could hear her father and the creature talk.

Mentally, she was thinking she needed a sheet or a rope or a curtain. But the open doors she passed—the doors to her parents' rooms—showed servants moving about inside. She ran madly, hearing her mother's steps behind her.

She must climb over the veranda railing. Perhaps she could dangle from this level onto the next one. Perhaps she could . . .

Blindly, she climbed over the railing, hands scratching at the rough stone. Holding on with one hand, the other grasping her carpetbag, she tried to feel with her foot for the railing below. But the railing was too far away and she couldn't manage it, and her mother was running and calling, "Sofie! Oh, you unlucky girl. Don't—"

And then her hold on the stone parapet gave.

THE DRAGON

Seeing the girl fall, Peter let go of his final shred of self-control. Urges and impulses he'd thought well under control ran through him. The urge to change. To become a dragon. And now...

He'd found out long ago, and through his own experience, how frail those railings were. They looked like solid stone, but the places where pieces joined often crumbled under the joint action of the climate and shoddy workmanship.

He coughed and contorted. Without knowing quite what he was doing, with long-practiced haste, he removed his clothes, blindly, by touch, even as his shape shifted. The foot with which he kicked them under the edge of the Holwell Monument to the Black Hole disaster was already changing to something taloned and much larger than a human foot ever was.

Before he could check himself or think of what he was doing, he was flying through the dark, scented night, toward the balcony and the falling girl. He was barely aware of a woman's shrill scream splitting the night. He was aware of excitement and babble from the native houses, but none of it mattered.

There was the air, and his wings cutting through it, lifting him higher and higher.

He couldn't think in dragon form as he did in human form. While his reason remained, submerged within the blind irrationality of the brute, thoughts came haltingly and slow—mostly sensations and the immediate results of those sensations.

And yet at the back of it, his the human self remained, conscious and aware, if rarely in control. He felt the girl fall, the weight on his back, felt the dragon fly away with only the thought of escape in its head, even as the girl straddling it screamed and pummeled its scaly back with what felt like a small, clenched fist.

This scared the dragon and confused him. It had been too long since Peter had allowed it sway. The dragon wanted to escape, both from the closed-in society of humans and from the human on its back. It started to turn its head, the half-formed idea of flaming the creature off its back taking over its befuddled brain—and beyond that there was the distant plan of flying away to some forest and hunting in peace. It had learned that Peter wouldn't normally allow it to eat humans, and after the energy burned in the transformation, it longed for food in the quantities the human form couldn't take.

But Peter, at the back of the dragon's mind, knew better. He couldn't just fly to some wilderness with this lost child on his back. He could feel her heels kicking at him as her panic mounted, and he wasn't sure that he could fly much farther without her jumping from his back in a fit of sheer terror.

The dragon flew, madly, to the outskirts of Calcutta, and Peter got a sharply delineated black-

and-white panorama of the town, lively even at this hour—with turbans and Red Coats, and servants in white, and carriages. To Peter, at the back of the creature's mind, slices of what the dragon felt and saw were relayed in snatches and bits.

The Hooghly—the branch of the Ganges that ships took up to Calcutta—was crammed with vessels of many nationalities, from transport ships to pleasure cruisers. Farther out were the great sandbanks built by the muddy waters, which made navigation so difficult and made the pilots of Calcutta such a close-knit guild. And stretching ten miles down the river were the warehouses and other necessities of international trade. On the opposite side of the Hooghly was Howrah—the end point of three railway systems, and headquarters to countless factories. There was the carpetport, where flying carpets—with the necessary buildings upon them—flew in from destinations around the globe.

Enough of Peter's sense remained in the dragon's mind that he did not wish to be seen by landing carpetships.

If Her Majesty's Were-Hunters should come after him, things would become ugly. Yet the rumor held—and Peter hoped it was true—that there were so many weres in India at every class of society that though Gold Coats had landed in all the great cities, they dared not hunt them.

Even an outsider had heard of the fearsome elephant soldiers of Jaipur. They'd sown fear and destruction in their wake during the rebellion of 1857, and had then vanished into nothing, melting back into the locals, with many, doubtless, returning to their posts in British regiments.

In fact, it was the Gold Coats' attempts to destroy Indian weres that had led to the current rumors of new riots, a new revolt.

No, should the Gold Coats in India become active, they would have their work cut out for them. And meanwhile, Peter would be safe. Maybe safe long enough to find Soul of Fire, though he was starting to doubt the existence of the historic ruby—and certainly his ability to find it.

He reached into the dragon's mind and managed— desperately and through long practice—to turn the creature around, lead it back to the balcony.

Every instinct in the beast—that, somehow, was also Peter—struggled against his dominion and control, demanded to escape the confines of Calcutta.

But Peter, feeling himself in command of paws and claws and powerful wings, was trying—desperately— to control as much as he could without forcing the creature's reversal to human.

Balancing on that precarious edge, he bent back toward Calcutta and the foreign palaces that stood out very white in the dragon's field of vision. Tilting, banking, but not so much that he would lose the burden on his back, he tried to get close to the balcony where two men and a woman were calling out confused demands that he bring *her* back.

One of the men had a powerstick. This did not worry the dragon, who knew it took especially bespelled powersticks to hurt his kind, and a veritable barrage of such fire to kill him. It worried Peter, a little, since he knew for certain sure that about half the powersticks in India were bespelled against weres. They had to be, considering how often one's own servant was likely to turn into a fearsome beast. At least, those were the stories of Indian expatriates who were forever talking of the dangers of native servants—and were just as determined to not give them up. After all, Sahibs could not be expected to do the menial work themselves.

But all the same, Peter—still at that edge of control, where he could move the dragon without forcing it to become human, something that would be at best disastrous, midair and with a girl on his back—thought his best bet was to return his fair charge to her place.

"No, please. Anything but that. Don't make me go back!" the girl screamed as they approached the balcony.

The dragon thrashed to remove the unwanted burden from its back, which only caused a fresh panic of shrill screaming. Peter reached for the dragon's mind, and conveyed without words *easy, easy, easy*.

What was left of his rational capacity—seeming very remote from the senses of the body the beast occupied—struggled to reason through. The girl did not want to go back. Why did the girl not want to go back?

And like a nettle piercing through skin, suddenly came the thought that of course she did not wish to go back. After all, she had been walking around outside the railing of the balcony. What creature did that who did not mean to leave home and family behind?

He did not know why, but this much he was sure of. The demoiselle now straddling the beast's back, warming it with a heat that Peter could feel even through the beast's scales, was a runaway. It was not his place to wonder why. And besides, the beast, in a panic, let Peter see the gentleman on the balcony leveling a powerstick at the dragon yet again.

Peter released some of his control and he could feel the great wings struggling to beat down the air, propelling the dragon away from the balcony at all speed.

Behind the dragon, the powerstick erupted, but all Peter felt—distantly—was a warmth on the dragon's flank. Not hit. He knew what hits felt like. This was merely the far-reaching warmth of the power explosion.

He should land, Peter thought. Land and change back. And then Peter thought of his clothes, shoved behind the Black Hole Monument. Normally he would not have cared to go back and retrieve them. Normally he'd have directed the dragon to the vicinity of the house in which he was a houseguest. But he had a female on his back, and he couldn't be walking around, naked, with a girl. Besides that, he didn't know who the girl was or what she meant to do with her hard-won freedom. And he could hardly show up at his hosts' home with her.

But the monument was not far. So he directed the beast's flight at housetop level, then lower down. Its outspread wings grazed the edges of buildings on either side, and its senses—sharper than those of the human Peter—could taste cardamon and curry, while its ears were assaulted by a multitude of musical instruments and, from one home, a female voice raised in sweet song.

Confused, almost lost, since he could not see through his human eyes or orient himself with his human sense, Peter was relieved to glimpse the scant moonlight reflecting off a vast square of black marble paving—which exactly defined the dimensions of the Black Hole, in which 146 Britishers had been locked away, and from which the next morning only 26 had emerged alive, having survived the close confinement, the lack of air and the heat of a Calcutta summer.

It was almost certain that the deaths had resulted from nothing so much as miscalculation and the natives' fear of waking their nawab, who had retired to bed after ordering the men confined. Still, it was counted in England as one of the many reasons the Indians should not be allowed to rule themselves.

This thought was in Peter's mind—not so much in clear words, but in a certain feeling of frustration and despair—as the dragon's paws touched the sun-warmed black marble. The dragon tucked its wings in and Peter—madly, with all his strength—tried for control of their joint mind before the dragon could flame his burden. He felt said burden slip down his back scales and step to the side. He heard the sound of her soles on the marble—but only as through a haze.

With all his willpower, he was holding fast to the dragon, preventing it from turning and flaming, forcing it to yield control to Peter and give up its form for Peter's. It was not easy. The dragon disliked turning into Peter as much as Peter disliked turning into the dragon. There had been times in his life where if he could have separated himself from the beast, Peter would have willingly—nay, gladly—killed the creature.

But now he felt no hatred, only urgency, as he gentled the brute into giving him control of their joint mind and into allowing him to change their body into human form again. The dragon contorted and danced in a mad rictus of pain as bone slid over bone and flesh altered its shape. Wings and tail melted away and back into the body, and legs became long and human, and the teeth shrank to Peter's accustomed, well-shaped human set.

The transformation, though fueled by magic, wasn't easy. Peter felt the pain wrenching the creature's body, the grinding of bones, the seeming tearing of flesh. Lost in the mortal pains of change, he thought the girl must have run away by now. She must be running madly through the streets of Calcutta to alert her compatriots that there was a were-dragon on the loose, to call the wrath of the Gold Coats upon him.

Trembling, he found himself human, his hand holding on to the foot of one of the heroic statues that surmounted the black marble. Sweat covered his body, cooling it even as the warm night breezes blew upon him. Panting, he blinked to clear his remaining eye of the sweat that had run into it, making it sting.

He must get his clothes. He must leave this place as soon as possible. By the time the girl found someone to listen to her wild story, he must be well away, back at the home of his kind hosts, who had lodged him in Calcutta for six months, without ever suspecting that Peter might be a were-dragon. They'd vouch for him and he'd...

Something—he'd never be sure quite what: a sound of indrawn breath or perhaps a shuffle of shoes upon the marble—called his gaze. The girl had not run away screaming. Granted, her pink, well-shaped lips were opened in what could be construed as shock, and her hands were clutching her carpetbag a little harder than strictly necessary. But still, there was in her dark blue eyes something that was very akin to curiosity.

And that seemed to be enough to keep her silent, whatever else she felt.

"I beg your pardon," he said, his voice coming out shaky, like the voice of someone very tired, which he was after his transformation. "I beg your pardon, miss." The words were automatic, as he fumbled under the monument for his clothes and quickly pulled on his underwear. "I should not be in a state of undress."

She didn't answer for a long moment, and neither did she move. He wondered if he'd so wounded her sensibilities that she'd lost her senses. He should probably be very grateful she wasn't swooning, or else crying, but he didn't know what to do if she presently suffered an apoplexy of some sort. He knew nothing of first aid. For too long, he'd known more about killing humans than helping them.

The girl cleared her throat. Her voice shook, too, as she answered, though her words strived, at least, to be sensible. "I imagine it must be very inconvenient," she said. "To change shape like that. You must ruin a fair number of suits."

Peter let his gaze sweep over her. He didn't notice any horror of his missing eye—lost in circumstances he was loathe to explain—nor any squeamishness because of this deformity. Instead, she stared at his face, her own grave and attentive, like a schoolgirl's. Except always for that twinkle that seemed to hide at the back of her eyes and which might be, in fact, nothing but his own imagination. He wondered if she was making fun of him. But it was too much to imagine that a young girl of respectable birth, probably delicately nurtured, would find anything funny in a man who became a dragon or a dragon who became a man.

Still, his suspicion of her amusement made his voice dry as he answered. "You can't imagine. Fortunately, I've learned to undress very quickly." As he spoke, he fastened his pants and proceeded to put on his shirt with fleet hands. There had been a time, in his early youth, where he'd have shrunk from the thought of performing this task without a valet. But years and circumstances, not to mention exile in foreign lands and extreme poverty—as well as the secret he must keep—had changed him. He now found it very odd to have a valet assigned to him at his hosts' house.

Something flickered in her gaze in response to his words, and she frowned a little, bringing very straight, dark eyebrows down over her eyes. "It must hurt..." she said. "The transformation. It looked as if it hurt." She looked uncertainly up at him as he fastened his sleeves by touch.

Like being drawn and quartered, he thought. Aloud, he said, "Yes," and looked away, quickly pulling on his waistcoat and his coat and checking the pockets of the coat for the letters, which he felt—one crisper than the other—rustling under his fingertips.

They recalled him to the memory of his obligations. Nigel was moving from place to place around the world, trying to keep the other ruby, Heart of Light, safe—moving, always moving to avoid those who would snatch the jewel from him—waiting for Peter to meet him and give him Soul of Fire, the ruby that Peter was starting to believe no longer existed, or perhaps never had existed and was a cosmic prank on him. And there was Summercourt, in far distant England, with its somnolent home farm, its flocks of white sheep upon the green hillsides. Peter must write and renounce it, no matter how much it hurt.

He put on the patch that hid the closed lid over his missing eye and turned smoothly to the girl. "You'll pardon me," he said. "Why . . . why didn't you wish to be taken back to your house? What happened to make you leave? I suppose you think I kidnapped you—or . . . or the dragon did. And I'm sure your good parents think the same, judging from the powerstick that greeted my attempt at returning you."

She bit the corner of her lip. She started to shake her head. Whatever arrangement her hair had been in, it had become wholly disarrayed through their flight, and it now hung in enchanting tendrils around her face, making her look less like a proper miss and more like a fairy or an elf of legend—an escaped woodland creature not quite at home in the human world.

She turned her eyes to him, and he was shocked to see they were not just dark blue, as he'd thought. They were a blue almost black, deep and textured like the sky over his father's estate at twilight in summer. If he stared long enough, he swore he would see stars shining back at him from their depths.

She sighed in turn, and her eyelids, fringed with long, dark eyelashes, fluttered half-closed. "I ran away," she said, "to avoid marriage. Even being kidnapped by a dragon would be better than that union."

SAHIB STILL
WOULDN'T LISTEN

Captain William Blacklock woke up to screams. They were the shrill, toneless screams of an aged native.

In the heat of the Indian summer, the captain had gone to sleep in nothing but his underwear, and now he arose from the camp bed, not quite awake, and grabbed for his sword with a hand made slippery by sweat. He stumbled on bare feet across the Chittai rug made of woven rush.

When his feet hit the cold, damp stone of the *ghuslkhanah*—what passed for a bathroom in these parts, though it rarely contained more than a thunder box and a hip bath—his eyes half opened and his mind became alert enough for him to understand that the man screaming was his *bhisti:* his assigned water carrier. And what the man was screaming was "Snake, snake," or as close to the English pronunciation of the word as he could get with a near-toothless mouth.

Bringing his eyes fully open with an effort, and forcefully pushing back the remnants of his dream, William saw the offending creature: a shiny, wet-looking green-and-red serpent coiled on the stone floor

and raising its head to attack. It was not a very scary
sight, as it was quite common for snakes of all sorts,
poisonous as well as inoffensive, to crawl into the
ghuslkhanah through the hole in the wall that served
to empty the bathwater. They were doubtless attracted by the damp and the coolness, more hospitable
than the heat everywhere else in the merciless sun of
summer.

William did not know if this snake was poisonous or
inoffensive. And it did not matter. He swept his sword
in an arc. The snake turned its attention to him at the
movement, but it was too late to strike. The head went
flying to a corner of the room, while the body contorted
on the stone.

The water carrier—an elderly man, his dark face
wrinkled like a dried plum—stepped back, looking
with something that might be disgust at the remains of
the reptile, and William sighed. The rules of caste in
India. He knew, vaguely, that there were four castes
and that many of the sepoys came from either the warrior class or the Muslim population, which, like the
Christians, stood quite outside the caste system. As for
domestic service, he very much doubted that anything
but out-castes would work for the Englishmen. And
yet, it was clear that there were distinctions among
them and that one of the distinctions made it impossible for anyone but the so-called sweeper caste to have
anything to do with dead animal flesh.

On the other hand, it was quite possible that his
water carrier was hoaxing him and simply didn't want
to deal with the dead snake. William neither knew nor
cared. A few months in India and he was feeling as if it
were a punishment that would never end. He used the

tip of his sword to flick first the body and then the head out of the hole in the wall, and ignoring the obsequious bowing of the *bhisti,* stomped into his bedroom.

He couldn't even say why he was so resentful of the man, so uncomfortable with everything here.

Except...except that having refused to marry Sofie Warington, whom his superiors had tried to press him to offer for on the principle that the feel of the jewel they sought was thick all about her—a cause he considered insufficient to tie himself to the lovely and resourceful girl with whom he was, unfortunately, not in love—he'd been sent to India to find the jewel himself. Some rumor had been concocted, something to explain his presence here—about resentment among the natives for the presence of the Were-Hunters. Gold Coats had been dispatched first, to major cities, to create an opportunity for the rumor.

Blacklock didn't for a moment doubt that the natives must indeed resent the Were-Hunters with all their hearts. They lived a life closer to the beasts of the field—as William's clergyman father was all too fond of saying—and as such tolerated those who changed from beast to human more easily than Englishmen did. In fact, with their gods who took animal forms, and their idea of reincarnation up and down the scale of creation, their attitude was no surprise. So though weres were forbidden under Her Majesty's rule, the law had never been enforced, or not seriously.

No, the Gold Coats had been sent to India—that William knew—for one reason only: to find the were—the British were, at that—who had been reported to be in possession of the jewel Heart of Light, taken from the primal temple of mankind. And so far the Gold Coats had failed at that mission.

But their presence on the subcontinent, and the largely imaginary native resistence to it, had been used as a pretext to send William and another twenty-five officers to India, to reinforce far-flung garrisons.

As a reinforcement they were inadequate. As a cover, they were good enough. They had allowed William to spend a month in Calcutta, gossiping and looking about. But the document that reported the existence of this mythical were said nothing else about its human form—whether he was a sailor or a soldier, a merchant or a nobleman. From what William understood, the rumor had reached Lord Wiltington—the new head of Her Majesty's Secret Service since poor Lord Widefield's death—through curiously broken channels of native tribesmen, railroad employees and finally operatives in the north of Africa.

It was said that a dragon had taken the most magical jewel in the world—Heart of Light—to parts unknown. The twin of the jewel—Soul of Fire—had been stolen by an envoy of Charlemagne and used to bind the magical power that existed in small amounts to the descendants of Charlemagne alone. It should have guaranteed the permanence in Europe of order and of the one true monarchy.

Unfortunately, noblemen were as prone to sins of the flesh as other men. Or perhaps more. The descendants of Charlemagne had spread their seed with abandon, so that eleven hundred years later everyone from high nobility to country squires like William's own great-uncle to a few enterprising peasants had magic enough to challenge the holy rule of monarchs.

The result had been revolutions spreading across the world—from Britain's loss of the colonies in the Americas, to the revolution in France, to anarchy and rebellion in every corner of the globe. Worse, the enterprising members of the lower classes had banded together to introduce things like trains and flying carpets and textile factories operated wholly by magic.

While this was, William supposed, good in itself, it enriched the lower classes above the noblemen and gentry so that even those who weren't revolutionary were starting to get their claws on the nobility—through loans, through mixed marriages, all of it resulting in a great leveling and a complete dissolution of order.

This William understood, and he understood it very well. His father had told him early on that the worst possible thing that could happen to the world was to see chaos loosed upon it, and also had shown him through history that the only reason Europe had risen above the other lands was Charlemagne's action. Only that had allowed noblemen to impose order and forward civilization.

William knew, therefore, that it was imperative that Her Majesty get the ruby and rebind the power to the proper people. He even understood that finding Soul of Fire, spent though it was, had become imperative, as it would, unfailingly, point to the now-vanished Heart of Light

And he understood, though for personal reasons he very much wished he didn't, that it was necessary to come to India, the last place Soul of Fire had been. But William wanted out of India as soon as possible. Before he died here.

He'd been dreaming again. Dreaming of the hordes of weres descending on them from the nearby forest. Worse than that was the idea that the rebellion of 1857 and the massacres that had surrounded it would repeat themselves. The excuse given to send him to India seemed all too plausible an outcome to his stay. He knew it wasn't rational. He knew it was superstitious fear. But in the dark of night, it seemed much too real.

He sat down heavily on the side of his narrow bed and frowned at the sweat-soaked sheets. From everywhere around the cantonment came the sound of military men waking and getting ready for the day. The smell of the cow dung used to warm his bathwater, and for cooking breakfast, stung his nose. He heard the stomping of feet and native voices calling. Somewhere, farther off, there was the sound of men's feet falling in cadence, accompanied by what sounded like a marching song.

There were maybe, all told, one hundred and fifty Englishmen in Meerut—even including the ten officers, William among them, who had arrived here in the last two months. Surrounding them were thousands of sepoys and native officers. It seemed foolish, crazy, with the rebellion having happened less than fifty years ago, to keep such low numbers. But how else could they do it? The British could not hold India by numbers. It would empty their small island to send forth enough people to command this mass of humanity. So they must control the natives by bluff and courage. And that required as few officers as possible, to impress the natives with their daring.

And then, William thought, the fact was that the

rebellion was well forgotten. He remembered it only because his grandfather had been killed in it, among the wretched garrison of Cawnpore, fortunately leaving his wife in England, alone with their child. She'd been scheduled to join him but had not embarked before news of his death reached her.

There were books and stories aplenty, all over England, about both the mutineers' barbarism and the heroism of the defenders. Though very young, he remembered wondering how the writers could know what had happened in those many places where every Englishman had been killed.

Worse, no one remembered those stories *truely* anymore. And no one remembered them enough to take the lessons that needed to be taken from them.

Having read his grandfather's letters to his grandmother—many of which had arrived well after his grandpapa's death—William, the second son of the third son of a fairly prosperous esquire, had signed on to the secret service and agreed to a cover identity as a captain of the regulars, but he'd sworn he'd never go to India. Never.

And now here he was. Here because of the rubies and Her Majesty's determination to secure them. And yet, he dreamed of riots. It wouldn't worry him so much if his magical power, such as it was, didn't run to scrying, to foreseeing.

He sighed deeply again, as his blood-soaked dreams visited his consciousness in vivid and glaring images. These gifts of his were so scientifically ill-defined and so often wrong—in everyone—that his dreams were not enough to alarm his superiors. They would say he was going all to nerves and pieces and that the dreams came from that, not foreseeing. His superiors had, in fact, got into the habit of dismissing him on anything relating to India.

He was aware, without paying it much attention, that his *bhisti* was carrying back and forth can after can of water. They were recycled kerosene cans and it took so long to heat the water for the bath in these that by the time the tub was suitably full most of the water was barely tepid.

In many ways, it seemed reprehensible to have commanded a daily bath, but sweating as he did every night—between his nightmares and the close-in humid air—he didn't feel he had a choice. Whatever was said about vapors or humors, his grandfather had written to his grandmother, and William had grown up believing, if you washed yourself, you were far less likely to succumb to one of those fevers that were often ascribed to the climate of India.

While the *bhisti* went back and forth, William thought of the man who'd come to see him yesterday. Was that a corroboration of his dreams? Enough at least to call them prophetic and to mention them to his superiors.

Gyan Bhishma, one of the sepoys, had come to William with hints that there was something brewing, but he'd been reluctant to talk because there were other sepoys nearby. William remembered the word *tigers,* and presumed the man meant were-tigers.

As the water carrier entered the room, bowing to announce that Sahib's bath was quite ready, William said, "Would you tell Gyan Bhishma, the sepoy, to come to me?"

The *bhisti* bowed again, and William hoped that

meant he would tell the person considered appropriate, by whatever the protocol was, to run such an errand. He felt tired and impatient. Some part of him, the child who had read his grandfather's letters and heard his grandfather's acerbic comments on people who ignored native culture, despised the way he didn't take in the local customs or the ranks of the servants. But William didn't want to be here. Ever since he'd read the letters of his grandfather, for whom he was named, William had feared he would die in India.

He submerged himself in the tepid water and washed briskly, savoring the coolness of the room and the water. It was shortly after sunrise, but the sun would soon be a fiery ball in the sky and the air would be heating till it felt like an oven. And William wondered when the monsoon rains were supposed to come, and if they would be soon. He wanted the promised coolness he'd heard about. He felt as though if it were only to rain, everything would cool down, the tempers of the natives with it.

He had dressed and was shaving in front of a mirror when Gyan came in. He was what William's grandfather would doubtless have described as a "likely lad" or some other similarly approving epithet. He was tall for a native, just shy of the six feet reached by William himself. He was close-shaved; his hair, longer than regulation, was combed and tied into a ponytail at the back; his uniform, impeccable and spotless; his eyes, clear; his features, regular and almost European in their cast, or at least made in such a mold that might have befit a statue of antiquity. He saluted William and took the other man's wave to mean that he could stand at ease. Only, he must have been in the British army a long time, because his version of at-ease still retained a hint of military poise.

"Sahib wished to see me?" he said. His voice was pleasant and his accent near flawless.

William looked around the room and listened for sounds that indicated anyone might be close by. His *bhisti* had withdrawn after emptying the bathwater, and he would now, doubtless, be doing whatever he did during the long days, till it was time to set up things for William's bedtime. And there didn't seem to be anyone else close enough to listen in.

"Yesterday," William said, casting his voice just above a whisper, "you told me something about tigers?" In the mirror, he saw the shadow overtake the man's eyes. "I presume you meant were-tigers?"

The man looked away. "I was foolish, Sahib. Forget it," he said, and stood just a little straighter, as if he were in a defensive position.

"No," William said. "You said there was a Kingdom of the Tigers nearby?"

The man said something under his breath that might very well have been a curse, then sighed heavily. "Sahib, here in the Punjab, it is said there are more weres than men. We all know the empress"—he spat out the title Victoria had given herself as if it must be got out of his mouth as quickly as possible—"thinks there is a risk of new rebellion over the were laws."

"So why did you need to speak with me yesterday?" William asked, feeling as though he were fencing with an invisible foe who shifted position every time he thought he had him pinned.

Bhishma took a moment. His eyes were half-closed—to veil his expression or to give him time to think, William could not guess. Finally, he sighed. "Sahib, if the empress had any idea how close the danger and how awful, why would she send only twenty-five officers, and more than half of those bringing women and children with them?"

William blinked, involuntarily. "That large a danger?" he asked softly, afraid the words would scare *him* as he pronounced them. "A . . . plot?"

Bhishma looked all around, as if to assure himself the room was quite deserted. He tiptoed into the *ghus-lkhanah* and looked about. When he returned, he stepped close to William. "Sahib," he said, leaning very close, his breath tickling William's ear, "it is said that the local ruler of the Kingdom of the Tigers—"

"The—?"

"Kingdom of the Tigers." Bhishma pointed vaguely west. "There are cities in the middle of the forest where it is said that the men who live in them by day all become tigers by night. Do you understand, Sahib?"

William nodded and Bhishma sighed, as though he were absolutely certain that William did not, in fact, understand. "They have their own maharajah. It is said he's very old, as weres live longer than normal men, and don't die easily. And it is said that he's used dark magic to extend both his life and his power."

"It is said," William repeated, with a hint of impatience in his voice. He'd read his grandfather's letters, true enough. And he'd learned from them, as well as from everyone else, that there were a lot more weres in India and China than anywhere in Europe. Because whatever Charlemagne had done all those years ago to concentrate magic only on his descendants had made it less likely a European would have the power—or the curse—of changing forms.

The other continents were supposed to be lousy with it, filled with men who were half-beasts. William had heard it often enough, starting with his grand-papa's spidery writing.

But he'd been in India for three months and he'd not seen any more evidence of this than of any other legend.

"Sahib," Bhishma said. "Remember that before the last riots, the sahibs didn't listen, either."

William started to respond, the words hot on his tongue. But he thought of the line on his grandfather's last letter, written from the doomed barracks at Cawnpore and rescued from the ruins before the burning, sent to his grandmother by who knew what means.

He remembered the scrabbling handwriting and the many-times underscored warning. *My dear Harriet, I wish to God we'd listened to the natives.*

Feeling cold all over, he turned to Bhishma. "What can I do?" he asked.

PROVIDENCE ON THE WING

There were many things that Sofie had heard about weres, and far more that she was prepared to believe. But as she stood on the black marble of the monument to the Black Hole disaster, while the man who had been a dragon dressed himself with expedience clearly born of practice, she thought: *No one told me they could be beautiful.*

It had been the beauty of the beast—fire-winged, luminescent-scaled—that had caused her to fall on the dragon's back and not to fling herself from there once she had dropped on it.

The scales, which should have been cold, had instead been warm and felt strangely soft beneath her body. And the wings... the wings rising and flapping on either side of her had been like captive fire. Like... a million fireflies captured within a frame of gold. But not even that, for where the fireflies would project white light, these were blue and green and pale gold, shifting and changing and looking now like jewels and now like stars.

When the dragon had set her down, she'd meant to run. She'd heard and read stories—mostly in England, in the papers, and in the novels that all her classmates smuggled into their rooms and hid under their mattresses. Journalists and novel writers alike maintained that those people subjected to turning into weres were the basest of creatures, so crude as to defy belief.

So, despite the beauty of the dragon, Sofie had thought the man whose other form it was would doubtless be an Indian servant, or else one of those drunken young men whose respectable families sent them to India to avoid the embarrassment of having them on hand.

But then the beast coughed hard, mercilessly, twisting and writhing in the pain of it.

And then . . . it changed. And the process of change itself was fascinating to one who had only read about it. The accounts were quite wrong, she now realized. There were not buckets of blood lost, nor did the body become, for a moment, something inexpressibly gross and strange. No, instead of evoking disgust, the process seemed wondrous. The dragon glowed with a blue light, as its lines blurred and changed.

For a moment in the middle, the dragon was neither beast nor man, and did look quite odd—like a man with reptilian wings or a dragon with a bipedal stance. But then the whole resolved itself into a man who, like the beast, was of uncommon physical beauty.

He was tall, very tall. Taller even than Papa, who had always been accounted a very tall man. This gentleman—for there could be no doubt he was one—was straight of back and limb and golden all over, a color just slightly lighter than her own.

His features managed to be beautiful without in any way deviating from the straightness of line to be expected of a gentleman's physiognomy. A squarish chin was emphasized by an aquiline, high-bridged nose, on the right side of which his single eye—she hadn't noticed the dragon had only one eye, and now she wondered in what brave act he'd lost the left—was wider than average, and soft and green, the deep green of a tree in winter. And his hair, soft and dark and curly, fell over a forehead beaded with sweat. The blue light faded around him and, as if from very far away, she heard him apologize for his state of undress and then, disbelieving, heard herself muse on the inconvenience—the *inconvenience*—of being a were. He dressed by rote, and quickly, as a man who often found himself naked and in public or semi-public situations would. And all she could do was make inane small talk. At least until he was fully dressed—in a linen suit of impeccable tailoring, which emphasized the lines of his body and his long legs—and insisted she must go home.

But she couldn't. Of course she couldn't. She'd rather die a thousand deaths than face the raj again. She didn't know what she expected, but she felt her body shift and tense as he bent the intent gaze of that soft and pondering eye upon her face.

In such circumstances, at least as far as she'd been led to believe, a gentleman of breeding—which this one certainly appeared to be, even if he was also a dragon—would tell her she couldn't run away from home and would demand that she return to her parents. Or perhaps he would be so shocked by her declaration that he would instantly turn away in disgust from one who had to be lost to all propriety.

But the dragon-man merely raised his eyebrows

and looked at her very intently, then nodded once. "I see," he said. And Sofie had the uncomfortable notion that whatever he saw was not the propriety of her behavior. "Look, Miss . . . ?"

"Warington," she said. And—training defeating reason—she dropped him a hasty curtsey.

He smiled a little at it, as though he recognized in the gesture the unthinking response of the body. "Miss Warington." He fished in his coat pocket for a cigarette case, from which he extracted a thin cigarette that he proceeded to light with a nonmagical flint lighter fished from the other pocket. He expelled a neat cloud of smoke, and looked at her. "I assume you were running away from home because you had a disagreement with your family or some such thing. I've never had sisters, but I understand from overhearing friends that this is not uncommon with girls your age. I beg you to believe me, the events you'd be exposed to on your own in the world are worse than anything you might have left home to avoid."

She shook her head, quickly—too eagerly, her mind told her—and said, "I don't want to marry the maharajah."

This got her a widened eye, showing she had surprised him. "Your parents wanted you to marry—"

"They accepted his suit while I was away in England," she said. "And then presented it to me as a done thing. I was to marry the maharajah, and he said I'd be his only wife."

The eye sparkled with something like amusement. "Yes, I can see how that would drive you to despair. I'm sure it has always been your secret and active ambition to be part of a seraglio." And then, as though

reading the shock in her eyes, he added, with quick so-
briety, "I'm sorry. That was ill-spoken."

"No, I beg pardon," she said, confused. "I ex-
pressed myself poorly. What I meant is that he had discussed marriage with my parents before ever he met
me, which seems . . . very odd."

"Though done often enough in India, which is, in
that respect, a more traditional society than ours.
Marriage is made for other reasons than sudden and
unavoidable love." He pronounced the last word as if
he didn't quite know what it meant—a foreign word
culled from an unknown language.

She shook her head, unable to tell whether he was
joking or just persisted in misunderstanding her—and
feeling, somehow, deep within, that it was all her fault
for failing to explain it more coherently. After all, she'd
never before had problems getting words to obey her
and she'd always been able to make her meaning quite
plain when she chose. Why was she now tongue-tied
and unable to explain this matter, when it was of the
utmost importance that he understand her? "I know
that," she said, curtly. "My father's grandmother was
Indian and we— I know that." Then she shook her
head. "But you see, there is no reason for him to
marry me. My father is not very important. He tried
to make a go of a shipping service, but it did not prosper and our ships kept sinking. The whole family is terribly unlucky," she said bluntly. "Always has been. If
we were to make hats, boys would be born without
heads. So, he didn't prosper, and though our house is
well enough, or at least I thought it was till today,
and . . . and I . . . I suppose I'm well enough, too, though
not *beautiful.*" She rushed on, afraid he would dispute

this point, and even more afraid he would fail to dispute it, "I am nothing special and neither is my family, so why would a native want to marry me sight unseen? My maid says there are rumors he saw me once in a vision, but that seems unlikely. And he can't have gone to England, because he's something special in the way of looks and I'm sure there would have been talk about him if he had visited London."

"Something special?"

"He's ... ugly," she said, and tried to convey her feeling of disgust and fear in that one word, sure that she was coming short of it. "A face broad and scarred, and little slits of eyes, which are quite yellow."

"I see," the dragon-man said again, this time making it obvious that he did not. "And so you don't want to marry him. But, my dear girl, surely you know that in this day and age no one can force you to marry anyone else? There are laws against that sort of thing."

"I know. And yet ..."

"And yet?"

"I feel that if I go back, somehow I will be forced to marry him."

He should have disputed that, but he didn't. He just frowned at her for a while. "And what do you plan to do with your hard-earned freedom? Surely you didn't count on me?"

She shook her head yet again, then said, her voice coming out oddly young and breathless, "Oh, no. You were quite ... providential."

"Yes, that's me. Providence on the wing. But we can't stay here talking. Sooner or later they'll look for you, and I don't care to explain why, exactly, a dragon took you and now they find you with me."

It crossed her mind suddenly, and with some surprise, that he stood under a penalty of death for the
mere fact of having been born a were. And yet he'd
gone out of his way to rescue her, which doubtless
would attract attention to himself and his condition.
The penalty of death had always been justified by saying that weres ate people. Sofie had never doubted it
till this moment. And in this slice of irreality in which
she was living, she blurted, "Do you eat people?"

He didn't even look surprised, just said, "Rarely,"
with that hint of carelessness that might mean he was
joking or else might mean her question had injured his
feelings. But before she could apologize, he said,
"What are we to do with you now, though? Did you
have any other plans than dashing your brains out
falling from that balcony?"

"Yes. I intended to go to Meerut."

"Meerut?" he repeated. "In the Punjab? Good
God. That's a long way away. How were you meaning
to get there? Do you have friends here who'll lend you
transport?"

"No," she said. Her plan—forged in the heat of
panic—had seemed perfectly reasonable, but now appeared as if it was not so much a plan as a fever dream.
"You see . . . all my friends are in England. I lived there
since I was very young. In . . . in an academy for young
ladies."

"But why Meerut? What were you intending to do
there?"

She felt color come to her cheeks. She had never
really spoken of Captain Blacklock to anyone, and she
didn't wish to confide in this man who was taller than
William Blacklock and—though she was loathe to ad-

mit it—even better-looking. "I ... You see ... When I was in England, there was this captain of the regulars, a ... He was a very good-looking ..." She cleared her throat. "What I mean is, we were very good friends, through meeting at balls and parties a good deal, and we went riding together sometimes, and ... and we formed an attachment."

"Oh, so you're engaged," he said, sounding indefinably relieved.

"In a manner of speaking. I mean, he said that he would marry me in a second if he could. But you see, he was the child of the second child of a mere country squire, and he didn't have any money and he thought my parents would never accept his suit, which might very well be true. He was ordered to India three months before I left England myself. Something about were unrest?" She looked at him, hoping desperately he would think of that, not of the obvious confusion of her situation with William.

But he dismissed were unrest with a toss of his cigarette onto the ground and a flicker of his eyebrows upward. "Never heard of any were unrest," he said. "At least, not in Calcutta. Not that I've met any other of ... my kind. Well, properly speaking, I've never met my kind anywhere, since I've never come across another dragon, but ..." He shrugged. "So Captain Blacklock is in Meerut and you wish to go to him and throw yourself in his arms?"

She felt the blush in her face become a raging fire. She imagined, having seen herself blush before, that she presented a very pretty picture with the pink coming up in her cheeks and her eyes averted. But she wished three times more that she might have more control of her reactions. "That's an abominable thing to say," she said. "He . . . he said that if things were different and he had a chance, he would have very much liked to marry me. So, you see, now things are different, because my parents have forced me into this position, I don't see why I shouldn't marry him."

The dragon-man didn't speak for a long time. He looked at her in silence till she felt she would burst into flames out of sheer embarrassment. But at last he opened his mouth and said, levelly, "Miss Warington, it won't do. Even supposing you had some way of making it across the wilds of India to where Captain Blacklock is stationed—are you sure he is stationed there, by the way?"

"He told me he was being sent to Meerut in the Punjab."

"So supposing he wasn't lying for some specious reason of his own—and before you look too shocked, madame, let me assure you that men do lie—and that his orders didn't change, nor that he didn't catch some horrible disease on ship—which, yes, also does happen—and die and get buried at sea, nor die shortly after debarking, from the shock of the climate or from tainted food—if all these conditions apply, then he is on the other side of this vast subcontinent. And supposing you travel to him by bullock cart, which is the fastest means of transportation you could command—supposing you could command it—to reach such a region as the Punjab . . . you'd take three weeks, perhaps more, to make it to his side. And all on the strength of a comment he made to you during a party, which was that he would be well pleased to marry you, all other things being equal."

He reached the end of this devastating recital and stood looking at Sofie, as if challenging her to recognize the flaws in her plan. She saw them all, and starkly enough, and she felt about two feet tall, but she would be cursed if she would admit to this man, this stranger, that she hadn't thought things through perfectly well.

"It won't *do,* Miss Warington," he said at last, very softly. "Your plan is impossible."

"Oh, you're wrong," she said, and stomped her foot, even while she was aware of his being absolutely right. "It will do." It had to. "William was not just flirting. You don't understand. He was *quite* head over heels in love with me. All the young men in his regiment were. They brought flowers and sent gifts and were all desperately, madly in love with me."

"Were they? And yet none offered?"

"Oh, you are vexing. I've no doubt they would have offered had I remained in London. Only, Papa wrote demanding that I return home immediately and I—"

"And you returned. Leaving behind an entire regiment in love with you."

Said like that it sounded like the craziest thing she could have said, but she was not about to admit that, either. She exhaled forcefully. "Still, I know Captain Blacklock was neither flirting nor lying. Wherever he is right now, I warrant you that he's thinking about me and wishing he could be married to me. I'll warrant you that he—"

"Perhaps he is," the man said. "Wherever he is— *wherever* being the operative word here. It is quite likely you'd get to Meerut only to find your love-struck captain has been sent elsewhere. Or perhaps, if you haven't misremembered and he was sent over due to some unrest, you'd discover that he is in the midst of a devilishly dangerous situation in which the last thing a man wants is a bride hanging on his arm. And then there's the fact that even if he's madly in love with you and wishes to marry you, his circumstances might not be such that would permit his taking a wife. In which case, all his love, and all your arduous travel—which, since you'd have to depend on strangers kindly furnishing you with transportation, is likely to take months—will have been in vain. And by then your reputation will be ruined and your parents, doubtless, in great anxiety over your fate. You can't do this, Miss Warington," he said, softly.

"But I have to!" she said, finally voicing her despair. "Oh, I know that William might not be able to take me in, that he might not be able to take me as a wife, but I will find some other way to survive, then. Perhaps I can be a maid to one of the officers' wives. Or a governess to the children."

"What? When there's so much local labor offering at very low prices?"

"Then I'll . . . I'll join a mission, or something."

At this he cackled, almost derisively. "I don't see you as a missionary, Miss Warington."

"But I must. I'll do anything but go back home."

"Come, you're young, but don't be foolish. Surely you realize this is just a scary fairy tale you've been telling yourself." He ignored her attempts at speaking and continued, "Your parents would not make you marry this native, or indeed anyone you didn't wish to marry, any more than they'd sacrifice you to a local god." He walked toward her, swiftly. "I rescued you from almost certain death, and therefore I am in some measure responsible for you. I do not wish for you to get lost in the wilds of India, with no other choice but to appeal to a mission for your barest sustenance. Come with me," he said.

"Where?" she asked, confused, putting her hand on the arm he offered.

"Home," he said. "I'll walk you back and we'll say I found you alone after you escaped from the dragon—or, if you require that I be a hero in this, that I chased the dragon away from you. Whichever you prefer. I'll walk you home and then—"

She pulled her hand from his arm and stepped away from him. "Never. I will never ever ever go back." She felt a body-long shudder run through her. "I couldn't. Ever. They'll make me marry the raj."

"You're being quite foolish, you know. Of course they won't make you marry him. At most they'll demand and thunder, but you look more than able to withstand such pressure."

"No. Mama says that we are quite ruined and the prince is offering a bride price and they cannot refuse him."

He looked exasperated. "Not after you proved you were desperate enough to run away from home to avoid it."

He should have been right. Sofie wanted him to be right. He should, by all that was holy, have been speaking the truth. No mother—no *parent*—in her right mind would force her daughter to marry someone after she'd almost killed herself escaping from the match.

But against this rational thought, Sofie felt a certainty that rose from within her like a suffocating

pressure brooking no dissent. They would make her
marry the creature, no matter her protests. She was as
sure as she was of standing here and being alive. If she
went back home tonight she would never emerge from
that house again as Miss Warington. She would only
leave it as the creature's bride.

Feeling as if the air were all quite choked out of her,
she said, "Never. I could never . . ." Her breath seemed
very loud. Her heart beat like a deafening drum.

The dragon-man stretched his hand to her. "Don't
be foolish," he said. "Come. You're being fantastical."

She shook her head. Through her fear and her
swirling panic, she said, blindly, "I . . . I will call for
help. If you make me go back, I will denounce you. I
will scream that you are a dragon and that you kidnapped me."

IN THE HALLS OF
THE MONKEY KING

Lalita ran, hurrying through the streets, her bare feet slapping now dirt, now cobbles, the jangle of thin silver bracelets around her ankles making a musical sound. She penetrated deep into the native quarter, where everything was bright with life and light, even after sunset.

She ran past women in saris, past houses whose open doors showed dancing and music. She ducked around the advancing bulk of two elephants—carrying the principals in a marriage procession—squeezing herself against the wall, as the elephants took up almost all of the alleyway between makeshift buildings and hovels and tents.

It had been a long time since she'd taken this path. There had been no reason to take it since she returned from England with Sofie, but there were things one didn't forget—paths and experiences engraved on the mind and soul that resounded across all the years. She remembered this as she remembered her position and the protocol ingrained in her from a very early age. She turned unerringly down alleys and paths, never doubting—despite the many new buildings—that she knew the way to where she was going.

She had come this way many times before being sent to England. She'd come with her father. She'd come on important occasions, on hallowed days. It was not something she could forget easily, or indeed at all.

She stopped sharply in front of what would have looked to the uninformed like little more than a miserable shop, merely a tent made of silks of varying age, at the door of which sat a man, his legs crossed, surveying the passersby with a calm and indifferent gaze, as though they had nothing to give him and could take nothing from him, either.

Lalita looked at him and bowed, and he lowered his eyes fractionally and bobbed his head a very slight amount right and then left, then right again. Consent enough. She walked past him, into the tent, where there were bolts of silk everywhere. The last time she'd come here, those had been tables with produce. It did not matter. The nature of the shop might change completely, but what mattered, truly, was the establishment beneath it.

She walked past the colorful silk, paying no attention to the two obese men who guarded it and who did not seem at all interested in selling the fabric. Perhaps she expected a more British attitude. She'd been away too long.

At the place she remembered—the spot where she could feel the power surge beneath her feet—Lalita stopped and made a gesture, which was known as a "wave of revealing" in the magic of her people. To other people it was unknown. It made visible what had been hidden by the magic of her kind. In this case, what had been hidden there at the back of the dingy shop, in the shadows that smelled of silk and the street outside, was a massive door, set in an old, time-weathered stone doorway.

To this door, Lalita bowed three times, and the door opened to reveal a man. He was triple the height of a normal man and wore only loose pantaloons of violently red silk. In each of his hands was a sword, gleaming and polished and lethal-looking.

Lalita wondered if he were truly that big, or if it was only an impression conveyed by some sort of magic. His look—a sword in each hand, his shaved head, a grin on a face that appeared, otherwise, oddly blurred—led her to suspect it was the last, but it didn't matter. She viewed him as what he truly was, the guardian whose job it was to protect the inner sanctum from profane eyes.

She bowed to him, and pulled up the scarf part of her sari to cover her head and half of her face in its soft folds. Then she ran her hand, palm up, in front of her face, without touching it. In that gesture, she allowed him to see her true aspect. In that gesture, she revealed who she was.

The guard jumped back with a grace that would have looked unnatural to someone not acquainted with the nature of this place. He sheathed his swords with blinding speed, and bowed to her—hands joined at his chest. "Welcome," he said, stepping out of the way, to allow Lalita to pass through.

Past the guard was another doorway—the massive, hammered gold doors standing wide open. And past the doorway was a hall that seemed to Lalita's gaze as immense and long as it had looked the first time she had entered it.

It was of golden stone, built deep and narrow. It had side walls and—high up on them—windows, through which came a diffused and filtered light, like the sun seen through several layers of dazzling white cloth. From the walls inward, a profusion of columns—tall, seemingly endless columns—pierced the gloom upward. Covered in faded golden writing in an alphabet that no one had ever seen outside these halls, they held up—high above the heads of even the most towering giant—a ceiling like the inside of a boat keel, arched and peaked and high.

There were paintings on the ceiling, but they were not visible from Lalita's humble height. But the paintings on the wall were fully visible. They represented—mostly—monkeys frolicking amid ancient palaces. Monkeys wearing rich apparel and jewels.

The same monkeys—or their real life counterparts—ran along the walls, amid richly dressed men and women. Lalita glimpsed them there, in the shadows, rustling and moving—their eyes, seeming too human, staring at her in something like shock.

Lalita fell to her knees and bowed her head. At the other end of the hall, vaguely visible in the filtered-light gloom, stood a tall, shining gold throne, covered in strange carvings. When Lalita entered the room and knelt, it was covered in monkeys, running this way and that.

But now a deep voice rumbled from the throne. "Lalita?"

She lifted her head to look up. On the throne sat a man who didn't appear old so much as timeless. He looked at her with piercing, dark brown eyes. Even if she couldn't see his face very clearly from this far away, she could see the eyes, or feel them, like a caress upon her face. And at the same time, a slow and steady examination.

"Sire," she said, speaking in little more than a whisper, and yet knowing that he would hear her as clearly as if she'd shouted.

A long-fingered, mobile hand stretched forward and gestured for her. She got up and walked the length of the hall, to fall to her knees again, closer to the throne, her hair down her back, the silken bit of the sari she'd thrown over her head slipping to reveal her young and awed face, gazing up at her king.

He smiled kindly at her—a human and gentle expression. "What brings you here, Lalita?"

"I . . . came back from England. We were summoned four months ago and we just arrived," she said, struggling with her words as though they were an unaccustomed foe. "Two weeks ago."

"We know," the king said, his voice vibrating with what, in a lesser being, would be amusement. "And what brings you here?"

"I was, as you know, sent to England with my mistress, Sofie Warington, whom we believed to be the only descendant in her generation of the family that inherited Charlemagne's spent ruby."

"Yes. Our memory is not that bad," the king said, and now the amusement was quite obvious even in his regal voice.

"If you remember . . . the mission you gave my parents, and them to me, was to find if her family was indeed in possession of the ruby—which I found they were, though they don't know what it is. Only that it's very valuable and magically powerful. However, they don't know *how* magically powerful. They only know enough to hold on to it tightly. But not why they do so."

"All this we know," the king said, now bewildered as well as amused.

"Yes, but... why would anyone need my mistress as well as the ruby?"

The king didn't speak for a long time. She heard him take in breath, a suddenly loud sound in the silent hall. "I don't understand," he said.

Lalita shook her head. "I don't understand, either," she said. "And yet, it must be so, because my mistress has been kidnapped and because... because the tiger wanted her as well as—"

"Kidnapped?" the king asked, his voice booming oddly in surprise. "She was kidnapped? By whom?"

"By a dragon. That's why I came. Before this, I've suspected... When we were in London, Sofie would dream, and she would walk in her sleep and I would find her far away. I thought she might be a shifter, only I found that what was making her walk at night was a compulsion, laid upon her. And I think the compulsion, though it's hard to tell, was to seek out a certain group of people. From the magic, I would think the tigers. Then we came back home and I found..." In short, incisive sentences, she told of Sofie's betrothal to the raj who was king of the Kingdom of the Tigers. She told how she'd warned Sofie of this—she hadn't had time to come here for instruction, nor had she wished to exceed her orders or risk being followed here.

"But now you risked it?" the king said.

"Now I had no choice. My mistress ran to the balcony, you see, and the railing gave, and she fell . . . onto the back of a dragon. Once, the dragon looked as if he'd return, but then he flew away." She bowed again. "I don't know where Sofie is, and though I am, to her, only a servant, we've been friends—almost sisters— these years. I don't know what the tiger wanted with her, and I can't imagine what the dragon wants with her, but we must save her."

"How do you know"—the king said, standing— "that he wants anything with her? Or that the tiger did? Even if he laid a compulsion, she clearly didn't come to it. He asked for the ruby in the dowry, didn't he? Depend upon it, it was the ruby he wanted, and nothing more. And doubtless the dragon means to hold her hostage for the ruby as well."

Lalita shook her head slowly. "Sire, it can't be. Because I heard her father tell the tiger he would give him the ruby if only he'd leave his daughter alone."

The king rubbed his chin pensively. "That is . . . interesting," he said. "And a dragon took her, you said?"

Lalita bowed her head by way of affirmative.

"Did he take the ruby also?" The king tilted forward on his throne, as though trying to read Lalita's expression.

She shook her head, and the king licked his lips in quite an unconscious reaction. "And the house is in disarray, is it?"

"They were on the balcony when I left, trying to find where the dragon might have taken Miss Warington."

"Would the ruby . . . be attainable now?"

Lalita hadn't thought of the ruby. Her mind had been full of her mistress—of her being stolen by the dragon and of what might be befalling her now. She had not spared a thought for the ruby. It had always been with Mr. Warington, but under heavy protections. Though he didn't know it was the mystical Soul of Fire, he knew it was powerful and magical. And there was an ancestral legend about horrible things that would befall the family should they lose the ruby. And since Lalita and Sofie's return, Lalita noticed it was still protected. Enough that no one would be able to touch it. Lalita was sure Mr. Warington had started using dark magic to keep the ruby secure from the tiger—and in the process was keeping it secure from everyone else. But the tiger had somehow hooked the Englishman through the dark magic, somehow snagged his magical power in his own dark, roiling magic. And now he was forcing his hand.

"I think it would still be protected," she said, and swallowed. "Unless I'm mistaken, the tiger will get the ruby."

The king narrowed his eyes, as if deep in thought, and slowly puffed out his cheeks, then let them deflate again, suddenly. "Very well. I shall send sentinels to watch for the ruby. To see if it leaves the house with the tiger, and if so, where he takes it."

"But...my mistress!" The words came out as a wail, which Lalita hadn't meant them to. "My mistress was taken by the dragon. Something horrible could be happening to her."

"That's not very likely, is it? Even if the tiger thinks he needs both her and the ruby, surely nothing can be done with her only?"

"The dragon could be holding her hostage," Lalita protested. "Or...or hurting her."

"Oh." The king looked at Lalita a long time. "And this would distress you? Even though she's an Englishwoman whose parents came here attempting to make a fortune off of our land and our people?"

"Sofie didn't try to make a fortune off of anything," Lalita said. "And besides, her great-grandmother was Indian." Personally, Lalita couldn't understand why it mattered what Sofie was. Oh, she wanted freedom for her people and for them to have the right to govern themselves. It galled and distressed her that Englishmen thought her people too infantile, too savage to govern themselves. She wanted the Imperial authority out of India—the East India Company, too. But until this moment it had never occurred to her that her own king wanted everyone of English blood out. There were decent people and there were people who weren't decent. Sofie Warington was silly and often strange, but she was a good person. She might not show it in public, but in private she treated Lalita as one of her friends. No, better. Because Sofie had never felt at home with the girls in London. She'd never felt at home at all. Both girls had longed for India.

"And she's your friend, milady?" the king asked.

"Yes. Oh, yes."

"Well, then. Because she is your friend, we will find her." He paused. "Besides, it would be good to find out what the dragons want with her. Perhaps the Chinese..." He looked toward the shadows to his right, where amid the soaring columns courtiers pressed together, and he waggled a long, agile finger.

From the shadows slid a man, dressed in loose white pants that seemed to shimmer with a pearlescent sheen. His tunic, too, was white, but embroidered in shimmering gold patterns. He wore a turban that hid most of his hair, save for a few straight, black tufts sticking in disarray from the edge. A pearl of considerable size secured his turban, and gold earrings dangled from his ears. He glanced at Lalita furtively, giving her a glimpse of heavily lidded, sultry black eyes. Then he turned to the king and bowed deeply.

"Hanuman, you will go with the princess, my niece," the king said. "And you will find her friend for her. And if you can find the ruby, too, and keep both from the tiger, I shall give you whatever your heart desires."

The courtier thus called was named after the monkey god Hanuman, and Lalita couldn't remember anyone of power or influence—nor any of the main families of their were kingdom—who would give their child such a name. She stared at him, trying to discern his caste and his standing, but saw nothing save his finery and his cinnamon-colored skin. And she remembered nothing but those sultry eyes of his.

He bowed to the king and said, "How am I to do it, Your Majesty?"

"I trust your resourcefulness, my friend," the king said with a chuckle.

Lalita didn't, and would have said something, but at that moment the king twisted and writhed. His royal clothes were suddenly empty, sitting on the abandoned throne, and a monkey scampered amid the columns to the ceiling, whence it called in sharp cries to its court.

Following suit, all lords and the few ladies who could change shapes let go of their clothes, and their human form with them. Lalita stared at Hanuman.

From Hanuman's look at her, the smile on his mobile face, he might be thinking it would be great fun to shift now and chase Lalita along the rafters of the long-hidden palace.

Lalita shook her head severely at him. "My mistress is lost," she said, "and we must find her before the horrible creature hurts her."

A SLIP OF NOTHING

The dragon fluttered within him at her words, but Peter Farewell stopped it, reflexively. When threatened with being exposed, the very worst thing one could possibly do was shift into dragon form.

Besides, he was tired. The transformation into dragon always seemed to exhaust him—drawing more strength from his body than a full day's work or a night's wakefulness. And he hadn't been feeding the dragon. What he ate, and the quantities he consumed in his human form, barely fed the one transformation. If he changed into the beast now, he'd be ravening.

No. That he could not do. As a human he calmed the beast, held on to it with an iron hand, thinking soothing thoughts. He was so busy with those it took him a few breaths to realize how angry he was.

This slip of a girl had said she'd bring the Gold Coats down on him. They'd come eagerly, too, stationed nearby as they were—and perhaps her family had already called them. Peter Farewell chewed on his lip to prevent words emerging that he would not be able to control. She was young and beautiful and angry... and he would hurt her if he stayed here.

He turned neatly on his heels and started walking away before he realized what hurt him most was her ingratitude. He had saved her from a plunge to her death. He'd risked his life—the discovery of his other form would surely lead to his public execution—to rescue her.

And yet she was willing to deliver him to death.

He felt tears prickle at the back of his eye and chuckled bitterly to himself. This was what came from trusting people. Any people. When his own father had disowned him for being what he couldn't help being, he should have learned not to trust humans. But perhaps because at least half of him was human, he couldn't seem to break himself of care for the creatures. And then there was Kitwana and Emily and Nigel...He thought of the people who'd shared his African adventure and the risks they'd all taken together.

They were good people. But none of them quite considered him one of them. Nor should they. There was the beast that lurked within him, dogging his every thought, his every movement, influencing his actions more than he liked to admit. And perhaps the girl was right, too, in showing him no gratitude. After all, how much of his saving her was true heroism, and how much was the dragon's impatience, making him change forms under the impact of emotion? He was a beast and he must remember he was a beast, and thus not fit for the company of men.

A sound of steps behind him—light and hesitant, as though afraid of themselves—and he turned around. And there she was, Miss Warington, less than ten steps behind him, her carpetbag in one hand, looking quite confused.

"Why are you following me?" he growled through clenched teeth. "Are you afraid of losing your prey? Are you, then, determined to collect the reward for turning in a dangerous were?"

He knew the moment the words left his lips that they were unmerited and possibly cruel. He didn't need to see her eyes widen in shock and surprise to know she'd thought none of that and had no nefarious intentions toward him. Mentally he complimented himself on informing her of the reward. Perhaps she hadn't known of it, and now he'd given her a truly strong motivation for turning him in.

Color drained from her face, leaving it a curious tone between milk and caramel, like the palest of brown sugar. She lowered her eyelids to hide her shocked gaze and dropped a curtsey in what must have been an unthinking impulse. "I beg your pardon," she said, her accent frosty, her diction better than he'd heard it before. "I merely thought, as a woman alone at night, I might..." She stopped, and confusion painted itself on her features. "Foolish of me, when I've decided to run away from home on my own, to wish for protection."

"Yes," he said, and he thought that she was quite the most foolish young woman he'd ever met.

She shook herself a little, like someone wakening, or perhaps like someone who's been languishing and decides to be about her work. "Of course," she said, her voice flowing easier. "You are absolutely right. Since I will have to make my way to Meerut on my own, then I will make my way on my own. I beg your pardon for having bothered you. It won't happen again. And you might as well forget my threat to turn you in. I'd never do that. I owe you a debt of gratitude for saving my life."

And, like that, she turned on her heel, as neat and military a movement as Peter would have expected from a soldier, and marched down the street, holding her carpetbag. Peter frowned after her. She was so small. Her head had barely reached his shoulder. Small, and weak, and proud as hell. He observed the straight setting of her shoulders. A little slip of nothing, with a determination that would dwarf many a general's.

Determination and courage, because she didn't look nearly as much the fool as she acted. She knew what dangers she faced and yet faced them, unflinching. Peter had seen the look in her eyes as he described the unlikelihood that she'd find her beau waiting for her. He knew well enough she was aware of her folly. She might have run away from home in a sudden panic, but now she would be aware of how impossible it was for her to make it to Meerut. She would be aware of the dangers on the way.

Well, perhaps not all the dangers, Peter thought, observing how her narrow waist gently flared to well-contoured hips. At least, he hoped she couldn't imagine what some—if not all—of the men she'd meet on the way would want from her. But then, he doubted she was as innocent as all that. They never were. Girls might never have met depravity in real life before, but they'd have read enough about it in lurid novels. And the smart ones understood easily enough what hid beneath the veiled descriptions. So she knew what she faced. And yet, she would go into India on her own, rather than face her parents back at home. She would brave almost certain death—or worse—rather than marry the native they'd chosen for her.

He frowned. His instinctive feeling was to dismiss it all. She was young. She was sheltered. She was deluded. He knew better than to imagine her parents would marry her to someone against her will.

And yet . . .

That small figure with squared shoulders was ready to face untold dangers, but not the danger that waited back at her parents' home.

He stared at Miss Warington's retreating form. She was leaving everything behind just as he must do. He felt bile sting the back of his throat at the thought of giving up Summercourt. His destiny had always been to end up alone and in exile, but that didn't mean that he should let the decent people in this world go to their horrible fate without trying to stop them.

A shadow detached itself from a wall and surged toward Miss Warington. And Peter leapt forward. The native—whatever he was, probably no more than a beggar—took one look at Peter and fled.

Miss Warington, on the other hand, continued walking as though she hadn't seen him loom large in her peripheral vision, as though she hadn't heard him fall in step beside her.

Not knowing whether to be amused or scared, Peter cleared his throat. When no response came, he sighed. "Miss Warington, I am a fool. But not such a fool that I would let you walk to Meerut, or whatever other scheme you might have in mind."

She shook her head, not looking at him. "There is hardly any question of your allowing me. Or not allowing me, for that matter. I am neither your ward nor your child."

Peter thought about it. He'd talked to many women in his life. While his entire amorous experience could be written on the head of a very small pin, his travels around the world had brought him into contact with women of many classes and nationalities. But he would swear that he'd never met a creature as prickly as Miss Warington. Choosing his words carefully, feeling as though the wrong one at the wrong time might be his undoing, he said, "I beg your pardon for my rude words and for having insisted you should return to your parents' house. It should have been obvious to me from your horror of returning, since you don't seem at all to be disordered in wits—" He floundered as it occurred to him that taking a were-dragon in stride might well be considered insane by most people. But he charged ahead, thinking that, after all, the dragon had saved her.

"You must have reason for it. I will not force you to go. But I must beg you—indeed, I *do* beg you—to allow me to escort you on this travel to meet your ..." Again he floundered, but decided to go with her view of things. "Your fiancé."

For a moment, he thought his gambit had failed. She continued to walk, as though she hadn't heard his voice or refused to acknowledge his words. But slowly her steps seemed to lose impetus, and finally she stopped and turned to face him. "Mr. ... Oh, this is abominable! I don't even know your name."

He smiled. He could not help it. She had seen him naked, but she did not know his name. They'd both be disgraced before any polite society imaginable. To his surprise, he saw his smile echoed in her expression. He quickly bowed, lest he should stand there smiling at her like a smitten fool. "Miss Warington, permit me to present myself. I am Peter Farewell, Earl of Saint Maur." He stood straight, and smiled again at her expression of surprise, this time deprecatingly. "A few buildings and a farm, plus some tenants. Not enough, I assure you, to support the title in any style. Quite eaten up from the inside and worthy of no greater a representative than I." But even as he said it, something in him flinched and he realized he was proud of his title. He, who'd always believed in the equality of man. What a fool he was.

"Oh," he heard her say, and was not sure what that sound meant. It seemed to express dismay and surprise in equal amounts. "I am Sofie Warington," she said. "My father is of the Yorkshire Waringtons."

Peter allowed himself to look into her eyes. "That means little to me. I left England many years ago."

She shook her head, as though embarrassed to have brought it up at all. "I learned to say that in England. Everyone asked, so . . . In fact, my father and my grandfather before him born and raised in India."

"I see," he said. He only knew that she didn't seem to be surprised at a man who became a dragon, that she didn't sneer at him for his moth-eaten title and that she was silly enough to propose she'd find her own way across India. "Miss Warington, will you let me escort you?"

She hesitated. For a moment, he thought she was going to refuse him. But instead, she looked suddenly scared and dropped her bag, and her face crumpled a little, like faces do when someone is about to cry.

"Lord Saint Maur," she said, in a thread of voice, "I don't know. . . . That is, you might be right about my course of action. It will take months all in all to get to Meerut, and what if I do get there to find that Captain Blacklock is dead or . . . otherwise occupied." She swallowed visibly.

Peter couldn't console her. He, himself, had pointed out to her the folly of her ways. And yet, if she wouldn't go back to her parents' house, what other course could he urge on her? "Miss Warington, you must understand that if you can't go back to your parents' house, there is nothing else I know to do with you. I am not . . . so situated that I can give you asylum."

"It will take us months," she said. "Months, and I—"

He shook his head and went a little mad. He knew, even as he spoke, that in later years he would look back on this moment in utter bewilderment, wondering how he could have suggested such a course of action, how it might have seemed reasonable to him. But at that moment, he was carried on the crest of a feeling he couldn't describe. It was partly his admiration of this tiny thing who was ready to brave an unknown continent on her own rather than submit to a repugnant fate. And partly it was the intoxication he felt, like music distantly heard, whenever he looked into her dark blue eyes.

The final part . . . the final part might very well be the dragon, speaking in the back of his mind with a voice composed of longing to be out of the confines of the city. "Miss Warington," he said, "I can't help you find a place there, if your Captain be dead or ailing, or . . ." He couldn't say *or not interested*. Not to her.

"But, madame, I can get you to Meerut within the week."

"The week?" Her voice squeaked as she spoke.

"If you don't mind traveling dragon-back," he said. And it *was* madness. The purest madness. Because Peter knew well—too well—what the beast could be like. And how, sometimes, it was difficult to control the dragon. And yet, here he was, proposing to take a defenseless woman with him, across the wilds. What if he should lose his grip on the dragon?

And yet...The dragon didn't prefer to hunt humans. On the contrary. If other prey offered, then it took it. And if Peter could be sure to have the beast eat often, so it never got hungry enough...In the wilds of India there would be nonhuman food aplenty. And then there was something he couldn't even understand, much less express: there was something to Sofie Warington, to the scent of her, which seemed to be from some fragrant tropical flower, that made the dragon...like her. Or perhaps Peter himself—he didn't want to think about it—liked her so much that the dragon liked her in turn. It had tolerated Emily Oldhall. And Nigel, for that matter. But it had never before approved of a human.

"Would you mind?"

She looked up at him, serious, her eyes scrutinizing his face as though it were part of a puzzle she couldn't quite decipher. "I...No, I would not mind." She smiled a little. "Though I'm sure people would find it very odd. But people find all sorts of things odd."

She was the strangest woman he'd ever met, and Peter couldn't imagine why he found her so fascinating. He bowed, offering her his arm. "If you'd accompany me," he said, "to the home where I'm staying, I

can get myself some changes of clothing and other...
necessaries for the voyage."

"But..." she said. "The dragon doesn't wear clothing."

He had to smile at that. "Undoubtedly. But I won't
always be a dragon. And tell me, how strange would
people find it if you were to travel with a gentleman in
a state of nature?"

This brought a blush to her cheeks, which made
her, if possible, more lovely. "Oh," she said. But she
accepted his arm.

It was stupid—foolish at least—to take time to
pack, or to go to the house where he was staying.
Surely her parents must be raising the alarm and
sending out a search for her. He would have to count
on their not having any idea who he was, or that he
was a member of the gentry.

And he would have to leave a note for his hosts,
who would be in bed by now. It couldn't be helped. By
tomorrow, the story of the maiden kidnapped by the
dragon would be all over town, or at least the part of
town inhabited by expatriates. And if he disappeared
at the same time, leaving no trace and no account of
himself, and having taken no clothes, he might as well
announce to one and all that he was that dragon.

No, he must leave a note. And he must pack like a
decent human being—even if he was not quite one.
Easy enough to find a justification for his leaving. He'd
been apprised of the death of his father. He could tell
them that he was trying to see men of business, to set
his affairs in order.

No one could find any problems with that. And
Peter only regretted that it wasn't true.

A JEWEL BEYOND PRICE; THE COST OF A CHILD; TIGER!

"We should have changed," Hanuman said, *a quick* smile on his mobile face. They stood outside the Warington house, looking at the balconies above. "We should change now."

Lalita gave him a quick appraising glance. She could see his point in a way, but she was conscious of one thing only, and that one thing overwhelmingly: she didn't want to change in front of this stranger. Foisted on her by her king, he might be, but he still had the marks of a commoner about him—the quick glances, the impertinent looks and definitely that name. That horrible name that no real member of the monkey clan would have given their child, for fear of appearing too obvious.

"No," she told him curtly, setting her mouth more primly than she otherwise would have done. "Monkeys will still be noticed in Calcutta. And two monkeys..." She shrugged. "At best, they'd bring brooms to chase us away. At worst...the powersticks. And while I know they might not kill us, remember they are ready for the tigers. The powersticks are likely charmed for weres. We'll be more invisible as ourselves. Remove your earring. And your turban. It's too fine by half for a servant."

"Oh, I'm to be a servant, am I?" He flashed her a quick smile, even as he obeyed her instructions and stashed his finery in a fold of his tunic. The hair beneath the turban was very straight and dark.

"It would be better if you had another headdress," she said. "Something less fine. But it can't be helped."

He didn't answer and she chose not to pursue it. Instead, she led him to the back stairs. No one asked her any questions as she started up the steps. They wouldn't. There was enough movement in and out of the house. People hired for this task or that, and sometimes just friends, countrymen or family of servants. And the last ones to notice anything would be the Englishmen.

They kept the jewel in a small room off the master's study, on the third floor—a room warded with enough dark magic to damn an angel. But she stopped just shy of it, when she heard the voices of Mr. and Mrs. Warington and the hissed, threatening accents of the king of the tigers.

The voices came from the drawing room, which—the house having been built in some ways like a labyrinth—impeded the progress to the study. Seeing a broom abandoned by the door, Lalita seized it and thrust it into Hanuman's hands. "Here, hold this."

"A sweeper?" he asked, with a quirky grin. All these things seemed far too amusing to him.

"Why? Are you afraid you'll lose caste? You only have to hold it. No one will notice you if you do."

Hanuman's eyes sparkled at her—in response to what thought she wasn't sure—and he grabbed the broom then followed her into the room. Lalita, conscious that as the miss's servant she was a little more noticeable to her employers than most others, draped her sari over her head, hiding her features without seeming to do so.

Thus, looking like two servants of no particular account, they slouched into the room. Hanuman went to the corner and shuffled—she had to grant him that—like a very convincing dispirited sweeper. He did something or other with the broom—she was sure it wasn't actually sweeping—and mumbled to himself in the tone of a man who doesn't even realize that the rest of the world exists.

As for her, she started toward the table where a tray with various biscuits and such was sitting, untouched. She didn't want to actually pick up the tray because she didn't want to leave the room, but being near the tray would give her an excuse for her presence there if she absolutely must disguise it in some way.

Once near the tray, she looked up. And her mouth dropped open involuntarily. Because the ruby was there. Right there. *Soul of Fire*. She'd never actually seen it, not close like this. She'd heard about it, and sometimes she'd sensed it, though Mr. Warington had worked very hard indeed to prevent that happening. He'd used forbidden magics, despicable ones. He'd used blood sacrifice—not human blood, she judged, but blood nonetheless—to bolster his own inconsequential hereditary power. He'd tried to keep the jewel hidden from all. Though Lalita wondered if he even knew what he was hiding. Or else, why he'd bothered to hide it so well, at the risk of his life and soul?

At the moment he held it in a trembling hand. He looked at the tiger, who was in human from—that same human form that Sofie had disdained as ugly—and who stood before him, hand held out. "I don't even know why you want it," Mr. Warington said. "Much less why you want my daughter with it."

The tiger smiled. Showing huge teeth, all out of proportion with even the broad features and sharp canines, the left one broken short. "Never mind that. Give me the ruby. I know my purposes. They're none of your concern."

"But Sofie is gone."

"Oh, I'll find her."

Now Mrs. Warington stepped to the fore. "Can't you leave our daughter alone? Take the ruby, if you must, but leave Sofie be. She . . . she saw you. And she doesn't wish—"

"Oh, I'm not pretty enough for the fine Miss Warington, I see," he said, and laughed a sound like a cat hissing. "Give me the jewel, Warington. What do you think would happen if I told your own people that you've been using the dark magics? Do you think its stink is not all over you, visible if someone cared to look for it? Or do you think that jewel would preserve you from the death penalty, should it come?"

Mr. Warington paled, and licked his lips in an anxious gesture. "It has been in my family forever," he said. "It's the only jewel that came down from my father's house. And it is not worth very much."

"Quite the contrary, Warington. It might not be worth anything to you, but for me it is a jewel without price. And since the value is such, and so skewed, I clearly need it more than you do. Hand it over. Now."

Mr. Warington hesitated. He stretched his hand forward, the ruby sitting on it, flashing erratically with sweeps of magical light. You could see that the jewel had suffered some injury in the past. The center of it was dark and split, like the center of jewels that have given up all their power. Only this one hadn't. Or not quite, since it still flashed and trembled.

It wouldn't have, Lalita thought. Since this jewel anchored the first and most primal magic of mankind, it might be impossible to harvest all of its power. It would still show the way to its twin jewel. And it might, perhaps, be able to be repaired. Maybe. She didn't know. All she knew was the mission she'd been given by the monkey king.

"Only, I say..." Mr. Warington mumbled. "Perhaps... My wife is right, you know. We'll let you have the jewel, but I've told you before to leave my daughter alone. And now the poor thing will be in enough trouble, what with the dragon and all. We'll attempt to recover her, but you..." He licked his lips again. "Could you not leave her be?"

The tiger laughed. There was something very primal and lascivious to his laughter. "Oh, no, my dear Warington," he said in impeccable English that, somehow, made him seem more terrifying and alien. "Your pretty little daughter is part and parcel of the deal. I'll take Miss Warington *and* the jewel."

"But the dragon—"

"Don't worry yourself about it," the tiger said in an impatient voice. "I'll find her easily enough and take her home to Jaipur. The next you hear of her—if you hear of her at all—she'll be my wife."

Lalita didn't like the sound of those words, and once more she wondered how the Waringtons could ever have thought to use their daughter as a bargaining chip. The jewel might be unique, but surely Sofie was, too. She was their only daughter.

As she was thinking this, and worrying for her friend who was somewhere in the hands of an unknown dragon, she heard Mr. Warington sigh. He extended his hand farther toward the tiger's waiting hand.

"Come, release the jewel," the tiger said. "The alternative is my denouncing you, and your execution. Surely you prize your life more than that."

"Sometimes," Warington said, "I prize it so little that I wish I was shed of it." But even as he spoke, he tipped his hand, overturning the ruby into the tiger's hand.

And in that moment, Hanuman jumped. He dropped his broom and sprang toward the tiger, hands extended.

Mrs. Warington screamed, and the tiger roared, even as he contorted and twisted and . . . changed. All of a sudden, the silks and finery the man had been wearing slipped to the floor, as the form that had supported them altered. In the place of the portly human who'd presented himself as a native raj, there was now a huge tiger, roaring with open mouth, snapping at the man who was trying to take the jewel from beneath the tiger's paw.

Mr. Warington, pale and trembling, drew back. And Hanuman shifted, too—somehow in the merest blink of an eye—and was now a monkey, jumping and leaping and seeming to run on the ceiling itself as he taunted the tiger.

Lalita, staring, could only think the idiot was going to get himself killed. And while he was no kin of hers, and certainly none of her responsibility, her uncle had given him to her as a partner in this mission. She must take care of him.

What could he hope to gain by playing these tricks? This was not just a tiger. It was the king of all were-tigers. She did not doubt he had as much power as their own king. After all, the reason he was their king was not hereditary only. He had the magic of their clan. He could even call their magic to him.

As she thought this, the tiger seemed to get tired of the monkey taunting him. He looked up to where Hanuman was now screaming and puffing his cheeks at him, and Lalita could feel him gathering magic, ready to let it go.

It had been years since she'd changed quickly. In London, she'd changed a few times only, and under very controlled circumstances, careful that no one would see her. Or, if they did, that they would assume her to be some lady's pet monkey, momentarily loose. And she and Sofie had been back in India only a very short while. She'd had neither the time nor the opportunity to change shapes.

But she found that, when needed, she could do it with very little trouble. There was a trembling, a fluttering, a brief, painful wrenching, and she let her monkey-self toss aside the clothes, and jumped upward at the same time that she felt the tiger let go a bolt of raw magic.

Hanuman shrieked and went stiff. He fell. And the tiger waited, mouth open.

One of the good things about this state, Lalita thought, was that she could pick up weights she wouldn't otherwise have been able to. Also that Hanuman weighed not much more than she did. She got hold of him with a single arm, even as he started to fall, and swung herself from the ceiling with another limb.

Once, in London, she had accompanied Sofie to a variety show and been amused at how the acrobats duplicated what came naturally to her while changed. Now, with the natural ability of her race, her unconscious comrade held by one long arm, she swung from one ceiling beam to the other, while the tiger roared below.

Doubtless, the tiger would get help. He was a king and he would have to be particularly stupid not to already have infiltrated this house, and to not have his emissaries in every nook and cranny of it, ready to do his command. Though Lalita could not see them, she could almost feel tigers shifting shape all over the house. She could hear subdued roars.

But then, valor was knowing when you were outnumbered and not staying to fight a battle you already knew was lost. She ran along the ceiling beam toward the open door, and then, shifting the burden of Hanuman, prepared to jump.

The tiger roared, what he doubtless meant as an order for the Waringtons to close the door to the balcony outside, but fortunately he could not speak in a human voice while in tiger shape. Lalita calculated the jump and swung. The tiger ran into position and snapped.

She'd overestimated her ability while holding a burden. For a moment, she felt the tiger's breath on her fur, but then her hind hands touched the balcony railing and she swung, letting her somersault carry her and her burden to the lower rail, where the branches of a tamarind tree almost touched it. She swung onto the tree and ran along the branch, and then swung again, farther off, to another tree.

Behind her, she could hear the roars of the tiger, and wondered how long he would pursue them. It wasn't till she was quite far off—past the edge of the garden, past a multitude of roofs and in a distant alley, that she set Hanuman down and allowed herself to become human once again—a naked girl standing in the shadows of the alley. She would have to find clothes. She would have to find Sofie. If the tiger was so determined to find her, then Sofie must be protected.

But right now none of it counted so much as making sure that Hanuman was well, that he was alive. She wasn't sure how much magic the tiger had loosed in that burst, and she very much feared that her companion was dead.

But as she looked down at the long-limbed furry body she'd deposited on the ground, its eyes opened, the broad mouth made a very good imitation of a human grin and the left eye winked impudently at her.

She almost screamed, but controlled it just in time. This area of town was relatively quiet, and people must be within the tall, dark, stone houses, possibly even asleep. But she could hear a conversation somewhere overhead, and she didn't want to call the speaker's attention to her. Instead, she looked down at Hanuman as he shifted, and once he had changed shapes, she glared at his mobile face. "How long were you awake?" she asked.

"Only the last few roofs," he said, and tried to look regretful, or at least serious. Neither worked very well. Hanuman's face was not made for gravity, and his dark eyes sparkled with unholy mischief. "I thought," he said, as he put his earrings back in his ears, and how had he managed to get them from the pile of his clothes? "that if I'd moved or given a sign of being awake, it probably would have thrown you off your stride, and it might have been very painful for both of us."

Lalita exhaled. She had long ago discovered that reproaching her clansmen for not being serious enough was a waste of time. "What were you thinking?" she said instead, her voice harsh. "What could you be thinking to change shapes like that, in that room, with the tiger there? What did you think you could earn by it? Did you not know that he was the king of tigers? Did you think you had the slightest chance to get the cursed jewel?"

"Well, as to that . . ." Hanuman said, and smiled—a wicked, twinkling smile. He brought up his right hand, which he'd kept clenched through the shape-shift, and opened it, displaying a red, glowing jewel. "You see . . ."

Soul of Fire pulsed with magic like a beating heart. And Lalita was, for once, speechless.

CLOTHES; TRAVEL; MADNESS

Sofie couldn't pretend to understand why the dragon must bother packing. Of all things the novels and stories she'd read about weres had told her, they had neglected to mention that dragons were unusually concerned with their own appearance.

Or, for that matter, that they would dither—audibly—over what to do with their lady companion while they changed. But St. Maur—who looked so self-possessed while completely naked and having just shifted from a dragon state, who as a dragon was powerful and magnificent like a force of nature—had started muttering to himself as he approached the house. "Can't leave you in a grotto in the garden. Really, it won't do. Someone might come upon you and ... It doesn't bear thinking. Besides, someone is bound to be looking for you. I don't know if or how they'd find you, but people saw us come here. In my own shape, I mean. We passed so many people. If your parents send out servants to ask ..."

He didn't seem to expect a response from her, and she gave him none. If she'd been forced to speak, she'd have wondered why he thought it would be safer to be found with her in the house than to have her found in the garden and have it thought he'd kidnapped her. Then again, she supposed the worst that could happen if they found her alone in a bedroom with him would be they'd assume she'd somehow been in collusion with him, that they were eloping—they'd have to think of a story to explain the dragon, but she'd found herself in such odd and unaccountable situations in London, and been able to account for them perfectly—and then they'd force her to marry him.

Lady St. Maur, she thought. Money or not, dragon or not, if she had to choose between this man, clearly a gentleman when not a dragon, and the horrible creature on her parents' veranda . . . Well, there was no contest.

She shook her head at the whole thing and followed him quietly—or as quietly as she could—through the front door and up a spiral staircase. She wondered if he knew that three or four servants would be up and unobtrusively watching from various places. Part of this, she knew, was that servants tried to be on hand if you needed them. The other part was that they would be curious. She knew—from being closer to Lalita than was expected, having found herself more at home with her servant than with English misses—that the main topic of conversation for servants was their masters. And in India it wasn't any different. Perhaps it was even more so. The sahibs were strange, wonderful creatures, to be marveled at, censured, criticized or mocked.

But she assumed that Farewell didn't know that, and she would not be the one to destroy his illusions.

Besides, in her experience, when a young woman tried to inform a gentleman about some area in which he was woefully ignorant, she was likely to find herself ignored or—worse—put in her place. She didn't want to start an argument here, in the middle of the night, in some strange people's home. Farewell had been dismissive about his hosts.

"The Holferns," he'd said as they'd entered the immense, carefully tended garden that put her parents' to shame. "Really quite good people. Friends of my father's from way back. Possible they were, initially, my late mother's friends. Not sure about it all. But at any rate, they welcomed me with open arms, and in six months haven't so far as hinted that I leave. Really, quite hospitable. You see why I can't disappear without leaving them a note?"

Which had brought up yet another fact none of the books on how arcane dragons were had disclosed: They were punctilious about etiquette. And now they were on the second floor of the house of these quite hospitable people, where St. Maur commanded a room as large as Sofie's own at home, but far better furnished. It was stocked full of good, solid English furniture: a broad, curtained oak bed; a delicate, painted oak desk by the window; a huge mahogany wardrobe, which St. Maur was consideringly turning out as he packed various suits and hats and walking sticks. Really, Sofie was starting to think that, dragon or not, the Earl of St. Maur was a dull man. The sort that one's parents (though perhaps not *her* parents) said would make a splendid husband. He'd put his ivory-handled brush and comb into a silver-plated toiletry case, containing any number of specifics and powders.

He finished packing the suitcase and looked at his closet, which remained half-full. He sighed with an expression of resignation, and muttered under his breath, "Only so much to carry."

Then walked past her, quite abstracted, to the small writing desk. From a drawer he pulled stationery. He opened the ink bottle. Dipping the handy quill, he wrote quickly. Placed as Sofie was, she could read—in fact, would have trouble avoiding reading— what he wrote with his broad angular hand: *Dear Molsy*—or it might be Moldy, but Sofie very much hoped it wasn't. Squinting, she decided it was probably Maisy, and then she wondered if it was a woman's name and why he'd been addressing his hostess and not his host. *I'm sorry to leave so quickly, but as you know, I got word via mail this morning that Father had departed this vale of tears.* The wording struck Sofie as funny. She'd never have expected even this seemingly conventional English gentleman to use such terms. *Please forgive me, and rest assured I will attempt to return as soon as possible, to claim my clothing and to take a proper leave of you and dear Funny*—or possibly Furry, though more probably Fanny, she supposed. *It is simply that I must consult with Father's local man of business before I make any decisions about my future.* He'd signed it *PF* and then, after an hesitation, *St. Maur.* And then he turned, and caught her looking at the paper.

She expected him to be upset, or perhaps shocked that she was reading over his shoulder, but instead he flashed her a quick smile and spoke in a low voice. "Damned thing to get used to a new name at my time of life." Then he frowned. "And not much chance

Marty will believe that I have any men of business in India, or that Father had one. He knew Father well enough to know all Farewell money has long ago done what the name indicates." He shrugged. "Then again . . . Mother had properties, and perhaps he'll think it has something to do with her dowry. Who knows?"

She didn't, and therefore forbore to speak until he asked directly, "Ready, Miss Warington?"

She nodded, once. "Yes."

"Very well," he said. "We'll go, then. It would be best leave the way we came, through the garden, and for me not to change shapes until we're a while away from the house, so that—" He stopped, as a series of loud roars split the night. "The devil," he said. "Tigers within the city?"

In Sofie's mind, the image of the creature on the veranda appeared. "Lalita said . . ." St. Maur turned to look at her, his eye gazing with a vague expression, as though he didn't really expect her to say anything important or as if he wondered why she was talking at all.

"Lalita said that the raj my parents wanted me to marry . . . She said he came from a place that was called the realm of the tigers, and that anyone who went there . . . wouldn't . . . that Englishmen did not come out of it."

For just a moment the vagueness in Farewell's eye remained, and he looked at her deliberately, from head to toe. It wasn't an interested look. More a considering look, as if he was trying to decide how trustworthy she was. Sofie wanted to scream at him, and possibly throw things. Her quick anger surprised her, so she held herself still by an effort of will.

But then he blinked and nodded. "Kingdom of the Tigers. I've heard. . . . Mind you, I've seen no evidence of it in all my time here; but then, I'm very much an outsider. I've heard that India is shot through with shape-shifters, and with realms and clans of shape-shifters, all holding nothing but their own kind in loyalty."

The roars sounded closer now.

"It's like they're calling to one another," Sofie said. "Showing one another the way." She reached down, almost involuntarily, to pick up her bag. "Like they're telling one another where we are."

"It's possible." Farewell said. "I was never around weres myself. They're not that common in England. Well, other than myself, I mean. I've been around myself, but it's not the sort of thing—" Having muddled his words, he ground to a halt, his brow furrowed above the patch that hid his eye. "The legends say," he said at last, "that witch-sniffers can smell out a were. It is said the Royal Were-Hunters have trained sniffers for that purpose, though I don't believe it, as I've often been quite near companies of them. . . ."

She blinked at him, in turn, confused as to what he could possibly mean by that. "I haven't noticed any particular odor," she said tartly.

His mouth quirked, just briefly. "No," he said. "I bathe." Then seriously, "But you see, if there is an odor to the magic of transformation, then witch-sniffers who are used to having more of our kind around and . . . who are organized might very well have developed a method of smelling us out. And perhaps even recognizing what kind of were."

"How could they smell your path?" she asked. "We flew."

He shook his head slowly. "I don't know, but listen to the roars multiplying out there. If the creature is in town and has a number of his subjects with him, wouldn't he have . . . I mean, how hard could it be to send them to crossroads and . . . and to places a dragon might shift without being seen, and then send them out. To sniff the way the beast went."

"We shouldn't have landed," Sofie said, as a black panic welled within her, threatening to submerge her reason, "We should never have landed. We should have stayed aloft. And we should never have come here."

St. Maur shook his head sternly. "We had to, don't you see? If we hadn't come here, then as far as Marty and Fanny are concerned, I'd simply have disappeared. And if I disappeared at the same time that rumors of dragons flourished, at the same time that a disturbance indicated a dragon had fled town in some hurry . . . My dear child, I might as well have sent an invitation to the Royal Were-Hunters and invited them to hunt me down. And though I've been all over the world and often very much the pauper, my name is something I've never had to abandon. In fact, my name and family connections are often the only things that have allowed me to *survive*. I have to leave a note to account for my absence."

"But now we're going to be killed for it," Sofie said, her heart beating at her throat, her voice a strangled bleat. "Oh, I can't let him catch me. I can't!" She stooped to grab her carpetbags, and started toward the door.

But St. Maur grabbed her arm. "No. Not that. They're in the garden, can't you hear? Quite soon they will be on the staircase, inside the house."

"I will not be caught," she said. "I will run. How can you stand there and—"

Only, Peter wasn't standing there. Instead, he was, with efficient, cool calm, undressing himself. Was he insane? Did he think the tigers would be balked by finding her in a room with a naked man? Did he think that would be enough to cause him to drop any idea of marrying her? But then, he'd never seen the man, and couldn't imagine the animal ruthlessness in those yellow eyes.

St. Maur might be a dragon, but in human form he was a man and a gentleman. He simply did not have the resources to imagine what a true villain would feel and think. He had no way at all.

She shook her head at him, but he spoke calmly, in a stage whisper. "There is no way to avoid it. I'll try to make it quick, but I have to shift in the air. Or shift and leap at the same time, from the balcony. Then I will circle and come back to get you." He removed his cuff links and put them, carefully, inside his bag. "Bring the bags with you, though the dragon...I will take them, once we are airborne. It's what I usually do when I travel. If you just leave them on the edge of the balcony as you climb on his—my—back, I will be sure to grab the bags." He removed his shirt to reveal his smooth, muscular torso, covered in golden skin and glowing, faintly, with the magic glow that she imagined prefaced his changing. "The dragon will be very hungry," he said. And she thought he seemed to have the oddest relationship with his other shape, talking about it as though it was something quite other, something quite separate from his human self. "And I must stop just outside town and let it feed—as soon as we can be sure of finding some wildlife. But I will try to make it brief and I will stay aloft as much as possible, till we're far away from the city."

In her mind, slowly, she was processing that he meant to shift here, on the balcony. That he was actually trying to do something to save her.

He was now completely naked, and she tried not to look at him. Yet, even with the approaching roars of the tigers, even with the panic welling up in her, Sofie could not help looking him over and thinking that he was magnificent. Smooth and golden, like a statue carved in gold—he didn't look like someone any woman could ignore, unless she were dead. Thoughts came to her mind, unbidden, of running her hand along his shoulders, of feeling the smooth strength of his muscular arms. She wondered what it would feel like. She'd never touched a man before. She'd never seen a man naked before, save a crazy beggar in London who was wont to remove all his clothes and walk around proclaiming that his body didn't belong to him.

"Miss Warington," he said, recalling her to herself. "No point being frozen in fear. Please take my bag as well. I must go." Turning, he walked with the broad stride of an athlete to the balcony. Before he got there, she heard him cough—once, twice. Then his body twisted.

She heard roars in the house, roars up the stairs.

She stooped and grabbed the bags and hurried to the balcony, where St. Maur leapt into space even as he was shifting shapes.

He leapt from the balcony railing—and for a second, she thought that they'd both imagined it, that he wasn't going to change shapes, couldn't change shapes. That he was, in fact, just a man like other men. That he would dash his brains on that neat cobbled path they'd passed while entering the house.

It was easier to believe that she'd imagined his transformation before than to see what was taking place before her very eyes—that smooth, golden body twisting and writhing midair; a sound like a strangled scream escaping his lips; a tail, wings, paws, scales extruding themselves from that mass that seemed much too small to contain them. And then the wings spreading...

The beast took to the air with a grace that denoted this was its natural environment, the wings spread between her and the sky, and the dragon described a broad circle over the gardens, before coming back to her.

Sofie resumed breathing, not aware she'd stopped for a moment. And then she realized that the loud roar behind her was closer, just a tiger's leap away. She looked over her shoulder and caught a glimpse of a tawny, sleek hide, and the vague impression of lifted hind quarters and lowered front, as the creature prepared to jump.

There was a sound from the other side of the balcony that might have been a sneeze or a dragon-sized exclamation of alarm. Forcing herself not to panic, she turned forward, to see the dragon just by the balcony.

Dropping the bags, she jumped onto the broad, green back.

The dragon grabbed both bags at the same time she saw the tiger leap. But it had arrived too late and could only roar in frustration as the dragon took wing.

Sofie, holding on to a sort of ruffled skin around the neck, wondered if she was hurting it. Beneath her, the Ganges flowed sluggishly, and the expanse of the park looked dun-gray in the night, showing the colors of the drought before the monsoon.

She clasped the warm, scaley body with her legs. There was no way of riding a dragon sidesaddle with any safety, so her skirts were hiked to mid-thighs, which made her feel indecent, until she realized it couldn't be nearly as strange as riding this beast who was only so recently an English gentleman. The Earl St. Maur. She wondered how much of the gentleman remained in the beast's form, and what he thought of having her ride him. It seemed almost too debauched for words.

"It would be much better, really," she said, speaking to distract herself from the strangeness of the situation, "if one could use a saddle."

It seemed to her as though the dragon convulsed beneath her, but she was not at all sure what the spasm meant.

Below, the teeming metropolis of Calcutta dwindled to the size of a toy village. And she took it all in with wide-open eyes. It was really a much better view than from a carpetship, where there were always other people in the way, and partitions of glass designed to keep the wind out.

It was cold, here on dragon-back, and her hair

flapped in the wind. But it wasn't too cold, since Calcutta sweltered in the premonsoon heat, and not even the breeze of their motion could cool her fully. She saw her parents' house—or thought she did—as they soared out of town. She wondered what her parents were doing, what they thought of her disappearance and whether she would ever be able to return to a calm and conventional life.

SAVING THE JEWEL;
THE DRAGONS AND
THE TIGERS; DECISIONS

Lalita heard the roars of the tigers and stood, shaking herself. So Hanuman got the jewel, which would probably make him insufferable, at least judging by the impression of incredible self-satisfaction he managed to give without so much as batting an eye.

"You would be dead," she said, tartly, "if I hadn't saved you."

He got up in a single jump and bowed to her, a smooth movement. "Indeed, Princess. But you did save me, did you not?"

There was no answer to that. "We must hide that jewel. If we don't, we'll have them all on us."

He bowed again, and she could feel him doing something with his magic. That she couldn't tell what it was disturbed her. Not only did she have more magic than practically anyone she'd ever met, her magical knowledge had been grounded in early teaching and childhood training, and she could instinctively sense spells and read the magic works of those around her. Not for her the kind of half-baked spells and pretty-

pretty mage-workings that had been taught to Sofie at Lady Lodkin's. She knew real magic, and she could read it as easily as she could read human expressions. Or better. But she couldn't tell what Hanuman had just done, and she would rather be flogged in the public square than admit her ignorance.

"The jewel is hidden, Princess," he said, smoothly. "Now, what are your orders?"

She was irked by finding that not only couldn't she feel the ruby—which should have been distorting her magical perceptions and feelings—she couldn't see it either, and she shook her head in frustration. Then she listened to the roars and said, "Are they looking for us or the dragon?"

"Both, I imagine," Hanuman said, "though I can't understand their roars. If I were them, I would look for both. You heard them talking in the house. They want both the ruby and your friend."

"But why? Why Sofie?"

Hanuman shrugged. "Your guess is as good as mine. If I were the dragon, I would be well out of town by now. But I've said the spell to activate my witch-sniffing, and if it is not deceiving me, he's not. The air is thick with the smell of dragons."

"You are a trained witch-sniffer? And you know the smell of dragons?" she asked, raising eyebrows at him and wondering what could have passed through her noble uncle's mind to saddle her with such a strange and trying companion as Hanuman. And who was Hanuman, exactly, to be both so trusted and so exasperating?

He shrugged at her and grimaced. "I know from China."

So he had traveled? He spoke the local language without flaw, so surely that meant . . . But her head was spinning. "And you can smell dragons? More than one?"

He nodded. "Most strongly I smelled one of them in the square back there, when we swept over the roof near the monument to the Black Hole disaster. But then there was another one—I think following close behind—that joined him. And they came through here, and went that way." He frowned. "Probably in human form."

'The dragon who took Sofie had help?"

Hanuman shrugged. "This, I can't say. You know how things are in China. Their own and ancient Imperial line—the dragon line—has been deposed by the English, and another installed in its place. One that is neither magic nor dragons. What would you do if you were a deposed emperor and there was a jewel that could give you what this ruby can?"

"Take it," Lalita said.

Hanuman nodded. "Indeed."

"But that means that they must be planning to do something with Sofie." She didn't ask him if he could smell Sofie. One human smelled much like the other, and even a sniffer would have problems isolating Sofie's inconsequential amount of power. "We must follow. We must see if we can rescue her."

"Perhaps," Hanuman said, looking down at himself, then back up at her, unholy glee in his eyes. "It might not be a bad idea to dress oneself, though. I know the very poor go around naked, but, Princess, neither you nor I look like the very poor."

She hated to admit he was right, but of course he

was. Slick and well fed, neither of them could pretend to be destitute beggars. "We'll go back to my uncle's palace, then, and get clothes."

Hanuman shook his head at her, and she tried to explain. "After shifting shapes in front of the Waringtons, I can't go back to their house," she said. "Oh, I know they didn't recognize me before I changed, but they will have had time to look at the clothes. And they will—or at least they might very well—remember them. And you know what Englishmen do to weres...."

He shook his head again. "I didn't mean that. But we don't have time to go to the palace. Do you hear the tigers? They're closing in. Both on us and on your friend. If they find her, with the dragons or not..." He shrugged. "I would guess there are thirty tigers or so in the city right now, and two dragons. And while dragons can fly, you saw what the tiger can do with his magic. Even if one of the dragons is the hidden emperor himself, this far from his land and his clan, he can't command as much power as the tiger king."

"No," Lalita said, conceding. "But then...why shouldn't we go as monkeys?"

"They're looking for monkeys," Hanuman said. "And though they surely can smell us in human form, the smell will be less strong, and there are...things we can do."

"But where can we find clothes?"

"Hold this, kindly, Princess." He shoved the ruby into her hand. She still couldn't see it, but she could feel it, hard and faceted, in her hand. And the next moment, he was a monkey again, flitting and climbing the nearby buildings.

It seemed to Lalita that the man was indefatigable. How did he manage that much energy when he had just changed shapes moments before—and had been hit with a magical blow by the king of tigers? You'd think he would be tired. She was tired just looking at him.

Not that she could follow him clearly or for very long. She knit herself deeper into the shadows as she watched him flit up the wall and around windows, until he plunged into an open one.

She thought he would be a while, and she prepared herself for screams of outrage or shock when someone spotted a monkey in their bedchamber. But there was nothing. Nothing but the distant sounds of the city. And suddenly, he was back, jumping in front of her in monkey form, then changing to human very rapidly and bowing smoothly, extending her a bundle of green-and-gold clothing. "I hope this is acceptable finery," he said. "I know it is not worthy of your beauty, but it is the best I could do in the dark and in this neighborhood."

Lalita wrapped herself in the sari, which was clean but fairly worn cotton, and did not deign to dignify his needling with an answer. Instead, she said, "You said there was something you could do for our scent. I thought you meant to steal sandalwood or some of the other perfumes that dull the ability to smell."

He shook his head. "Those would inevitably work, but then they would also dull *our* ability to smell. And that would lead to our finding ourselves adrift, with no possibility of finding your friend before the tigers do. Unless you propose to ride a tiger without being noticed?"

Lalita hoped he was joking, but she could not be sure, and she shook her head at him. "Then, what?"

"Magic," he said. "Like what I used for the ruby." He'd dressed himself while he spoke, in loose pants and a tunic. Not quite peasant attire, but not nearly as rich a fabric as he'd lost back in the Waringtons' house—in what Lalita still thought was an ill-considered act, even if it had got them the jewel.

"Shouldn't we bring the jewel to the king?" she asked. She was aware that if they did take the time to deliver the ruby to the secret palace, going through the various bodyguards and barriers, they might be too late to save Sofie. But the king wanted the jewel, and the ruby must be their first priority.

Hanuman shook his head. "Time enough to take the ruby when we have found your friend," he said. "After all..." He shrugged. "If the dragons and the tigers think they need the girl and the jewel together, perhaps they do. What would be the good of giving the king half a solution?"

Lalita thought he was lying. Or at least giving her a superficial reason to hide a deeper one. She got a feeling, as she'd had back at the palace, that Hanuman played his own game. A trusted servant of the king he might be, and even perhaps loyal—within reason. But he had his own plan, and his own agenda. And he'd been in China. She wondered what that meant. What had he been doing in China? Who was this monkey-man who had a peasant's name and a nobleman's arrogant certainty?

"Come," he said, displaying that certainty as he walked assuredly down an alley and up another, following a scent that Lalita could not sense.

They went down the alleys, and up streets, past parks and fountains. People crowded on either side and several discussed the tigers that had invaded the town. A few seemed aware that they were weres— enough of their conversation reached Lalita for her to know that. But Hanuman did not slow down and neither did she, so there was no time to ask what the locals had seen or what they knew. Which in a way fitted with Hanuman's seeming arrogance, and certainty that he knew where he was going and what to do.

She followed him as the roads they traveled became less crowded and more spacious until before them loomed the huge mansions of the Englishmen in the most fashionable area of the city.

"What would a dragon be doing here?" Lalita asked Hanuman's back, but he only shrugged. Then, reaching over, he pushed her against a wall. Before she could protest, she felt as though a warm hand were pressed over her mouth—even though Hanuman had squeezed against the wall by her side and was only touching her at waist level, to hold her still against the wall.

She squirmed against his hand. How dare he? She had saved his life. She had brought him here, too. And she was better born than him, of that she was sure.

He looked at her pleadingly. That stopped her movement. She didn't even know his bold, handsome face could look that humble. She was sure the impudent cuss didn't mean it, but that he could look like that at all was enough to arrest her movement.

In the next second, she felt as though a blanket were thrown over her, smothering her. She could see everything, and she could breathe, but there was a flicker before her vision, as if some translucent veil interposed between her and the street with its huge mansions and graceful palm trees. And she could only hear and breathe as though through that veil.

She couldn't make a sound, because the feeling of a hand holding her mouth shut was still over her lips. But she could see and hear and smell as a tiger came padding down the street, looking this way and that, roaring softly with the appearance of a man talking to himself. Or perhaps calling signals to nearby companions.

Lalita's heart beat fast at her throat, and she felt as if her blood had turned to ice in her veins. The tiger would see them. It would see them and turn on them, and weres always knew how to kill other weres.

As it passed, it turned in their direction, looked straight at them. It opened its broad jaws and roared loudly.

From an alley behind them, another roar answered it. It was calling its comrades. It—

Lalita fought for breath, to scream. Her mouth was still magically shut, but she refused to die silent. She fought with the magic, and found it overpoweringly strong, much stronger than her own.

And then the tiger turned, slowly, and roared again, looking at the other side of the street. It got an answer and padded on. It took a moment of hasty swallowing, of taking a deep breath—of feeling like she was drowning—for Lalita to realize that the tiger hadn't seen her, after all. She was free.... *They* were free. Whatever strange magic Hanuman commanded, it had defeated what must be the personal bodyguards of the king of tigers.

"Who are you?" she asked Hanuman, as the tiger disappeared around a corner. She was surprised to hear her words echo back at her, actually audible. He'd removed the obstacle to her speech.

"Your humble servant," he said.

She shook her head, annoyed. She wanted to interrogate him right here and now . . . but what good would it do? She didn't have time to look for a proper answer. And besides, her uncle, whose duty it was to protect the kingdom of monkeys, thought that Hanuman was trustworthy. And what galled her most was feeling the charm of the creature. But she should know better than to allow herself to feel his attraction. She must remember how annoying he was and stay on guard.

"I don't think we should go any nearer," he said, and pointed. "The dragons went there." He pointed to a white mansion enclosed by tall walls and set like a jewel in its casing deep within a rich garden kept verdant even in these premonsoon dry days. How many gardeners did they employ? How many servants?

"The tigers went there, too," Hanuman continued. "All of them. That garden and that house will be lousy with them."

"What about Sofie?" Lalita said.

Hanuman opened his mouth to answer. Before he could, there was a rush of wings overhead. Lalita stared, unable to believe. Sofie sat astride the dragon that had first taken her from the balcony. That much was easy to understand. The beast could have overpowered her or somehow forced her to climb on its back again, so it could take her wherever it meant to. But what magic, what strange twist of events could have caused the dragon to carry Sofie's carpetbag and another one—one in one claw and one in another—like some sort of supernatural porter?

Lalita stared and fought back an urge to laugh at the incongruence of the sight. And before she could fully absorb it, another dragon flew by overhead. This was a different dragon, lacking the bulk of the first. It was a wisp or a serpentine creature that shimmered like a flash of lightning across the sky, and which had no visible wings.

By her side, Hanuman was not so constrained. He laughed, a full gurgle of amusement.

"Princess," he said, "I think we might have got the whole situation wrong. I don't think your friend was kidnapped."

"No," Lalita said, reluctantly. "But who was the other dragon? I suppose that creature was a dragon?"

Hanuman nodded. "Oh, yes. It was a dragon from China."

CHINA TEA AND HUNTING
HOUNDS; THE UNCONCERN
OF THE GENTLEMEN

Inside the Wheeler Officers' Club in Meerut, one might have been in Mother England. Captain Black-lock looked across the small table, set with delicate china and plates of artfully piled sandwiches, at General Paitel.

It had been a matter of chance and—for a change—good luck to find that General Paitel was in fact an old Eton friend of William Blacklock's father. He was also the man that William's superiors in Her Majesty's Secret Service had instructed him to tell his fears to. They had gotten tired of the minute explanations of William's blood-soaked dreams, and so had told him to tell the general of his suspicions—though William presumed they still meant for him to hold on to the secrecy of his placement there. And it came to him, with sudden bitterness, that perhaps even that didn't matter. Perhaps they were so disgusted by both his failure to find Soul of Fire and his refusal to marry Sofie Warington that they just wanted to punish him.

It shouldn't be possible, of course, but William had

found that the secret service, like any other large orga-
nization run by humans, could often descend to ap-
pallingly childlike behavior. So that left William with
General Paitel.

The note sent around to the captain's lodgings and
brought in with almost reverence by his carrier had
seemed fallen from heaven. He didn't know how much
he could tell the general. He was sure he could not reveal any of the knowledge that came to him from the
secret service. Not that it mattered.

After all, all Lord Wiltington's knowledge, delivered to Blacklock as it had been, at several removes—
and probably delivered to at least fifty other young
secret service men spread around the various parts of
the empire, from China to Africa—was scant enough.
Yet, perhaps because General Paitel had known
William's father, William wouldn't need to reveal all.
Perhaps he could just explain his premonitory gift that,
after all, ran in the Blacklock family.

Now he'd poured out all that his subaltern had told
him—and more, his vague feelings and fears—into
General Paitel's ears. He'd spoken in an undertone,
conscious of the natives all around—one of them,
uniformed and smooth shaven, wearing a European
haircut, standing behind the General's own chair and
moving swiftly, now and then, to refill their cups.
William wondered what he'd heard, and what he understood of William's careful half-whispers.

He also wondered what General Paitel thought, or
understood of what William had said. A fatherly man,
portly and powerful, his rounded face fringed with
white whiskers and beard, the general was the sort
who could have posed for a sentimental portrait of an

old man surrounded by grandchildren, enjoying the pleasures of home. Instead, he was out here, in an alien land. Experienced in India, too. He'd first come to the country at twenty or so, so he had been there almost his entire adult life. There and Back Again Paitel, his troops called him, and it was said he commanded the fanatical loyalty of his native sepoys.

Even in his short time in India, William had seen how General Paitel interacted with his troops and how they treated him, with deference and respect. If anyone here could make something of William's misgivings, it would be General Paitel.

But the mild blue eyes looked Blacklock over with almost a hint of amusement. "Now, boy," he said, softly, making William feel as though he were about three years old, "how long have you been in India?"

"Three . . . three months," he said, a stammered response, which he knew sounded infantile. He was talking to a man who had been in India for twenty years, a man who knew everything about India.

The general didn't improve on William's frame of mind by laughing. He leaned across and grabbed a sandwich, which he ate in three precise bites before answering. "Listen, you're young, and I don't doubt you're as sharp as they come. Your father always was, when we were both at Eton. Sharper, in fact, than I. But the thing is, India is not like England. It is not at all the same thing. If you are going to put much faith in the words of your subordinates, you'll find yourself hoaxed more often than not. Melodramatic, the natives are." He spoke in a big, booming voice that could be heard all over the dainty tearoom, with its elegant white-covered tables and its occupants—English officers and their wives and daughters, and countless native attendants.

Reflexively, William looked to the man standing behind the general. His face remained quite impassive. Blacklock tried to convince himself that perhaps the man did not speak English, but this was hardly probable. Everyone who worked at the club and was brought in daily contact with the Englishmen there understood at least enough to encompass the theme of the general's remarks. So what did he think of them?

"But, sir . . ." he said, and in a reflexive gesture that he hadn't repeated since he'd been teased for it at Eton, he swept his raven-dark fall of hair from his forehead and back, to stare with seemingly too young and innocent eyes at the experienced general. "But sir, you know the Blacklock men—all of us—have the gift of premonition."

The general nodded, but his mouth twitched just a little in the beginnings of a frown. William was familiar with this reaction. It had followed him all through his public schooling and his career in Her Majesty's service. Foretelling, premonition, prophecy. Oh, they'd first recruited him because of it, but when it became clear he wasn't always right, they stopped listening. And they never trusted soothsaying. Whatever you called it, it was considered somewhat less than respectable. The great mages of the last few centuries—Locke, Lavoisier, Descartes, and Hume, whose quantifying of the laws of magic and their application to reality had taken magic from the secret mutterings passed from master to apprentice to an exact science—had changed all of magic except prophecy. That alone remained uncontrolled and unquantifiable. Better men than William, finding themselves possessed of that gift, had kept quiet about it for fear of being thought crazy. His own father rarely spoke of it—though when William had visited home, just before shipping out to India, he'd caught his father opening the Bible and reading a passage within (in a clear act of bibliomancy) then closing both the Bible and his eyes and looking very pale. He'd parted from William as if he'd never see him again. Which might be true, or it might simply be William's imaginings.

General Paitel shook his head slightly, as if relegating the whole idea of prophecy to that realm about which no decent man should talk. "A great pity, I say," he said. "And I always thought it was because your great-grandmother had Irish blood. Or at least I remember her portrait in your father's house—all milky skin and blue eyes, with pitch-black hair. Yes, very attractive and all that, I'm sure, but these curses come into English blood from mingling with other races, and there's no getting away from it. And the Irish are as full of mad prophets as—" Perhaps catching William's eyes and the plea in them, which had nothing to do with his ancestry and all to do with his dark dreams of blood and roiling massacre, the general sighed and dabbed at his moustache with the tip of his linen napkin. "But I know you have a gift of prophecy, at least if you're like your father, who would often wake screaming in the night before some tragedy or other.

"I remember this one time when three boys drowned while swimming in the stream—before it happened, for days on end, Arthur would wake up screaming that he lacked for air. But you see, it is always like that. I found it marvelous that he could have such a gift, and yet that his gift should be of no help whatsoever. Because he never dreamed the results to a test, or even the results of a roll of dice in those games we held after hours."

William smiled, despite himself. It was a taut and controlled smile, more dismissal than amusement, but still he smiled. "No, sir, they never reveal that. And even what they do reveal is often occluded and hard to interpret. But..." He paused as the servant filled his cup. The aroma of fragrant China tea tickled his nostrils. "But, sir, ever since I landed here at Meerut, I've had blood-soaked dreams every single night."

"Eh? Blood-soaked?"

"Dreams of blood, of..." William waited while the server backed away from the table. In the lull, he could hear the clink of teacups and, behind him, a loud discussion of someone's hunting dog, a fine bitch. From the other end of the dining hall, a female's voice sounded, saying something about sleeves. The native stepped back and William spoke just above a whisper. "I have dreams of riots, like the ones in 1857."

"Pshaw. A morbid imagination, my boy," the general said, then gave the younger man a kindly look that did nothing to calm William. "Your grandfather died in those, did he not? I remember your father telling me that."

"Yes, sir. Here in Meerut."

"And you're named for him, are you not? Your father told me that, too."

William nodded. "But—"

"Doubtless enough to get anyone's dander up. I mean, same name and you find yourself in India? My boy . . . sympathetic magic is a strange thing, and your being here, same blood with the same name . . . Has it never occurred to you these might not be premonitions at all? That it might be no more than your grandfather's . . . memories?" Warming to his idea, the general's voice gained impetus and enthusiasm. "Wouldn't surprise me at all. You know, with the memories being his last in life. And there was so much death here at that time."

William said, "But . . ." even as his eyes strayed again to the native standing behind the table, and he wondered if the man's ancestors, or his relatives, had been part of the massacre. Had they been among those servants and sepoys who had remained loyal? Were they among the ones who had never broken faith with their British masters? Who could tell? More than a generation had passed. Perhaps more than two, in this land where people married early.

"No, depend upon it," the general said, reaching for an apple from an artfully arranged tower of fruit, and peeling it with a little silver knife. "That's all it is. Your grandfather's memories, poor sod. You know, without being papist . . . Well, it might benefit you to say a prayer in his memory, maybe visit his grave. I'm sure your father would tell you the same."

"I'm sure, too," Blacklock said, then hesitated. "But, sir . . . it can't be memories."

"Eh?"

Blacklock realized that his words, instead of a semi-whisper, had come out as almost a scream. He saw that the general was looking at him and waiting for an explanation. He managed to lower his voice. "There were weres in this dream, sir. Elephants and...and tigers. And monkeys and...dragons."

The general's laugh pealed out like a bell, startling the club into silence. "Dragons? Now I know you're simply imagining things. What would a dragon be doing here? Now? We're not in China. And even in China, since the Arrow War dragons have been scarce enough."

William wanted to talk of the English were who was somewhere with that jewel the Queen wanted, but he could not. It was not his secret to betray. And yet, an English were would certainly not be a dragon. The most exotic creature he'd ever heard mentioned in his books was born of the soil of Albion: Richard the Lionheart, who shifted to lion form. And given how long ago that had been and what a mingle of nationalities royalty was, he supposed it wasn't so surprising.

But then...if the jewel in play truly was everything the Queen thought, and if Soul of Fire—which William hadn't been able to see in his visions at all—was truly in India, then what pieces would that attraction not bring to the game?

For a moment, for just a moment, William Blacklock had a flash of premonition, something that rarely happened to him when he was awake. He saw himself on elephant back, while all around him, animals and humans fought, and blood and corpses piled high, and in the middle of it all, the girl he knew from London— Sofie Warington—and a flying dragon.

It was all too quick for him to understand what it meant. The vision happened between one breath and the next, and left him tasting bile and gasping for breath.

"Are you well?" the general asked. "You look white as a sheet."

William nodded. He couldn't explain, any more than he could avert a doom that he didn't understand, a doom that was headed for him.

THE DRAGON WAKES;
WORSHIP AND PANIC;
WHERE THE EARL OF
ST. MAUR REALIZES
HE'S LOST HIS MIND

There was a feeling like a spiderweb being dragged behind Peter's eyes as he turned in his sleep, but he did not wake. Instead, his mind followed the web, silver bright, through a dream where he tripped—he wasn't even sure in which form—blindly through a landscape shrouded in amorphous wrappings. Trees, bushes and—he would swear to it—wildlife were all swathed in the sort of covers that people used for furniture in abandoned houses.

He stumbled through the shrouded landscape, searching... And then, suddenly, he stood on a slight rise and looked below, at his ancestors' home— Summercourt, with its untidy garden, its neglected fields, its ivy-grown walls. But there was something about it, a glow, a feeling—and he knew this time he was coming home for good and no one would ask him to leave again.

"Home," he said. And the word startled him

awake, having come out of his lips in something like a moan. He blinked awake to green-filtered light, and realized he was in human form, lying beneath the low-hanging boughs of a tree.

Almost everything around was the blinkered dun that people who had been in India far longer than he assured him was normal during the season of drought before the monsoon. But this little clearing, where he'd chosen to spend the night, was green from a brook running at the periphery, like an oasis in thirst-parched lands. Peter looked at the sky through the boughs, trying to order his mind. There had been the dream... but that was foolishness.

He didn't turn to look behind him, where Miss Warington should still be asleep. From the look of the sky, turning rosy-pink but not quite bright yet, it was very early, and they'd lain down late. They hadn't lit a fire. There was no point lighting a fire. No creature in its right mind—or even in its wrong mind—would come near Peter.

Only humans, with their foolish disregard of instinct, would be silly enough to come near the dragon—at least in his human form. But Peter had lain down as a dragon, something he rarely did. It was strange, but he hadn't felt right, laying beside Sofie as a man. Not alone like this, in Darjeeling. Sometimes, lying with the dragon could be dangerous—though since Peter had allowed the beast to feed just out of Calcutta, he didn't think there would be any danger at all. And strangely, the dragon behaved to Sofie as he'd never behaved to a human being before. Around Sofie, the creature went all mellow and biddable, and allowed Peter to control it better than it ever had before.

To be honest, though the thought seemed strange, Peter trusted the dragon better around Sofie than he trusted himself in his human form. Last night, she'd ducked behind some bushes to change into a white nightgown not so different from the muslin dress she'd been wearing when he met her. But by the light of the moon and the eyes of the beast, Peter had seen that the nightgown lacked a collar and sleeves. It exposed her shoulders and the base of her neck, and that space at the base of her throat, where a little hollow looked as though some enamored divinity had lingered his finger too long upon the clay.

Even now, remembering it, Peter groaned. From the back of the beast's mind, Peter had dreamed of touching that spot with his lips, and seeing if her skin felt as silky soft as it looked. *And what good at all would that do, Peter Farewell, Lord St. Maur?* he asked himself. *She's beautiful and young and foolish. And you are not human. Or not quite.*

But here, for just a moment between the night and the morning, he sighed deeply and held on to an image, not quite a dream—he'd long ago given up on that dream—of a time when he could be a man like others, a man who loved and was loved in return. A man who could inherit his father's paltry lands and his honor.

A sound like something scurrying at his feet made him sit up, alarmed. Images of snakes, or some animal dangerous enough not to fear him, slithered through his mind. But as he blinked, what he saw were two girls. Pretty girls, of the local type, perhaps all of twelve or thirteen, dressed in heavily embroidered clothes and arrayed in gold and sparkling stones. Their hair was braided in heavy plaits down their backs.

They had circlets of pink corals about their heads, and they were blushing and pressing into each other, as if looking for protection or comfort. They'd been setting heavy brass trays at his feet. He looked at the trays in wonder, for they were full of what appeared to be fruit and roast meat.

He looked back up at the girls, who hadn't moved and who, though they were blushing, didn't seem to find anything strange about the fact that he was stark naked and sleeping outdoors. Without seeming to do so, he let his hand fall to rest on his lap, partially covering his privates, to protect his modesty if not theirs. And he tried to understand what was happening. They bowed to him. First one, then the other.

Why would mountain maidens—probably from some nearby village, since the city of Darjeeling proper was quite a bit away—come bearing trays of fruit this early in the morning? Was this some strange form of hospitality? And if it was, what did it mean? There were rumors about the tribes in these mountains. Some so different they did not seem to be part of the culture of India at all. It was said that there were even cannibals in this area. And thinking of that, Peter almost smiled. Let the cannibals come, and welcome. He hoped they liked dragon. But why would they send two barely nubile girls with food? To ensnare their prey by making him feel safe?

He cleared his throat, and with a ray of hope of being understood—because his countrymen had the bewildering ability of insinuating themselves into the strangest corners of the globe—he spoke. "Hullo. Good morning. What is this about?"

The girls exchanged a panicked glance. Seeing that

look, he knew they didn't understand him. Or at least he thought so, until the girl on the left—perhaps the prettier, and certainly the most developed of the two—stepped forward hesitantly and fell on her knees, giving him a full bow, forehead touching the grassy ground. He scooted backwards. She raised her head from the ground and spoke in a lilting accent, in hesitating cadences, "Sahib dragon."

Oh. Well. That was something. They knew he was a dragon, then? He raised his eyebrows, not quite knowing whether to wonder at their calm acceptance of the fact or at their innocent offering of fruit to something like his other form.

The girl clearly took his expression for questioning, and she blushed and stammered, "Our father chieftain of village. He send food and greeting. He say 'O Lord Dragon, leave our flocks and our children alone. Take instead this food.' " She gesticulated to the tray of fruit with its few slices of meat with a gesture that would not be out of place in amateur theatrics in an English girls' school. "And . . . and . . ." She blushed even deeper, the red like a blotch on her cheeks, and glanced at her sister, who blushed in turn, but gave her a little determined nod. " 'And my daughters. They are . . . they are virgins. Take them as offering, O Dragon.' "

Peter felt his eyes widen in shock. He was not absolutely sure why he was being offered these barely grown maidens. And indeed, he had no idea if he was supposed to eat them or disport himself with them. And he was as likely to do one as the other, he thought, since neither was something a decent human being would do. They were beautiful in the way girls were beautiful when they'd not yet reached full adulthood.

They excited his pity and his amusement, his tenderness and his desire to protect them. But they did not arouse him. And as for eating them—never while conscious had he allowed himself to eat human flesh. Much less young and innocent human flesh.

He must have looked truly bewildered, because the girl went from looking scared to looking puzzled and then, by degrees, looking faintly disdainful. "You dragon," she said.

He nodded. Admittedly, him dragon. There hinged just about all his problems.

She sighed, and suddenly assuming an expression that reminded Peter very much of his nursemaid when he was five and being particularly dense about learning his first letters, said, "You dragon. We virgins. You take us. Both. You make babies."

He didn't know whether to laugh or cry. He coughed instead, and for just a moment hid his face in his hands, not trusting his expression not to offend them mortally. "It . . . it is very good of you to offer," he said at last, looking up. "Kindly thank your father, and tell him I wouldn't hurt his flocks nor his people, but, you see, I travel with my own virgin." And on those words, his lips quirking with the repressed urge to laugh out loud, he looked over his shoulder at where he fully expected Sofie to stand.

But she wasn't there. He got up, panicking, and looked all around the clearing. Her bag and clothes were where she had left them last night, where she'd lain down for the night, with her head on the carpetbag. But no Sofie.

"Sofie," he said. Then more loudly. "Sofie?" He

turned back to the girls. "Where is she? Where did she go? Did your men take her?"

He felt the beast writhe within him, struggling to emerge. But he couldn't allow it, not now. Rage surged like a black tide within him, and he was barely holding it at bay. He could not allow the beast to take over. He'd lay waste to this whole area. Then he would be a true danger to these two maidens, who stood staring at him with wild, scared eyes, shaking their heads ever so slightly.

Turning his back on them, he called into the tall trees and the enclosing greenness. "Sofie! For the love of heaven, Sofie, if you're there, answer me!"

From very far off, it seemed to him, a faint call came. Not quite an answer as much as a surprised "Oh!"

And in that direction he plunged, naked, through the woods, feeling bushes and trees introduce themselves to his acquaintance quite forcefully, bruising and scraping him as he ran barefoot on the uneven ground. "Sofie," he called.

And this time more definite, there came an answer, in a tone of great surprise. "Milord?"

She'd called him milord or Lord St. Maur in the very few words they'd exchanged yesterday, something he would have to change. It didn't matter if it was his true title. It wasn't real. He'd never live in his domains on his father's land. So he didn't feel right being addressed by his title. Certainly not by lovely Sofie Warington. But he called back, "Sofie?"

Through the trees, he caught a glimmer of pale skin and dark hair, and he ran forward . . . and stopped, abruptly. Sofie Warington stood before him, her abundant hair loose down her back, framing her face in lush black curls.

"Sofie," he said, and he felt himself blush. "I woke and you weren't there. I thought . . ."

She looked sleepy, confused, like a child woken from a deep sleep who has not got his bearings yet. "I just woke," she said. "Back there." She pointed. "When I heard you calling."

His hand went up to his hair and clutched there. "You just woke . . . but how?"

She shook her head, as though the answer she was about to give didn't particularly satisfy even her. "I used to sleepwalk in London," she said. "A few times I found myself outside the school at night. It is part of the reason my parents said I should come back to India, where I could be with them. They thought it was the stress of living so far away from them. Or at least they said so. It's possible . . . no, it is certain, they just wanted to marry me to . . . that thing."

Her mouth set in something between a pout and an expression of grief, and Peter wanted to kiss the pain away from those lips, but it was not possible. Was this what being in love felt like? If so, it was a very foolish thing, and it had come on him as suddenly as a fever. He was a man of the world. He'd seen many, many women, several of whom would have made Miss Sofie Warington pale in comparison. He'd met them beautiful and he'd met them witty and he'd met them wealthy. But never till now had he come so near to losing his head over a woman.

Probably just lust, he thought. And it made sense, of course. Among Mr. Farewell's many exploits, the one he couldn't brag of was carnal love. He'd discovered he was a dragon just before becoming a man and it hadn't taken him long to realize that the same dizzying tension that women quickened in his body could cause him to change shapes and become the beast— and a particularly uncontrolled beast, at that. The thought of what might happen should he actually attempt to complete the act that made humans and beasts the same—the idea of some poor woman caught, charred and half eaten in his bed—had kept Peter from bedding even the most beguiling courtesan or the most abandoned of loose skirts. And he was now close to thirty. Most men his age were married, or at least had found *bibis,* or mistresses. The body would demand its dues. This Peter had discovered in both forms. He knew vaguely that papist clergymen and monks stayed celibate, but he supposed religious faith helped with that. *I know nothing of her, or next to nothing. I just want to touch her and hold her. Lust, definite lust. If only there were women who could—*

And with that, the thought intruded of the two girls back in the clearing, who had been expecting him to do who knew what to them, and whom he'd left standing by the trays of fruit. He wondered what they'd done. And he felt a sudden fear for his luggage and Sofie's, and for what the girls might tell their father, too. After all, he did not want to have to fight the local tribe. Not when he was with Sofie, who was vulnerable.

Aloud, he said, "Oh, Lord, the virgins," and, to Sofie's look of surprise, he explained, "Two girls from a local village. They woke me with trays of fruit, which I fancy will do very well for our breakfast, if you will follow me back to our suitcases—which I hope are still there."

"Fruit?" she asked.

"It appears their father is a local chieftain." He led her through the trees, back the way he'd come—quite easy to discern, the way he'd broken the branches and torn the leaves in his rushed panic to find her. Now that he was calmer, he realized he must have stepped on a thorn somewhere along the line. He felt the pain every time he rested his foot fully on the ground, and he started favoring his foot as he walked. *Perhaps if she removes the thorn from the dragon's paw, the dragon will follow her to the end of the world.* "Apparently he thought it prudent to ply me with fruit, which would keep me, of course, from eating his herds and his children."

Immediately after saying those words, he repented them, because she had seen him feed yesterday—eviscerating a buffalo, eating pretty much everything save some bones and the horns. That gory, blood-splattered spectacle—on which she'd turned her back, but which had nonetheless rendered her very pale by the time she'd got ready to climb on his back again—would be present in her mind. He'd thought it funny they tried to feed the dragon with fruit, but perhaps it was not so funny for someone of more delicate sensibilities?

But from behind him, he heard only a little gasp, like a sigh. "And they're virgins?"

"I presume," he said. "At least they told me so."

"They told you . . ."

"I don't understand it, any more than you do. It appears their father had some odd idea I should mate with them. But I assure you, they look far too young to appear to me in that light."

"I see," she said. And he wondered if, in fact, she did. He very much suspected not. But he could not ask, as at that moment he and Sofie emerged from the trees and were back at the clearing, where the two girls stood, staring at them.

He reached over, instinctively, and grabbed Sofie Warington's hand. *As if she will protect me from the unbridled lust of virgins.*

She gave him her hand readily enough. It felt warm and fluttery in his hand. Once, when he was very young, he'd picked up a little baby bird—not yet full-fledged—who had fallen from its nest. With infinite care, he'd held it in his hand as he climbed the tree and replaced it.

Now as an adult, he understood that the bird had probably not survived. Birds would kill their own young that had the smell of a predator about them. Wise creatures, birds.

But at the time, he'd felt he was doing what he must, returning the bird to a place of safety. And he remembered the bird's warmth upon his hand, the softness of it, and its little flutters. Sofie Warington's hand felt just like that as she stepped forward to take her place beside him.

The two girls looked . . . not surprised, he decided. Relieved. Clearly the idea of mating with a dragon alarmed them as much as it alarmed the dragon. He bowed to them slightly.

They bowed back. The older one smiled at him and said, grandly, in the tone of a queen granting a boon, "You keep the fruit."

And then they turned and ran, swift and assured like mountain goats on uneven terrain, down the slope and toward the trees, in what he presumed was the direction of their village.

CLOTHES AND FOOD;
SYMPATHY AND COMFORT;
MISS WARINGTON'S VERY
PUZZLING EPISODES

Sofie felt horribly embarrassed. She had gone through these episodes sometimes in London. She'd find herself outside Lady Lodkin's Academy, somewhere on the streets of London, some place she couldn't imagine and had never before visited in her waking hours.

Always, she felt tired and bewildered. Between herself and Lalita, they'd agreed that Sofie must be walking in her sleep. Often, they'd find a door unlocked—or someone would, leading to a lecture from Lady Lodkin herself. Lalita had advised Sofie to report it to her mother. In turn, this had led to her being called home. Or at least it was part of what had led them to that. Now she wondered if they'd sent for her because they thought she was defective—ill. If that was why they'd agreed to her marriage to the horrible creature.

But she was beyond that now. And as the two mountain girls scurried away, her only worry was whether Lord St. Maur would think she had walked away from him because she feared him.

She let go of his hand and hurried to the other side of the clearing, where, after rummaging through her bag and getting a bar of soap and a comb, as well as a set of clothing for the day, she went to the little rivulet that ran around the back of the clearing. The girls had jumped over it without much concern. To Sofie, the water—clear, pure, deep and running fast—seemed like a miracle. Everywhere around Calcutta, the rivers were sluggish and choked with mud—worse now than at any other time of the year. Water had become a precious commodity down at lower altitude.

Of course, the Earl of St. Maur had told her last night that the water here came from the glaciers high in the Himalayas, the same as the brisk air that allowed trees to grow more akin to the vegetation of Europe than to the lush tropical plants she was used to seeing in India. They were partway up one of the lower peaks, and around her the Himalayas climbed like the tops of a crown, majestic and overwhelming.

She washed in this unexpected water quickly, noticing small silver fish in the current, and hoping her soap wouldn't harm them. But surely such a small amount in so much water wouldn't. At any rate, they didn't seem inconvenienced, though they did swim a rather wide berth around her hands as she splashed in the water.

Having washed herself and put her hair up as well as she could without a mirror, she dressed briskly and returned to the clearing. He had dressed, too, she noted. Though he had the gift of making it appear perfectly normal to be naked—an ability doubtless born of long practice—she confessed she felt better about his being dressed and looking like the gentleman he was.

And how strange life could be. All the time, in novels, the hidden were was some chimney sweep or rough laborer. Never a peer of the realm. Much less a peer of the realm of such distinguished appearance as Lord St. Maur.

He was barefoot, and doing something with a small knife to the underside of his foot, so absorbed in his task that he did not look up as she entered the clearing. "Have some fruit," he said. "I think you'll have to content yourself with water with your breakfast, though, Miss Warington. I hope we can stop somewhere where there is a bazaar—though not in the city of Darjeeling itself, as I'd prefer not to fly that close to a place that is sure to have some British troops stationed—and buy some tea. Judging from the region we're in, and how much tea I've seen growing on these slopes, we should be able to purchase something." He paused a moment, then suddenly pulled what looked to Sofie like a finger-long thorn from his foot. A spurt of blood followed it, pulsing over the grass in long jets. St. Maur dropped his knife and pressed the palm of his hand hard against his foot, then looked at her. "Though, myself, I prefer Ceylon, Darjeeling is probably preferable to nothing. And while this water looks very pure, you never know with the water in these places. We should also buy a little teapot to boil the water, and something to brew the tea in. I suspect drinking only tea will save us from getting one of those mysterious fevers that everyone ascribes to the climate of India."

The blood that had been gushing around the edges of his hand had now slowed down, and Sofie stood paralyzed by the incongruence of the conversation. How could he talk of brewing tea and what tea he preferred and other such drawing-room conversation when he had just extracted a huge thorn from his foot and was actively bleeding?

"Is anything wrong?" he asked.

It occurred to her that a gentleman who became a dragon must have a very high tolerance for contradiction and strange events, and she stammered out, "N-no. Not . . . Does it hurt?"

He grinned and shrugged, then removed his hand to look at his foot. "Not as much as it did while it was in. I suppose I should now go and wash, before I join you for breakfast." And before she could answer, he got up, visibly limping, and extracted a silver-plated case from his luggage with his clean hand, before hobbling to the rivulet.

Sofie wished she understood what she was feeling. Why was it that the man who'd saved her from killing herself with a fall from that balcony should infuriate her so? Why was it that the fact that he could be perfectly amiable and at the same time show the kind of dark, sparkling humor that warned of dangerous depths make her angry or impatient? And why was it that she could admire his restraint and his self-containment as he tended to his own needs, and at the same time want to grab him by the shoulders and shake him?

It must be, she thought as she nibbled on some orange pulpy fruit she didn't have a name for, and which tasted almost sickly sweet, *because he is, ultimately, a zany. What need was there for him to do that to himself? Surely, he could have asked me to extract the thorn and assume I might do it without carving a big slice out of his foot. After all, most women are trained in looking after the sick.*

The fact that she herself had been raised in India, surrounded by servants, and then sent to one of the most expensive academies in London—and had therefore never been exposed to the sick or to nursing directly—didn't mean anything. True, if Sofie had been faced with his foot and asked to remove the thorn, she might have felt powerfully tempted to go into hysterics. Hysterics, she decided, would probably save her from having to remove the thorn—an operation she was sure she would completely fail at. But that didn't signify. Any sane male would ask the woman with him to remove that thorn before attempting it himself. Of course, the question must follow if a man who spent a good portion of his time being a scaley, winged beast—no matter how sublimely beautiful that beast (or the man) might be—could, in fact, be sane.

"You are very pensive," he said, walking up behind her.

She turned to see him—combed, washed, and wearing his shoes. And she blurted out the first thing she could think of. "Don't those shoes hurt? Or at least one of them? On your injured foot?"

"Not a lot," he said. "At any rate, I heal very fast, and I think wearing the shoe till I change shapes will prevent me from bleeding more, which is the only worry, as then I might have to let the dragon feed again before nighttime."

She didn't know what to answer and ate another piece of fruit to hide her confusion. He seemed to take it for an inquiry, and explained in a matter-of-fact way. "Bleeding always seems to weaken me. And when I'm going to be the dragon and fly all day, as I did yesterday—and what's more, fly at a high enough altitude not to be easily visible from the ground or the stray flying rug or occasional carpetship—I must not be weak or tired. The greatest danger with the dragon is that it will get too hungry, and I would prefer not to allow it to feed before nighttime." And then, as he sat down and reached for the fruit tray, he added, with every appearance of haste, "It's not that you'd be in any danger, you know. But others . . . others might not be as fortunate."

She wondered if he meant he'd eat people. Also why, if that was so, he thought she wouldn't be in any danger. And before she could still her tongue, she found herself asking, "How does it work? Yourself and the dragon, I mean. How much are you him? How much is he you? It seems like you talk of him as being something quite . . . other."

Immediately upon the words, she flinched, wondering how could she be so uncouth. In the back of her mind, she could hear Lady Lodkin growling: "Miss Warington!" in the tone she used when Sofie committed a social solecism in her presence. And yet, Sofie would challenge Lady Lodkin herself to navigate *this* situation correctly.

At any rate, St. Maur did not seem upset. He looked at her, more startled than shocked. "Oh," he said. Then with a small chuckle. "You know, no one's asked me that before." He took a bite of his fruit and chewed thoughtfully.

"Other people know? What you are?"

"A few. My father, for one. My late father. He knew." Something in the expression of his eye warned her this was not quite a safe subject. "And my friend Nigel and his wife—his ex-wife, Emily, and her new husband, Kitwana, and..." A sudden, startling smile. "A Masai girl somewhere in Africa at this moment. All of them know. But none of them ever asked me that." His dark, well-delineated eyebrows lowered, and his eye looked troubled. "I don't even know that I can answer."

"You speak as though the dragon were an animal you own," she said, emboldened by his calm acceptance of the topic. "You will let it do this, and you will let it do that, and—"

He shrugged. "Part of it is wishful, I think," he said. "It's just easier that way. You see..." He frowned harder—an expression that would be intimidating were it not so obvious that he was simply trying to comprehend, in his own mind, the whole process.

He sighed deeply and she thought that this thing he was doing, this searching of his mind and trying to understand something he'd prefer not to think on—by his own admission—might be very similar to carving up his own foot to extract a thorn. Then the thought that, like removing the thorn, it might be a needed and beneficial act surprised her, but before she could speak again, he continued.

"You see, I started changing when I was..." He looked up, as if struggling to remember. "Why, I guess when I was about your age. I'd just left school and gone home for the summer, to rusticate a while until I decided what to do with the various possibilities open to me. I was a good student and fairly adept at the social world and, I've been told, not wholly bad-looking." A faint smile twisted his lips. "The army would have been happy to have me. The diplomatic service vied for me. If I'd had an interest in politics, there were any number of people in positions of power willing to sponsor me. Or I might have made an advantageous marriage. My father did, and he had little more to recommend him than regular features and a polite address. I also considered writing peotry and becoming the toast of fashionable society. It seemed to me, you see, as though I had so many avenues open to me that I was spoiled for choice and didn't know which way to turn.

"I shouldn't have bothered, because all those avenues were about to close. At first, I knew nothing of it, save that my father was missing sheep. My father knew nothing of it . . . nor did anyone else. I suppose if my father had ever suspected I might be a were, he would have thought of those English, or at least European, shapes that are common in the nobility—a wolf, a fox, a bear. But the creature eating the sheep was none of those, see. It was . . . something quite new to our rural scene. In fact, it ate everything of a sheep but the horns and some stray bits of bone."

Sofie remembered him the night before—in dragon shape—eating the buffalo. The voracious mouth and those sharp teeth dripping blood and gore. Now his very human, well-shaped teeth glimmered at her as he smiled—a smile without mirth at all. "My father gathered his shepherds and his villagers, and me, of course, and we stood watch in the night. Hell's own jest, isn't it? Me keeping watch for myself?" He shook his head and his voice dropped and seemed somehow younger as he said, "This sickness came over me, like a wave of nausea, and I started coughing. I think it had only happened while I was asleep before. Or perhaps I was awake, but the mind refused to accept it. They say such things happen, that when something horrible happens, your brain erases all trace of it and you forget. At any rate, I went behind some bushes to cough, so I wouldn't startle our prey. And next thing I knew I was a dragon and I was aloft, going for the sheep.

"My father saw me change. I don't know how he talked the others into holding their fire, or if he did. I doubt their powersticks were charmed for weres, and if they weren't, the shots would have felt like little more than painful slaps. Mind you, I don't remember feeling them, but I don't remember much of that night. I *do* remember waking up in the morning, in my room. And my father telling me I would have to clear out and stay out."

"Oh, no," she said. She couldn't help it. He looked so young and so lost as he talked, she longed to do foolish things—to hold him in her arms, to console him. To do who knew what nonsense.

Her exclamation startled him and he looked up quickly, seeming suddenly older again. "He had to," he said. "My father had to send me away. If you think about it, it was quite the only thing he could do for me. The were laws might be winked at here, but they are quite implacable in England, you know. If I had been found and in such a dangerous form, they'd have killed me. No second thought about it, and no mercy such as might be evinced toward a fox or a wolf—or smaller, less dangerous weres." He ate a piece of fruit quickly, almost choking on it. Or at least that was an explanation for the tears in his eyes. "It was probably for the best for everyone," he said afterward. "I doubt I'm cut out to be a country squire, and our fortune doesn't run to being a light of society. But you asked how much of

me there was in the dragon, and how much of the
dragon in me. I don't know. I left home and I traveled
the world, at times living in ways I don't care to explain to a lady. For a while I believed in anarchy, and
that if I could but eliminate all European noblemen...
Ah, but that doesn't matter. About what you asked...
I think that I'm me in both forms, but the form itself
dictates some of the impulses and the feelings that I
experience."

A small flash of an almost genuine smile. "My human self has never looked upon a live buffalo and experienced the slightest bit of appetite. My dragon self,
on the other hand, seems to regard it much as I'd regard a ripe apple. But I think, if I should own the
truth, that both forms are me and that referring to
them as separate is just something I do to keep myself
from sensing the full strangeness of the situation. Like
playing chess with yourself and pretending not to know
your own thoughts when working the other side of the
board. I know when necessary I can control myself
about as well in both forms."

One last bite of fruit and he got up briskly, without
looking at her. "I will now change, shall I?"

By the time she finished eating and looked up, he
had undressed, put away his clothes and changed. In
the middle of the clearing stood the dragon, green and
gold and magnificent. Yet in the dragon's eye she read
the soft vulnerability she had, for a moment, glimpsed
in St. Maur's. And as she climbed atop his back and
held firmly on to the neck ruffle, she thought, *He has
three forms. A dragon, a man, and a lost boy.* And she
wondered why the thought made her wish to cry.

THE PRINCESS, THE
MONKEY AND THE RUBY

Lalita woke and rubbed her eyes. She had fallen asleep in one of those safe havens available to her kind when they traveled across the country. Like the hidden palace in Calcutta, this place had a magic-guarded entrance that would go unnoticed by any but monkeyweres. Lalita had sensed the place just before nightfall, and realized that Hanuman had been steering them this way all along.

She hadn't asked. She had no intention of increasing Hanuman's good opinion of himself. His smile was infuriating enough already. Now, as she woke, she looked around the chamber—so old that the stone appeared to have a golden cast and the floor mosaics were worn in depressions.

It was a single chamber, the back wall ornamented by a magnificent relief of the monkey god Hanuman. The columns—ornamental, not functional—in each corner were covered in carvings of monkeys climbing up. Though there were signs of burning incense and perhaps candles in the distant past, now the place was abandoned, empty and resounding in its echoing loneliness.

Lalita had set a magelight burning on high in the middle of the recessed ceiling, to which bits of gold patina clung together with a curiously vivid red paint. Now she rubbed her eyes and sat up in dismay as she realized Hanuman was nowhere in sight. Where had he gone?

He had made such a point—their both being naked after changing shapes—of sleeping in the far corner from hers, to preserve her modesty. But now she was the only one here, as she looked around, breathing in a sudden hiss of impatience. The fool. Where could he be? Their whole time together had been like this. He resisted admitting her superiority, or her right to rule over him. Her uncle must hear of the impertinence his favorite courtier so clearly displayed when away from his eyes. But right now her alarm was clearer and more immediate.

Hanuman had the ruby. Though no longer masked—that spell took too much energy to maintain—the gem was safely hidden in a pouch they'd taken from a poor family's hut—and marked the place, too, to remember to send the family compensation for their theft. Had Hanuman headed back to town without telling her? She didn't think he'd dare appear before her uncle, telling him he'd left the king's niece behind to fend for herself.

So, where could Hanuman have gone? She assumed that he couldn't be trusted. Also, she knew that he had intents different from her own, and despite his denials she suspected him of still intending to return to the city and give his king the ruby he'd recovered. The only reason he was looking for Sofie was to find out why she excited the interest of the dragons and the tigers—why the tigers thought they needed to have her as well as they ruby. But she couldn't believe he'd leave her alone.

She heard a muttering from the doorway, and then it sprang open, letting a thin trickle of daylight into the old buried temple. A man stood in the entrance, and thinking this must be a were-monkey she didn't know, Lalita jumped up, standing against the wall with the monkey god on it, ready to explain who she was and to command help and obedience from someone who had, by necessity, to be less wellborn than herself.

But the person at the entrance, fully dressed in turban, tunic, pants, bowed deeply to her before any introduction was made, then walked into the temple, uttering—softly—the word that closed the door behind him. Closer to her, he bowed again. Then lifted his face, to reveal Hanuman's irreverent, self-satisfied smile. "Good morning, Princess," he said. "Did you sleep well?"

Lalita glared at him. "Where did you go? What are you doing? With whom are you in league?"

He bowed slightly at her. It was strange how his features, well sculpted and beautiful in human form, somehow gave the impression of being as mobile and impish as his simian face. "I am in league with you, Princess. Per His Majesty's instructions."

She didn't believe it. She didn't believe it for a moment. He was too impertinent, too self-sufficient, too hardheaded. She frowned at his smile. "Where did you go?"

"It occurred to me," he said, and for just a moment his features acquired a pensive cast, as though he could be a thinking, responsible human, "that it is very foolish of us to try to chase down a dragon on foot. Or even"—he smiled—"on hands."

They had spent a good part of the day before swinging from branch to branch and making very good progress—certainly much better than they could have made on foot as either humans or monkeys. But she would agree that a dragon—as it was—could move much faster than they ever could.

"Is she still . . . with the dragon, do you think?" she asked, somewhat taken off balance. She still remembered, all too well, the image of Sofie sitting astride the dragon as it climbed high in the sky. She remembered it, but she couldn't understand it, much less accept it.

She'd been to England with Sofie. She knew the girl better than probably anyone else, her parents included. She had been Sofie's closest thing to a friend and confidante. Their different stations in life, such as they were—and such as Sofie thought they were, which was something else again—had created some distance between them, but not nearly as much as it would have, had Sofie been different. The English girl's naturally affectionate and sociable ways had met with the impenetrable barrier of English manners and English prejudices, and had made Sofie turn to Lalita for all her confidences and talk.

And Sofie had shared with Lalita the novels she read. Weres were a recurrent theme of the English novels. Usually as villains. At first, Lalita had thought that the stories about these weres—strange, savage creatures that attacked and tore people apart without knowing why or what drove them; who could kill their loved ones and not remember; who changed without control and without hope of stopping it—were written by people who had never heard of weres, much less met one.

But then she was not so sure. She had read legends and true stories of weres, and she knew a little more about Britain and the British. She knew, for instance, that there were no kingdoms of weres within the proper British society. As far as she could tell, in fact, British weres were so rare and so kept in terror of the laws against shape-shifters that they rarely met others of their kind, much less learned from them. Isolated, ashamed of themselves and in fear for their lives, they went through life in a very strange state, indeed. It was quite possible, Lalita thought, that they denied who and what they were even when they knew otherwise. And that as a result they ended up a little mad and unable to control either form properly.

This would explain the legends. What it didn't explain was why someone with Sofie's view of weres, acquired through these stories, would allow one of them to kidnap her. Or as her position on the dragon's back indicated, would willingly go with one.

What could have possessed her? Was it some threat it was holding over her head? What threat could control the brave, impetuous Sofie Warington?

"Are we sure, then?" Lalita asked. "That she's with him?"

He nodded to her. "It was part of the reason I went out. Since you wish to find your friend and I'm honor bound—ordered by my king—to do what you want me to, I went out and bought clothes, and have—"

"Bought clothes?" Lalita asked.

"There is a bazaar an hour's walk away, and I got up very early."

"But . . . with what money?"

He smiled that annoying, knowing smile of his, as though he were an adult and she a little child with no knowledge of the world. "Princess, in the walls of this temple, this refuge of our kind, there are always . . . What would you call them? Safe money repositories, for those of us who are traveling and who've lost our clothes and possessions to sudden changes." He touched the wall, said a word, and at the bottom of the wall a compartment opened, where gold glimmered. "See, Princess? There is a fortune in any of these shrines. The locals will leave money, often, in jars at the entrance, or give it to one of our kind who's staying here."

"But . . . it's not ours," she said. She hated his calling her Princess, but she would be cursed if she allowed him to call her Lalita. And she hated his superior smile and self-assured manner. On the other hand, she felt as though she would long ago have died or worse without his guidance and attention. The sad thing is that she knew nothing about India; having been sent to England so young, she'd never learned the manners of her own people or how to be an adult among them. She was a princess, yes, but counted for little more than a waif who had no idea what her new life entailed. So she contented herself with shaking her head at him. "It must be a gift to the god Hanuman."

"Sure it is. It is left here for wayfarers of our kind. To whom else would the god himself wish the money to go, but to his mortal children?" He grinned at her, and she wished she had his easy assurance. But before she could muster the words to refute him, he said, "At any rate, I took the money and got clothes, and I looked for those of our brothers who live hereabouts."

"Why?"

"I thought they might have heard something, or know something," he said. "After all, there will always be those of us who have contact with the tigers, or who might have heard about the dragons. There will be others, like me, who can witch-sniff easily and will know if there have been dragons here, and where they might have gone."

"And did you find anything?" she asked.

"Yes," he said. "As I bought these clothes and..." He bowed and somehow, from the folds of his tunic, produced a bundle of blue-green silk shot through with gold. "This for you, Princess."

He extended it to her, and she shook it out, to see it was a magnificent sari. "There is not much point in dressing in it," she said, as she noticed the little lotus flowers embroidered in gold all over the fine fabric, "since we'll have to change to continue on our way."

"Indeed, no," he said. "You see, I did find one of our kind that I could question. And he told me that not only have the dragon and the girl been seen—and they do seem to be traveling together with no coercion—"

"But...how is that possible?" Lalita asked. "How can she be traveling willingly with a dragon?"

"I don't know," he said. "Perhaps because she thinks it will get her away from the tiger? Perhaps because she's willing to do anything—everything— rather than marry the king of tigers?"

Lalita thought of Sofie on the veranda; Sofie looking afraid of the creature and repulsed by it, in equal parts; Sofie screaming she couldn't marry him and try-

ing to . . . Lalita wasn't even sure what her friend had
tried to do. She thought Sofie had wanted to climb
down from the balcony, though she had no clue how
the girl thought she could do that, when she had neglected to provide herself with a rope or any other
means of descent. But the very fact that Sofie had forgotten how frail that railing was, and how likely that it
would fall to pieces, spoke to her desperation. A
dragon could be a way of escaping. But how could a
dragon seem *less* dangerous to her? Lalita started—in-
sensibly—to wrap herself in the sari. She didn't like
being naked in front of Hanuman, and even if this
meant she would have to undress when she changed
again, it was a risk she was willing to take. "I will not
believe that Sofie had a rendezvous with the dragon, or
that she meant to run away with him."

Through her mind, fast and ridiculous, crossed the
notion that William Blacklock, on whom Sofie set such
store, might have been a dragon shifter. The idea almost made her laugh out loud. A sound between a giggle and a sneeze escaped her, causing Hanuman to
give her a very odd look before saying, "No, milady.
Undoubtedly not. But once she'd found the dragon, he
might have seemed to her the least of two evils. And
then, if you remember, you told me your friend wanted
to go to Meerut, and they seem to be headed in that direction, from all the gossip I've heard."

Meerut, where slim, elegant William Blacklock
had been stationed. Still, he could not be the dragon.
Lalita knew better. Even in English legends, dragons
were rarely mentioned as weres. And when they were,
they were always mentioned as foreign creatures,

somehow trapped or lost in England. Never as native forms.

What were the chances that William Blacklock had Chinese or Indian blood? Or even blood from those distant Estern European countries where it was said some dragons also lived?

Not high. Though the man had dark hair, he had pale skin, smoky-gray eyes and his features looked English. No, the dragon wasn't William Blacklock, but it began to seem as though Sofie had convinced the dragon to take her to Blacklock. Lalita shook her head and spoke from bitter experience. "She was always capable of convincing people to do the most insane things for her."

Hanuman grinned at that. "Well, if she is going to Meerut, and if they are flying, it would be very poor of us to have to walk, would it not? After all, what's the reason for that? I could take the money and buy us"— he smiled, like an adult unveiling a treat for a child— "a flying rug." He pointed to a rolled bundle at the entrance, which he must have set down before approaching her. She was not sure how he'd managed it—so many of Hanuman's tricks were like an illusioner's art, the hand faster than the eye. "Just a small one," he said. "Enough to allow us to sit on it with comfort and fly in style."

"And be far more visible in the air," she said. "And announce to all our passing, so that our direction and intentions in turn will be divulged to the tigers and, perhaps, to the dragons as well."

"You think they wouldn't be, otherwise?" he asked, and shook his head as though at her naivete. "Of course people—our people—know where we are, and probably who we are, too. You're too high a personage to travel incognita. Surely you know that."

"Still, traveling in a flying rug, you must admit—"

"We don't have a choice, Princess," Hanuman snapped. "You see, the king of tigers bought a rug also. The grapevine has it they'll all be stopping at the sacred city of Benares. I think we must go there as soon as we can."

FAKIRS AND BODIES;
SAFETY AND DARING;
TIGERS

*They descended near Benares, in a patch of impene-*trable forest. Sofie wondered if he did that because he feared that whoever watched them land would call the Gold Coats, or because he was afraid of receiving the sort of embarrassing worship that the two girls had attempted to bestow on him on the mountain.

She rather thought the latter. She suspected she was starting to know St. Maur better than he perhaps knew himself. The look in his eye and the veiled pain in it as he spoke of the circumstances under which he'd left his father's house would haunt her forever. Sofie imagined, from that glimpse, that she now knew or understood why he'd picked her up when she would otherwise have dashed her brains falling from that balcony, and why he had agreed to come with her across India. Having been, himself, cast out and lost in an uncaring world, he could not now allow anyone to be caught in the same trap. His kindness, born of pain, had earned her admiration as sheer goodness might never have.

Sofie realized she had forgotten he was a dragon—though she was sure it would be very improper to be sitting astride him like this in his human form—when she heard herself saying, as she looked idly over the landscape of the Ganges, with its throngs of pilgrims and its burning pyres, "Is this where they burn the corpses?"

She realized, right after asking it, that he couldn't answer, or not with words. Though the dragon could hiss words, she doubted he could do it while flying—and so was surprised to see him dip his head in what was clearly an attempt at nodding. Confused, she patted distractedly at his neck ruffle.

St. Maur—or the dragon he became—was flying very high to avoid the traffic of low-flying rugs. He dipped suddenly toward a thick massif of trees. Landing softly on the mossy ground, he waited till Sofie dismounted.

She averted her eyes as he started twisting and writhing in his change of shape, and did not turn back even as he spoke to her in human voice, the detached manner of a tour guide. "Yes, those are the burning ghats. It is believed that anyone whose ashes are thrown in the Ganges will have a better life in their next reincarnation. So anyone who can possibly do it will come here to dispose of their beloved relatives' bodies." Mixed with his words came sounds of his rifling through the bags. "But I understand it's very expensive, as they will not do the cremation out of charity, and you must pay for the fuel plus a good fee to those who burn the corpse. Who are all low caste of course, as they must be to be willing to touch dead bodies."

"You know a lot about this?" Sofie asked, hesitantly.

"I've traveled here and there in India," he said. "I've been here six months, after all. But surely, having grown up here . . ."

She wanted to ask him why he'd been here six months, but she didn't. It probably sufficed to know that India wasn't likely to call the Gold Coats on him. At least hadn't been until recently. "I grew up here until I was ten," she said primly. "And burning bodies are hardly what you'd consider a good subject for a child that young."

He chuckled softly. "I imagine not," he said. And then he added, softly, "You may turn now, Miss Warington."

She did. He was fully dressed, holding his walking stick. "I seized the chance to land in this spot, since it seemed the farthest from any great conglomeration of people. You know, this is an important pilgrimage area, and therefore it becomes hard to find a place that's not crowded with people." Something like a shadow passed over his face. "It's going to be difficult to find a place to hunt, but that's a worry for another time. Perhaps if I eat, in human form, it will be enough to hold me for the night. Then tomorrow, when we get a little away from this heavily populated area, we can find me some place where the dragon . . . er . . . I can hunt."

She noticed the correction and wondered if, having become aware of his split, he was trying to mend it. Trying, somehow, to make himself one. But it was not the time to ask. Nor was it the time to ask if he was sure about being able to hold off his hunger if he fed tonight only in human form.

Though nothing had been explained, she'd seen his hunger when he ate meals as a dragon. She suspected no meal consumed as a human could satiate that hunger. She suspected he knew it, too, from the worried expression on his face. But she could well imagine that in such a heavily populated area, to have the dragon hunt could cause a definite panic. "Are you afraid they'd try to worship you if you hunted as a dragon in plain sight?"

He looked at her, and his mouth quirked just a little, before returning to a more serious expression. "No," he said, with some finality. "I'm afraid what they would do if I ate one of their prized sacred bulls."

And while she was turned to him, she saw, just by the corner of her eye, movement amid the trees. "There," she said, speaking before she could think. "There was someone over there." She pointed to the green-brown forest, where a pale body was seen fleeing—it looked like an adolescent or young woman, running.

St. Maur took a few steps into the cover of trees. Then his hand went out to the trunk of a nearby tree and he came to a stop, staring. He returned to Sofie, wearing that brisk, businesslike look that he'd worn when he'd first let her walk away in Calcutta. She wondered if this time, too, he was unsure of his decision.

"Who was it?" Sofie asked.

He shook his head, shrugged. "I don't know. Looked like a native to me. Someone slim and young, or perhaps just slim and small."

"Oh. Did he, or she, overhear us?" She tried to locate the source of the uneasiness she sensed in him.

"It hardly matters." He set his lips tightly. "After all, it is not at all likely that just any native will speak English well enough to understand that conversation of ours. It is even less likely that a native who overheard us would hasten to tell the Gold Coats. As we've seen, natives' attitude to weres is . . . different from English attitudes. Also, if pressed, we could say the talk of my being a dragon was a joke. Who could disprove it?"

They stood in silence. Sofie could tell he wanted to go on. He took an hesitant step in the direction they'd been walking, but came back when she didn't move.

"Is there . . . some distress on your mind, Miss Warington?" he asked.

She realized she'd been frowning, heavily. "Only that . . ." she began, and hesitated. Then took a deep breath. "I know something about all this is causing you some uneasiness."

"How can you know that?" He looked very pale and tired, and she understood—for the first time—why they'd stopped near the sacred city of Benares despite its being one of the most heavily frequented places in India. One that anyone could tell would not offer them shelter.

She shook her head. "I don't know, my lord. I just know I do. I can sense you are uneasy and questioning your wisdom in letting that person escape."

"The person . . . I hardly had the option of catching up with him, you know? He was very fleet among the trees, and as tired as I am it would be folly to cede control to the dragon. The dragon looks only for one thing, and that is consuming as much food as possible. I'd be lucky if the only thing it savaged were the corpses in the burning ghats. It is far more likely it would go after the sacred cows and bullocks."

"Yes, but all the same, the fact that you allowed him or her to escape, that you did not pursue the spy further, preys on you. And before we go into a more populated area in search of food, I would like to know what it is."

She expected him to argue or to tell her that it was none of her concern. Instead, he nodded once, curtly, like a man faced with a difficult hand that he must yet gamble. "Very well, then, Miss Warington. What worries me about that man or woman who ran away is that this person was stark naked. I could not tell, at a distance, the gender or the age, but I did have an unobstructed view of a naked backside."

"Oh," Sofie said. It occurred to her that she did not in fact know how prudish he was. Certainly, he'd been naked in front of her and been able to carry on a conversation while dressing. But then, surely, being a were-dragon, he'd long since had time to be used to finding himself naked in odd places. However, how prudish was he about other people's nudity? She'd forgotten, for a moment, that he hadn't grown up in India. "But, surely, you see ... In India it is not unusual for someone to go around stark naked. They lack the rules of modesty we have in England, and it doesn't seem to disturb them in any way. If they are in financial distress, or else if clothing isn't very important to them because of a vow or something, they will go around naked." She shrugged. "I know it's a great lack of modesty, but it is quite normal for them—you must not let yourself be disturbed."

He'd looked a little bewildered as she spoke, and
Sofie flattered herself that she was giving him new information. But on her last sentence, he made a sound
like a hiccup and said in an utterly shaken voice,
"Disturbed?"

He was taking this far harder than she thought. "I
daresay it is very bad and immodest of me," she said,
"to not be disturbed by it, myself. But you see, I grew
up in India, where this is viewed as quite normal, and
therefore I have had time to get used to it. I know your
views of modesty might be different."

And now his hand went up to cover his mouth and
his shoulders shook and it took her only a moment to
realize that his eye was shining with a manic glimmer,
and that he was not, in fact, shocked. Instead, he appeared to be laughing almost maniacally.

"Lord St. Maur!" she said, shocked in her turn.

He removed his hand from in front of his lips, giving
up what had clearly been a vain attempt to conceal his
laughter. "I know." He gave her a quick, feral smile.
"And I apologize for laughing, but . . . surely, my dear
Miss Warington, you understand I do not heed the
modest standards of British maidens. I find them, to be
honest, a little boring. And I told you I've been all over
the world for the last ten years. Surely—"

"I don't know the standards of modesty in the rest
of the world," she said, sullenly, resenting that she
showed her feelings in her voice. "I only know that
India is very different from England. And you've
hardly been in India at all."

He nodded, while he made a visible effort to get his
expression under control. "It's just . . . the thought of
me being so shocked by a naked human being, it undid

me. I beg your pardon. I was not laughing at you, only at the image of myself swooning a drawing-room faint and needing to be revived by means of smelling salts. Tell me, would I need to wear a cap, too, or would my own manly curls suffice?"

The image made her giggle, in turn, but she shook her head. "I don't understand. If you're not shocked by the creature's nudity, then why did it disturb you?"

His expression sobered immediately. "Because it is a condition weres often find themselves in unexpectedly." He shook his head. "I daresay I'm being silly and imagining too much. As you say, it is not unusual in India to see people in all conditions, including quite naked. It's all a mare's nest, an unfounded fear, I'm sure."

But despite his reassuring words, her mind leapt ahead to the inevitable conclusion. "You mean you think he might be a spy for those were-tigers who tried to capture us in Calcutta, do you not?"

St. Maur shrugged. "I'm jumpy and confused. And very, very tired. I'm sure it is nothing. I can't imagine why they should pursue us this far. In fact, I'm not sure why they pursued us at all. I would give something to know why a were-tiger ruler finds it vital to have your hand in marriage."

"It is possible," she said, slowly, doubting her own words even as she pronounced them, "that he is madly in love with me. My parents said it was so. That he'd even agreed to have only one wife, provided I would be that wife, and I suppose it takes something to get a local ruler to give up his seraglio."

"Then he'd known you before?"

"Oh, no. My maid, Lalita, said he claimed to have

seen me in a dream. And there, you know, is where my doubt hinges. While I'm eager to believe he's madly in love with me—and, in fact, while I'm as capable of vanity as the next delicately brought-up English miss—I find it very hard to believe he would have fallen in love with me that way, without ever having seen me up close. without knowing me in any way."

He looked like he would say something. At least he opened his mouth and took in breath as though to speak, but then bit his lip and shook his head. "It is," he said, "a trifle strange. Would it change your mind about him if you found out that he truly loved you?"

She shrugged. "If he truly loved me, he would endeavor to conquer my affections by romantic means, not to as good as buy me from my parents. Or, worse yet, to send his henchmen after me. I'm willing to believe he might be smitten by me—oh, I don't think myself any great beauty, but then again, it is possible that local tastes vary—but I do not believe he loves me. And even if he did, surely that is not a cause to love someone? Just because they love you?"

He nodded at that, but his mind seemed to be elsewhere. He spoke, softly, between barely parted lips, as though he were talking only to himself. "I would give something to know why you are so important to the were-tigers, and what game is afoot right now. While they are less at risk from the Gold Coats in India than anywhere else in the world, still it seems a little brazen to follow us across half a continent, trying to capture you. Unless you are vital to their plans in some way that we can't guess at."

"If they are, indeed, following us," Sofie said.

"If they are," St. Maur agreed, nodding. "And if

this is not all madness brought about by tiredness and sleep deprivation. But in either case, Miss Warington, I think it would be good if we were to leave these relatively depopulated areas. They are far less likely to be able to strike at us in a populated area."

Sofie nodded. She took his arm again, and this time she allowed him to lead her down a path, which appeared to have been beaten by the feet of generations of pilgrims. She could imagine throngs of barefoot people making their way to the Ganges. Or, as the Indians called it, Mother Ganges.

"I wonder what the purpose is," she said, lightly, more trying to draw him into conversation than truly wanting to know. She could sense his tension, his worry. She suspected that the incident of being spied upon disturbed him more than he wanted to admit. She imagined, too, that this must be part of being a were. If you lived with a death sentence over your head simply for being what you were, you would grow a little jumpy, scared of every shadow. And if you were a gentleman, you wouldn't show it. She wanted to ask him if there were were females. The novels she'd read had never mentioned any. But she dared not. Instead, she said, "Why they bathe in the Ganges, I mean. I know that water is not abundant in the dry season, but the river can hardly be clean with this many people bathing in it, and cadavers being burned there and whatnot. Certainly not enough to justify the throngs that come from all over the country."

"They believe that any Hindu who bathes in the river has all his sins forgiven. And those whose ashes are thrown in the river after death will incarnate higher on the scale of things in their next life. Why, they even believe that Muslims and Christians who come and bathe in the Ganges will benefit from it."

She almost said perhaps they should try it, but the time seemed strange for levity. Unable to find anything else to speak of, and afraid that any topic would lead her into weres—a fatal conversation now that they'd reached areas filled with pilgrims who might, any of them, be spying for the tigers—she remained silent, holding on to his arm.

Fortunately, the scene before her eyes was wholly absorbing. As they neared the Ganges itself, she saw that, contrary to what she expected, it was all built up with palaces and villas, which she supposed belonged to princes and rajahs. And amid those were mud-walled hovels and what seemed to be very ancient shrines. And of course, a throng of humanity.

She could smell the sickly sweet cremations out in the river, could see flames here and there, flaring against the setting sun. The smell seemed to touch something primal in her and make her wish she could run away. Somewhere up the river, a group of pilgrims were chanting.

"Where shall we bed down for the night?" she asked.

"There are . . . rest houses and houses of accommodations. Wealthy philanthropists build them for the benefit of their souls," St. Maur said, speaking as if from a great distance. "Some of them, perforce, must be for low- or no-castes, and they won't throw us out."

"Do you think . . ." She hesitated. "Do you think that it will be quite comfortable?"

He chuckled, then shook his head. "I'm fairly sure it will be devilish uncomfortable, Miss Warington. But amid all those people—and those houses are always crowded—there will surely be some safety."

"Oh."

"Yes. I beg your pardon if I subject you to discomfort, but my goal is to keep you safe."

Indeed, faced with the multidinous strangeness of India, Sofie wondered if she'd even have made it so far without him. Surely not with the tigers pursuing her. And she, too, wondered why they'd pursue her. Surely a raj or king—and she'd heard him referred to as both—of a city would have more choices than one in matrimonial affairs. Perhaps it was connected to the ruby that was meant to be her dowry? No. Impossible. The ruby was flawed and cracked.

"Come, Miss Warington. We must find food."

She felt like doing anything but eating just now, but looking at his pale, drawn countenance and the dark circle under his uncovered eye, she remembered he needed it. And because of his nature, so did she—she had no intention of being left alone because he'd been killed for feasting on a sacred cow.

It was dangerous, she thought, traveling with a were. But not nearly as dangerous as it would have been traveling without him.

AN UNRELIABLE REFLECTION; FIRE AND BLOOD; MIRRORED FACE

William Blacklock chased his carrier out. This was his most constant servant, and he suspected in England he would have been called a butler or a valet or something of that nature. Here in India, even—in a proper household, constituted of a married couple and children—he might have borne that title.

But William's carrier was just his main servant while William lived in a household shared by several young men, all serving Her Majesty in these distant climes. And while most of the time the carrier's skills in communicating both with William and the rest of the staff were welcome, William didn't want him now.

Not that he was doing something illegal. Just something his commanders and superiors would laugh at him for, and hold him in contempt for. Divination was the stuff of fools—the work of women at country fairs, or the work of entertainers in crowded theaters. Not in any way serious. And no business for an officer of Her Majesty's Secret Service.

But it was his talent, and after another uneasy

night, it was his only hope. He'd bathed, and the sun was high in the sky—a ball of fire bathing a landscape that didn't need any more heat—stippling brown upon every remaining bit of green and making the dirt underfoot look like clay hot from the potter's oven.

Looking out, William longed for rain with an almost physical ache, and wondered if he would be alive to see it—if he would live to see rain ever again. In his mind was the image of a British street—the street where his club was located in London—under a gentle, drizzling autumn shower. If he closed his eyes, he could almost taste those drops falling through the gray fog of an English sky. And he wanted more than anything to melt the space between him and that cherished place and find himself there, among the well-known landscape and the things he understood. He wanted to be in his father's study while rain fell outside and a servant laid out tea by the blazing fireplace. He longed for the smell of wool, the embrace of the encompassing leather armchairs. He longed for his father's voice reading from the Book of Common Prayer. He longed for home.

Instead, he faced this foreign inferno, sweltering under an unkind sun, and the kind of dreams that must be used as torments for the damned in hell. He knew he had forecasting ability. He'd never questioned it. But he'd never done anything to bring it about. And none of the disasters that had inspired his premonitory dreams before had been this vivid, this unavoidable. Back then, he'd dreamed of a train coming down the tracks and then blackness for days before a train wreck in nearby Sheffield. And he'd dreamed of pain and hurt before a friend had been wounded in a hunting accident.

But never had the dreams been this long or this blood-soaked. Never had the impression of them hung upon his waking moments like a mourning wreath. So the question was: what event roiled the stream of time, casting its reflections back as well as forward, that gave William these dreams and this truly, unsettled feeling?

He closed the curtain over his desk with a brisk gesture. The curtains, thank the Lord, were heavy stuff, dark. Apparently the previous occupant of these rooms could not sleep if the slightest bit of light penetrated from outside. William wondered how he took to the suffocating heat that rose in the room as soon as he walked over to the veranda door and closed that curtain as well. He could feel the heat rise slowly, and prickled in sweat, which made him itch beneath his uniform. He could never sleep like this. But right now it suited his purposes.

He went back to his suitcase, which he'd opened on the bed. His clothes and the other things he used daily had long since been removed from the suitcase by his servants. All that remained were those items either too precious or too rarely used to need to come out. Or those things he didn't wish his servants to see. He moved aside his last primer in magic, which he'd used at Eton and brought along with him, should any elementary formula evade him; the well-worn copy of the New Testament that his father had given him at parting; a half-dozen handkerchiefs embroidered for him by Victoria, his little cousin whom all the family hoped he'd marry someday. There in the corner, in its own

wrappings of silk and satin, was the gift his grandmother had given him in parting. He pulled it out and
set it on the desk, removing the layers of cloth that obscured it, one by one.

Small enough that it fit in the palms of his hands, it
was white and perfectly clear. A single piece of crystal,
hewn from virgin rock by magical means. It had never
been melted, formed, blown, touched by metal.

He heard his grandmother's voice in his head,
telling him, *It has been a Blacklock legacy, always.
Your grandfather had it from his grandfather, who had
it from his grandfather. It was passed on, along with
the gift of foretelling, from who knows which ancestor,
lost in the mists of time. Your grandfather said the
story was that an old crusader ancestor had found it in
Jerusalem, and feeling a bond with it brought it home
to use. But your grandfather said that didn't feel right.
That the rock feels older than that, and more closely
related to the Blacklocks too. He said that touching it
was like putting a finger in the stream of time.*

William had used it exactly once, and he hadn't got
anything from it. It had been upon his arrival in
Calcutta, after a party in which he'd heard a lot of nonsense but no good leads to where Soul of Fire might be
hidden. In his quarters at the home of friends that
night, he'd set the crystal ball out and tried to find the
stone with it. He'd seen nothing—not even those
flashes of white light that the uninformed thought was
all the soothsayer could see and interpret in the reflection of the glass.

Now he set trembling fingers at the edge of the ball
and stared into its depths, wishing that this time would
be different, that he would see what he needed. All

other questions vanished from his mind, along with all coherent thought.

He wanted to know so many things: where Soul of Fire was; what exactly Gyan Bhishma was talking about when he spoke of the danger of a were uprising—and mostly, whether William Blacklock was destined to die in Meerut, like his grandfather of the same name. But these could not be put into a clear question.

So, his hands on the cool crystal, he cleared a throat that felt much too dry and said, "Show me what I need to know that I might survive."

For a moment nothing happened, and William took a deep breath, telling himself he'd been a fool and that there was nothing here, nothing to this hunk of crystal. His foretelling power, which came in bursts and spasms, could not be controlled, not even to the extent that other soothsayers could control theirs. The crystal would not show him even shadows or hints. He'd been a fool.

And yet, a sense of relief twined with his disappointment, and he released a deep sigh and started to stand up.

At that moment, the globe flared with a blinding light, like a magelight suddenly striking up in utter darkness. Like the sun, without warning, piercing the deepest night. It flared bright and vivid and William screamed, holding his hands to his injured eyes. Even through his hands, he could feel the light filling the room. Were it not for the fact that he felt no heat at all, he'd have thought that the room had caught fire. As it was, he was not sure what to do. He couldn't call anyone into the room, not with this light blazing all over.

What would they think? What did he, himself, think? What had he caused to happen?

From behind the fingers clenched in front of his insufficiently shuttered eyelids, he felt the light diminish, slowly, till he dared to pull his hands down and look, between half-open eyes, at the globe. He expected it to be cold and dead again. It was not.

No longer flaring, and not exactly luminous, it glowed with a subdued light, and showed ... He made a sound like a half-suppressed laugh. The globe showed him the features of the most perfect male he'd ever seen. Possibly the most perfect one anyone had ever seen. The man's chiseled features seemed to have been hewn by a skilled sculptor—even his skin, the color of light honey, and his crown of wild curls. Only one injury marred the otherwise perfect face—a patch hid the left eye. But the eye that remained uncovered, it was bewildering, and the most perfect of all the features, with a deep green-black iris, in which, if one looked closely, he might find hints of gold or traces of the sea or perhaps the ice of the never-ending glaciers.

William had barely recovered his breath, and his ability to think—and to wonder what exactly the Greek god might have to do with his dilemma and why the crystal thought this was what he needed to see and know right now—when the scene changed. The man didn't exactly disappear. It was more like the colors of a kaleidoscope shifting positions and twisting till a different picture emerged. The colors ran and shifted, and suddenly William was looking at a picture out of his memory—the beautiful Sofie Warington, with hair loose down her back, with shining eyes and moist lips, wearing the sort of white muslin dresses favored by girls of her age and station. Her lips were parted in an "Oh" of confusion and bewilderment.

But what could Sofie have to do with all this? Well, clearly she did, because the Queen herself had wished for William to marry her. She thought that the ruby was in Sofie's family and that this would be the easiest way of obtaining it. But Sofie was safely in England, and if her family had the ruby in Calcutta, not all of William's powers nor all of his social connections had been able to find it.

He blinked as the scene changed yet again, and it was now the inside of his father's study, with the fire blazing in the grate and the tea set out, and his mother sitting in a chair by the fire, embroidering while his father sat in another and read. A servant came in with a letter on a silver tray. His father opened the letter, then dropped it with an exclamation. And then there was William's mother—her horrified face, her disbelieving eyes filling the crystal globe.

So I am to die in India, William thought, and with a hoarse cry swept his fingers so that they backhanded the globe, rolling it off the desk. The globe flared again with white light, and William knew, even as he closed his eyes and felt the light diminish, that it would show him more, that it *was* showing him more. With his eyes half-open, protected from the flare by his hand, he fell to his knees and crept toward the globe.

His damn temper. His damn intemperate lack of control. He could have been able to see more if he had not lost his patience. But the grief and horror in his mother's eyes had goaded him, as though the crystal was showing him her suffering to mock him. No, he couldn't have held back. He couldn't have controlled himself.

He fumbled for the globe, feeling the light die down as he approached it. When he got close, the globe was filled with the image of a tiger, its mouth open in a roar, its teeth stained red with blood. And behind it, after the colors swirled and changed, came two monkeys.

They looked like normal monkeys, swinging from tree to tree, except that one was wearing golden earrings—although, he didn't know, that might not be too unusual among the sacred monkeys of India—and the other held a bright ruby flaring with red light.

Behind them came—William recoiled, jumping back. It was this outpost, this cantonment, the barracks and buildings he'd see if he looked just out the window. But everywhere there were dead bodies. The roar of a tiger could be heard, and William felt as though he could smell the stench of death. He looked—desperately looked—for his own body amid the bloodied, twisted remains, and found nothing.

And then the image shifted again and he saw an elephant filling the crystal. A large elephant, with a European man held limply in its trunk, heading for the line of trees in the distance.

He couldn't tell who the European was that the elephant was carrying, and he leaned closer, trying to see.

"Sahib," came a voice, and a door opened suddenly.

William jumped and gave a horse cry, and the crystal was filled with the face of Gyan Bhishma, looking anxious, and in the next minute dismayed.

Looking over his shoulder, William saw the sepoy,

looking just as dismayed as his reflection in the crystal. Bhishma managed to collect himself into an appearance of military posture, and swallowed hard. "Pardon, Sahib, but your carrier said you were alone in your room and I heard you scream, and he had heard a thunk, and I thought . . ." The dark eyes looked toward the crystal, but he gave no impression of wishing to laugh at William or mock his exploits into foretelling.

William picked up the crystal, scooping it in one hand, and set it on the desk, amid its wrappings. "Well," he said. "I was . . . trying to see my way through this. Done now. You may open the curtains. As you see, I had an accident and the crystal fell."

Bhishma walked past William, and opened the curtain to the veranda, then backtracked to close the room's door and reached past William to open the curtain over the desk. The crystal was dead and quiet; it now looked no more arcane than it had when William's grandmother had handed it to him.

"That is a very old instrument you have there," Bhishma said.

"Yes. It's been in my family for generations. Perhaps for millennia."

"Then everyone in your family has the gift of the sight?" Bhishma asked.

William shrugged. "Something like that. Only the men but . . . Though sometimes it is more a curse than a gift."

"It is always so for those who can see the future. Seeing it is one thing, averting it another. What did the crystal show you, Sahib?"

THE MONKEYS OF DURGA; A SUDDEN ALARM

"Why must we go to the monkey temple?" Lalita asked.

Hanuman only smiled at her, flashing his bright, sharp teeth, in what would be a threat had he still been in monkey form. Lalita and Hanuman had landed outside Benares proper. They had remained in human form the whole day. Having hidden the flying rug and locked it with spells that would only allow the two of them to take it, they were now walking into Benares proper. The roads were thronged with pilgrims in various modes of transportation, from human-drawn chairs to bullock carts, to poor wretches on foot carrying their meager possessions tied in bundles on their backs.

"I do not think it would be a good place for us," Lalita said, squirming. "They must sense the jewel and its power." She spoke in an undertone, rapidly. "And if they do they'll come after us. They know we're monkey shifters, and if they follow our trail here, they will look in the monkey temple."

"Ah, yes, Princess, they will." He gave her a long,

lazy smile. "But then, it is where we must go, to get information on other shifters in the area and where they might have gone. And it is in here we must go to find those of our kind who are in touch with the tiger-weres, or who might have heard rumors of their passing through. That is our only chance to find out if the tigers have come through here, and what they plan to do with the jewel." He nodded, then as an afterthought added, "And with your friend, too."

"But if we find the tigers, they will find us, too. They will track us by witch-sniffing or following the jewel."

He shook his head. "Remember, I've taken care to use a spell to veil the jewel, and our magic as well. It won't last more than a day or two. Such spells never do. But it should be enough to see us safely on our way and out of this very crowded city." He frowned as they walked past a poor man on foot who carried what appeared to be his only possession—a spectacularly polished brass bowl. Or perhaps it was an offering of some kind for one of the temples, Lalita thought, but stared at it as she heard Hanuman add, "The thing that I find strange is that the dragons haven't used this spell to hide their trail."

"It's not so strange," Lalita said. "I didn't know such a spell even existed."

"Ah, but, Princess," Hanuman's voice assumed a patronizing tone, "you were not trained for the sort of work that I was . . . and that any emissary from the dragon king perforce must be. More, since their rightful throne is occupied by an usurper and the true heirs have lived in secrecy and hiding." He shook his head, then said, in a distant, considering tone, "No, Princess. I do not like the way it smells."

"What do you mean, the way it smells?" she asked, in as low a voice as she could and still be understood as they passed a fakir, who held a hand high up above his head. From the withered and contorted condition of that limb, he'd been holding it in that position for a long time. It was the demanding discipline of these sages to mortify the flesh, often by holding themselves in positions or on surfaces that caused parts of their bodies to wither and die. Lalita knew this was a holy practice, but all the same, she looked away from the contorted man—before whom passersby were laying coins—and drew her head scarf a little closer as she said, "What do you fear?"

"Why, a trap, of course," he said. "Which makes it all the more imperative that we go to Durga's temple."

Lalita sighed, resigning herself, as they walked into the city streets proper. She didn't think she'd ever seen so many people together—or at least not so many people from so many different regions, who spoke so many different dialects. The babble of accents and the clash of many different appearances and of clothing as varied as silk and rags pressed close on every side and she felt as though she'd entered a madhouse.

Not even my uncle's court when we all celebrate some great festival and change shapes back and forth is this mad. And even as she thought it she wondered if it were true. She could barely remember the ceremonies in the monkey palace before she'd gone to London. She'd been in London too long, she decided. People didn't press you close in London. At least they didn't if you were the maid or companion of a well-dressed and well-educated young girl. She felt as though she were seeing India through the prism of her London years, and almost wept. It was as though she had lost something essential that should always have been part of her.

Hanuman, she noticed, cut through the crowds seemingly without noticing, and not giving the slightest impression of being bothered by being pressed close, or even by having beggars rudely tap a bowl against his arm, demanding alms. He looked back at her with a quizzical smile, and she wondered if she should tell him that she was bothered by all this. No, she decided. It would be foolishness. Admitting it would only make him smile ironically at her and possibly treat her either as a child or a pampered noblewoman. Instead, she hastened to catch up with him as he walked past many temples filled with pilgrims.

None was more magnificent or more crowded than the Golden Temple, right in the heart of Benares, with its gold-plated spires. It was a beautiful building, climbing above the crowds and seeming to transcend them. It was dedicated to Shiva, in his role as lord of the universe. A priest at the entrance made sure that only Hindus of the upper castes could enter and adjured them not to offend the monkeys in any way. Through the doorway, one could see that there were all kinds of people inside, wearing all sorts of clothing—from the coarse homespuns of the Hymalayan foothills to the white costumes of the Bengalis. Rich elbowed together with the poor.

Within it was a pool where anyone who drank from it would be transported to paradise. At least Lalita remembered her uncle telling her so, when she was very

young. She wondered if that was true, and what paradise would mean for such as them.

They traced the sinuous street until suddenly a
temple with elaborate columns and filled with monkeys playing on its broad stairs came into view. Lalita
had only heard of the temple of Durga, goddess of
slaughter. She had never seen it.

From Hanuman's sure-footed approach, she assumed that he'd been here before. She wondered once
more about this strange companion foisted on her by
her uncle, and how far he'd traveled and from whence
he'd come to guide her on her quest. And why.

The temple was as full of people as any other in the
city, and Lalita and Hanuman waited patiently while
the woman just in front of them purchased popcorn
from a vendor. Then Hanuman bought some. Lalita
had no idea why he was buying popcorn. After all, at
their last stop they'd eaten fresh fish hastily roasted
over a campfire. But Hanuman seemed intent on acquiring popcorn, and Lalita waited while he hailed the
merchant and the proper bargain was struck.

Carrying a clay plate of popcorn, they walked into
the temple, and Lalita couldn't help saying, "Hungry,
Hanuman?"

Hanuman shook his head. "No. This is for you to
feed the monkeys of the temple." As he spoke, he
handed the plate to her.

"Me? But why?"

"You will see," he said, as they reached the edges of
what appeared to be a crowd of unruly monkeys chat-
tering and screaming in the courtyard. "Here, come a
little deeper."

Monkeys clawed at her legs and pulled at her robes

as Lalita walked farther into the furry mass. She was sure that a few of these were shifter monkeys. Her uncle had told her that often those who were tired of the court and civilized society would retreat to the temple of Durga to be monkeys among monkeys and thus undisturbed in their own nature. She didn't know whether the thought that the owners of the tiny paws scrabbling at her clothes might be as sentient and informed as she was comforted or appalled her. It seemed to do both—all of it mingled with a sense that these creatures were probably teeming with lice, which were crawling onto her flesh and hair even as she stood there.

Which wouldn't be exactly surprising, as monkeys were climbing on her head, and pulling at her headdress, and generally trying to reach the popcorn she was holding. Covering it with her hand, because she wasn't sure that Hanuman meant to give it to the monkeys, she remembered the words of the priest at the entrance, who had abjured them not to strike, scare or insult any of the monkeys, and she turned in bewilderment to Hanuman, wondering why they were subjecting themselves to this.

Only, Hanuman wasn't there. Where he'd been there was only a pile of clothes on the floor. Reflexively, seeing a monkey reach for the clothes, she put her foot upon them, as her companion's plan became clear.

He'd wanted them to advance far enough that they were covered in monkeys—more or less literally. A place where he could shift shape into a monkey and not be noticed. She wondered how long he expected her to stand here. She didn't doubt that he expected her to keep holding the popcorn inviolate—because if she distributed her largesse, then the monkeys would lose interest in her and the returning Hanuman would not have cover for his nude human state before he got into his clothes.

Wedging her foot more firmly atop his clothing even as she felt grasping hands trying to pry them away, she thought that it would serve him right if she just let all the popcorn go, and let the monkeys take his clothes, too. The arrogant fool could have told her what he intended to do.

But as she was thinking this, she realized that a monkey came swinging through the air, seemingly running on the heads of the other monkeys. He hit the plate bodily, with a sort of flip, and the popcorn was flung upward, to rain down on him and his fellow monkeys, causing a brief flurry of activity.

Lalita gave a scream of frustration. Now she must go outside the temple again, she thought, and there buy yet another plate of popcorn. She turned and bent to grab Hanuman's clothes to carry with her, and realized that they were being gently but perseveringly tugged from under her foot by Hanuman himself—a human and naked Hanuman, smiling at her confusion.

He dressed more quickly than she could even imagine dressing and grabbed her arm, pulling her from the crowd of monkeys. On the steps to the temple, Lalita stopped to adjust her headdress, which had been pulled about and twisted during the brief battle for the popcorn, but Hanuman only tugged at her wrist. "Come, Princess," he said. "We have no time to lose."

She still simmered with surly resentment at his trick, leaving her to fight off the unruly monkeys and to keep his clothes from being stolen—all without so much as the courtesy of informing her of what his plan might be. "You seem to have forgotten, Hanuman, which of us is of royal blood and which one was sent as her helper and protector."

His features fell. She'd seen him happy and mobile and interested and horribly self-satisfied, but she'd never before seen his features fall like that, in utter dismay. He seemed to be struggling for words, then he said, "Yes. I'm sure it was very bad of me, but we have no time to lose."

"Good. Then you may wish to undertake the expedition on your own," she said. "I am not used to being a lackey who will act on unspoken orders. That is not my caste nor my station in life, and I—"

"Princess," he snapped, making the word sound like a whip cracked midair. "I will apologize most humbly and for as long as you wish me to at our earliest convenience, but now we truly must go, and fast. Come."

"Not until you tell me where we are going. That was a vile trick in there, and—"

"Yes, I'm the worst of villains, the last of the lackeys, and I'll put myself to death in a manner pleasing to His Majesty's niece as soon as my mission permits, but now, Princess, please, I beg of you, we must *go*!"

"Not until you tell me why," she said, crossing her arms, pleasantly aware of the fact that there were several people staring in their direction. Let them see Hanuman discomfited. He deserved it for treating her so badly.

But Hanuman only shook his head. "I can't tell you. Not right now."

"Well, then neither shall I go with you."

He exhaled with a sound like an explosion, then stole close to her, till his mouth was almost at her ear, and she expected him at any second to turn into a monkey, scrabbling at her head, scratching with tiny, clawed paws. "Princess, your friend does not know me! And we must go because I heard in there that the dragons are here, in town, and that the tigers are hot on their track."

Lalita stopped resisting him. She allowed him to pull her down the steps and into the town proper. "We must find them," he said, as soon as they were far enough away from the people of the town. "Those monkeys in there—quite a few of them are of our own kind," he explained. "And they said that the tigers were by, sniffing around and asking for us. But the monkeys found your friend and her escort of dragons easily enough. Or at least the dragons. We'll have to assume your friend is with them. They said that the dragons came through with their smell wholly unmasked, so it was easy enough for the tigers to track. But they're not sure where we are or what we're doing. I think they half suspect we took the ruby back to your uncle, the king. As maybe we should have done."

But Lalita was not in the mood to listen to his expounding on how, by duty, they should have taken the ruby back to her uncle. In fact, she was not really in the mood to listen to him expound on anything. For some reason, the fact that his stratagem in the temple had succeeded and that he'd been quite right when saying that they should go as soon as possible only served to make him more annoying.

"Use witch-sniffing," she told him, "to locate the

dragons. We'll snatch Sofie to safety as quickly as we may, and then—"

"I can't use witch-sniffing. Not with the tigers this close to us. The use of power will call their attention. It would also give away to them our possession of the ruby. No, Princess, we'll have to ask around, and find where your friend might have gone by description alone."

THE PILGRIM LODGING;
MIDDLE OF THE NIGHT
ALARM; FINDING SOFIE

Peter woke up in a startled panic. Part of this was not a surprise. They had fallen asleep on the floor of a pilgrim house in Benares proper. It was the safest place Peter could think of, being so full of people. While he knew that the Hindus in general had a very relaxed attitude toward all forms of weres, he also knew that the were-tigers would be shy of attacking them in the midst of other people. After all, even in India, someone as young and beautiful as Sofie being dragged off by weres would excite interest. And Peter thought—though he wasn't sure how right he was—that these creatures did not want light shed on their doings.

So they'd bedded down in one of the guesthouses created by some philanthropic believer. It was not, as it would have been in England, an almost monastical environment of tiny rooms. There might very well be private rooms somewhere in the sprawling building, but if so, they would be for high-caste pilgrims. As foreigners and out-castes, they'd been shown into a sort of courtyard with flagstones beneath and a high roof,

supported by columns. Someone had handed out what
looked like blankets, though they were truly more like
cloaks made of cotton, and not scrupulously clean, but
he and Sofie had taken them and bedded down, side
by side.

She'd fallen asleep much faster than he; he'd remained awake long into the night. He'd been hungry—
though they'd eaten some sweetmeats bought from
a side-of-the-road vendor—and he was afraid that
hunger would bring the dragon-shift, something that
was unthinkable in this crowded room, with innocents
all around. The stone under his body didn't bother
him—from Spain to Italy, from Greece to Africa, he'd
slept on the same or worse—but the people around
him *did* bother him, due to fear of what his other form
would do to them should he shift in his sleep. If only
there were some way he could control himself and
make himself change only when he wished, not at the
command of his body's imperatives. He turned and
looked at Sofie's sleeping face with a kind of bewildered surprise. She'd thrown the blanket halfway over
her head, and in sleep her face was even more beautiful than when awake. Gone were all learned expressions, all mannerisms, leaving only the clean lines of
flawless skin, the slight arch of the nose and the long
black lashes resting on the skin. He wanted to trail his
fingers down her jawbone, to her neck, to caress the little bit of ear that peeked from amid the wealth of black
hair.

He told himself he was foolish. Very foolish. It was
the infatuation of a man grown to almost middle age
without having given any vent to the passions of a
young man. He'd never been in love. There were

women he'd admired terribly, but there had never
been love as such, not even the awkward puppy love of
young adolescence. And he'd never held a woman
close, never felt that most basic of consolations that
other men took for granted. No. But he was not other
men. As a were, with an alternate—dangerous—shape,
he was forever set apart from them, as doubtless in the
primeval garden the serpent had been set apart from
all the other animals. Which might very well explain
all the business with the apple. Being set apart, unable
to fit in, unable to partake of humanity, would do that
to you.

Somewhere between philosophy and self-pity, he'd
fallen asleep. And woke now with a feeling that something was terribly wrong. For just a moment, caught
amid one of the spasmodic coughs that usually pre-
saged his changing shape, he trembled, and tried to
control his mind and body.

Deep breaths. He drew deep, slow breaths, sup-
pressing the need to contort and writhe and allow his
flesh to change shape. Cold sweat covered him. It was
always much easier to change than to fight the change.
Fighting it required all his strength, all his not-
inconsiderable willpower. He clenched his fists and
closed his eyes tight. He felt the blood pound behind
his forehead. He felt his heart already trying to shift
into the much larger heart of the beast, beating, beating against the cage of his ribs, seemingly fit to break
out. And he panted like a dog, and moaned, and hoped
that whoever heard him thought it was just a nightmare.

He didn't know how long he spent fighting the
change. It didn't matter. That kind of state, like the

measured time of a nightmare's scream, had no beginning and no end. At last the need to change abated, and he found himself conscious of his all-too-human limbs clenched so tightly that his leg muscles burned with cramp and his arms were folded across his torso in the position of one who died by painful means.

His throat was sore, as though he had screamed, and his eyes, still closed, pulsed with flashes of red light, as though he'd done violence to his optic nerve. Sweat covered him, the rank sweat that accompanies certain illnesses. But he was a human, and there was consolation in that. He took deep breaths, measured and slow, concentrating on them, until breathing was the center of his existence and all he could do.

At last, sure that he wouldn't change, he opened his eyes. And saw that the place where Sofie had lain was empty. Her blanket was gone, Sofie herself was gone.

Deep breaths. Deep. Nothing alarming. Perhaps she got up to look for a place to tend a call of nature. Women do that, too, even devilishly pretty women. Or perhaps she got up for a breath of fresh air. I'm sure it's nothing. Deep breaths.

He stood on shaky legs and made hasty passes with his free hand to secure their possessions—the bags they'd been using as pillows. Sofie's pillow was still there, he noted, as was the one he'd used. *Just gone for a breath of fresh air. Nothing to it. Nothing at all. You must breathe, and you must not—you must not—change. Not in this crowded room, with so many meals on two legs around. You will not change.*

Slowly, he got up. Everyone was asleep. Everyone looked calm. Nothing bad could have befallen Sofie. Oh, it was insane of her to go out anywhere on her own, without escort, but she was, after all, a creature of impulses. He thought of her on that balcony. No, Miss Sofie Warington did not understand the normal boundaries set upon life or the normal cautions imposed on a girl so young and pretty.

The thought that she might have walked in her sleep, as she'd told him she was wont to do while in England, made him frown. He must find her, the sooner the better.

Blindly, he wandered around the first floor of the shelter, which turned out to be exactly as he had anticipated. Just rooms such as the one they had bedded down in, strung together one after the other, all around a sort of central courtyard that reminded Peter of the open areas in Roman ruins throughout Italy, with tiled floor and fountains and a sort of little pool in the center, surrounded by fragrant flowers.

He tried to go up one of the staircases, but there his progress was barred, by a tall man who spoke to Peter in a rattling tongue, of which Peter understood not a word—though the intent was obvious. It was clear that as a foreigner, he could not be allowed to profane the lodging of the higher castes.

Sighing, he realized that if he couldn't go up, neither could Sofie. And since she was not in one of the other rooms, it stood to reason that she must be in one of two places: either the central courtyard or outside.

Assuming she had gotten up and gone somewhere under her own power—and Peter very much wanted to assume that, given that her leaving had done no more than disturb his sleep and had certainly not wakened him fully—she had probably gone into the courtyard. As likely as not to get a breath of fresh air, and perhaps to look for facilities with which this house was unlikely equipped. Steeling himself, he walked through the recurved archway at the end of the sleeping room and into the night, filled with flowers and smells and the warm summer night.

The courtyard was planted so as to make it difficult to see it completely with one sweeping glance, and Peter started walking around, telling himself he was sure to bump into Sofie any step now. And he would not scold her. If she chanced to be asleep, the poor thing, what would she know of the worry she'd caused him? And at any rate, she was very young. Almost, he thought, with a start, young enough to be his daughter. And then, with a frown, he corrected himself. After all, it was not at all normal to sire children when you were eleven. But all the same, she was young enough that he would have thought her a very charming infant if he'd met her in his boarding school days. Or perhaps not a charming infant. He'd never had much patience for the mewling bundles that tended to be wet at one end or the other, and altogether full of unpleasant smells.

Realizing that his thoughts had taken a hysterical edge, and were little more than a mad scrambling away from thinking of what to do if she had truly disappeared, he scrambled past a little circle of brambles and into what was a clearing within the courtyard. And stopped. On the ground, there, under the moon, was a pile of cloth.

It can't be anything. Nothing at all. Just some cloth. There are piles of discarded cloth here all abouts. And it means nothing. Probably one of those wretched blankets they gave us.

But the blankets were pale blue, and atop the pale blue pile, pink flashed, the color of Sofie's sash. She'd been wearing it so long, it was dirty and crumpled.

He knelt down and felt the fabric. It was Sofie's sash. But where was Sofie? A faint scent of her came from the pile of blankets, and Peter sighed.

He remembered her walking out of the high forest in the Himalayas. He knew next to nothing about sleepwalking. In fact, what he didn't know about sleepwalking could fill several very erudite volumes.

More frantic, he searched everywhere in the courtyard, but he could not find her. Which left only one option—one he was loath to think on. She must have removed her sash and headed out, through the sleeping room and then outside. In fact, it might very well have been her walking past, and not her initial waking up, that had woken Peter.

Convinced now she couldn't be in the courtyard, he took a step toward the sleeping room. But there, at the back of his mind, insidious like a dagger slipped in under the cover of a silken mantle, came the thought that the dragon would see much farther, much quicker.

He shook his head. The dragon was also hungry. *And so what?* the thought answered, bringing with it a reptilian slither that once more made him think of the serpent and the dragon. *And so what? What does that mean? Surely he'll have to eat—I'll have to eat—before the morning is through. And that being the case, I might as well do it here and now. Surely enough of my mind remains to control the beast, that I can make sure to find some food no one is guarding, something that's neither human nor sacred. And the dragon would never hurt Sofie.*

Rash, full of the urgency of the moment, he stepped behind the same hedge that hid Sofie's blanket and sash, and undressed. Absently, he cast a spell over his clothes so no one else would see them or be able to pick them up. And then he let go of the iron will that had been keeping him human.

His body writhed and contorted. Flesh ground on flesh and the unutterable pains of transformation took him. And the dragon sprang from the courtyard, full of the intent sense of his own needs, his desire to feed. At the back of his mind, Peter reigned the dragon in, with a mental scream: *We must find Sofie. We must find Sofie* first.

Slowly, like a man turning a boat against the force of the wind, he commanded the creature's great wings to turn, tilting and spinning in widening circles. In Peter's own mind, like a mad refrain, the words repeated: *Where can Sofie be? Where can she have gone? Let her not be in danger!*

His concern was such that though he'd have been hard-put to say whom, since he had trusted no divinity since discovering the colossal joke played on himself, the thoughts rose like a prayer, overwhelming even the dragon's mind and the beast's brutish hunger.

Through the dragon's eyes, Peter saw the city tilting and spinning, seemingly with each pass of the beast's flight. And with each pass, he looked closer and closer—dipping into a courtyard where a knot of people assembled, only to see it was the temple of Kali and that even at this late an hour the priests were sacrificing a goat to their goddess. By the light of torches, the goat had been tied so that its neck rested on the crook of a forked post.

One fast stroke of a sword, and the goat's head rolled, and blood spurted upon the priests and the statue of Kali—which, it seemed to Peter, appeared to smile. Scenting blood, the dragon rushed. Before Peter could stop it, it had snapped up the still-warm goat in its massive jaws. Lest the creature decide to return for the priests, Peter urged it upward, even as the dragon-mind was full of the sensations of appeasing its hunger, or at least making it controllable—of the taste of fresh meat, of the texture of crunching bone. Up, up and up. He must find Sofie.

He registered, in some surprise and as though from very far away, that the priests of Kali had not protested. In fact, they had made no sound at all at his unexpected theft.

And then at the edge of town, cowering against the crumbling wall of an uncharacteristically dilapidated temple in this pious town, he glimpsed something. Something white, something black, something human. He should not have recognized the form.

But something in that person clinging to the ruins of the temple called to him. Closer he drove the beast, flying in circles to approach—great wings spread to the sky and hurting with the force of his precipitate descent. He must see. He must know.

Closer, and he was now sure that the figure was a female. A female wearing a billowing white dress, with jet-black curls loose down her back. She was climbing the crumbling pile of rocks, tripping and restarting, and tripping again.

How did she get here? How did she get so far, walking in her sleep? Why would she come here to a crumbling ruin at the edge of town, where there are almost no people?

Peter, locked inside the beast's body, flinched when the girl tripped and lost her footing again, then swooped closer to save her.

Which was when he saw that she was awake now—whatever her state might have been in getting to this location. She was awake, her face a mask of terror, her eyes wide, her mouth open and panting. Looking over her shoulder now and then, she led him to look—for the first time—away from her, at those pursuing her.

They were tigers, with powerful heads and large, dangerous paws. Well-fed tigers that did not fear the weapons of man. Were-tigers, Peter would bet on it.

Then he looked on the other side of the rocks that Sofie was climbing blindly, hoping to find safety beyond them. But on the other side, he saw, other tigers waited—a very large one holding center stage. One he would bet was the king of tigers himself. Out of his kingdom and looking for . . . Sofie?

He tried to flame, but no flame came. Perhaps the concentrated magic of the tigers prevented him from flaming. He didn't know. There were places he'd gone in the past where the dragon couldn't flame. Places protected by spells of power, somewhat like the shields used in battle. Was the tiger kingdom protected by such?

TIGERS; MAIDEN
AND DRAGON;
A STRANGE KNIGHT

Sofie had woken—or at least come to herself—by the crumbling temple, surrounded by tigers. She couldn't say at which point her consciousness returned, at which point she was aware of being she—herself, Sofie Warington—here, amid unknown buildings, and near some horrible ruin at the edge of town. She assumed it was still Benares, the same town she'd fallen asleep in, because she could not possibly have transversed the distance to the next town by herself and on foot. Though in London, sometimes her nocturnal excursions had taken her farther afield than she'd ever been on her pleasure walks.

To the total strangeness of her surroundings, there was added—by degrees—the knowledge that she was alone. Where was St. Maur? Had he not noticed her leaving?

The situation was so clearly a nightmare that she would have closed her eyes and wished herself back in bed. But no more had she started doing so than a soft growl made her look up, to see tigers closing in.

There were three of them, and though she couldn't know for sure they were were-tigers, they were moving like no natural beast ever did. They were closing in on her by steps—small steps, at that, and languidly taken. It was, she thought, as though they were savoring her terror at their approach.

She backed up, step by step, till her heel hit the ruins behind her. And then she started climbing, madly, blindly. Oh, she knew tigers could climb. She knew tigers could leap. But what else could she do? How else could she escape them?

She climbed, and climbed—her feet balancing precariously now on this stone, now on the next. They hurt. She thought she must have skinned them on some stone, but it didn't matter. She had to keep going. She had to keep pressing on. Up and up and up, while the softly rumbling tigers closed in behind her.

Only the cold on her cheeks made her aware she was crying. Perhaps she had been foolish to run away. Perhaps she had been foolish to escape her parents' protection. Had they not nurtured her all her life? But they wanted to give her in marriage to a were-tiger. And yet, perhaps she had exaggerated the danger? Perhaps they would have listened to her fears?

Too late. She was going to die here, amid strangers, her body torn apart by savage weres. She thought of St. Maur—the dragon that St. Maur became—devouring the buffalo, and something like a scream escaped her.

A sudden sound, like a sheet being shaken vigorously, or like a sail creaking under the power of the wind, called her attention. She looked up, despite herself, in time to see the dragon plunge out of the sky, his claws extended. For just a moment, her body wanted to fling itself away to run back down the rocks, safe from the oncoming beast.

What stopped her, more than anything, was the sense that this was a dream. It had to be a dream. Because this one-eyed dragon was, unmistakably, St. Maur. And she'd never been threatened by St. Maur, nor did she have any cause to run from him.

In that moment of confusion, the claws surrounded her. She felt them, like gigantic calloused fingers around her middle, and closed her eyes. It was just a dream. She would wake. She would wake and find that there was nothing around her middle—it would happen at the exact moment the claws squeezed the life out of her.

Only the claws never squeezed. They held her with the gentleness of a young boy holding a wounded sparrow. She felt herself lifted, her legs flailing midair, and when she opened her eyes, she saw that she was being flown—carefully flown—over the city, toward the house where they'd lodged.

Her thoughts were such that they didn't bear exploring. There was the sudden realization that she'd been rescued by a dragon—that a dragon had indeed fulfilled the role of the white knight so prevalent in all the novels she'd read in England. She clasped both hands around what in the man would have been a wrist. And started, as she realized that on that wrist there was a slight, protruding dark spot. She remembered St. Maur's wrist, as he reached for something that displayed the skin normally hidden by his cuffs. He had a beauty mark in the same spot. The dragon was the man and the man was the dragon, she knew

that, but to be brought to understand it this immediately was almost shocking.

She looked up as the dragon looked down. The eye
had an expression of thinking and worry. Then he flew
lower, and retraced his path to the boarding house,
where he set her down on the alley.

Sofie averted her eyes, as he shifted to human. She
could hear gasps and a quickly stifled groan, but she
also could tell he was trying to keep down the noise associated with his shift. She wanted to run. Not from
him, of course, but from this alley, where the tigers
must have seen them landing—from this entire city,
where the tigers now knew they were.

She disciplined herself to say nothing and to wait,
clenching her fists to allay her impatience. And she
waited, as she normally would wait, for someone to
change clothes with back turned.

Only then St. Maur's voice said, softly, "Wait
here," and he walked past her, affording her a glimpse
of his naked body. For some reason, it didn't seem very
shocking. But to see him mid-shift—that, for some reason, had come to seem a violation of his privacy, as it
hadn't that first time. Perhaps because she knew now
how much he resented the change.

It seemed an eternity until he returned, an eternity
measured in pounding heartbeats and in blood rushing
in her ears. She thought he must be dressing, while the
deeper, more scared part of her thought he must have
left. Left her behind and saved himself from the pursuit of the tigers. Or would the tigers not be interested
in her if she weren't with him?

She thought back on the raj on her father's balcony,
the peculiar shape of his face, his yellow eyes that had

no white at all, and she shook her head. It was her they
wanted. She was sure of it. And now St. Maur had left
her here all alone, to face them as she could. Or
couldn't.

"Miss Warington." St. Maur's voice woke her from
this particular nightmare. He was still naked, holding
his clothes.

She almost yelled at him, asking him why he'd
taken so long to return. But before she could speak, he
said, "I came out immediately, so you'll pardon me if I
dress here."

He'd returned at once. That meant her perceptions
had exaggerated time. Annoyed at herself, at her fear,
and at—though she hated to own it—being more
touched by his rescuing her than she thought she
should be, she turned away. She could hear the rustles
of his clothing, but it was quite a while before he spoke,
and when he did it was in a slow and considering tone,
"I don't suppose you know how you got there? To that
perilous a position?"

"I . . . woke near that ruin, with the tigers."

"Yes," he said. He said it as though it meant far
more than the single, monosyllabic word should mean.
"But perhaps . . . It's hard to conceive, you see."

"What is hard to conceive?" she asked, turning to
face him, and seeing that he was fully dressed.

"That the tigers were following you." He frowned.
"They should have been able to catch up with you in
no time at all. I don't have figures, but I have seen
tigers leap and I'm quite aware of the speed at which a
human can run. They could have overrun you, and . . .
devoured you or captured you, or whatever they mean
to do with you."

She pulled back the hair that had fallen in front of her face. Really, the worst of this was that she had neither brush nor comb nor the leisure to tidy herself, as she did at home or at school, nightly before the mirror. Her hair had grown to be a tangled mass and quite unruly. While normally it didn't matter, some part of her did not wish St. Maur to see her wild and unkempt. "I know," she said. "And I confess I don't understand what they were doing either, nor how they keep tracking us down."

St. Maur nodded. "A witch-sniffer would be able to find me." And, as she was sure her features reflected her confusion at this, he added, "So I can imagine that having seen you in Calcutta, escaping on dragon-back, they realized they could use a witch-sniffer to find you. But here, in Benares, it shouldn't apply. You see, though I quite lack the witch-sniffing sense myself, I can imagine how it works. Here, all the sniffing should be too confused. There is the gods' power, for one, and the worship of their devotees, all of which are magic of sorts. And then, at least if rumor has it true, there are any number of weres in the city proper—monkeys and, as we've seen, tigers.

"Homing in on me would have been a difficult enough feat. Homing in on you . . . Well, considering you're nothing but an average magic user . . . it shouldn't be possible at all."

"And I haven't been using magic," she said, in some bewilderment, following his thought. "None at all. They would have had to track me based on my appearance and my description."

"I suppose they could have." He put his patch on and adjusted it, covering his empty left orbit. "But if

so, why? Why are you so important to them? Why
would they care?" He bit his lower lip, pensively, as
though trying to think his way out of a difficult maze.
"Miss Warington, I don't think we can continue with
this journey without knowing why the tigers are following you. Nor what they mean to do." He shook his
head, not so much at her as at some imaginary opposi-
tion. "You see, you cannot mean to rejoin your captain
only to be killed or kidnapped under his nose. And
from what I understand, Jaipur—the area around
Meerut—is the main hold of the were-tigers and were-
elephants. If it is indeed were-tigers pursuing you—"

"I'm sure it is," Sofie said. "I mean, you saw how
they were creeping up on me and enjoying my fear.
Those are the actions of a human, not an animal. Only
humans, being civilized, can take cruelty to such a re-
finement. I do have a house cat," she thought, thinking
back. "Or we did at the school. And Mrs. Thisbes was
quite cruel to the poor mice she caught. But that is cat
cruelty. What the tigers were doing, enjoying my fear
as they approached, was human cruelty. Oh, I'm ex-
plaining it very badly!"

He shook his head, his brow knit. "Not so badly at
all. I can follow your meaning quite well. You mean
that to know you were suffering anxiety at their approach, it required that the tigers creeping their way
toward you be aware of human modes of thinking and
human emotions. Something only a were could
achieve." On the last word, something like a sad, fugitive smile pulled at his lips, but it was only a shadow,
flashing and then gone.

"Yes," she said, looking away, embarrassed. St.
Maur was not a tiger. And yet she felt as though she

were discussing his own kind with him. Perhaps, she thought, it was because he had more in common with other weres, no matter how different from his other form, than he did with other humans? And, in the wake of that, she upbraided her errant mind. *No, no. Horrible. Despicable. How can I say that of the man who has twice saved my life? How like a knight of old he was rushing to my rescue, even though in his other form.*

He looked away from her, in turn, and spoke to the roofline of the opposing houses. "You see," he said, "if they are were-tigers, you're likely to be surrounded by them in the Jaipur area. It is said a lot of the sepoys—being of the warrior caste—are, in fact, weres. In the rebellion of 1857, they seemed to be mostly were-elephants, but I suppose were-tigers aren't out of the question and... I wish you'd understand, no normal man could have rescued you as I did. You were surrounded by tigers. A man who did not have a were shape—or even a man who didn't have a flying were shape—could have done no more than come in and die at your side. Something I'm quite sure you don't wish on your captain."

"No," Sofie said. Then again, more firmly, "No." Though Blacklock, in her mind, had become no more than a vague memory, the image of his smiling face, the boyish tumble of hair that forever obscured his forehead, only reminded her that she didn't want to bring death on him. She wasn't sure she wanted to bring anything on him. She wasn't sure she even knew what he thought about or wanted. And she was no longer so sure that his comment about marrying her if he could have meant any more than social gallantry pronounced at a party.

"We must find out what the tigers want," St. Maur said, his face set rigidly, like a bitter sculpture. "We must find out what they wish from you." He shook his head, slowly. "And I see only one way to do it."

"What?" Sofie asked.

"We must capture one of them. Preferably a young one of their number. And we must get him to talk to us."

"But," she protested, doubt assailing her, "it's not very likely that he would talk, is it? Even a young and powerless one? I hear they have... I mean, all these people have a fanatical devotion to their native leaders. How much more so it must be for weres."

"I wouldn't know," St. Maur said, stiffly, "never having met, face-to-face, another of my kind." He shrugged. "As for getting one of them to talk, it can't be that difficult. I have... some experience in the matter."

The flash of whatever it was—memory? thought? bitterness?—in his eyes made him appear more naked than even the transformation, and Sofie looked away from him hastily.

"Oh, never mind," St. Maur said. "I'll do what needs to be done. The trouble of this is that I don't dare leave you alone, or not for long. And that even though I have enough magic—as do you—to cast a hiding and locking spell over our luggage, I cannot do it for a living being such as yourself." For a few moments he was quiet, deep in thought, then he said, "I know. I will get your luggage, and we will walk a while before I change. Hopefully whoever is hastening in our direction, having seen me change, will then be thoroughly

lost. I will change shapes when I'm closer to the outskirts of town, so we can fly out relatively unnoticed.
Then I'll find one of the tigers and bring him back."

He sighed deeply. "The downside of this is that you
will have to be by—close by—while I interrogate the
creature. But let's hope he doesn't make it too difficult, and therefore doesn't make the spectacle too
shocking for you. And at least you'll be safe, should his
compatriots track us down."

"Yes," she said distantly, and stayed in place while
he went to get their luggage. After he came back out,
and while they were walking down the darkened
street, she said, "But how are you to find one of the
tigers after you take me out of town? You are not,
yourself, a witch-sniffer."

He shook his head. "No. That gift is even more rare
among Europeans than the ability to shift. From what
I understood of my comparative magic theory, it's
damned rare even among other populations. Our
teacher always said that most witch-sniffers were
shams and that their depredations, in fact, caused untold harm in Africa and India and other such regions.
You know, someone would be killed by magic and the
supposed witch-sniffer would put on a great show of using his gift and finding out who did it, when in fact they
were just accusing their personal enemies, knowing
they would be implicitly believed. A lot of people, I
understand, are put to death for murder on no better
testimony than a witch-sniffer's erratic word." He
shrugged. "I don't know how true this is. All such
reports, you understand, will be biased one way or another, but I have heard that our army's own witch-

sniffers ran tests of the witch-sniffers in west Africa and found not one of them even mildly capable."

Sofie nodded. "But then—"

"Miss Warington, they're tracking us. Mostly in tiger form, I think—at least in this region—because it saves them time, by keeping people from interfering with their quest. No one questions a were. No one pauses to ask a tiger where he's going. They're tracking us, relentlessly, ruthlessly. I don't understand by what means, but they won't give up just because I confuse them at little. At least, that's the best I can hope for—confusing them. They will be somewhere near where I take you. Tracking you."

Sofie shivered. She couldn't help it.

"Yes, see?" St. Maur said, as though answering a question she had not asked. "That is what I mean. We cannot go on like this. Nor can I leave you in some garrison post with a new husband who doesn't know how to counter this menace. I would feel responsible."

"I don't know why you should," she said. "You owe me nothing."

He flashed her a smile. "I don't know if this is true, but I've heard it said that if a Chinese man saves your life, he will consider himself henceforth responsible for you."

"That seems like a great deal of nonsense," Sofie said, hearing her own voice echo back far more assured and full of certainty than she felt.

"Does it?" he asked. His lips twitched into a lopsided smile. "Perhaps it is. And perhaps not. After all . . ."

"After all?"

"After all, if I hadn't saved you from your fall from the balcony, you would now be beyond all cares."

"I would be dead."

"Yes. At least it would have been a quick and painless death, though. I'm not sure what the tigers intend would fit the same description."

She wanted to speak, but the way he spoke of a quick and painless death put a chill in her chest, and made her mouth unable to form words.

"No, Miss Warington," St. Maur said, as though she had spoken, "I do have an obligation to you. An obligation to see you safe where you wish to be, and to set you up, safe, in a position such that will allow your life to go on with at least no more pain than you would have suffered from that fall. And that means..." His voice lowered until it was no more than a desolate whisper. "I will have to do what I would very much prefer not to do."

SAHIB AND SEPOY;
SUPERIORS AND
SUBORDINATES;
LEGENDS AND RUMORS

"It...The crystal showed me..." William could not command his words. He ran his hand backwards through his hair, but his unruly lock only fell down over his forehead again. "I can't speak of it."

"I'm sorry," Gyan Bhishma said, standing in the almost military pose he seemed to think meant at-ease, and looking across at William, who was conscious of a blush burning in his cheeks as he put the stone away. "I should not have asked; I should not have come in. Except that I heard you...I thought you were..."

William shook his head. "You did right. I might have needed you." In fact, he was fairly sure, from all his knowledge of both protocol and military discipline, that Bhishma had not done right at all. Almost any other officer would be punishing him for his trespass, coming into a European's room without warning. But then, William thought, in an emergency sepoys had to be able to think for themselves. The loyal ones had to have as much or more freedom of action as the rebellious ones. And that wouldn't happen if one held to strict military protocol.

He looked at the man's face—the gravely disposed features, the concerned brown eyes—and thought he'd meant well. And though a great part of colonial administration was convincing the natives that the colonials were demi-gods, set apart, protected by their own strangeness and strange ways, perhaps it wasn't all for the best. Oh, sure, in peacetime it made an officer who wasn't overly capable—and who, in England, would never have gone very far in the army—capable of instilling holy terror in the hearts of several rational, well-trained natives. But in wartime...He thought back on his grandfather's letters. In the 1857 rebellion, it might well have been responsible for most of the massacres. The Indians had felt forced to execute captive Englishmen—even helpless ones. Even women and children. Because had they left them alive, it would be viewed by the other Indians as proof of the Englishmen's invulnerability and it would eventually have killed the rebellion and brought the English to power without the slightest effort.

"Sahib?" Bhishma asked, his voice sounding hesitant.

"No, no, you did right," William said, answering more his internal thoughts, than the man looking at him with the concerned expression of one consulting an oracle. "It is, of course, a breach of military discipline, and all that. But the ultimate need is that you protect Her Majesty's interests in this region, and therefore protect the officers placed here. And I think you were trying to do that. And though discipline and

proper procedure is essential, I've always thought..."
He floundered.

"Yes, Sahib?"

"I always thought it was important that each man
be allowed to use his head," William said. And was
surprised by seeing the other man startle and then
smile—a fugitive smile, quickly hidden. "What is hu-
morous about what I said?"

The man looked surprised, perhaps at his expressions being observed, then shook his head, vigorously.
"No, Sahib, you misunderstand. I was smiling at something foolish. Something that I thought..."

"What did you think?" William Blacklock asked,
trying to appear forbidding, threatening. Of one thing
he was sure, through all his reading and his military career: you could let them hate you, you could let them
worship you, you should never allow them to laugh at
you.

Bhishma shook his head. "Only that most of our
officers would not care that much for what an Indian
sepoy might think."

Ah. Not laughing at him, then, merely at his own
surprise in finding an Englishman who cared. William
thought back on his grandfather's letters. *We should
have seen this coming, but none of us talked to them,
or not as fellow human beings. The truth, I am afraid,
my dear Harriet, is that even those who commanded
sepoys for a lifetime, and were the quickest to defend
their virtues, their courage and their selflessness,
thought of them as undisciplined children, not as
grown men.*

Well, he might be making a mistake of his own—so
often people did when correcting mistakes of the

past—but he would not repeat the errors of his grand-father's time. "You are a human being," he snapped, "and you seem intelligent enough. Why shouldn't I allow you to use your head?"

"No reason I can think of, Sahib," the sepoy said, his face solemn. "But . . . I came to ask you, you see, if you'd spoken to . . . to General Sahib."

"I did," William said, and tried to find words to explain that he, himself, had not been treated as an adult man. "I'm afraid his response was much the same as if I'd been a sepoy."

It took Bhishma only one moment to understand. His mouth set. "Oh."

"Indeed. He told me I shouldn't listen to rumors encouraged by a tropical climate and fervid imaginations."

"I see," Bhishma said. "I was afraid he might. I must admit, since I can offer no proof and there is nothing I can do or say that would convince you, that it sounds childish and overheated, but . . ."

"But it's true?" William asked.

"To the best of my understanding, yes, Sahib. In fact, there are . . . well, some people in camp who can understand the codes of weres and the messages sent about by weres, and they say that the tiger kingdom is agitated about something. That the tiger king is looking for a mystical jewel. That with it he intends to . . ." He hesitated, then said, all in a rush, like a horse taking aim at a barrier and suddenly clearing it, "To expel all the English from India."

And why are you telling me this? William thought, looking at the man. And in the same thought he reproached himself for thinking that way. There were

loyal sepoys. In fact, rebellions and mutinies notwith-
standing, he would say the majority of the sepoys were
loyal to England, loyal to the English queen, loyal to
the officers who commanded them.

They might think their officers tiresome and stupid. William had spent enough time in the regulars in
England to know that most enlisted men thought their
officers tiresome and stupid—or worse. That made the
Indians no different.

Then why did he view this man with suspicion, as
he told of his compatriots' intention to depose the current regime and overthrow English rule over India?
He couldn't say, except he did view him that way. It
seemed like a violation of natural order, somehow.
Bhishma, unless William mistook himself, was quite a
different breed from the water carrier or the sweeper
who tended to daily needs. He was a warrior and
caste-proud. That much was evident in his way of
standing and in his look, in his proud military bearing.

So, why would he come to William with rumors and
stories? For just a moment, William wondered if this
was not a trap. Had Gyan Bhishma come to him with
a mad tale to distract him from the real danger?

That surely dovetailed with the man's next words.
He said, "I shouldn't have asked you what you saw in
the crystal, Sahib, but . . . did you see anything worri-
some?"

"Nothing," William snapped, half impatient at the
questioning, half frustrated at himself. In his mind was
the panorama of the encampment, such as he had seen
it—the bodies strewn everywhere, ripped by the fangs
of were-tigers, stomped under the gigantic feet of
were-elephants. A beautiful young woman holding a

little boy, still trying to shield his little, dead body, even in death. A mad vision, nothing else. "Nothing of any consequence. I saw a girl I used to know back in England."

"A . . . girl?" Bhishma said, stumbling over the word, as though it was not at all what he'd expected.

"A pretty girl. Met her at a few balls and went dancing with her a few times and . . . went riding in the park and . . . *someone* wished us to marry," William said. His mind, quite divorced from his mouth, was working feverishly on the puzzle of what he had seen. He shouldn't be considering it. Foreseeing was so unlikely an art, and so ill understood, so poorly controlled even by those who had the greatest supposed control over it.

Louis XVI's court clairvoyant had not warned him of the coming rebellion. Queen Victoria's own and much-feted royal soothsayer, the Earl of Sandwich, hadn't warned her of the Zulu rebellions—nor, for that matter, of the Indian mutiny of 1857. And yet these were people trained in the best centers of magical learning, men who had taken their specialty in the University of Avignon, where the great Nostradamus, himself, had studied. Who was William Blacklock to think he could compare his own puerile skills to their great learning? Who was he to think his forecasts were right, or even rightly interpreted? He wasn't a fool. Though foretelling wasn't formally taught in England, he'd read compendiums and books on the subject. And he knew that often what one saw was no more than a symbol for what might happen. So what could hundreds of dead bodies strewn about this space mean? What could it be a symbol for? The death of his position? The death of all his dreams? The death of his quiet life in England? Perhaps that was it. Then thought of his father's and mother's faces, receiving the news, whatever it was, and going all wooden and still.

He wondered what that letter had said. And then he realized that would tie in with his seeing Sofie Warington in his vision, too. Sofie Warington was the reason he was in India. If he'd agreed to marry her . . .

But that thought brought his mind back to what Bhishma had said, and he looked at the sepoy, who was standing still and dismayed, and gazed sternly at him.

"Is that what you were asking, then?" Bhishma asked. "About some girl you left back in England?" And then, as though realizing the unutterable trespass of both rank and familiarity that his words represented, he drew himself up to almost full attention and said, "Begging your pardon, Sahib. I was just surprised. I heard you cry out, and I thought . . ."

"Never mind my private life," William snapped. He'd allowed the man too much familiarity already. It was always so with him, even back in England. He had a way of becoming friends with servants and subalterns, of seeing them as people and not just as the functions they fulfilled in household or army. And inevitably, he was repaid with daring and abuse from his subordinates. He had to learn to guard himself better.

His father had said that William's characteristic came from caring too much for everyone, and that it would be an admirable trait in a parson. He'd said it with a kind of hopeful tilting of the head, again, at their last meeting, just before William had shipped out to India. And though William had long ago decided that the Church was not his destiny, nor would it ever be his profession, he now wondered if it wouldn't have been better for both his father and himself if he had decided it was. If he hadn't been so obstinate about Her Majesty's service. After all, if he'd gone into the Church, he wouldn't have come to India. He would hardly have volunteered to come as a missionary.

He shook his head at his own foolishness, dragging himself back from morbid thoughts about his past choices. "You said something about a jewel?" he asked Bhishma.

A curt nod answered him, even as the soft brown eyes looked somewhat bewildered, as though he was trying to work through a puzzle of his own. Had he, then, been setting a trap for William? And was he starting to think it would backfire.

"There is a jewel, the were-tigers' codes say, that would have the power to lead them to . . . something with greater power; I'm not sure I understand their communications exactly. They are different, you see, from—" He stopped abruptly. "That is, the people who tell me about them say that their codes are different from others. The roars in the night, the sequence of them . . . They are a slightly different code from those that my friend understands. But my friend says that they speak of some jewel that will lead them to something else—perhaps another jewel—which will give them more power than anyone else has had in all the world. They say it will bind all the magic to them and that the British will be left without power to run their magic trains and their magic carpets—without the magic to enchant powersticks, even."

Soul of Fire. Soul of Fire would lead them to Heart

of Light. And Heart of Light would give them power to do all that. Of course. All that and more, perhaps. Only, Blacklock couldn't imagine how the Indian would have come to knowledge of that, unless he was himself in on the conspiracy to steal the jewels.

He turned an analytical gaze on his subordinate. "Tell me, how do you know this? You say the tigers have codes?"

"All weres have codes," the man said, looking a little taken aback. "That is, at least all the weres in India. I'm not sure if English weres do, but then, of course, they don't have kingdoms, nor belong to groups, nor do they organize themselves or know what other weres are thinking. Or even," he seemed very struck by this, "if there are other weres about. If I understand it right, from the English newspapers, the only time a were is sure that there is another were in his region is when that other one is caught and publicly executed."

"Never mind the English weres," Blacklock snapped. "Tell me, rather, about who heard these were tiger codes. How can those codes be interpreted by a normal person? How would you learn to?"

Bhishma looked off balance, confused. Blacklock wondered if it was because he'd pushed him to the edge of his lies. *If he was telling me something, feeding me a line . . . If he thought I would fall all over myself to do whatever it was he thought more likely . . . yes, my interrogating him about how he came by his information would confuse him. Perhaps General Paitel was right all along. Perhaps these were rumors and an attempt to get me off balance. Or to make me go haring off and get myself and everyone else into some strange state, waiting for a rebellion, when the danger is from quite another quarter.*

Try as he might, he couldn't imagine another quarter from which the danger could be greater than from a rebellion of sepoy weres who outnumbered their superiors and were far stronger than them, even without special were powers.

But Bhishma had started to answer, haltingly. "There are ... friends of mine who are weres. And some of the were code is instinctive, though the instinctive part doesn't have a very specialized vocabulary and doesn't, of course, allow one to talk about modern life and the things that happen now. But all were codes have been modified somewhat, for the present time and for the species using them. And the tigers are in this region, see, and all the weres in this region understand their code, though perhaps not with the same fluency as if they were, themselves, subjects of the king of tigers."

It took Blacklock a moment to think through these words. Indeed, he felt as though the words were a labyrinth, through which he must make his way without a light, and with only a thread to mark the way he'd come. Things jumped at him, though, statements, out of the confusing argument that Bhishma had made. "There are weres in the ranks?" he asked, alarmed. "These friends of yours, are they sepoys?"

It seemed to him strange, almost shocking, that Bhishma should have friends who were were animals, that he thought nothing of it, that he didn't consider the association strange, nor feel guilty for it.

"Yes, Sahib," Bhishma said, looking puzzled in his turn, as though it was a very strange question to ask him. "Always some number of sepoys are were-elephants, and sometimes were-tigers."

"Were-tigers! Are they, then, subjects of the king of tigers?"

"We're all someone's subjects," Bhishma said, and he shrugged. "I mean, in India, you're always the subject of more than one person, the member of more than one group. It can't be helped." And then, as though belatedly realizing how his words could be taken, "They are loyal, these friends of mine. Loyal and true to their oath."

Yes, but loyal to whom? Blacklock thought. *And to which of their oaths?* Aloud he said only, as he regarded Bhishma with what he hoped was a forbiddingly stern gaze, "And why would you—or any Indian—wish to warn us of plans to overthrow the English rule? Why would you not wish this?"

Bhishma looked startled. "Because I swore my oath to the Queen, the Empress of India."

"But she is not of your breed, nor of your kind. She has not, in fact, ever set foot in India."

"There are many breeds and many kinds in India," Bhishma said "Men of all colors, all beliefs, many modes of living. Before the English, we were ruled by other foreigners, and I think we'll be ruled by foreigners again in the future."

"You don't wish for your country to rule itself, then?" Blacklock asked.

A sound like a cackle escaped from Bhishma's throat, but he didn't look amused at all. Instead, his eyes looked very sad. "Ah, Sahib," he said, "I have long ago realized that is impossible." He swallowed convulsively, as though trying to keep at bay some emotion that William could not understand. "My kind, as such, is not..." He shrugged. "Maybe India will rule itself one day, but if so, it won't be achieved by killing innocents. Death will only bring reprisals and killing among my own people, and besides..." His voice trailed off.

William thought of the horrible reprisals after the 1857 massacres. Had some of Bhishma's ancestors been involved in the uprising and been severely punished for it? Was that what he meant by "my own people"?

"And besides...?" William asked, sharply.

"And besides, knowing the sahibs in the encampment... Well, one knows that not all of them deserve death. And one would grieve, as a human being, if the innocent should be killed."

"The women and children, you mean?" William asked.

"The women and children as well."

CONFUSION; THE ROOFTOPS OF BENARES; A HINT AT LAST

"They're gone," Hanuman said, *shaking Lalita awake* and managing to give the appearance that Lalita had let them both down by falling asleep and by not seeing their quarry vanish.

They'd located Sofie last night—by dint of asking around until someone pointed them to the hospitality house—and they'd reassured themselves that Sofie was within. Further, they'd been told she was with only one man, a lone Englishman. This had led to spirited debate between them, and made them conclude that Sofie and the Englishman must have lost the dragons— or perhaps the Englishman had somehow rescued her from the dragons. They couldn't really probe the man's power and see how much he had, but he acted like the upper class, and the upper class of British society often had quite a bit of magic. It came, after all, from being descended on various sides from Charlemagne, who had originally stolen the power for himself and his descendants.

However, they couldn't be sure that the dragons

weren't about, somewhere, watching, as the tigers were. All around, they could see people with the characteristic broad faces of the most staunch members of the Kingdom of the Tigers—those who had only mated with their own kind for generations on end. There seemed, in fact, to be some sort of patrol going on, with members of the Kingdom of the Tigers passing back and forth in front of the door to the hospitality house.

"They are afraid of doing anything open while in town," Hanuman had said. "Any aggression against the English could bring the entire might of the British Empire cracking down on them. The revolt of 1857 is still remembered, and the reprisals against our people even more so. The tigers will wait till your friend and her escort are in a more isolated area, then they'll take them."

Lalita agreed. It was the only explanation for the situation. Satisfied, they had decided to bed down in one of the adjacent rooms in the same house, and after much argument, they had settled for rooms: spartan, bare rooms on the upper floor, which had the advantage of not having them bedding down elbow to elbow with untouchables—the idea of which caused them both to recoil.

But now Lalita wondered if they shouldn't have done it anyway. Caste when you were a monkey was a slippery thing, not as easily defined as for the normal population. There were rules, yes. And none of the weres were ever low or out-caste. But they were more flexible about violations of their status. And the fact that they were following inviolable orders of their pre-ordained king protected them from loss of caste.

So they should have slept downstairs. Instead, they

had settled into a system in which each of them stayed awake half the night and went down at intervals to see that Sofie was still there, still sleeping, and still side by side with her protector—whom Lalita had verified was indeed an Englishman of most superior appearance.

"How are they gone?" she asked, grumpily, getting up from the mat upon which she'd been sleeping. "I thought you were watching, Hanuman. Did you fall asleep?"

He let forth a string of curses. "I did not let them go. I watched. I was looking from the top of the stairs as often as I could, and the last time I looked they were both there, both asleep. And now they're both gone."

Lalita felt a sting of irritation. "If you mean that they both have gotten up and that neither is in that room anymore, that could mean anything. She might have needed to go outside to answer a call of nature, and he would of course accompany her. I mean, I doubt she would ask—the English are odd about that—but if he rescued her from dragons, he has to know she's threatened, and I doubt he would let her go outside alone."

"Am I a fool?" Hanuman asked, at the same time he slapped his not-inconsiderably muscular chest. "Would I come and wake you, Princess, were I not sure they are gone from all the rooms downstairs? They have disappeared, Princess, like snow brought down from the top of the mountain will vanish on a summer day."

"You have looked?" Lalita asked, hints of alarm creeping upon her. "Looked everywhere? And yet, you cannot find them?"

"I looked all around downstairs, and even in the streets and alleys near here, Princess!"

"Sofie... my friend sometimes walks in her sleep. Perhaps it is not so very bad. Perhaps it was just that she woke and walked out in her sleep and he walked out after her?"

"Not so very bad?" Hanuman clasped his hair in both hands and rocked back and forth, moaning. "Please, tell me, Princess, what your idea of very bad is. Don't you realize, if they're out there—if they go to a lone spot at all—the tigers will snatch them up? And then—" He stopped abruptly.

"And then?"

"And then I saw a dragon, downstairs."

"A dragon?" Lalita asked, starting to wonder whether her confederate was, in fact, hallucinating, or perhaps prey to vivid dreams. "A dragon, here?"

"In the central courtyard." He waved vague fingers in the general direction. "When I arrived there to look for her, there was a dragon, just taking off."

"That's impossible, Hanuman!" she said. "A dragon? Why, his wings by themselves would take up almost all of the central courtyard."

"I know that. I am not a fool. I'm sure he was not in dragon form when he came in. And even if he is from China, in this holy city Chinese people are not altogether unseen. And it is nighttime. And who would deny them entrance to the hospitality house, provided they didn't try to get access to the upper floors?"

Lalita, barely awake, tried to think through all this new information. So the dragons had tracked down Sofie and whoever the Englishman might be who had accompanied her. But Sofie had left before that. Or had she?

"Did they leave before you saw the dragon?" she asked Hanuman, sharply.

He shrugged, a mobile gesture. "As to that, I can't swear to anything," he said. "You see, the dragon's wings were spread. For all I know, they were on its back."

Sometimes, Lalita reflected, it was very hard to keep from screaming and throwing things at Hanuman's head. She knew part of the reason her uncle had chosen her to go to London with Sofie was that Lalita was one of his closest relatives and therefore trustworthy. And though Lalita had been only twelve—just two years older than her charge—when she was sent to London, she remembered the speech her uncle had made to her. All about how if the royalty of monkeys had one abiding fault, it was their volatility. They lost their temper, or were amused, incensed, enraged, happy—all at the slightest of provocations. This defect of character caused them to not be taken seriously by the rest of the world—weres and not—and gave them a reputation of tricksters and jesters.

Her uncle had hoped that, in London, Lalita would learn to control herself. The English were, after all, so restrained, and she would be taking a servant position, which called for yet more restraint.

Now Lalita pressed her closed fists on either side of her head, and wondered if pairing her with Hanuman had been a further test. The gods alone knew that this man—or monkey—in either form could tempt the patience of the most devoted mystic. "You're telling me," she said, slowly and dangerously, "that you failed to observe them get up. That you don't know where they are, only that they are not anywhere near the building, and that, having seen a dragon take off from the courtyard, you did not stay around long enough to see if the dragon had anyone on its back."

"I couldn't have seen it anyway," he said coolly. "The dragon was too near, the courtyard too confined for me to get a view of the beast flying away."

"But how are we to find them?"

Hanuman's gaze played amusedly over her, as though this were all a big joke that she had, so far, failed to get. "Well, Princess, we'll assume that they are with the dragon. Your friend was with the dragon before, and it was never fully clear whether she was held captive or she went with him of her own free will. So we'll assume the Englishman is just someone who joined their traveling party. We'll assume that the dragon came and collected them by arrangement."

"What about the other dragon? The Chinese one?"

"We'll assume he's watching their backs."

"And after we're done assuming all that," Lalita said tartly, "will we be any nearer to finding her and making up your appalling error in letting her disappear from under your nose?"

She expected him to take offense, which was probably stupid. After all, she'd been traveling with this man for a few days now, and she should have known better. Offense and other reactions that might result from pride and honor were quite unknown to him. He was all mobile and ethereal, like the smile that flitted across his lips at her words. "Hardly under my nose, Princess," he said. "More under my feet, since they were on the floor below. However, take heart. We found them before and we can find them again."

"If they're traveling dragon-back?" she said, hesitantly.

"No matter how they're traveling," he said. "You forget that here in Benares, there are monkeys everywhere, though mostly centered in the colony in Durgas's temple. They'll be all over the rooftops, even at this time of night. We can ask information as we go."

Lalita hesitated only a moment, then said, "We'll go in changed forms, I presume?"

"Of course." He was already doing something to the belt around his waist, which held the ruby. Adjusting it, she thought. So it would stay put when he shifted shapes. As she thought this, she started unwrapping her sari, while Hanuman, more efficient at his task—as though changing in and out of monkey form was a far more common activity for him than it was for her—took off his loose pantaloons and his tunic and wrapped them neatly in a bundle, which he tied at his back, using the pants legs as a tie. Lalita followed suit with her sari, tying it, bundled, around her shoulders. It would slow them down, of course, but in a city this crowded it was easier to be able to put clothes on at an instant's notice, should the situation call for it.

Hanuman had already shifted when she finished tying her bundle on her back. He shifted quickly and painlessly. Lalita shifted painlessly, too, right after Hanuman, but with more of a struggle.

When she managed to become a monkey, Hanuman was at the window, looking at her with a very good imitation of his human grin. She bared her teeth at him, regretting that in this form she lacked the eyebrows and the expressiveness of facial muscles for a really good scowl.

The roof of the hospitality house, onto which they swung in one smooth movement, was low for Benares, only two stories tall. Worse, around it crowded other low-roof structures, hovels and makeshift shelters for the pilgrims who wished to stay in Benares but lacked the money.

Though it was night, there were people on the streets—of course, this was Benares. Chants went up from nearby temples. From the river below came the glow of burning ghats and the faint smell of burning human flesh.

They took the roofs of the hovels at a trot, with Hanuman in the lead, swinging easily from roof to roof. And, at last, from them to the roof of the temple of Kali, where the statue of the goddess, with its garland of human skulls and its necklace of dead men's hands, stood in the courtyard, her outstretched tongue seemingly reaching for the place of sacrifice, where a bifurcated post marked the area where the sacrificial animals were tied and offered.

In that sacrificial area there was a goat's head and a concerned knot of priests of Kali. "It was a dragon," someone said. "I wonder if the Lady sent him to take the goat?"

Lalita and Hanuman fled the temple of Kali, and up to the glistening cupola of an adjacent temple. In the street below, someone was gently leading a herd of sacred cows. A Brahman priest was consoling what appeared to be a bereaved family. Lalita and Hanuman jumped over the bridge and onto the roof of the Golden

Temple, next to it. This impressive structure should allow them a good view of the city and surrounding areas.

And, indeed, it did, showing the city of Benares in its multidinous worship and prayer. But it didn't show them a dragon. As for the monkeys in whose presence and observing eyes Hanuman had placed so much confidence, Lalita could only imagine that he'd dreamed them. She hadn't seen them on rooftops before, and she didn't see them now. The only place she could discern any group of them was around the temple of Durga. Which meant that unless the dragon had made it an express point of checking in with the monkeys of Durga, they would be quite out of luck.

But just then she heard, behind her, the half-vocalized call of a monkey—in fact, the call of her kind. She turned around sharply.

A male monkey stood behind them, one with the characteristically slim and agile build of the princely monkeys that belonged to Lalita's own family. Her uncle had a dozen sons—princes all. But she hadn't seen them since they were very young, when most of them were still unable to change shapes.

This one now bowed to her, consciously, acknowledging her superior rank, and in that one gesture making his obeyance to her.

Then he moved his fingers, fast, in the gesture-language they used when in this form. All were-creatures had ways of communicating with their kind. Tigers and elephants used mostly sounds, some of them modulated so that the human ear could not discern them. She didn't know what dragons did, though the legends spoke of their using a peculiar type of hisses and clicks that mimicked human language, so that each dragon spoke the same tongue he spoke as a man.

Monkeys, however, with their mobile digits, had long since created an extensive and all-encompassing language of gestures. The new monkey used it now, his long brown fingers flashing in the dark at a speed that made it difficult even for Lalita to follow.

One flying—no, one dragon, carrying a human female . . . headed southeast out of the city. Tigers before. Tigers following.

Lalita groaned inwardly. Of course the tigers were following. That made it harder to find Sofie—at least, presuming she was trying to evade the tigers—and equally difficult to rescue her, should they reach her in time.

The monkey, however, had taken the lead and Hanuman was following him, temple to temple, golden spire to golden dome, flat roof to hovel thatch, then up again, south, southwest.

If only Hanuman had managed to detain them, somehow. If only Hanuman hadn't been such a fool as to look around in the alleys after they'd disappeared, thereby delaying when he'd come to wake her. If only—

The if-onlys were obscuring all other thoughts, when Hanuman gave a sharp monkey-cry and pointed a long finger at the sky.

There, stark against the night, was a dragon—green and gold, its wings sparkling with captive fire. On the dragon's back was a girl, and Lalita would be willing to bet it was Sofie, though she was too far away to see details of form and figure.

And caught in the dragon's claws, screaming and roaring, was a young tiger. At a loss for what to think, Lalita stared, mouth open in shock.

The dragon dipped below, to the forest floor, and disappeared from view.

AMONG BEASTS;
THE DRAGON'S FURY;
BEAST AND MAN

Sofie was scared. She couldn't have explained it to anyone. She wasn't scared of St. Maur. It was hard to be scared of a man who had saved your life twice over, and who was determined to protect you at all costs.

He'd said that as they reached a small clearing in the woods. He undressed, briskly, hiding their bags and his clothes under a nearby tree and locking it under various spells of secrecy and invisibility—or as close to it as spells could get, carrying the strong suggestion that anyone noticing them should immediately stop doing so and look away as soon as possible.

Then he turned around. He'd removed all stitch of clothing, including his eye patch. His deformity should have scared her or shocked her, but it did not. Instead, with his eyelid closed on that side, he presented the aspect of someone who'd been through a great battle and not escaped unscathed. The only explanation he'd given her for his wound was that it had been "a sacrifice and a worthy one." She didn't know what that meant.

In her mind, she'd conjured up a lot of stories about his fighting many battles and being wounded in a noble charge against the enemy. The enemy in these daydreams was always indefinable, but she could see St. Maur clearly—being very noble and self-contained and self-sacrificing. She could see him losing his eye and telling his men to charge on, to not flag.

All of this would have made much sense had it actually fit in with the story of himself he'd told her. Of course, it didn't. And yet, that didn't deter her. She realized perfectly well that in the story he'd told her there were holes—places left dark. She supposed he thought they were too rough and ready for her maiden ears. And, as such, she was sure he would tell her the whole story, someday.

She realized she was certain of this as she watched him turn around. And at the same time, she realized she'd been a fool to think that friendship or any sort of intimacy between them could subsist or grow. Or, indeed, that anything about him was human and soft and the same kind and order of being as she was.

Naked, his face bare, standing in that clearing, St. Maur made one think more of a blade, naked and ready, shining in the sun, than of a man with human frailties. Sofie shivered, and couldn't say why. There was a set to his jaw, all angles and sharp decision. His cheekbones looked more starkly planed, his shoulders thrown back, showing all his muscles in sharp relief. His body looked perfect—the even skin, the muscles of his torso, his perfectly shaped legs. He was almost hairless. The whole contributed, Sofie thought, to make him look more like a statue on display at a museum than the man who had rescued her. The man who, she realized, she'd been building up as some sort of knight-errant in her mind.

"Where . . . What do you mean to do?" she asked him, somewhat frightened at the implacable gaze of his single eye and at the straight line of his folded lips. What had brought on this change of expression and demeanor, and why did he look, of a sudden, so pitiless, so devoid of mercy or humor?

"I'll do what must be done," he said.

"Oh," she said, the exclamation wrung from her by emotions she couldn't quite put into words. "And what is that?"

He shook his head and looked at her, and his mouth set in a firmer line yet. His fingers seemed to stretch forward, and with it, to grow into something resembling the dragon's claws. She knew it wasn't true. It couldn't be true. When he shifted shapes, he shifted them in pain and with effort, not inconsequentially and in response to a mood. But his gesture made her think of dragon claws, and his expression, too, had something of the voracity of the beast.

She stepped backwards, confused, and just as the expression had appeared on his features, it changed and shifted, and something like a soft tenderness crept over him. "I'm sorry," he said, "but this can't go on. I cannot allow you to go your way, cannot leave you at Meerut, without knowing why these tigers are following you, or what they wish of you."

"But . . . surely you know what they wish of me. Their leader wants to marry me."

He shook his head and crossed his arms on his chest, and managed, suddenly, to appear formal, an older gentleman introduced to her at a London party.

"Don't be more of a fool than you can help, Miss Warington."

This was uttered in such a tone of pity and protective gentleness that it took her a moment to realize he'd insulted her.

"No matter how lovely you are, you are not so foolish as to think they would set this determined pursuit, that they would try to catch you by any means, simply because their leader wishes to put a wedding ring on your perfect little finger. You know better than that." He frowned and looked over her shoulder, and for a moment seemed to be quite abstracted—quite . . . immersed in another reality. "No, they want you for some purpose of import, a purpose for which no other woman will do. No other Englishwoman, even." He brought his gaze to bear on her again. "You see, when I first rescued you, I thought that perhaps they just wanted an Englishwoman of a certain class—not the English riffraff they easily can get hold of—to kill publically and incite a greater revolt against British rule in India. I studied how revolutions are started, you see, and this seemed to me a plausible ploy. He'd take you to his distant kingdom, and there kill you publically, and when his followers saw that no chastisement followed the transgression, they would have the heart to take on the English—all of them."

"Oh," she said, because she could picture the scene he was describing. She could imagine it all too well— being butchered before a crowd of natives, serving as an incitement to rebellion. In fact, it seemed all too likely to her.

"But I don't think that's what he meant to do," St. Maur said, curtly. "Because if it were, there would be no point at all in pursuing you halfway across India, particularly not after the raj saw you snatched up by a dragon, who could be presumed to put up a fight should you be taken from him. No. They would have moved to other, easier pickings. In as desperate circumstances as your parents might be understood to be, they are not alone, you know? There is more than one family ruined by India and ready to sell their daughters in matrimony to a titled native for a reasonable consideration—or as well to be bribed or coerced by other means. You, no matter how beautiful and accomplished you are, you are not worth the game. Not if all they wish to do is kill you."

"So..." A strange hope took hold in her—a hope that the tigers didn't mean to kill her. Moments ago, this wouldn't have been her assumption, but now... "You mean that they want me for some other purpose? Than just killing me?"

"I have to assume so," St. Maur said. "And such being the case, they're not likely to give up simply because you're in Meerut and married to a young English soldier. They will continue pursuing you. And I can't allow that."

"Why not?" she asked, caught between anger at him—he'd as good as said no one would risk much to marry her—and confusion that he seemed to feel some form of responsibility for her well-being.

"Because..." He opened his mouth, then closed it, suddenly, with a snap. "Because I saved you. And therefore what may happen to you is my fault. Even falling from the balcony would be easier than what might happen to you in the tiger realm."

She shivered at his words, and thought of the novels she'd read in London, which delighted in describing in vivid, purple-streaked, blood-soaked detail the perils of captive maidens. These heroines would talk, at length, of their feelings, and of how their fate was shocking and cruel. In fact, they adorned horrors with big words and careful description that seemed to thunder and echo in the back of the scene, ominously, a Dies Irae of doomed musical accompaniment. But it wasn't that way, was it? It wasn't that way at all. Instead, horror came with a sort of matter-of-fact quotidian air. It was like...if one were to be killed by one's own mother in the kitchen, it wouldn't be with some arcane ornate dagger used by the priestesses of Isis, but rather with the wooden-handled knife that had all one's life served to cut the bread.

Thus St. Maur's description of what might happen to her. The idea seemed all the more obscene when stated in those simple, unadorned words. She turned to him a face that she could feel draining of color, and he looked conscience-stricken and worried.

"It's not like that, Miss Warington. Not like that at all. They might have plans. They might have nefarious intent." He shook his head, and for a moment the chiseled look was gone, leaving in its place that curiously vulnerable look he'd shown her before. "But nothing will be done to you. Not while I live and take breath. I am responsible for you, Miss Warington, and I take my responsibilities seriously."

His responsibility. Why did her heart seem to close upon itself, as on an impenetrable shell at the thought that this was all she was to him—all she would ever be? It was foolish, unaccountable. A responsibility was more than she should be. She nodded primly at his

words, and was rewarded with one of his rare smiles—
the one with what seemed to her a shadow of brittleness
in its quick appearance and just as hasty disappearance.

A wrinkle formed, vertical, on St. Maur's forehead,
as he said, "Now, listen. As soon as I change shapes,
you will climb on my back. No, don't protest. I can't
leave you alone here, you see. I want you to hold on as
well as you may, because I'm going to be hunting for
the tigers, and that might necessitate sudden maneu-
vers and turns. Do you understand?"

She ducked her head, to indicate acquiescence,
and as was likely to happen when nervousness seized
her, she heard her voice say unthinkable words: "You
know, all this dragon riding would be far easier if you
came provided with reins."

There was a moment of silence and she thought
that she had offended him mortally, but when she
raised her eyes to his face, she saw that he was smiling,
his eye crinkled at the corner, in a way that denoted
true enjoyment of the joke. "Indeed," he said. "Undoubtedly it would. But for now, I must ask you to hold
on as tight as you can."

And with that, he started glowing with the soft blue
light that surrounded him on such occasions. She
looked away from his torment, and did not look back
until there was a sound that she had come to identify
as a sort of dragon chuckle.

He extended his front paw and dipped his wing, to
allow her climb, as had become their habit in these
days of traveling together, and she leapt on the
dragon's back with an ease that would, doubtless, have
scared her family, and all her friends back in London.

For all the descriptions of dragons in books, they had neglected to say the dragon would, in the end, be much like the man they were in their other form—honorable or villainous, cruel or gentle. On the crest of this thought, she ran a hand down the dragon's neck-ruffle, that protrusion of skin to which she normally held. It looked like gossamer silk shot through with gold thread, a thing too beautiful to be practical, but St. Maur had told her she could hold on to it as tight as she wished. She ran her hand down it, feeling its folds, surprised at realizing, for the first time, that it was not cold, as one would expect of a reptile, but soft and warm like one's eyelid or the skin on the inner curve of an infant's knee.

The dragon made a sound—a sound she could neither identify, nor remember its ever having made—and turned back, its eye—so disturbingly St. Maur's eye—looking at her with something she could not identify, then closing partway, much like a cat's on being caressed.

Rather proud of herself, Sofie held on to the neck ruffle with both hands and said, "You may start, my lord. You may be aloft as soon as you think it good."

TIGER, TIGER; THE CODE OF HUNTERS; THE MOST PRECIOUS OF GOODS

Every time he changed shapes, Peter realized more and more that he was the dragon and that the dragon was himself—the two inextricable and linked. He realized that pretending to be two different creatures was just a game he'd played with his own mind, to make himself feel normal.

And yet, this time, the situation was uniquely suited to make him feel like two people. The dragon was looking for tigers amid the forest and the undergrowth—now flying above, now dipping in for a close look at something moving down there. And Peter— Peter's mind that was composed of memories and thoughts and feelings—felt Sofie on his back. That warm weight, that dear burden for whom he would gladly die.

The thought shocked him. It shocked him as much as the acts of barbarism he had first committed as a dragon. That thought, crossing what he could only call his most human of minds, reverberated through him as much as the frisson of being locked in a body that devoured sheep whole. The dragon dipped and wobbled, for a moment losing control of his glide upon the air.

Sofie screamed. Peter shook his head—or the dragon did—and Peter forcefully willed control upon himself. The dragon's wings stretched as it found its balance again. And the girl on his back relaxed her death-grip on the neck ruffle, and gave it a long caress instead.

What did she mean by it, Peter wondered. Did she mean anything at all? Perhaps she was a good horse-back rider in England and that had simply translated to her trying to gentle him on this ride. He felt her hands grip the neck ruffle again, and frowned at him-self, before he realized that the dragon face was uniquely not equipped to show much emotion at all.

It didn't matter, since she couldn't see his face any-way. And why did she matter? He couldn't understand it all. She was just . . . a girl. He would grant that she was one of the most beautiful he'd ever seen. And she was daring, as no girl he'd ever met before.

But six months ago, while traipsing through Africa with his friend Nigel Oldhall and his friend's then-wife, Emily, he'd thought he'd never again meet Emily's like—for bravery, for unconventional accommodation to impossible circumstances, nor for beauty. And yet in all of those, Miss Sofie Warington either met or sur-passed what he'd presumed to be the most superior fe-male. But there was more than that to his feeling. There was also an ache, a feeling of belonging.

Peter Farewell had no conscious memories of his mother—or at least no coherent ones. She had died when Peter was just three, and all he could call to mind when he thought of those situations to which other people attributed mother's love, was his nanny—a great Scottish woman with a large bosom and a permanently strached apron.

Of his mother, he retained but one memory—at least he thought it was of his mother, because there was no one else he could attribute it to. His nurse had had pale blond curls, arranged—or so it seemed—with iron bonds. But Peter remembered being very young, lying in bed, huddled in a mended nightshirt, and having a woman lean over to kiss him. Again and again, in dreams and awake, he'd pursued that memory, and tried to see the face of the woman—but this was never granted him. Instead, the memory replayed itself in the same manner. A soft voice talking to him, saying words he couldn't quite understand, then a woman leaning over him—a scent of powder and rose water, a billowy, lace nightgown, the touch of soft lips on his forehead, and then the woman rising, her dark hair enveloping him like a curtain through which the light of his bedside oil lamp shone diffuse and rich, like the dawn of a new day.

Though Sofie looked nothing like his mother, and though he wouldn't say that she struck him as particularly maternal, the feelings she aroused in him were of the same intensity, the same disconnected, deep-echoing nature—an attraction, a feeling of need that surpassed all the constructions of his well-schooled mind.

As the dragon swept closely in an area where all the undergrowth was tawny-yellow—the color of a tiger—burned and parched by the drought before the monsoon, Peter wondered if this was what people talked about when they spoke of being in love.

He didn't know. All he knew was that he would give his life for her, and give it willingly and without thinking—and that there was no rational reason for this. There was nothing she'd done for him that merited such a return. And there was nothing particularly special about her. She was an excellent woman, superior in all parts—but, within those parts, just a woman.

And yet, if he could—he realized with a shudder of wonder—he would marry her tomorrow and take her away from the were-tigers and whatever they wished with her. He'd take her away from India, with its warring factions, its multidinous clamoring crowds. He'd take her away from holy men and madmen. And he'd take her to Summercourt and install her there, as Lady St. Maur.

The thought startled him for a moment, and then he thought it was all a symptom of his age. It was one of those mad passions that men almost in their thirties developed for girls much younger than them. Just as well that his condition and her position prevented him making a fool of himself.

Unbidden, a line of poetry that he hadn't heard since school crossed his mind: "Ye Gods! annihilate but space and time." Alexander Pope, begging the gods to make two lovers happy. But Peter was not sure there were two lovers here. In fact, he was absolutely sure she did not love him. As for himself, he was just a fool. Besides, Peter Farewell, Earl of St. Maur, did not believe in gods. No gods—or at least no sane gods, worthy of being believed in—would have laid this curse on him.

At that moment, as the dragon swept low once more, he saw the tigers in the forest below. There were ten of them, and none of them was looking up, though they were all excited by something—probably the feel of his presence nearby.

Ten of them, and one clearly the leader—large and built and muscular. Yet, at the edge, were a couple who—without Peter being able to explain why—looked scrawnier and younger. More defenseless.

He dipped in toward them in one long flight, mentally hoping Sofie was holding tight. There was an art in this, like there had been an art in picking Sofie up before. It was one thing to grab prey and silence its screams with quickly plunged talons. And another entirely to grab prey and keep it alive while you flew with it thrashing and shrieking in your grasp.

Peter held on to the creature a little harder than he'd held Sofie—Sofie had made no attempt to escape—and tried to think clearly despite the dragon's firm decision to fly away as far away as quickly as he could.

He could return to the clearing from which they'd departed. But alas, it was too close to the prowling tigers for his comfort. They would find him too quickly.

So he'd fly farther on, look for an area totally isolated—a rocky area, where perhaps the tigers would have more trouble going. And he'd cross a river—or as many courses of water as he could find. He didn't know if it was true that crossing water made it impossible for a witch-sniffer to discover you. He doubted it would be as simple as that. But if there was a chance, he would take it.

Grasping the tiger, he flew over forest and two small villages, away from Benares. He crossed the Ganges, and another couple of bodies of water, before he came across a clearing he thought perfect for his purpose.

It was desolate, the terrain raised a little above its normal incline. It would give him a look at the area near them. Enough, he thought, that if he saw or heard the tigers approach, he could reach for Sofie and take her to safety.

Landing, he kept his paw on top of the tiger, who was writhing and now coughing and spasming in the violent convulsions that Peter knew all too well. And Peter realized that in all his planning, he'd forgotten something. Turning his head so it faced the girl on his back, he concentrated on forming words with the dragon's mouth.

It was always hard. Almost impossible, in fact. The voice that came out was either a hiss'or a roar, and the roar was totally unsuited to communicating. But the hiss could hardly be modulated with unwieldy lips and a forked, thin tongue that could not form syllables. Something like words could emerge, though, and, struggling, Peter forced them to do so now. "Give me your belt," he told Sofie. "Your belt."

For a moment, she looked startled. Then, with nimble fingers, she untied the blue sash from her middle and handed it to him. Holding what was now a young, lank native under one paw, Peter picked up the belt with the other.

Tying knots while a dragon was even harder, but he had experience with it. He'd once tied up—and interrogated—Her Majesty's minister of magic. It involved holding the creature with his mouth, making sure his teeth didn't break skin, or not too much, while with his claws he tied the belt around the boy's middle and then, breaking off part of it, around his ankles.

When he stepped back, the native was writhing on the ground in front of him. He wondered if the young man understood English. If he didn't, this would all have been for naught. He couldn't, after all, get an answer if he couldn't interrogate the man. If he didn't speak English, Peter would have to go back and pick another tiger.

Hissing, he turned to the boy and forced the words to form within the dragon's mouth. "What's your name?" he said.

The boy—with lanky hair falling in front of his face—opened his mouth, but all that came out was a sort of growl.

For a moment, Peter was puzzled, then he realized that the young man was trying to roar—that he didn't even realize he had turned back from a tiger. Clearly the transformation had happened under the impact of panic and horror at finding himself captured by this immense and far more powerful creature.

Peter—who turned into a dragon and not a human when in panic—couldn't understand the reaction, but he supposed there was nothing to understand. It would be instinctive, taking place at a level of the self where the self didn't think, only feel. For some reason, the young man felt more comfortable as a human. Peter wondered why, since he looked horrified and terrified enough. One would think the tiger would be better defended.

"You can't roar," Peter said, his voice a loud, modulated hiss. "You must talk. What is your name?"

And then words came, a torrent, emerging from

lips gone pale with fear, in a voice high-pitched and crazed by the last vestige of hope. "I am Prince Yatin. I am a son of the raj of the tigers. You cannot hold me. My father will avenge me dreadfully."

Peter settled back on the dragon's haunches, a comfortable position, and showed his teeth in the dragon version of a smile—which he knew all too well was not reassuring to watch. "A prince, are you? Good. That means you will be well informed. Now, tell me, for what reason does your father want to marry the girl Sofie Warington? What does he want with her?"

The boy, though he looked very young—to Peter's eyes he couldn't be more than maybe twenty—didn't appear to be stupid. He looked at the dragon's back, at Sofie. Peter wondered what Sofie felt, and prayed—internally and desperately prayed—that this boy was young enough to spill everything. Spill everything now, and Peter would cut his bonds and take to the air and let him go.

He didn't want to kill him, he didn't want to hurt him at all in front of Sofie. He would protect her even from the disillusionment of seeing the dragon in his true colors.

"Come, boy," he hissed impatiently. "Answer me now, and I will let you go."

But the prince shook his head, revealing a small, sharp face, full of determination. He again looked at Sofie on Peter's back, and then at Peter's single eye, and pressed his lips closed, as though steeling himself. The Adam's apple on his neck bobbed as he swallowed. But his voice was creditably steady and strong as he said, "I will not talk. I have done only what my father told me to do. I will not talk."

All right. There were ways to do this—ways to force words from reluctant lips—and Peter was not unacquainted with them. The boy looked stubborn—or at least the boy was willing himself to be stubborn—but he was young. The easiest method was to threaten him, to get him to see that his best interest lay with speaking—and that, indeed, he could not avoid doing so.

"If you don't speak," Peter said, as he might have spoken to a child in the nursery who was too young or too stupid to understand the alphabet—supposing, of course, a nursery child understood a dragon's hissing—"I shall have to hurt you. Hurt you hard and long enough to make you talk."

"I don't care," the boy returned, shrilly. "You can hurt me as much as you wish. You can bring the might of China against me, but I will not break. I will not talk. I will never tell you anything. I am Prince Yatin, whose father rules the fearsome tiger kingdom of Jaipur, whose ancestors held the crown and the claw, and fought every enemy valiantly. I will not give in to you."

"Oh, are you sure? Well, that's too bad. Because I hate to hurt someone so young and brave," Peter said, making his hiss as threatening as he could. What did the boy mean, the might of China? Was he under the impression, then, that Peter was Chinese?

Peter shook his head. He wanted to pursue those thoughts. He wanted to pursue all possible thoughts, rather than continue to follow the logical course of this. Less than a year ago, in the English countryside, using the techniques and knowledge acquired all over Europe, in missions that had then—he thought—been destined to usher in anarchy, he'd tortured Lord Widefield, the queen's minister of magic.

How long ago that seemed, and how strange that, looking back, he felt nothing but regret. Widefield had been an old man, and an old courtier, accustomed to navigating the maze of power in Europe, and he was certainly no innocent. But this boy before him, tiger or no, of what was he guilty, exactly, but of following the narrow confines of his culture, and obeying his father as a living god?

The boy shook his head and compressed his lips and opened them only to say, in an English marred with a strong accent, "I will not talk."

And Peter, who would much rather not do this at all, cast about erratically for something that would cause the boy to break, and to break quickly. He'd start slowly, he thought. He'd start ... almost gently. He'd inflict physical hurt, but no real physical wound—something that would heal well and quickly in a were.

The boy's even skin, his uncalloused hands and feet, gave away his privileged status. A soft prince—possibly his father's heir—raised in comfort and luxury. He'd break at the first touch of pain. At least, Peter hoped so. He truly hoped so.

Carefully, using his incisors, which were sharp and fine like Toledo blades, he leaned over the boy and carefully, precisely, cut two long incisions on the boy's thighs. Blood poured. The boy's face went white. He screamed.

And Peter felt a little of his humanity melt away.

MONKEYS ON A FLYING RUG; DRAGONS AND TIGERS AND ENGLISH MISSES

"There, ahead." Maidan, Lalita's cousin, had joined them on their quest. Now he pointed an eager finger ahead, where some movement at the low level of the canopy seemed to indicate a flutter of dragon wings.

They were all on the small flying rug that Hanuman had purchased. Maidan was in front, and Hanuman, using his magic to steer the rug, was immediately behind. Lalita was behind the two of them, thinking that, very soon, the rug might not be safe, and wishing for the first time in her life that she had wings to fly on her own.

Maidan had followed them as they ran to the place where they'd hidden the rug, and had changed shapes when they had and jumped aboard. Maidan was as good-looking as Hanuman, though younger. Broad of shoulder and long of leg, with even cinnamon-colored skin and black hair that had the texture and sheen of fine silk, he was as princely as Hanuman was, but underneath it all, shoddy-plebeian. He didn't wear those bright-shiny gold earrings, and he did not call her

Princess. In fact, he hadn't yet called her much of anything. They had played together as children, and she remembered that, for a monkey, he'd always been unnaturally quiet and reserved.

Hanuman had looked thunderous at being forced to start the rug with the interloper aboard, and now looked equally upset at having to steer in the direction in which Maidan's finger pointed. Lalita was amused. You could almost hear Hanuman gritting his teeth, even though he tried to keep his face impassive.

As they neared the place, what had seemed like a flutter of captive fire wings resolved itself into a flicker of a bonfire, in which some shepherds were burning rubbish. Perhaps a dangerous pastime in this most perilous of seasons, but hardly a dragon.

"Why did you say you decided to join us?" Hanuman asked, his voice as deep and cool as the snows on the Himalayan peaks. He spoke without deference at all toward the prince, but Maidan didn't seem to take offense, which, in itself, was instructive.

Hanuman was, of course, baiting a hook, in a manner of speaking, because Maidan had never told them who had sent him, or why he'd decided to come. Maidan looked back over his shoulder now and graced Hanuman with a blinding smile. "Oh, most wise Hanuman, you know well I've told you nothing."

"I think perhaps you should," Hanuman said, straightening the flight of the rug and looking below as they flew. Lalita looked, too, but saw nothing but dun countryside and the occasional hovel.

Where could Sofie be? And who could she be with? If there was an Englishman with her, why was she on a dragon's back? And if she was on a dragon's back, why was the dragon carrying a were-tiger? Lalita, always used to considering her former mistress and friend too impetuous for her own good, now wondered if Sofie had got in so far that she could no longer see the shore and kept sinking further and further into whatever trouble enveloped her.

"Lalita," Maidan called, "do you also wish to know where I came from and why?"

"Yes," Lalita said. "With what is at stake, I feel..."

"That you must know who is friend and who is foe. Very well. My father, King Budhev, sent word to me to help you. Years ago, I decided it was not worth my while to reside in the court, and came here, to the temple of Durga, to seek enlightenment in the true ways of simian life." He released a sigh that she suspected was half theatrical and half heartfelt. "Into my retirement, yesterday, there poured a communication that has been passed from monkey to monkey very fast, since shortly after you left the capital. I am to render you assistance in anything you need. And they said you would be tracing a girl riding a dragon. Therefore, as you see..." He grinned over his shoulder. "I hastened to obey the orders of my father and king."

Lalita wondered how much of this—if any—was true. Maidan had always been less mischievous than other monkeys, but that did not mean he couldn't lie.

She thought he was truly her cousin. It was even possible that he was telling the truth about being requested to assist. Doubtless, the king would have investigated what had happened after Lalita left the court and would do what he could to help them on their way.

"And besides," Maidan answered, turning forward,

looking like he was talking to the tops of the trees and the distant mountains, "I saw you at the temple yesterday. And I thought it was time I came out of seclusion and met my lovely cousin again."

Lalita thought of the tiny monkey paws, everywhere, scrabbling at her clothing, and felt a hot blush suffuse her. It made her feel even more uncomfortable about having been briefly naked in the presence of this stranger. Then again, what he said clicked into an internal suspicion she had been entertaining, but refusing to admit to consciously.

Monkey-kind married as early as possible, because they had a very low fertility rate.

Of course, she was no more sure that she had any interest in spending the rest of her life—or indeed any part of it—attached to Maidan. "There," Maidan shouted, this time with decision, pointing in the direction of a slight rise in terrain. And Lalita didn't need field glasses to see the dragon upon the rise. Nor did she need the sharp hearing of the were to hear the hoarse scream coming from the clearing, followed by a high, outraged and shocked feminine cry.

Hanuman was steering the rug in a circle and very low—low enough, she noticed, that even if the dragon should give a cursory glance around, he would notice no more than a mere fleck of something at the top of the trees. Then he rounded again, and landed, behind the group.

"Why are you landing so far from the dragon?" Maidan asked.

"Shh," Hanuman replied, holding his finger to his lips.

"I think," Lalita said, whispering, "it will be better

if we round on him from behind, and listen to what may be going on before we reveal ourselves."

"Why?" Maidan asked, in his normal voice. "Are we to rescue your friend from the dragons while hiding?"

Hanuman rounded on the man, finger still on his lips. In a sort of angry whisper, his face stern, he said, "Listen, do you know what dragons can do? A single dragon could burn us all where we stand."

"So what?" Maidan asked, insolently. "We are all weres, are we not? We'd heal very fast."

"Not if he burns us to a cinder." Hanuman's whisper, impressively, managed to convey absolute fury.

"We can rescue my friend by stealth," Lalita said, supressing a grin. "It will work. And it is my wish." It wasn't that she found the fight between the two men amusing. It was more that she'd just realized that if Maidan hadn't been present, Hanuman would have been insisting on exactly the sort of rescue he was now decrying.

Instead, Hanuman—a serious, grave-faced Hanuman, looking as much as he could like an elder statesman of the monkey court—led them amid the trees, walking with the stealth that their kind was quite capable of.

Their approach would be no more than the occasional scrape of leaves touched by an inconsiderate foot, or the swish of a disturbed branch. Even on a quiet day, they made no more noise than a breeze, whispering through the trees. With the screams emanating from the rise above, there was nothing—and no one—that could have discerned the noise of their passage.

As they approached, Lalita could hear Sofie yell, "Stop, you're hurting him."

An unearthly hiss that modulated itself into words answered her. "Yes, Miss Warington. I am. That's rather the idea."

"But he's only small and scared, and doing what he thinks is right. How can you hurt him so?"

"Because you're worth more to me than all the tigers in the world."

And before Sofie could respond, there came again the male scream, inhumane and hoarse and ending in a sort of gurgle.

The three monkeys rushed ahead, tripping one upon the other, to look. In the clearing just ahead of them, there was a dragon. In front of the dragon, tied hand and foot on the ground, was a young man whom Lalita assumed was the tiger they'd seen in flight with the dragon. There were fine cuts all over the boy's body, and his blood ran freely. He had to be a were. Were he not, he'd already be dead, with all the blood he'd lost.

The dragon, leaning over the wounded boy, asked in a dreadfully intent hiss, "Are you going to tell me now? Are you going to tell me what your father wants with Miss Warington? Why is she so important that the ruler of the were-tigers is pursuing her across half the Indian continent?"

The boy on the ground rolled his head from side to side, in what might be a negative, but might also simply be a reaction to pain. And Sofie, standing to the side of both the dragon and the boy, splattered with blood, looking pale enough to faint, clasped her hands tight on her skirt while tears ran down her cheeks.

Lalita started toward her, but stopped short as the boy on the ground spoke.

"I will tell you," he said, in a voice so faint it could barely be heard. "I will tell you and be damned for all the good it will do you. My father wants the girl and the ruby."

"The ruby?" the dragon asked, with every indication of surprise in his hiss.

The wounded boy managed something that might have been a cackle. "You don't know about the ruby? You stuck yourself in the middle of our affairs and you don't know about the ruby? Is China so ill-informed, then?"

But the dragon reared back his head as if slapped, and let out in a hiss that seemed to contain the last of his strength. "The ruby! *Soul of Fire?*"

"Ah, you know about it, then. Yes, my father planned to marry the girl to get the ruby as her dowry payment. You see, she's the last of her line, and her parents are anxious to marry her well . . . And there's more. Her father used blood magics to make the ruby invisible, but my father found out about it, and got a hold on him through those magics."

Lalita wondered if he meant a magical hold, or if he meant that the king of tigers would denounce Sofie's father to the British authorities. She suspected it didn't matter. Both of those courses would result in death.

"But why did he want Miss Warington as well as the ruby?" the dragon asked.

The boy made a grimace that might have been a smile. "Why, because as it is, the ruby doesn't work. It is inert, and will not connect with anything. But once it is purified and made to work again . . . then it will show us the way to Heart of Light, the ruby that still has all the power in the world in it. And with Heart of Light my father will bind all the magic in the world to himself, and send the British scrambling from India. And then India shall be free, and her weres shall be safe."

The dragon's head reared back once more and he whisper-hissed something. It seemed to Lalita to be, "And destroy the world with it." But more loudly, he said, "Why does he need Miss Warington to purify the ruby?"

"Her blood is the last in the line that received Soul of Fire from the hand of Charlemagne himself, and she is a virgin. If she is sacrificed to the ruby, her blood will purify it. And only her blood—unless, of course, she marries and has a daughter. Then her daughter's blood, when she's a virgin and nubile, will be able to do the same. That means—"

The dragon's head moved through the air, very fast. Lalita knew, as it snapped forward, that the dragon would kill its prey. But the dragon stopped. Somehow, Sofie had surged forward as fast as the dragon had moved, and was holding on to a sort of frilly, glowing ruffle at the end of the dragon's neck. "No," she said. "Don't kill him. Don't you dare!"

The dragon turned to her, and Lalita surged out of hiding immediately. She couldn't help it. Seeing the blood-spattered creature turn on her friend that way, with that much intensity, it was clear that he meant to kill her.

But neither Sofie nor the dragon looked at her. They remained, gazes locked, staring at each other. "He meant to kill you," the dragon hissed.

"So he did. He is a beast, raised in a kingdom of beasts, and not knowing any better. You and I are different. We have been given the benefit of true moral instruction. We know what is due our humanity."

The dragon coughed, then writhed and twisted, like a man caught in an epileptic seizure. "Miss Warington," he said, in what started as a hiss and ended as a human words. Human words emerging from a tall, blood-splattered Englishman standing naked before Lalita's friend. An Englishman! Well, he'd clearly not been the Chinese dragon. But did he work with the Chinese? Lalita looked at the sky for a trace of the blue dragon, and didn't see him. If he was still guarding them, he was cunning and hid well.

"Miss Warington, I speak better in this form, and you must—you *must*—listen to me. This man is on a quest for ultimate power, a power that will doom all of the Earth if it should be obtained. Heart of Light, the ruby that they want to use Soul of Fire to find, will bring nothing but death and destruction. I...I was looking for Heart of Light, myself, a bare six months ago. And I entered that most ancient temple of mankind, and saw there the avatar of which the rubies were meant to be the eyes.

"What you don't realize—and apparently neither does our tiger friend—" the dragon spared a glance at the boy on the ground, who was now, seemingly, listening to him with full attention "—is that when Charlemagne took the ruby, he created a fracture in the fabric of the universe. Older and wiser ancestors than Charlemagne—ancestors of all mankind at the dawn of civilization—had anchored all the magic in the world to the avatar, so that people who had the capacity to use it could spin it out and use it in manageable quantities. But when the ruby was fractured and the power released, only a small part went into Charlemagne and his descendants."

"Right," Sofie said. "Only the power of Europe." She had on her stubborn expression, lower lip slightly advanced, upper lip trembling. In that way, she had faced out the dictates of matrons and the laws of Lady Lodkin herself when she considered them unjust.

The man who had been a dragon shook his head. "No, not even that. Granted, all the power in the continent of Europe was ripped from their rightful owners, but what Charlemagne captured—that seemingly immense power that made him the master of Europe and capable of turning trees into soldiers and back again— was in fact only a fraction of the power of Europe. It was no more than a little bit of it. The rest of it ... The rest of it took reality and splintered it, creating many worlds from our world, all radiating from that point. Can you understand that?"

Sofie tilted her head sideways a little, but nodded. Lalita knew that Sofie's books spoke of the variety of magic worlds, so this should not come as a surprise.

"Well, if Heart of Light is taken, then the rest of reality will splinter with it. It will all be fractured, destroyed. There will be nothing and no one to save us after that."

Sofie looked considering. "And beyond all that," the dragon added, "this creature planned to kill you to achieve this goal. How can you not want me to kill him?"

"Because he is still a man," Sofie said, thrusting her head forward and striking with the certainty that she used when discussing points for which she cared passionately. Lalita thus had heard her insist they hire a healer for Sofie's favorite mare in Lady Lodkin's stables, instead of putting the animal to death when she broke a leg. She had stuck it, too, even though Lady Lodkin had lamented the necessity of paying the healer's price, and even though the mare would, of course, never be as strong as before her injury. "Because, as a man, he shouldn't be killed just because he planned to do something he didn't know was wrong. His king and father told him to do this. How could he think it wrong? Don't we teach everyone to be loyal to their kind and their family?"

"But he's not a man," the dragon answered, furiously. "He's a were. A half beast."

"So are you."

"I know."

"He's lying to you," the tiger-man yelled. "He's lying to you, miss. He admits he was hunting for Heart of Light himself. And he knew about Soul of Fire. And he has been running across India with you, has he not? Why else would he be doing it, if his plans weren't exactly the same as ours?"

KNOWING ONESELF; OLD CRIMES AND NEW; THE BEST OF CHOICES

Peter hadn't known himself till the moment when he'd almost killed the were-tiger. Oh, he knew he was upsetting Sofie Warington dreadfully. He could hear her scream, even as he was torturing the young tiger prince, but he'd told himself it was necessary. He'd told himself it must be done. He'd told himself, too, that he was a fool to even care what she thought.

She was not for him. And he could attribute his infatuation to nothing less than how lonely he'd been, and for how long—so that now, on the threshold of thirty, he was ripe to fall for the first pretty face that came along. Not that she was just a pretty face, and even if just in his own mind, he apologized for implying she was such. However, Sofie Warington being what she was, his fall was guaranteed, and all that much harder.

But it would be criminal of him to stain her life with something such as himself. No, worse than that. It would be a horror to attach himself to her. And besides, he was sure she would never have him. He'd been sure

of it before, and he was more sure of it now as he faced
her, his face covered in gore and his mouth tasting of
human blood, and looked at the horror in her eyes.
And the doubt—the terrible doubt—that distorted her
gaze at the words of the tiger.

And yet, was he a fool? Was he insane? Because
having accepted that she wasn't for him, knowing that
he must no more attempt to defile her than he would
attempt to defile Summercourt—as much as it called
at him from the past, as much as his heart and soul
longed for the ancestral house and the familiar landscape—he still could not leave her in the full certainty
that he'd intended to kill her, or to steal from her.

He couldn't do that for the same reason he
couldn't—not even knowing it would save her life—
consider taking her virginity. Not when he couldn't
marry her. Not when the result might be a child with
his propensities. Or even a child without his propensities. She'd have no reputation, no standing, no hope of
an honorable life after such a fall.

He couldn't, because he couldn't stand injuring her.
Or having her think ill of him.

"Miss Warington," he said, "I beg you to believe . . .
never would I hurt a hair on your head. I have no intentions of getting Heart of Light. Indeed, if I did—"
He caught himself as he was about to reveal that a
friend of his had the jewel and that he could have got it
before this, had that been his intent. "No, truly. I did
not intend it, nor dream on it. I did search for Heart of
Light six months ago, in what now feels like another
life." And yet, here he was, torturing a man, just as he
had done six months ago in his attempt at getting the
first stone. "I was looking for the ruby not to get power

for myself, but because I thought I could destroy it and that would suck power from the noblemen in the world and redistribute it to everyone, so that no one had too much and no one had too little. . . .

"I thought at the time that I was doing it out of altruism, that it was my sworn mission to redistribute power in the world and make everyone equal and equally strong so that there was no injustice and no suffering. I was a fool. I now see the only thing I truly wanted was to reduce the power I was born with, because I hoped . . ." Something tore through his lips that sounded like half a sob, half mad laughter. "You see, I hoped that without power I would lack the morphic energy to turn into a dragon. That was all. Once I realized the only way to do that would be to destroy the whole world, I thought it would be easier to simply destroy myself. And that, my dear lady, I lacked the strength to do. I still do." He bowed slightly to her, aware that he presented a ridiculous aspect, naked and covered in blood. He was aware, too, that the tiger-prince's eyes were intent on him, and it seemed to him there were other people, barely noticeable at the corner of his eye. He didn't know and he didn't care who they might be. They were—he thought—not were-tigers, or they would have rushed to free their compatriot or to take revenge on Peter, weak as he was in his human form. So they didn't matter. All that mattered was that he wouldn't leave Sofie Warington with a bad impression of his character. He couldn't stand that she should be alive in the world and thinking ill of him.

In her eyes, blue and deep and unreflective, he found no echo of his argument, and he thought that of course she wouldn't be able to take any of this in, not after what she'd seen him do. Not while he was still covered in blood. He looked away from her white and set face and said, slowly, "I am aware that I am a beast. But I beg you to believe that the only reason I acted bestially today was because you...because I wanted to protect you. Now you at least know what they wish of you and I...I will take you to Meerut, if you'll allow me, and in Meerut you can tell your captain that he should protect you from the tigers. Though, perforce..." He felt a blush overcome his cheeks, and he forced a smile. "Perforce you won't be at such a great danger once you have become a wife."

She watched him a while longer, and her hands clenched and unclenched on her skirt. He thought she was very far away, and then he thought, with sudden shock, that he might very well have pushed her over the edge, forced her to lose her mind. But at length, her gaze returned to him, and she looked him over, head to toe. It was a curiously dispassionate look, and oddly old, coming from one so young. It was also a strange look, when they'd been friends, travel companions...almost a couple these days alone together. It was a look as she might have given a dumb beast condemned to slaughter.

There was no hatred in it, and in fact something very much like mercy might have shone at the back of it, but it was not the look of a fellow human being, much less of a woman who would ever think of him as a man.

"I would prefer," she said, her voice small and distant and giving, somehow, the impression that she was cold and marooned on an island of ice, "if you would not, in fact, take me to Meerut. I will . . . I will make it there on my own."

He opened his mouth to protest, to explain that she was as unlikely to make it there alive as she'd been to make it there alive from Calcutta, when someone spoke from the side—a young woman's voice. "You don't need to make it there alone, miss. We will escort you. And we have a flying rug."

Turning his head slightly—for the first time fully aware of that presence that had been there, just at the edge of his vision—Peter saw three natives. And one was an uncommonly pretty girl, with an impish face that seemed to smile even though he would guess she was trying to make it still and serious. He hesitated. What had they seen? What had they heard? Who were they?

Sofie turned to the girl and gave a deep sigh. "Lalita," she said. And then, like someone very confused, but also very relieved, "You found me."

"Yes, miss, I found you. I have been tracking you for days, with the flying rug. These are my . . . my cousins." She indicated the two native males who seemed, between them, to be sharing a single outfit, as one of them wore long pantaloons that left his chest uncovered. He also wore, incongruously, two bright gold earrings. To his left, the other man wore a long tunic that left the impression he wore nothing else underneath.

This was not unusual attire, not in this land where many people would go about naked, and others partially clad as a matter of course, but it was odd that they seemed to have shared a single outfit between them. However, whatever suspicions Peter had, they

were not shared by Sofie Warington, who looked from
the girl she'd called Lalita to the two men, then back at
Lalita again. "You've not...come to take me to my
parents?" she asked.

The girl shook her head.

"You promise?"

"I promise, miss. Besides, I'm afraid I'm in trouble
with them myself, having left after your mother
slapped me and blamed me for allowing you to escape
out the veranda door."

This seemed to make sense to Sofie, who nodded
but said, still in that tiny, cold voice, "Then, my parents didn't...repent? They didn't fetch you to collect me?"

The girl shook her head. "No. We came because...
Well, you'd told me, miss, that you intended to go to
Captain Blacklock, who used to be so besotted with
you in London. And I thought that perhaps you would
need an escort, and...and a means of transportation,
since the country is strange to you, as it is to me, after
all the time we spent in England. And so I got my
cousins, and Hanuman here," a quick, voluble gesture
toward the one who wore the pants, "borrowed a rug
from his employer. And we will escort you to Meerut.
You have nothing to fear."

For a moment, Peter thought of objecting. He
didn't know these people at all. How could he know
that they would take care of Sofie? How did he know
they'd protect her as he would have protected her?
But this Lalita must be the maid that Sofie Warington
had talked about in passing once or twice—the one
who'd gone with Sofie to England. And if so, then she
was the closest thing—or so it had sounded to him at

the time—that Sofie had to a friend. And she'd shown herself quite sensible in bringing her cousins with her to protect them both on the trip.

So while he hesitated to let her out of his sight, at the same time he had to admit she had asked him to leave her alone, and also that after what he had done—and after almost killing the tiger-boy in the heat of passion—he'd shown himself quite unworthy of her. Perhaps it was better to let her go, just like it was best for him to let go of Summercourt and of the family reputation—both of which his presence and his curse could only hurt. Yes, it was best if he let go of Sofie and let her depart into the great world beyond, where she had a chance to find happiness.

But there was one more thing he could do, one risk he could rid them of before he left. He stepped swiftly to the bound tiger-prince. An exclamation escaped Sofie's throat, and he realized she thought he was going to kill the boy. Well, that, too, he could dispel—and perhaps she would go from him with a better idea of his morals and character than he'd given her so far.

He knelt swiftly and, ignoring the young prince's look of abject terror, untied his hands and feet, then sprang back, ready to change and face him, should the boy attack. With weres, you never knew—and it was quite likely that the young man, weakened by blood loss though he was, would come at Peter with fang and claw. The dragon had been known to hunt after an evening in which it had been injured more seriously than the boy had been.

But the prince only looked confused for a moment, and then stood up, shrinking away from Peter as he did so. He stepped away—one step, two, three—without

turning his back on Peter, and then, suddenly, as
though deciding he was far enough away, turned and
shambled at a stumbling run into the line of the trees.
Before he reached them, he'd started to change, and
then he was leaping away, running very fast toward
the trees.

Peter, in his turn, faced Sofie once more. "I would
leave quickly," he told her. "He will go and tell his tiger
friends where you are, and you can't allow that to happen. He will tell them where I am, too, and also what I
look like in my nondragon form, and I imagine that his
father will be none too pleased with my continued existence. And so I must away." He turned toward Lalita
and the two men. "Is your rug distant from here?"

Both Lalita and the men looked as though in awe of
him, as though he had been doing something terrible or
scary. He realized they'd probably seen him in both
forms, and possibly what he'd done to the young tiger.
It didn't matter. None of their opinions mattered. He'd
disappointed the hopes of people who loved him before. What did it matter if he now disappointed the
views of strangers? Sofie . . . Well, Sofie mattered, and
part of him would ache forever that they'd had to part
like this, without her knowing that he'd done the
things that repelled her for her sake only. But it could
not be helped.

He wished, with a mad, overpowering desire, that
he could kiss her hand as he left. He wished, just once,
to have his lips touch that skin only his fingers had
touched, and even then lightly and constrained. Something to remember, and to carry with him all the years
of his life—or however long his curse allowed him to
carry on in the land of the living.

But he was not so lost to all propriety that he imagined he had the right to kiss her hand while he was smeared head to toe in human blood. And he would not further disgust her. He bowed stiffly, then let the change come. He was tired and there was a taste of blood in his mouth. He had to allow the dragon to feed, but not here, and not anywhere she might see him. He would go back to where they'd left their luggage and collect his own. He would eat. He would wash. And after that...

After that, his entire life seemed to stretch, a panoply of gray sameness. It no longer mattered to him whether he found Soul of Fire. It had been in Sofie's family. Was it now with the tigers? It did not matter. Nothing mattered. He felt like he imagined people must when they were very close to death—as though the whole vision of the world and everything in it had no consequence because they would have no part of anything in that bright future to which others were hastening.

The pain of change seemed less than normal. As he stretched his wings to the sky, he noted that Sofie and the natives were no longer in the vicinity. And as he gained altitude, he could see the four of them still on the ground, sitting on a little flying rug that looked barely large enough to accommodate them.

They'd not make very good time on that, but it didn't matter. After all, she would not make much better time with a dragon that must stop at intervals to feed. And they would fly faster than the tigers could run, which was probably the heart of the matter. Still, even as he felt despondent and disconnected from the world, he'd spoken the truth when he'd said he was too cowardly, too attached to his life to commit outright suicide. He could not bring himself to do anything so foolish.

In that spirit, he kept an eye out, and watched closely as he flew over the forest, to make sure the tigers were nowhere close. He saw them, gathered, not far from the clearing where he'd interrogated the young tiger, and he was glad to see the rug take off at the same time.

As he was collecting his luggage, he realized that he had her luggage, too. Then he realized that—worse— they'd all been so surprised and out of their minds that they'd discussed Meerut and Sofie's intention to go there in front of the tiger. Of course the tiger that he'd let go, in his fine attempt to impress Miss Warington, would even now be telling his father where the girl—on whom his father's hopes of world domination rested— was headed.

I blight all I touch. How could I even dare think of making her my bride? But he'd brought this danger on her, and having done so, it was incumbent on him to save her from it.

He'd bathe and eat, and then he'd fly to Meerut. He didn't have to worry about Sofie Warington grow- ing too tired to hold on to his neck anymore. He could push himself to fly longer distances. He'd flown across continents in a single night before. Surely he could do it again.

In Meerut, he'd drop off Sofie's luggage, and he'd hope with all his heart that the young captain whom she intended to marry would be worthy of her.

A BELLICOSE BOLT OF LIGHTNING; A SERVICE DONE IN HUMILITY

As Peter rose above the clouds, he saw a flash ahead of him. For a moment he thought it was a bolt of lightning. And even after he focused and could see the thing, it took a moment for his mind to absorb it.

A dragon, was his first thought, but it was a dragon of a type he had seen only in Chinese illustrations. A serpentine creature, with a rounded face and fins... This one had many tones of blue, but it had no wings at all, and yet it was here, above the cloud layer, moving in a way that suggested it was swimming on the air.

It took a moment before Peter reasoned that this was a dragon—a dragon moving in a way that had to be magic, a way that couldn't possibly be explained rationally. The thought should not have shocked him so much. After all, there should be no way his own relatively inconsequential wings could carry such a weight as his aloft. None.

And even while Peter was thinking on the strangeness of this beast, and looking into its slanted, catlike eyes, trying to judge its mood, the dragon that was in command of his body screamed in rage and hatred. In Peter's mind the word *Kill!* formed.

He felt his front claws open and drop the luggage, and he spared only a brief look, through the cloud layer, to see his bags fall onto a grassy clearing. And then the dragon surged forward, toward the creature that every fiber of his being believed was a foe.

Peter, in the back of the dragon's mind, called for a halt. He felt himself reach past the reptilian mind and hold forcefully the creature's claws and fangs. *No. No. No. We don't kill. We have become altogether too bestial. No.*

And then the blue dragon hissed. "What, leaving the pretty girl unguarded? Did she send you away?" And with an intensification of the hiss, which might be an effect of gathering magic, the creature threw itself at Peter.

Taken by surprise, Peter didn't react, until he felt a trickle of hot fire like concentrated, liquid heat blistering his chest. This awakened Peter from his dream, from his attempt to control the beast's nature. He saw a mouth open in a snarl before him. He saw the thing... swimming closer, like an aggressive lightning bolt, its cheeks puffing out in wrath.

Peter could not have controlled the dragon if he tried, and he didn't try. It surged forward, gripping at the other dragon and flaming it. Only, the flame was repelled by what appeared to be a shield of magic, similar to that which had protected the tigers. Peter—in the dragon's mind—felt a stab of annoyance that he'd never met other dragons, that he'd never learned how to use this defensive magic. He felt again the stab of the other dragon's fire, and he flapped his wings and climbed, then fell, quickly, on the serpentine dragon beneath, grasping it around the neck and squeezing.

The creature didn't appear to have any claws. Only small talons at the end of two ineffective, foreshortened arms that could not reach Peter's clawing legs. Its head didn't seem to turn far enough around to hit Peter's body with its jet of blue flame. Fire flew past Peter's leg; he felt only a distant heat.

But the dragon was mad; the dragon lusted for blood. It sank its claws deep, feeling the enemy's flesh rend under their power. And then it bit. Once. Deeply.

The Chinese dragon screamed and drooped, and Peter's dragon let go. The other dragon's body fell through the cloud cover, even as Peter wondered if it was dead. He'd heard the only way to kill weres was beheading or burning. Or, of course, specially spelled powersticks.

The dragon wanted to follow its enemy to the ground and finish it, but Peter couldn't do that. The other dragon might have had designs on Sofie—perhaps. Or perhaps not. What did he know about how dragons behaved when they met each other? He only knew that he didn't like the way the beast had overpowered him. He didn't like the way it had made him dance to its tune. He would not let it have its way. He remembered the look in Sofie's eyes as he tortured the tiger-prince. When he thought of following the Chinese dragon and killing it, he felt as though her eyes were fixed on him again. With such reproach!

Instead, he flew back to where his undisturbed luggage sat in a peaceful glade.

He drove the dragon down, picking up the handles of the portmanteaus with its bloodied, taloned feet.

A RUDE WAKENING; DRAGONS AND MEN; THE EYE OF THE DRAGON

William Blacklock woke to the sound of wings. Wings unfolding, beating. At first, he thought it was part of his dream—perhaps a premonition of change. But the sound was too persistent, and it was followed, close on, by a distressed wail from his sweeper.

A snake. It's another cursed snake, William thought as he lurched out of bed, his sword in hand, and started across to the *ghuslkhanah,* when he realized that the screams—and now, joining it, the sound of a voice speaking steadily in English—came from the veranda.

In the suffocating heat of the drought before the monsoon, it was beyond William's power to close the door and sleep in the confines of his room, with all the air unmoving. Instead, his veranda door was open, and only a curtain at the door—and a curtain at the window—protected the room from the nocturnal insects. In truth, only the gauze tent around his bed kept him from being eaten alive.

Now he twitched the veranda curtain aside and

looked out. Who could be talking out there? And why?
Had one of his superiors come and violated the sanc-
tity of his quarters? It must be a very important
matter. William found himself gaping at the most in-
congruous of scenes.

There was a man standing there—looking perfectly
composed—wearing only his pants, quite bare-chested.
He was speaking to the sweeper in exact, precise sentences that, clearly, meant nothing to the man.

William recognized the stranger at a glance, and his
breath caught in his throat. It was the Greek god from
his vision in the crystal.

"I am a friend of Captain Blacklock's," he said,
very carefully. "I come to speak to him, to bring him
news he will be glad to hear."

The sweeper looked up at the man out of rheumy
eyes and screeched, "Sahib? Who Sahib? What Sahib
want?"

The stranger had started on a repetition of his same
declaration yet again, when William, still sleep befuddled, erupted through the curtain, sword in hand. His
first thought was that the man was not his friend. His
second thought was that the man was quite informally
attired. And his third thought was that he, himself, was
less than formally attired, in his underwear and carrying his sword in one hand. But all these were overrid-
den by his need to find out who this visitor was.

The man turned to him, not at all discomposed,
and said, "I don't believe weapons are needed,
Captain Blacklock." He bowed formally. "I am not exactly a friend, but I bring you a message from a friend
of yours. Indeed, one who would like to be more than a
friend."

"A . . . friend?" William asked, and ran a hand backwards through his hair. "A friend of mine?"

The man bowed again. "She would at least have me believe so. Her name is Sofie Warington."

"Miss Warington?" Blacklock asked. "What—What message from her can be that important?" He saw a minimal look of surprise in the man's one eye—the other eye being covered by a patch and, presumably, missing. But there was more than that to disturb him in this stranger. For one, as he spoke, and waited for William to answer, he'd resumed dressing, putting on his shirt and coat as though he wasn't even aware of what his hands were doing. He dressed himself by touch, with ease of someone long used to dressing himself like this. But why? Why would anyone need to dress himself that way? By touch? Blindly? To do it often enough to acquire an unthinking skill at it?

And then . . . there was the man himself. Something about him made William feel very odd. The chiseled features, the square shoulders, that golden, almost hairless skin, so brazenly displayed when he'd approached. All of it made William's blood race and his mouth go dry, and he could not explain it. And the single eye, green and deep and cold, gave him the impression he'd seen it before . . . and not just in the man in his glass. But where could he have seen it?

"Now, Mr. . . . ?"

The man smiled—just a fugitive smile—and colored a little as he said, "Peter Farewell, Lord St. Maur."

"Milord," William said, frowning more. In his station in life, he didn't associate with many titled heads, and those he did associate with didn't normally show up on one's veranda early in the morning, when the sun was just a suspicion of pink against the darkness in the east. He still wondered how St. Maur had made it up here. Had he perhaps come in one of the staircases, walked through some unoccupied room on this floor and— But no. All the rooms on this floor were occupied just now, the company being at its fullest.

Besides, he remembered the sound of wings in his dream. What had that dream been all about? What had he heard to inspire it? In his mind, he had an image of this man descending from the sky, naked, flapping his clothes like gigantic wings, and shook his head. About as implausible as all other ideas he'd had.

He indicated that the man should precede him into the room, and carelessly flung a lighting spell toward the magelight on his bedside table. By its pale glow, he was able to see more of the man. He'd thought— hoped, perhaps—that in this light St. Maur would appear less perfect than he did in the half light of the dawning day on the veranda. No such luck. St. Maur remained as perfect as something chiseled out of stone by a master sculptor.

Thou shalt make no graven images went through William's head in his father's stern voice, and he gave his mental confusion relief by turning away from St. Maur to set his sword against the wall next to his bed. He took two deep breaths and turned around, to be overwhelmed once more by a vision of human perfection. "Milord, you were saying?" he said, trying to keep his voice as steady as he could.

"I was saying that I brought you a message from Miss Sofie Warington. Or not a message, but word . . ." The man seemed to be overwhelmed by confusion himself, and opened his hands in a gesture of exasperation. "It is hard to explain, but I . . . You could say I made Miss Sofie Warington's acquaintance as she was escaping her parents' house."

"Her parents have joined her in London?" William asked, knowing he was not thinking straight.

"No. They are, as they always were, in Calcutta. She was escaping their home here."

"She came to India, then?" William asked. He wondered why St. Maur thought it important to tell him this. And what he was supposed to do with the information. But his mind was too clouded just now by his feelings for him to know exactly what to do. It wasn't just that he found St. Maur disturbingly handsome, he also could not look at him without the nagging feeling that he had seen him—or at least his eye—elsewhere.

"Yes. Some weeks ago, I understand. Her parents had arranged . . . they had betrothed her to a native prince, the ruler of a state near Jaipur. Only Miss Warington didn't like the look of the man, and therefore jumped from her window."

"Jumped from her window?" William asked, wrinkling his brow. "Good God! As impetuous as that?" The Queen had ordered him to marry Sofie and he refused. He didn't love her, but of the various society women with whom he found himself in company, she was one of his favorites. Not that he was attracted to her physically, nor that he ever felt anything toward her that indicated they should be united in matrimony. No. It was more that she struck him as an impish child would have, a creature quite out of control but always filled with the of best intentions. He liked her company, and had lived half in fear of what she might do next. But . . . jump from a window? He wondered how far up the window was.

St. Maur smiled and shrugged. "Actually, from her veranda. She was, you see, quite desperate. Not only did she intensely dislike her intended, she had heard from the servants that his kingdom was normally referred to as the Kingdom of the Tigers, and that no European had ever entered it and come back out to tell the tale."

"The Kingdom of the Tigers!" William said. His hands clenched and opened of their own accord. "He told me about the Kingdom of the Tigers. I thought—"

"He?"

"Bhishma. A sepoy. It doesn't matter. But he did tell me that there was a Kingdom of the Tigers."

"It is nearby, then?" St. Maur asked, tilting his head.

"So I understand. He said that some of his friends heard their . . . coded roars, and that they were on a quest for some jewel, something that would allow them to overthrow the Queen's rule in India."

St. Maur took a deep breath, as though William had struck near the truth. "Then you must hear this. It is urgent. . . ." He leaned close.

William smelled something that couldn't be quite perfume but was not the body odor of any human, something slightly sweet with a hint of spice like . . . cardamon and cinnamon mixed. It shouldn't be an alluring smell, but it was, and William found himself taking great deep breaths as the man talked. Fortunately, St. Maur's story was disturbing enough he probably assumed that William was breathing deep in fear.

In an unhurried, precise voice, with matter-of-fact words, St. Maur told William of rescuing Miss Warington from a fall from her balcony, and of running with her into Calcutta.

"That was very bad of you," William said sternly, holding on to a thread of sanity. "To entice her away from her parents' house."

"I did not entice her. If I hadn't followed her, she would have continued on her own."

"But . . . you were stronger than her."

"Are you truly suggesting I should have laid hands on her?"

Blacklock shook his head. "But—"

"*But* is precisely it. As she threatened to go, and actually started walking away, I realized she did know, fully, the dangers of her position. And yet, she was still determined to see it through, to walk here alone rather than return to her parents."

"Walk here?" William ran his hand backwards through his hair yet again. "Why would she walk here?"

"It appears she . . . Well . . . She said you would have married her if you could."

St. Maur said the words as though it hurt him, and while William stared at him in sheer horror, he looked back steadily.

To William, it was as though an abyss had opened where he'd thought to step. What had he told Miss Warington? What could he have said to her that gave her such an idea? The Queen wanted him to marry her, but he'd never even *courted* her. A casual acquaintance, perhaps a light friendship, was the nearest they'd got. He remembered her well—a pretty girl, a good dancer, good on horseback. She had spirit and she stuck out from the group of girls from Lady Lodkin's Academy that got trotted out at every ball and assembly and social event where young people would gather. She stuck out in part because for all her courage and determination, she looked more than a little lost. Enough to excite William's pity. She didn't know how to react to the flatterers crowding around her, and she often would put them off with too bold a dismissal, and end up alone throughout a party.

He ran his hand back over his hair again. What had he said? What had he told her? Had he mentioned marriage? It was possible he had, though if he'd done so, it would have been as something that could never happen. And there, perhaps, she had misinterpreted him and assumed that he meant he could not financially do it, not that he could not ... Oh, but this was infamous. "She was coming here ... to marry me?"

St. Maur, looking at William, his forehead wrinkled in a concern that was perhaps not very far from just the slightest hint of amusement, nodded. And William, flabbergasted, looking at St. Maur's eye, suddenly remembered where he had seen it. "The crystal," he said before he could stop himself. And then, "The dragon."

St. Maur froze. His whole body went rigid. The lines of his face hardened, and it appeared to William as though he'd become, in that moment, a creature of stone or ice—something that had no human understanding and no warmth at all. His eye, too, seemed to ice over, to become empty of all sympathy.

Meanwhile, William's mind worked. He realized he'd seen the same eye in the dragon in the crystal. According to the legends, the eyes often looked the same between person and were-beast. But that meant...

He jumped backwards without meaning to, and flattened himself against the wall. Had it been possible, he would have melted into the wall and disappeared. The sound of wings. The sound of wings he'd heard before had been nothing less than the dragon landing. He swallowed again, convulsively.

What happened now? Would St. Maur change into a dragon and devour him? Surely he couldn't allow William to go, to spread the word that this man, a peer of the realm, was a were-dragon. It would be death for St. Maur, and surely a were-dragon capable of becoming a ferocious beast would not allow himself to be denounced and killed without fight.

St. Maur's rigidity had passed, and he was patting his pockets desperately. William wondered if this was some sort of preliminary to changing shapes. Was it necessary to touch certain pressure points? Was it something that William should be stopping?

But when St. Maur spoke, it was in a vaguely annoyed tone. "Damn. I appear to have lost my cigarettes when I carried my clothes up. I don't suppose you have...?"

Acting on some instinctive good manners, William grabbed his cigarette case from his bedside table and flipped it open. Then, at a pointed look from St. Maur, he found his lighter, and—getting a cigarette for himself—lit both. St. Maur took a deep puff and exhaled in a series of neat rings. "Please, Captain," he said. "Do not imagine I am about to change and incinerate you."

"But...how can you know...how can you be sure

I won't give you away? That I won't..." He was the Englishman linked to Soul of Fire. He had to be.

St. Maur shrugged. "Surely you don't imagine that I can ever go back to England, or claim my seat in Parliament, let alone any of the other prerogatives of my estate?" He shrugged again. "If you give me away, I imagine I'll go on living as I've been living for the last ten years, moving about from land to land, never settling, taking care no one finds out what I am. I probably won't even use the name." He took another puff of his cigarette. "I'm more interested in knowing what you meant by *The crystal*. And how, exactly, you found out."

William realized he'd neither taken a puff of his cigarette nor shaken from it the ash, which was growing very long. He shook the ash into a small bowl he used for the purpose, and which was set at the corner of his desk. "I'm a soothsayer," he said. "Is St. Maur your real name? Are you a real British lord?"

"Yes. And are you trained as a soothsayer?"

Shaking his head, William said, "The only properly trained soothsayers go to France or Spain to study, and I could do neither. My father is a curate—the second son of the third son of the local lord of the manor. Never much money there, and by the time you get to third sons..." He let the rest hang, then asked, "I thought dragons came only from China and Scandinavia. Do you know where the blood comes from? How it got in the family?"

St. Maur shook his head. "Not at all. To my knowledge, there have been no weres anywhere in the family, in any branch, at any time. I suspect the blood got into the family the same way you ended up not being trained as a soothsayer." And to what William was sure was his perfectly blank gaze, in return St. Maur smiled, just a little. "What I mean is that my family, too, was quite out of money. My grandfather, you see, loved gambling and women. Or men. Or whatever crossed his path when he'd drunk a bit much, which was another of his vices. As a result, he ran through our fortune like water through a sieve. So, my father, being responsible, married the daughter of a moneyed man. It didn't last—the money, at least. Though my mother didn't last, either. She died giving birth to what would have been my younger brother, when I was very small.

"But the thing is, though my mother had some minor gentry in her ancestry, the bulk of her ancestors were plebeians and merchants. People of little worth and with very few recordings left of their passage through the world. Who knows? Perhaps one of her maternal ancestors went to China and bought himself a wife or a concubine. Or perhaps, judging by my dragon form, the dragon gene came over with the Normans. I always thought genealogies were kind of a hoax, where you track one line absolutely—two lines at most. You might think all that is your ancestry, but in point of fact, it is impossible for a man to follow all his lines of ancestry in all time. At least for a sane man who wishes to stay so. I suspect at the other end of that type of madness lies the sort of person who shuffles about unswept rooms in his underwear, addressing pointed remarks at the walls."

William chuckled, despite himself, and realized he was no longer afraid. "You know, you seem quite—" He stopped short, as he realized he was about to use the word *normal,* and that he didn't know how his guest would take the remark.

St. Maur smiled, a feral grin. "Nice? Normal? Human? Ah, don't be deceived, Captain, it is but a show . . . as others have found, to their chagrin." The smile vanished, and a wrinkle, as if of worry, formed on his forehead. "The truth is, sometimes even I am not too sure where the boundaries of the beast lie, nor what it means to do . . . until it does it."

"Well, you seem . . . That is . . ." William could not feel a menace, and wished he could. Was he deceiving himself that this creature was perfectly harmless?

The worry vanished from St. Maur's features, replaced with slight embarrassment. "I'm sorry. I'm being a boor, and worrying you. Let me assure you that you are not at all at any risk from me. Not now, not ever, unless you should charge me or wound me or in some way that causes me to feel my life is immediately threatened. As for your soothsaying talent—I take it you used it, with a crystal, and therefore saw my image."

William nodded. "Yes. Your image and . . . Sofie Warington's. Now I know why."

St. Maur took a deep breath. "I take it, then, that you have not the slightest intention of marrying the lovely Sofie Warington?"

William shifted uncomfortably. He looked at the broad forehead, the mobile mouth, and an impulse swept over him that he was far too intelligent to avail himself of. It didn't matter if part of him wanted to touch St. Maur, to hold him. William was not an idiot. He knew this was likely to bring about the sort of reaction one got from threatening the dragon's life.

"If she thinks I made her a promise," he said, miserably, "then I will have to marry her. The truth is, I hadn't planned to marry yet. I can hardly support anyone from my pay, and besides ... At the risk of sounding mercenary, I thought when I did marry, it would be to someone who could help me establish myself back in England, or perhaps find my fortune in India. Not that—"

"Then you know Sofie Warington has no money? How?"

William could not exactly say that the ministry of magic had informed him of the fact. Instead, he shrugged. "It was open rumor."

"I see," St. Maur said, and unfortunately it looked very much like he did. "You've heard of Heart of Light and Soul of Fire, Blacklock?"

"Oh!" William said, feeling a blush climb to his cheeks, and in that moment feeling as though he'd been wholly unmasked. He tried to recover, saying, "I mean ... I've heard of the legend. Like every ... like every English schoolboy."

But St. Maur was not deceived. He said, drily, "Just so." And then he proceeded to pour on William's ears a tale William wasn't sure he could believe, not in its entirety. How the queen had sent an English nobleman, the younger of the Oldhalls—of whose disappearance William vaguely remembered reading in the paper—to Africa, to find Heart of Light. How his mission had been impaired by local tribesmen and bedeviled by a movement started by none other than the older Oldhall, whom everyone believed to be dead. How Peter Farewell, then not yet St. Maur, had joined the expedition under false pretenses, wishing to take the ruby and destroy it.

And then, softly, he described how they'd come to the oldest temple of mankind and mankind's oldest avatar, whose eyes the rubies were supposed to be. In this part, William could not, indeed, doubt him. St. Maur's face became grave with reverence and intensely focused, the way William had seen the faces of feverish people looked when they were fixed intently on a faraway mirage. No, St. Maur had truly visited that temple, and in it understood that the rubies had to be returned, so the splintering of the worlds could end. He had truly been there and truly lived it... or else he was the greatest madman alive.

The other details rushed out in a torrent. It appeared that Nigel Oldhall and Peter Farewell had separated six months ago, so that when St. Maur found the second ruby, the two stones wouldn't be together. Because if they were together and fell into the wrong hands, the result would be the death of the entire universe—a painful though mercifully quick end. But Peter Farewell had failed to find the ruby in his six months in India.

Now the pieces of his story fell into place. He'd rescued Sofie Warington while in dragon form. And of course he could not drag her back to her parents, not while she had the power to retaliate by denouncing him.

And then he said, "I was a fool. I never thought... I never realized the reason the tigers were interested in Miss Warington... as I found out last night under circumstances that..." He shrugged. "The reason they wanted her and the ruby, both, is that she is the last of the line in which the ruby of Charlemagne has passed. He presumably gave it to his son. Even spent, as it was, it would have some value, some magical power as one of the oldest jewels of mankind. I don't know through what crooked channels of inheritance it ended up in Miss Warington's family, but there it is. And therefore the tiger wants to secure both Miss Warington and the ruby, so that by sacrificing Miss Warington, he can..." He shook his head, his eye reflecting a pain that William wished with a fatal, heart-deep longing, he could ease.

"I see," he said, mechanically.

"But you see, the reason she matters to them, the reason she can be used to this end is that she is... er...a virgin. I cannot marry her. I can even less... despoil her. I wouldn't thus mar a woman I hated, much less—" He halted. "If she marries, then the jewel can't be healed until she has a daughter who is nubile, but I thought...twenty years...The jewel can wait for twenty years. And...and someone else can take it to my friend Nigel, who...who'll have to travel around the world until then." Suddenly, he cackled, sounding like a man on the edge of madness. "And I thought, if she married you...I suppose it is not in the cards, then?"

William shrugged. He felt as if he were being pulled inexorably toward an abyss. And it occurred to him that beautiful Miss Warington deserved better than a husband who felt this way about it. He heard a moan escape his lips. "I wish...What am I to do if she comes to me, having already compromised her reputation irreparably? What can I do but marry her? But I—"

"No, by God. Don't marry her if you feel that way.

It would be shackles for her and she—" St. Maur stopped. In that one word, he had managed to convey all the enchantment and passion in the world. That *she* was a blazing summer breeze; it was the breaking of the wave upon a golden shore; it was the sun coming out after a long night, when all the Earth had looked dead. That *she* echoed with a longing that William had never felt and never . . .

"I was thinking," William said, "that she is too good, too kind to be shackled to that sort of marriage, where I would be marrying for obligation only. But what am I to do, then, about her reputation?"

"All might not be lost there," St. Maur said. "She . . . Her maid has found her. It could be said she is traveling under native escort, as so many other English misses do in India, and no one will know anything at all was amiss, unless talk spreads. I'm more worried, truly, about the other thing. While she remains a virgin, she will remain at risk. But . . . Don't worry about it, I will simply have to find another way to neutralize the tigers."

"They have the ruby, then?" William asked. "The tigers have Soul of Fire?"

The oddest looked passed over St. Maur's features. "You know . . . I did not ask. The tiger spoke as though we had it, yet I think . . . Oh, let Sofie not have been hiding it all along."

William did not say anything. He registered that St. Maur had referred to Miss Warington as Sofie, and wondered if this was how he referred to her in the secret of his heart. And then wondered why this pained him so, like red hot irons to the soul. "I'm sorry," he said, without even having any idea why.

"No, don't worry about it. I half suspected her claim was the imagination of a girl who had but little experience in the ways of the world and the ways of man." He stubbed out his cigarette and got up. "If you don't mind, I will fly from your balcony."

"I don't mind," William said. He remained rooted to the spot as St. Maur walked through the gauzy curtain to the veranda, to where the sun was coming up over the horizon, making it far brighter than the mage-lit room. William watched the silhouette as it undressed, revealing that perfect body he'd half seen before.

He examined his tumultuous thoughts and feelings in the dispassionate light of day, and frowned slightly. *It doesn't mean anything. It is in all the stories. In every legend. Dragons are fatally attractive to females.* He stubbed out his own cigarette. *But I am not a female. Therefore, I must be . . .*

In that moment, it was as if he'd always known it. He should have always known it. All the clues were there in his thoughts, in his feelings, in what he'd done and in what he'd failed to do. But until this moment, he'd never seen it. And now, having seen it, he wished he could undo it.

AN EYE FOR SEEING;
THE OBLIGATIONS OF A
RESCUER; THE MANY USES
OF A BROKEN HEART

Miss Warington was right about me, Peter thought, as the dragon took wing over Meerut, against the fast-brightening sky. *I've been giving the beast too much sway. Far too much.*

For a moment, when the word *dragon* had formed on Blacklock's lips, Peter had wanted to reach over and break the aristocratically high neck that held Captain Blacklock's aristocratic head. *And perhaps I should have,* he thought, tilting to take advantage of the air currents. Below him, looking like a child's model, were forests and villages and English troop encampments and citadels. All of it dun with drought and shimmering under a veil of heat. And he wondered where the enemy hid—the people who wished to kill Sofie.

No. Not Sofie. I have no right to call her that. She will be someone's wife soon. If not that fool Blacklock's, then someone else's. She's too lovely to remain unmarried long. And I can't think of another man's wife that way. Miss Warington. I must teach myself to call her that.

A sound startled him, before he realized it was a half-painful and half-wishful sigh escaping the dragon's mouth. He climbed higher, which was folly. In the full light of the dawning day, everyone could see him, and the troops in this area would have rugs and anti-were powersticks. But it did not matter. Very little mattered anymore.

Not for the first time in his long exile from house and father and ancestry, he wished he had the strength to kill himself. What was it Hamlet ranted on about? A dagger. With a dagger one could purchase liberty. Only Peter couldn't. First of all, killing a were was almost impossible, unless one got hold of a were-charmed powerstick and discharged it, at close quarters, against the head. And even then, it was unlikely to kill. More likely it would maim you, and leave you an idiot—half-witted and shambling and open to speculation as to how you could have survived such a thing at all.

The only way—the only truly good way—to kill a were was to remove its head, or put a charmed blade through its heart, or burn it. Peter thought that to commit suicide in that way would entail some truly careful engineering. And again, it left too much chance of simply crippling oneself in the attempt.

But no, there was an easier way open to him—to allow himself to be caught by the Gold Coats, the Were-Hunters with their magical weapons, in service of the queen. The powersticks wouldn't kill him, but they would weaken him long enough that he could be bound over to inspection by the Royal Witch-Finders. And eventually, on an overcast morning—in his mind

it was always an overcast morning—brought out by the
public executioner for his final walk. He'd imagined
the scene many times. When he was young—newly
thrust out of his father's house and the family's circle of
acquaintances—he used to dream of it and wake up
sweating. In more recent years, it had become a conscious fantasy, almost a daydream.

Because he was a nobleman, he would merit the attention—the public exposure—given to other dangerous weres who had been caught and condemned over
the last two centuries. Peter had read about them, almost obsessively, so he knew how the ceremony would
go. They would bring him to St. Paul's Cathedral and
make him kneel on a step leading up to the entrance,
laying his head on another. The rest for his neck would
have been constructed already, so the ax didn't mar
the stone. Above, the sovereign would sit—Queen
Victoria with her inert features, looking saddened and
somewhat out of sorts, lending her stolid bourgeois
presence to this most barbaric of spectacles. After all,
Her Majesty had ordered much bloodshed, but rarely
watched it. And then there would be the minister of
magic, on the steps above, yelling out to the assembled
crowd that England would now rid itself of this corrup-
tion in its body politic.

And then the masked man holding the ax would lift
it with solemn poise, and let it fall—hopefully swiftly.
Peter had read all he could about death by beheading,
including the descriptions of the deaths of members of
the French aristocracy under Monsieur de Guillotine's
merciful invention. That it was indeed merciful in rela-
tion to the British ax, he knew. Often enough the ax
would botch it, merely breaking the neck or wounding

the prisoner, leaving him suffering but not dead. Anne Boleyn, after her denunciation as a were-hare—hardly a dangerous animal, but the fact that she had concealed this crucial defect from the king constituted treason in a royal spouse—had demanded and obtained a French executioner brought forth, to behead her with a sharp sword. Peter doubted that impoverished Lord St. Maur—though descended from the family that had once upon a time supplanted the Boleyns; and just as fast, through treason and bungling, lost all their power—would have the political pull to ask for a similar boon. And then there was the whole question of how fast one died by beheading. There were indications that the noblemen so swiftly dispatched by the waves of revolutionary favor had lived for some minutes after the head was severed. The lips moved; the eyes looked at this or that person; the mouth emitted a peculiar sound, still trying to breathe. Coughing in the basket, they called it.

This half life before the final oblivion scared Peter more than that inevitable nothingness to come—if there was nothing on the other side. And if there wasn't, then he intended to have a word with whatever divinity ran the show. But those minutes—feeling life ebb away, knowing there would be no going back, nothing he could do—those moments terrified him.

It was easy to imagine all this. Peter had imagined it so often before, sometimes he got the impression these scenes played themselves over and over again when he closed his eye. There was only one doubt relating to the whole pageant, and that was what he would do. How would he react? What would happen to him, to his mind, in that position?

For years, imagining himself dragged to that most unholy of gallows for his end, he had wanted to believe that, like Monmouth, he'd rebel and shift and charge the crowd, having to be brought down again by the Gold Coats and rather dramatically beheaded on the fly. Or perhaps he would do what Anne Boleyn had done and rail aloud against his ancestors, the sovereign, the skies above and the indifferent faraway divinity—all of which had wished this curse upon him.

In his current mood, though, he imagined himself going quietly—almost indifferently—laying down his head and his life with relief. But his last thoughts would be of her. Not in sappy romance, but he would wonder where she was, and if she was safe, and what her life would be. The only way to avoid that, he thought, as he reflexively brought the dragon lower, was to make sure that Sofie Warington was well and truly disposed of. That there would be no need for his services in protecting her. That she was, as it were, out of his hands.

He'd hoped to do that with Blacklock, but—though he couldn't quite understand why—it was clear that Blacklock would consider the lovely Sofie no more than a burden upon his life. It was clear Blacklock operated on more rational principles, principles that didn't allow for the impetuosity of love, nor the sudden attraction to a mass of silky black hair, a pair of midnight-in-summer eyes. And though lying with him would save Sofie, Peter didn't wish that. Even if her life was safe, if she was chaffing in her marriage bonds, feeling a slave to fate much as he now did, it would not be any better. He would still feel responsible for her, and still seek to rescue her.

So he must first see Sofie properly established, with a man she could love and respect. Then, and only then, he could allow himself to be caught by the Gold Coats and taken to that awful last pageant that he'd been avoiding for a decade.

But he must first locate the ruby, he thought, as he brought the dragon down to where his luggage lay hidden, in a clearing in the middle of the parched jungle. And there was only one way to find the ruby. If he understood the babble of the tiger, the jewel had been hidden before by blood magics invoked by Miss Warington's father. That would not be true now, and so the one instrument that Peter had to obtain the position of the jewel should work.

He landed and let the clothes he carried in his foreclaw drop to the ground, before forcing himself to change. He ended up sitting on the ground—naked, disheveled and sweaty—and not caring particularly. There didn't seem to be anyone about, at least no one he had seen from the air. And for what he had to do, his attire made no difference whatsoever.

He made his luggage appear, and slid over to it, sitting on his heels while he rummaged inside for the object he was searching for.

It was round—about the size of his fist—and felt very cold to the touch through the silk scarf he'd enveloped it in. Bringing it out, he thought how strange it was that this had once been his eye. Having heard that a dragon eye was the favored instrument of scrying, and finding himself—and those who depended upon him—lost in Africa, Peter had extracted it, at knife-point.

And then he'd received proof of his mystical nature, which was not usually so obvious to him. For as soon as it was severed from his body, the eye had grown and acquired a crystalline solidity and appearance. Though it was still green—touched here and there by darker and lighter colors, like undercurrents—that was the only resemblance between its state now and when it had been attached to his nerves. Now anyone would take it for a blown-glass bubble.

He sat on the scrubby grass and pulled the eye-globe onto his lap. As he unwrapped it, it glowed softly, and he wondered if it would do that for anyone who owned it, or only for him, since it had been his. But it didn't matter.

Peter thought intently of everything he knew of the ruby Soul of Fire, and its surface seemed to swirl and move. Then, like the waters of the Red Sea under the staff of Moses, it parted. And in the blank of color, there appeared a scene.

He saw a clearing in a forest, and in it two men and two women. They weren't difficult to recognize. The men were the natives, and one of the women was the girl Lalita, whom they'd accompanied. But the other woman made his heart clench. Sofie. Miss Warington. She looked so sad and scared. Why, he wondered. What did it all mean to her? Had she cared that he'd left? Did she care he'd proven himself unworthy of her?

What was it that the Romans said about a man who is late in falling in love for the first time? I'm sure they said something, and that it wasn't pleasant. The classics master mentioned it once....

But the words were only a screen to hide from him the sight of Sofie Warington, as it only seemed to be something to distract him from his thoughts. He closed his eye, then opened it again. *I know where my heart is,* he told the green, glowing globe in his lap. *But I need to find out where Soul of Fire is. The jewel that Charlemagne stole and desecrated, the jewel that holds the key to power in this world for the queen of England and the king of tigers, and who knows how many others.*

The globe swirled a little, like stormy waters blown about by the wind. And then it cleared. And it showed him the same scene.

So the stone is with them. They have it, he thought, morosely. *Which means that Miss Warington has it. Of course she does.* He could imagine her running into whatever strong room the ruby was kept and stealing it, simply because they'd meant to give it as her dowry to the repulsive king of tigers.

But if she had it, she was in double danger. If the tigers captured her, they would have the ruby as well. And then it would be no time at all to her death by sacrifice.

And that was not something that Peter could contemplate—or allow to happen. No, he must stop it.

He'd go back to Miss Warington and her escorts. Oh, he would not speak to her. He very much doubted she'd listen to anything he had to say, not after she'd seen him act the way he had with their prisoner. But he would speak to Lalita and appraise her of the danger to her mistress.

And then, he thought, he would try to find from Sofie's very intelligent maid what could be done to protect her mistress. Of course, every glimpse of Sofie would hurt. But it didn't matter. Once your heart is broken, you cannot be tormented by hope.

FALLEN FROM THE GARDEN; AN UNLIKELY MEETING; THE KINGDOM OF THE TIGERS

This was how Adam and Eve might have felt when they fell from the garden, William thought. Except— though he'd never told his father as much—he didn't believe in Adam and Eve. Or at least, not in a real, embodied Adam and Eve. His father might not either, now that William thought of it. Reverend Blacklock was a scholar in Latin and Greek, and all too knowledgeable about all the archeology that took place around biblical sites.

For some reason, William could picture himself before his father's desk, asking him about Adam and Eve and the garden. And he could see his father removing his glasses and polishing them, and deliberately putting them back on before launching into a discussion on metaphors, and what it all meant.

But William knew what the story meant past metaphors, past literal retelling. *I have fallen from the garden,* he thought, as he stared at the gauzy curtains billowing in the very slight breeze. Somewhere, there were shouts and the clank of pots and pans. He didn't care. Nothing mattered anymore. He wasn't angry or sad. Instead, he felt a dry-eyed horror, as though . . . As though he'd woken up to find the entire world populated by spiders who acted like and carried on the functions of the humans they'd replaced.

And yet, that might be easier, he thought. That strange, unlikely state of affairs might be easier to understand and accept than this. Because the dry-eyed, blank horror was not at anything external, but at himself. There had been, in his Eton days, close friendships and young friends for whom he would have, gladly, laid down his life. There had been touched hands and bodies meeting in the hurly-burly of school games. But he'd thought, back then, that it was just how everyone felt—that mature feelings would come later, when he found the woman who was perfect for him.

He had listened many times to the story of his parents' first meeting. His mother had been in her garden, tending to a climbing yellow rose, and his father had passed along the road. Their eyes had met, and they'd known in that moment—in that first searing instant. His mother said she could feel all their life ahead of them, and the children they would have, and the years they were supposed to share. And his father would nod happily and assure William he'd felt the same.

It had seemed very odd to William to think of his plump and comfortable mother, with her faded blond hair, falling in love at first sight with his father, that calm man with his salt-and-pepper hair and extensive knowledge of ancient languages. But if it had happened to them, he'd assumed it would happen to him. And that if his passions seemed cold and his interest in women scant, it was because he was his parents' son and, as such, not given to great transports or much romantic thought until the moment . . . the moment when it would be right, when it would all come together.

Only it hadn't. And he'd gone on waiting. And now . . . it wasn't the dragon. He didn't think he was in love with St. Maur—and thank the heavens for that, because he suspected there were depths there he would rather not plumb. He didn't think he was in love with anyone, or had ever been. But he realized what the quickened heartbeat meant, the shallow breath and the pounding pulse, and the irresistible desire to touch. Even just thinking of it made images rush through his head that he would fain not confront. But there was nothing for it. He was what he was.

He thought of the men he had heard of who'd evinced the same disposition. No one spoke of it openly, and it was treated either as an object of fun or something that would occur only to the utterly abandoned or depraved.

William didn't feel like either. It wasn't something he'd come to, open-eyed, nor a thought he'd spent any time entertaining. The reality of it had burst upon his unwilling mind and forced itself upon his notice only because of one of the properties of dragon-weres—that unearthly attraction that had, through the ages, caused normal humans to sacrifice human virgins to them.

He didn't know how long he sat there, staring at the door. He became aware only after a while that his carrier was crossing the room, armed with the kerosene cans of warm water, and realized, faintly startled, that this was not the man's first such voyage.

The man saw him staring and smiled. "Sahib bathe now? Bath all ready."

But though Sahib was sweaty and felt bruised and tired—as though he'd run a long distance in a very short time—he did not want to have a bath. He wanted, he realized—suddenly and with a physical need—to leave his quarters and walk. To walk in the real world of real people, to reassure himself that everything looked as it had yesterday when he went to bed. That the internal explosion and leveling of all accepted reality was just that—internal only—and that no one need know about it. No one need see it, or even guess at it.

He dressed himself almost without looking—like St. Maur on the balcony—mumbled some apology to his astonished carrier and hastened down the central stairway. This early, no other inhabitants of the bungalow were awake, and only servants moved around, cleaning and cooking. They took one look at William and scurried out of his way as he moved toward the door.

Outside, it was markedly warmer than it had been when he'd stepped out on the balcony, but it was by no means as hot as it would get later in the day. He walked down the dusty road of the cantonment with some idea he would go to the Wheeler Club. He would sit at the white-cloth-draped tables and have breakfast. He would reassure himself that what he'd discovered within himself wasn't visible, like a mark on his forehead.

His steps felt erratic and ambling, as though he were drunk or just recovering from a hangover, unable to see his way clearly. Very few people were about. A couple of officers exchanged greetings with him, and two sepoys stood at rigid attention. And then, from William's side, there came an astonished, "Sahib!"

He turned. Gyan Bhishma stood there, frowning a little. William nodded and tried to focus on him, but was quite unable to make out the man's expression. He blinked and shook his head. Bhishma was looking at him with an odd mixture of concern and protectiveness—something quite inappropriate from a sepoy, a subordinate. William flipped the lank hair off his forehead and looked at the man, daring him to explain himself.

But Bhishma only drew closer, and asked, in a concerned whisper, "Sahib? Have you been ... using the crystal?"

Ah, so that was the concern. That the crazy Englishman had been practicing the soothsaying arts at which his people were notably inept, and that he had found only confusion. William started to shake his head, then decided that was as good a way as any to explain his present state, and shrugged.

The native looked interested, his eyes shining, "What did you see, Sahib? Did you see the dragon?"

William blinked. "The ... dragon?" he managed, in a voice that was all breath. What did Bhishma know? What had he seen? "In the crystal, you mean?"

"No, in the sky." He pointed. "There, over the encampment. A huge dragon, sparkling green."

All too able to imagine St. Maur in dragon form, William swallowed hard and said, "No," in a voice that was almost a moan. "A dragon?"

"Yes. I think," Bhishma said, "it is an emissary of China, coming to contract with the tigers. They know the tigers are on the verge of acquiring the ruby, and as such, they make their diplomatic ties now. That way, they can go ahead and trade directly with us, man to man. Were to were."

William drew a deep breath, trying to figure out the implications of that comment, and failing. Did Bhishma mean he had allied himself with the tigers? Bhishma's next words were uttered in almost the tone of a child begging a classmate to join in a game. "I thought Sahib might have seen this in the crystal and had come to go with me?"

William rubbed his hand down the front of his face, wiping away what felt like cobwebs. "What do you mean? Go with you where?"

"To the city of the tigers, of course. Their kingdom is, you know, quite nearby. We could take horses." Again there was that look, like the sepoy's invitation meant more than mere words could convey.

"Don't you have duties?" William asked. His own duties were scant and spotty. A few hours of paperwork a week, some pointless drilling with the native troops. Nothing much, because William was not, as such, a part of the garrison. Just a man on a futile quest. The jewel . . . among tigers and dragons . . . How was William to rescue it? Particularly when he couldn't seem to think straight.

Bhishma shook his head, black hair swinging. "Not today. And I thought your having talked to Sahib General and Sahib General not understanding, if I could go and spy on them and have proper explanation of why they are a danger, it would make it easier for you to make Sahib General understand what the tigers can do to all of us."

William wished he didn't feel like he had a hangover—or worse, like he was viewing the entire world through a haze of distorted perspectives and a fog of confusion. He could tell the sepoy that he didn't want to accompany him. He could, for that matter, order Bhishma not to go. He had suspicions about Bhishma—he had suspicions about everyone, possibly including himself. He could tell Bhishma to stay and mind his own business, and never mind William's or Sahib General's opinions and fears for things that mere sepoys couldn't control. He could do all that.

But in his mind was his grandfather's letter. *If only we had listened.* And before his eyes—as though floating in air, like a series of stilted woodcuts—were the remembered scenes he'd seen in the crystal...the broken bodies of the dead Englishmen and dead Indians together. Tigers and dragons and elephants had rampaged everywhere. Probably some of the dead were even weres. They reverted to human form in death, he'd always heard.

He struggled for the words to ask Bhishma how they could accomplish this, how he could be sure of not being detected, what his plan was for finding proof to show the general. But before he found them, there was a wild call from his right side, and he turned to look.

At any other time, the scene would have made him laugh. A completely naked blond boy of perhaps two or three was running full tilt across the dusty road, where exercises were normally held. Under the shadow of stunted trees, he ran, wild and free. In his wake came not the nanny that was to be expected, but a very young woman, also blond, her hair in trailing ringlets, her dress in disarray, screaming: "John, come back!"

Bhishma moved quickly, intercepting the child, grabbing him around the torso, under his arms, and offering him to his mother. The woman stopped in confusion, her cheeks coloring. "Oh, thank you. So kind of you. He is very naughty, you see. And our nanny is ill."

"Sahib must not be naughty," Bhishma told the child, in a deep, amused voice. "Sahib must obey his mother, always, always."

As the woman retreated, cooing to her child, William turned to Bhishma, realizing with a shock that those were two of the bodies he'd seen in the crystal— the woman fallen half over her son, trying to protect him, both of them shot through with the same power-stick discharge. And tigers. Tigers everywhere.

"No," he said, speaking to himself. "No. It must not happen. It must never happen."

"What must not happen, Sahib?" Bhishma said, his face concerned again.

"The massacres must not repeat themselves. There must be no rebellion."

Bhishma's mouth twisted, and for a moment it looked like he was about to say something. But he didn't. Instead, he nodded gravely. "There must be no massacres," he said, assenting. "Massacres will not make Indians look any more civilized. Brutal rebellion will never give us our own land back. Sahib will help me, then? You . . . You'll go with me to the realm of tigers, and see what they're planning? Perhaps if we can convince Sahib General—"

"Yes," William said, surprising himself. "Yes, I'll go with you."

THE PRINCESS'S MIND AND
THE MAIDEN'S HEART;
RIVALS ALLY

"I do not wish to discuss it," Sofie said, *putting down* her teacup. She had no idea where her companions had found teacups, or tea—or any of the other things they'd acquired seemingly overnight. Only that the two men had left for a few moments and come back carrying an elaborate chest that contained tea and a tea service. They'd also obtained full clothes, instead of the odd outfit they'd seemed to be sharing earlier.

All this, had Sofie been feeling as she normally did, would have excited her curiosity. But it did not. Once, when she was very little, she'd had the measles. She remembered very little about it—partly because she'd been all of three years old, and partly, she thought, because she'd had such a high fever. She remembered her mother covering every possible magelight in the house in red flannel. She remembered being given red pajamas to wear, and also that all the toys she'd played with had been burned after she got better. And she remembered sores all over her stomach that itched horribly.

The rest had been cloaked in a sort of confused juxtaposing of images—her mother's face, tea with milk, someone's voice singing an Indian song that she remembered understanding then, but no longer would now.

Now entire days were like that—a mishmash of images. She took the cup of tea from Lalita's hand because Lalita insisted on giving it to her. She sipped from it indifferently.

"What is wrong, miss?" Lalita asked.

Sofie said she did not wish to discuss it. But she might as well say that she didn't wish to think. The last few days, in her experience, had been like the measles. And anything that had touched them should be burned. The memory of riding dragon-back; the impression of loneliness and vulnerability from St. Maur; the feel of the neck ruffle between her fingers. And then, suddenly, the way the dragon had become a beast—fully as cruel and as villainous as anything she'd read about in the novels.

It wasn't that Sofie didn't realize the tigers were trying to hurt her. She still shivered at the thought that they meant to sacrifice her, in some beastly manner, to restore the potency of the ruby her family had held on to for centuries. And they'd thought it powerful for the family only. A bauble that was tied to them by blood and tradition. There were legends saying that if the ruby left the family, the family would be cursed. But it was worthless for the rest of the world. Worthless to make magic with. Unless it was purified with her blood.

She understood that. But for St. Maur to torture a defenseless being!

Sofie shuddered at the memory of St. Maur shifting back to human form, of his handsome features smeared in human blood, and realized with a start that Lalita had left her alone and that the two men were somewhere at the edge of the little clearing, near the flying rug, talking to each other in whispers.

In a way it was like waking from sleep, because she couldn't imagine what had happened in the meantime, nor could she remember Lalita walking away from her. She frowned at her cup of tea, in which the milk had taken on a curdled appearance. The cup felt quite cold to the touch.

She'd been thinking of St. Maur, and she could not even explain why. If St. Maur had mattered to her in any way, rather than being a chance-met acquaintance, she could explain why his sudden change had affected her so. Or if, perhaps, she had entertained any romantic thoughts at all about him. Which—despite how sorry she felt for his lost-little-boy moments—she did not entertain.

It was, she thought to herself, that his sudden transformation mirrored the transformation of her parents, the transformation of everyone she knew. He had changed so suddenly. Just as her parents, on her return to India, seemed to be quite different people. According to the tiger, her father had been dipping into dark magics to keep the ruby safe. It begged the question, why? After all, they'd known the ruby was terribly flawed, and there was no reason to imagine it would ever have any value. Strangely, this made her think of her father as he had been before she'd left to go to England—an amiable man, fond of tradition in an almost hide-bound way. Chances were that he'd decided to keep the ruby simply because it had been in his family for generations. Having kept it all this time, he would hold on to it with the force of tradition.

And to hold on to it, he'd sold his soul. Just like St. Maur ignored his very human soul to uncover the tigers' plot. She didn't know how else the dragon should have obtained it, but she was sure there were ways that didn't require his tainting himself with such dishonor. And then he'd left her . . . with people he did not know. With two people whom she, herself, did not know. How could he be sure he could trust Lalita's cousins? And if he wasn't, how dare he leave her alone? All his pretense to care for her and to feel responsible for her well-being had been just that—a pretense.

And Lalita wondered why Sofie was so despondent that she refused food and drink. As if it should be an astonishing thing! Had not the last person who had promised to care for her betrayed her, just like her parents had?

At that moment, she *heard* something. Or not quite heard. It wasn't a sound—or not quite a sound at the level ears could perceive. It was neither words nor shouts nor groans, just a suspicion of things sliding around. . . .

The sound St. Maur made when he changed shapes. Oh, it was ridiculous. But that sound roused Sofie from her stupor. Shooting a glance at the two men, now huddled—their backs to her—talking in a corner of the clearing, Sofie realized she could leave without being noticed.

Swiftly, she entered the verdant jungle to her right, hunching over so as to get lost in the confusion of vines

and bushes and ground cover. Hurrying, she realized
that a tiger might leap out at her, but that seemed a
distant fear. She must see what had changed shape
that way. She must see if it was St. Maur.

Her heart beat fast, her mouth felt dry and she
knew that she was a fool. But then, suddenly, forcing
her way between hanging vines, she saw another clearing. And in the clearing...

St. Maur was dressing in that careless way of his,
without so much as a glance as he fastened his trousers
and the buttons of his shirt. And in front of him stood
Lalita.

A surge of something—not quite jealousy, because
of course she could not feel jealous of a man for whom
she did not care at all—shook her. Lalita had secrets
from her. It only needed this betrayal to confirm her
impression that she was destined to be betrayed by
everyone in her life, mercilessly and without respite.

It was with some difficulty that she managed to
concentrate on the words that Lalita was speaking, so
she heard only the end of it.

".... a flash of wings, over the trees," she said,
"and I thought it best if I came to see what was happening, and whether it was you. Miss Warington is
having her tea, you see, and I thought she wouldn't notice I was gone."

Sofie's hands clenched into fists. Why was it so important that Sofie not notice? She suspected that
Lalita intended to betray her somehow, and it was
hard not to wonder how.

"It is good that you came out to meet me," he said.
His soft, cultivated accents made Sofie's stomach tie
into knots, and she didn't know why. It must be the

memory of his sudden transformation, which still felt like a betrayal to her. "I was wondering how to approach you without . . . without calling Miss Warington's attention. I do not wish to cause her distress."

He dared! And why would he think seeing him would cause her distress? Such monstrous conceit. And this from the man who had advised her not to fancy that every man she came in contact with her had a passion for her. He should take his own advice.

"Why do you wish to talk to me?" Lalita asked, visibly surprised.

"I don't know how much you heard of the tiger's words," St. Maur said. His face looked pale and set— the way he looked when he shifted into human form after having spent the entire night flying in dragon form. "I don't know how much of it you understood. Do you know about Soul of Fire?"

"Of course," Lalita said, hastily. "I know it is the ruby that Charlemagne used to bind all the power in Europe to himself and his family. I was in England." There was something vaguely defensive to her tone. "I read European legends and novels."

St. Maur smiled. Was that one of his ironic smiles, vaguely patronizing of all creatures not fortunate enough to be St. Maur, peer of the realm and dragon? "Yes, of course. I should have remembered. But what I mean is, do you know—"

"I heard the tiger say that the ruby demanded as dowry for Miss Warington was in fact that same ruby. I heard that the King planned to use it—after he sacrificed my mistress to cleanse it—to find the other ruby, Heart of Light, which would allow him to be lord of the world."

"Very well," St. Maur said. Why did he sound so tired, as though only his willpower was keeping him going? "You see, then, the danger in which she stands. I flew ahead, to Meerut, where the Captain Blacklock fellow whom she expected to marry lives."

Expected to marry? Sofie's doubt seemed to be reflected, at the same exact time, by Lalita's own sharpened look. "Expected?" Lalita said.

St. Maur shrugged. "I confess, I expected him to be more willing. You know what she is like. I can't imagine a man made of flesh and blood not wishing to unite his life to hers."

Sofie found that she had taken a deep, sighing breath, and was surprised the two interlocutors in the clearing hadn't turned to look at her.

"I know that the captain danced attention to her most faithfully."

"Yes, but apparently he meant nothing by it. I think he admired her excessively, but I don't think there was ever an intention to marry her. Rather, he was scared at the thought of marrying her—scared that he would have to do so to protect her honor. And I . . . I will confess that I told him he should not marry her unless he wanted to, because it seems to me indecent—almost insulting—to have her shackled for life to someone who doesn't love her."

Sofie took in a deep breath, more startled at the pain she *didn't* feel.

"But sir!" Lalita said. She looked horrified and had leaned against the trunk of a tree, facing Sofie. It was Sofie's impression that Lalita would have liked to fall to a sitting position, and would have done so had there been anything nearby upon which to sit. "Think how short her life might be if she remains a virgin and falls into the hands of the tigers. You must know they are following us even now."

"I know," St. Maur said, and his terrible tiredness was like a pall hanging over his speech. "I know. I flew to Meerut and back over two days, and I saw and heard it all. They have sentinels posted at intervals. They are in constant communication by means of growls that transverse the jungle."

"I've heard them," Lalita said, and shuddered in turn. "I've heard them, and I know that they mean trouble. So how can you say it's fine for the Englishman not to marry her? When her continued life might depend on her being a wife, not a maid?"

St. Maur shook his head. "I don't know what to do, nor what to think. All I know is that I cannot, in clear conscience, advocate she marry a man who has no chance of loving her, and who will indeed resent her if he has to offer her his name." And in response to Lalita's puzzled look, he added, "He has hopes of a rich wife."

"Oh."

"But that is not all—I have observed you from above, and attempted to make sure that Miss Warington was safe, but that is not the main worry. You see, I have on me a scrying device. I was sent to India—as you might or might not have heard—to get the very jewel the tigers want, though it is no part of my plan to sacrifice Miss Warington to it.

"But for finding it, I was provided with a scrying device that will point me to the ruby. I operated that device and . . ." He shrugged. "Try as I might, it shows me your group." Was it Sofie's impression, or did

Lalita look alarmed at these words? "Therefore, I must assume that Miss Warington has it."

Sofie almost stepped forward, saying, *No, you fool, you must not assume any such thing.* But of course he'd said he had no wish to see her, and she was too much of a lady to impose her presence on a man so wholly unwilling to be in her company.

"Yes, it is something she would do, is it not?" Lalita said. "We both of us knew where the ruby was kept, and Miss Warington went running madly from the room when she realized that her mother would force her to marry the tiger. I can very well imagine her stealing the ruby before she ran out into the balcony, as an additional revenge against her parents."

Sofie frowned. What was Lalita thinking? Why, Lalita had helped her pack! Lalita had seen everything that went into her bag.

"Yes," St. Maur said. "That is exactly what I feared. And, you see, that was why I returned. Since Miss Warington has the ruby, every effort must be made to separate her from it and to have one of your cousins keep it. Should Miss Warington—forbid the thought—fall into the tigers' hands, then all is not yet lost, provided you can be sure the ruby doesn't fall into their hands as well. This would allow time for Miss Warington to be rescued."

Lalita smiled—a pale, worried smile. "Yes, I see your plan. And meanwhile, we'll stay in the air as much as possible. That should keep the tigers from being able to catch up with us."

"That," St. Maur said, "is an excellent plan. I see Miss Warington is in most competent hands."

"Oh, sir, of course," Lalita said, blushing with

pleasure at the compliment. "She has been my best friend, and I have been her companion since she was seven. I will defend her to the utmost of my strength."

St. Maur surveyed her with an amused gaze and said, "I'm sure your moral strength is phenomenal, but perhaps you'd best trust her to your cousins when it comes to physical strength."

Lalita smiled back at him, and said, "I'm actually stronger than I look, but of course my cousins are better equipped to perform the duty of bodyguards."

"Very well, Miss . . . ?" St. Maur said.

"Lalita."

"Very well, Lalita," he said. "I will leave now. Remember, I entrust you with her life and her safety and I will be counting on you to keep both of those intact."

She bowed to him, but said, just as he started undressing, "Where are you going now?"

"It doesn't matter, does it?" he asked. "Somewhere. I thought . . ." He spoke slowly. "I thought all these years that I was too much of a coward to take my own life. And so I am. This is why, sometimes, it is useful to have a lawful and strongly constituted state at your back. It does that which you are not willing to undertake yourself."

"Sir!" Lalita said, in a tone of surprise and shock, though Sofie was not sure at all what was so surprising or shocking about his words. She couldn't quite understand what he meant by having a well-constituted state at his back, though.

"Never mind," he said, calmly. He'd finished undressing. The whole ceremony was familiar to Sofie, almost to the point of being comforting. She had seen him do it every morning, before changing into a dragon and letting her climb on his back.

She could imagine herself on his back now, her hands tangled on the golden neck ruffle. Remembered the feel of his muscles operating the powerful wings. Strange how one could be so high up in the air, over utterly alien country, knowing oneself pursued by vicious beings, and yet feel so safe, so utterly calm and protected. But that had been then, and that feeling was now gone forever.

Now she must get out of the vicinity of the clearing before St. Maur changed completely and took the wing. He might very well see her lurking and realize she had heard his conversation with Lalita. Sofie didn't know why she shouldn't overhear it, but clearly he thought it was important to keep his very presence here a secret.

"Are you sure you don't wish to see Miss Warington?" Lalita asked.

St. Maur, fully undressed, shook his head. "No. I would not wish to. She made it abundantly clear she did not wish to see me again."

Sofie started to move toward him. Then she remembered his relish in torturing the young tiger, and stepped back. Could he truly imagine himself to be any maiden's dream?

Part of her wished to stay where she was, to watch him change into the dragon. She wished, with a passionate intensity, to see the firefly wings spread against the sky. But she knew better. She made her way back, tracing the way she'd come by the broken branches and bruised leaves. She heard the roar of a tiger in the distance and wondered if that meant the tigers were near. Insanely, desperately, she wished they were.

It is a horrible thing, she thought, *to be young and female and to feel so lonely, so utterly devoid of protectors and of anyone who might care for me.*

She made it to the clearing just in time. The two males had disappeared. She wondered if they'd noticed her gone and gone searching for her.

Moments later, Lalita came into the clearing. "What, miss?" she said. "All alone here? Where have those two good-for-nothings gone?"

Sofie shrugged. She hoped she projected the same despondence she'd been showing since Lalita had found her. Internally, though, she was thinking furiously.

I don't have the ruby, yet St. Maur said his scrying device pointed him back at this party. And why would he think or say so, except that it was true? He wasn't trying to lie to me. He didn't even think I'd overheard it. And he certainly wouldn't be lying to Lalita, would he? Not when he flew back for a day, probably without sleeping. How tired he must be! And how hungry. All just to bring me warning of what he perceived as a danger. Surely he wouldn't lie to me. So he saw the ruby with us. And if I don't have it, who does? And why are they hiding it from me?

TIGER, TIGER!

They came through the forest at a gallop, following some ill-defined path that Bhishma clearly knew quite well.

Among the trees, breathing in the smell of leaves and dried grass—feeling the warmth of the sun come and go on his back, as light and shadow succeeded each other on their ride—William started coming out of his despondent state. Oh, it might all be true that he was attracted to members of his own sex, but what did it matter? How could anyone else penetrate into his mind and soul and see what was there?

Other men, he dared say, had faced this and bullied through it, by pretending—no, by convincing themselves—that they were something they were not. He was not a warm person. He'd never been. All his passion, his intemperate feelings, manifested only in his prophetic dreams. In his waking life, he was viewed as cold and correct, he knew. But none of these said anything of what he felt inside.

Before he'd realized this, he'd been afraid that he was never going to fall in love with anyone—that he never would know the companionship his parents enjoyed. Nothing had changed, or nothing much. He would never have that. At least he hoped he wouldn't, for it would be more difficult—painful—if he did fall in love with someone desperately, a feeling that must never be shown.

But he didn't think this likely. It was simply not in his nature. He suspected he was very much like his father—a conventional man with conventional thoughts. If he'd been normal, then his wife might well have become the love of his life, because it was expected. And over time and her retelling, he might even convince himself he'd not married the second daughter of a well-to-do man who could further his church career, but a blond beauty with whom he'd fallen in love at first sight by a flowering yellow rosebush.

Things being as they were, he might now and then feel a wild attraction, but he was unlikely to fall in love. Providing he could control his lust—and he felt as though he'd trained all his life to do that—no one would ever know, and the course of his life need not be altered. He would get promoted once the queen's minister forgave him his unwillingness to marry Sofie Warington. He would then marry a well-to-do girl of decent background. In the course of time there would be children, and quiet teas by the fireplace on a winter evening, with the English rain pattering against the conventional windows.

Having thought himself through this labyrinth, he felt more like himself as Bhishma slowed, then stopped and dismounted.

"Are we near?" William asked.

Bhishma put his finger to his lips, commanding silence, and spoke back in a quiet whisper as he tied his horse to a tree. "Not that near," he said. "But as near as I dare go with a horse, and in any state that might look like we're doing more than strolling the forest and talking of something relating to the garrison."

"Oh," William said, dismounting and tying his own horse beside Bhishma's, then proceeding afoot on a meandering forest path ahead.

It wasn't so much a path as a tunnel, William thought—with leaves ahead and leaves to the side, and light filtering greenly through to cast an enchantment upon the area.

Bhishma turned back and whispered, "This passage will keep us from being seen by the sentinels in the camp. They patrol this area routinely, but tigers are..." He shrugged. "They prefer to look down and keep sentinel from the top of trees. A virtue, of course, for tigers, who can then drop upon the unsuspecting prey. But also an advantage for us, if we are willing to be humble and follow a forest path with plenty of covering."

"And that was why we left our horses so far back," William said.

"Of course. We couldn't risk their being seen."

"You've spent a lot of time watching the tigers, haven't you?"

Bhishma nodded. The look he threw William over his shoulder showed a face knit in concentrated worry. "I've been watching them a long time. I don't like talks of mutiny, of destroying all the Englishmen... of sending them all from India."

"And you don't agree with them?"

Bhishma turned around, his eyes dancing with some sort of amusement, his face wreathed in smiles. "Sahib," he said, "I've answered this before. Are you arguing for Indian independence or are you testing me?"

"Neither," William said, mildly surprised. "I'm simply curious. I guess I've been curious since I arrived. You—all of you, though I suspect there is as much difference between you and my sweeper as there is between you and Englishmen—"

"May it please heaven," Bhishma said, still in a tone of great amusement.

"Well, yes, but all the same, you know, it has been working at my mind. I'm not of the school—I think very few people of my generation truly are—that thinks all natives are stupid or somehow incapable. You clearly are not. Or no more so than many Englishmen."

"Thank you," Bhishma said, with a slight bow, and an unmistakable impression of sarcasm.

"No, what I mean is, I don't know you very well, to know exactly how intelligent or . . . or accomplished you are, but what I've seen of you seems perfectly sensible, perfectly capable of rational behavior. I don't . . . I don't mean you are in any way inferior. That was exactly my point, and that being my point, it makes me wonder why you wouldn't desire independence or work toward it. It would seem foolish to me," he said, with sudden, startling realization, "if I were Indian, to submit to Englishmen sent from abroad simply because they were sent from an empress, who actually never set foot in the country."

Bhishma smiled a broad smile. "Admirable, Sahib. But truly, listen to what I said. I did not say that I wouldn't embrace independence, that I'm not proud of my own country, or that I think it right we should be ruled from abroad by another people. What I said, Sahib, is that I don't want a mutiny, a rebellion like the one of 1857."

His face went suddenly very serious. "My grandfather was one of mutinying sepoys in 1857. He was also one of those killed—horribly—in the retaliation. Cut to pieces in front of his wife and children."

"Oh," William exclaimed. And to Bhishma's curious look, he added, "My grandfather died in the mutiny. He was one of the men shot down by the boats, after being told he'd be allowed to embark."

Bhishma shook his head, his brow knit in an odd expression. "My grandfather was probably one of the shooters," he said, as though it were marvelous. "But," he went on with renewed vigor, "that's the whole point. You really can't go on making the same mistakes. The rebellion might have looked to my grandfather and his compatriots like a brilliant, daring feat. To the rest of the world, though, the massacre of innocent women and children only showed them as barbarians who should never be allowed to rule themselves. And to ourselves, too, I think, as time went on. And the reprisals . . ." He shook his head. "I don't suppose you have any idea of the reprisals—of men cut to pieces in front of their families, of . . ." He shook his head again. "You don't want to know."

"I can imagine," William said, more drily than he meant to. Partly because, of course, he *could* imagine it, all too vividly. It was of a piece with the images of the massacre—the gruesome woodcuts in period books, the story of the murdered English ladies thrown down a well and the two little English boys, whose ghosts are said to still appear, thrown in alive after

them. Men in regiments coming in right after the massacres—what would they not do? They would, of
course, do the same as they'd heard, only from the
other side. And then both stories would get exaggerated, handed down the generations, perpetuating the
hatred and injury.

"Yes, perhaps you can," Bhishma said, very quietly. "You see, then . . . you see how very important it is
that I should not allow this to happen again?"

"I suppose I do, yes." And both men resumed
walking in silence.

They walked what seemed to William a long time.
Here and there, growls erupted, making William shudder. But Bhishma seemed unconcerned, only pausing
occasionally to listen to the growls—trying to analyze
them, William thought.

They emerged into a small clearing that was like-
wise covered from above with vines and foliage. It occurred to William that the tunnel and the clearing
looked as though they'd been encouraged to grow that
way. Bhishma said he'd been watching the tigers a long
time. William wondered what he meant by that. A
weaving of a vine here, a twisting of two branches together, and it would probably be less than three seasons in the sweltering climate of India for the covering
to grow this way. Probably. Bhishma now appeared to
him far more calculating than William had thought
when he'd first met him.

Bhishma put his finger to his lips again, as though
thinking that William might ask questions, then, half-
hunched to avoid touching the canopy above, he led
William to the edge of what turned out to be a small
rise.

From there, they could look down on a city. It seemed ancient and magnificent at the same time. From their vantage, they could see past the walls that encircled it and into the main street, lined by tall buildings in golden stone. They were more elaborate than any William had seen elsewhere in India. They had the traditional verandas of Indian homes, but each of them was hung with either a bright and expensive-looking tapestry, or with what seemed to be the same tapestries woven of flowers. Everyone on the streets was dressed in what must be the equivalent of their Sunday best. And as William watched, the streets themselves were being decked in flowers—different colors of flowers weaving different patterns upon the yellowish dirt.

Bhishma said something under his breath that had the feel of an imprecation, and though William could hardly understand the word, he understood the tone of it all too well.

He looked sharply at Bhishma, and the man turned to whisper in William's ear, his breath hot and vaguely curry-scented—a spicy, not unpleasant smell. "They are preparing for some ritual ceremony. As they would if they are going on what they'd consider a holy war against the occupiers."

William turned and tried to whisper just as low. Bhishma's ear was surprisingly small and well formed, and the same bronze color as the rest of his skin. "This is the city of the tigers, then?"

"What we can see of it," Bhishma said. And then, shaking his head, as if in impatience at himself, or perhaps afraid of what William might ask next, "You see, every one of the were cities and towns has a . . . a veil

that only the magic of their members can penetrate—
something that doesn't allow anyone not of the
same . . . magic stripe to see all of it. What we see here
is part of their capital city, the part where they remain
human. The rest . . ." He shrugged. "The rest of their
kingdom has been magicked so that it folds upon itself." He looked at William, and must have read perfect incomprehension in his eyes. "There is . . . a portal
and an illusion, so that if you step over the border of
the Kingdom of the Tigers on the north, you will find
yourself suddenly on the south side without realizing
that you have transversed any great distance. All these
magics have been perfected by the weres from the
dawn of time, to keep themselves safe from hu-
mankind."

William digested this and nodded, wondering why
British weres didn't have the same contrivance. Or did
they? Had Charlemagne, by concentrating the magics
in Europe to himself, denied most of the Europeans
enough magic to be truly dimorphic? Or did St. Maur
have a secret dragon king to whom he owed alle-
giance? Somehow, William couldn't imagine that.

Aloud he said, "Are you sure it is not just one of
their holy days, or one of the festivals they observe?"

Bhishma nodded. "I know all their festivals and
everything they observe, Sahib. This is not one of
them. Besides . . . I have some capacity to understand
their language—their signals spoken in roads—and
what I've been hearing all morning . . ."

"Yes?"

"They expect their king to return triumphant soon,
with the restored jewel that will allow them to reclaim
control of their kingdom. And control over India."

SHADES OF MADNESS; WHOM TO SUSPECT; THE MOST DARING OF SOLUTIONS

"On board, now." The taller of the two men, whom Lalita called Maidan, came running through the trees, dressing himself as he ran. "To the rug!"

Running behind him, full tilt, was the other man, the one that Lalita called Hanuman. Sofie had noticed that the two males often fought each other, or at least wrestled each other, for ... supremacy, for Lalita's attention, for she didn't quite know what. But this time they were of one accord.

And Lalita, without a word, dropped the teacup she'd been holding onto the chest she did not bother to pack and close. Instead, she dove into the shadow of a nearby, overhanging tree, and from it extracted the rolled-up rug, which she spread on the ground in a single, elegant motion.

Sofie, still thinking about St. Maur and what he'd said, remained, her cup of cold tea in hand. The two men took hold of her, one at each shoulder. "On the rug, now," they said, as they half lifted her, half walked her to the rug and more or less forced her to sit. Sofie felt she should scream or protest, but it was all too much like a dream for her to muster the strength.

And then Maidan was grabbing Lalita's hand and pulling her. "Come, Highness." He pulled her onto the rug and held her, and got no more than a reproving look from Hanuman. Maidan, Sofie realized, had a powerstick—which, like the tea chest, seemed to have appeared during his excursion with Hanuman, with no explanation.

Hanuman was chanting the incantations that flew the rug. It lifted with a sudden tilt, much rougher than their previous liftoffs, and speeded ahead with such a brute surge that he felt it necessary to reach back and hold Sofie with his free hand. "Come, come, Princess," he said loudly, addressing Lalita. "Come, hold on by yourself so that Maidan can use the powerstick."

Why would he need to use the powerstick? Sofie thought. And as she thought it, she felt a ray of power singe over her head, and looked to the side to see that there were three people on a flying rug, catching up to them. They all had broad, flat faces, like the king of tigers, and while one of them steered the rug, the other two were kneeling, firing powersticks.

Hanuman made a sound that seemed to be something or other about a mother—though it was said in Indian—and shouted aloud, "Hold on," as he dipped the rug and then tilted it almost completely sideways. Sofie held on. What else could she do? Her mind might be in a fog, with St. Maur's words running through it, but she did not feel a great need to die by throwing herself from a height. Instead, she held on—tight—and behind her, Maidan knelt and seemed to shoot without needing to hold on. The way he kept his balance was almost preternatural.

"I guess it was inevitable," he said, between clenched teeth as he fired, "that they would have found someone capable of steering a rug the European way. Or commandeered a stranger."

Lalita said nothing, but Hanuman shouted, "I don't know how long I can continue to evade them."

"Don't worry," Maidan answered as he shot. A scream came from the other rug, and the man who'd been shooting at them from the left collapsed and fell from the rug.

"The rug controller," Lalita screamed. "Shoot the rug controller."

"What if he's been conscripted?" Hanuman asked.

"What are you, a moral arbiter?" Maidan asked, and aimed the powerstick at the man who had been in the center, steering the rug.

Hanuman reached back without looking, and his arm seemed, strangely, to lengthen as he grabbed at Maidan. "Maidan!" he said. "I have responsibilities. You will not shoot the driver. He might be innocent. Take out the other shooter. I'm ordering you."

At that point, the shooter shot again, and Hanuman dipped just in time, while Lalita asked, "Are those powersticks charged for weres?"

"Yes," Maidan answered. And on those words, he let fly a ray from his powerstick, which and pierced the shooter's heart. He fell off the rug, and the rug driver made a strangled sound and steered the rug down.

Maidan turned and sat down on the rug, taking a deep breath.

"I told you," Hanuman said.

"As you wish, my liege," Maidan said.

Sofie saw Lalita shoot Hanuman a sharp look, which Hanuman studiously ignored. And now that the primary danger had passed, Sofie was back to thinking of St. Maur and of what his visit had meant.

"Where are we going now?" Lalita asked, sharply.

"As far as we can get without stopping," Hanuman said, quietly. "I was thinking Jaipur, or as close to it, and Meerut, as we can get."

Jaipur, Sofie thought. A big city, a long way off. She wondered if St. Maur had gone to Jaipur. She wondered where St. Maur had gone. He'd sounded . . . She didn't quite know what to think of how he sounded. Tired? Despondent? He'd been flying too long. But he'd been concerned about her. Yes, that fact remained. He must have been very worried about her, to have flown for so long. She knew that ordinarily he never flew that far or that much. Not without rest.

She found herself wondering whether he'd eaten enough or if he was risking losing control of his mind and of his body when the beast needed to feed. She reproached herself for caring. He was the beast, she told herself, but it did not matter. It was as though her heart, quite divorced from her mind, insisted on caring, no matter what she said.

St. Maur was probably alone and hungry. She'd turned her back on him, as good as if she'd ordered him from her sight. She had done him a great unkindness. Oh, surely, he'd acted with no consideration for the tiger, but then . . . But then, he'd been trying to save her. That much was obvious by his return.

And this brought Sofie to another thought—he was worried about her and the ruby. And Sofie remembered how certain he was that she had the stone. He had seen it in his scrying object. But she *didn't* have it. So someone in this party did. But who?

She ran a curious eye over the two males and Lalita. She'd known Lalita for over half of their lives. And yet, now she felt she didn't know her at all. There had been that flash of surprise, that lurch of fear in Lalita's eyes when St. Maur had mentioned the ruby. What did it mean? What did Lalita think in that moment, when surprise and terror had dueled for supremacy in her eyes? Clearly it had to do with the ruby, and it probably meant that one of the three of them had the stone, and that Lalita knew it.

While forest and villages passed beneath her, Sofie frowned, reviewing the days she had spent with these people. They'd hadn't been deferential to her, as Indians usually were. More...kindly, as Lalita had been when telling St. Maur she'd look after Sofie.

And for the first time, it occurred to Sofie to wonder who Lalita was and where she'd come from. She'd only ever known Lalita by the single name. No father's name, no place of origin. A buried memory from the time when Sofie was seven came back. Her mother saying she had payed some insignificant amount to Lalita's family. "And glad to get rid of her, they were. In India, daughters are never very important to the father."

But Lalita had called on male cousins when in need, and it did not seem as though her family had either forsaken her or forgotten her. More like they answered her every command.

She looked at the girl sitting there, demure and composed in her sari. The two men called her princess or highness. And they disappeared and came back with whatever seemed to be the necessity of the moment. She narrowed her eyes. "Lalita? Why do they call you princess?"

"What?" The girl looked surprised. "Why... it's..." She blushed. "It's a family joke."

Hanuman looked at her, a quick, sly look, and smiled a little, but said nothing. And yet, Sofie was sure that this was a lie—as she was sure that Hanuman knew it was a lie. And what was the most common reason for someone to call someone else a title? Why, that the person had a title, of course. So, it was quite possible that Lalita was a princess of some sort. Rajs, princesses, kings and queens were thick on the ground in India. There were hundreds of them, thronging every corner, many with little more than their pride to support them. It seemed to Sofie that Lalita might very well be the daughter of a prince or a king, and Sofie's parents hadn't realized it.

But if that was so, then why would have Lalita's family have agreed to send her with Sofie to England? Only a few days ago, Sofie would have said that there was no reason at all, or if there was, it was poverty. But now she was not so sure. St. Maur had talked of his own mission, looking for the ruby in India. He'd talked of others seeking it. He'd mentioned how much power could ride on that ruby. Power to control the human race itself.

In Sofie's mind, a picture was forming. What if Lalita was the daughter of an impoverished prince and had been sent to England with Sofie so as to win Sofie's confidence, and to make sure Sofie would trust her at the crucial moment?

It was possible, she realized, that Lalita or one of her cousins had found the ruby. And having found it, they were now taking her somewhere to sacrifice her, just as the tigers meant to do. This was probably why they talked of going to Jaipur and not to Meerut proper. In Sofie's mind, Jaipur was associated with weres. Were-elephants, mostly. She remembered reading of what they'd done during the mutiny—the fierce, proud, terrible warriors of Jaipur who'd turned on their English masters. She felt a shiver run through her as she looked from Lalita to the two men and wondered if they were were-elephants. Oh, no one would think that elephants would be dangerous creatures. They were the beast of burden of all of Asia, silently bearing the weight of all the responsibilities the natives wished on them, but that was not the only face of the elephant. When Sofie was very little, an elephant in musth had run through the street in front of her house, attacking and destroying everything in its path, until two British soldiers armed with powersticks had managed to shoot it through the brain and end its rampage.

She remembered overturned carts, flipped-up stalls, people trampled and one small child—who must have been Sofie's age or less—lifted up by the creature's trunk and smashed repeatedly against a wall. She remembered the blood.

In her mind, that's what the elephant sepoys of Jaipur must have looked like in the midst of the mutiny. And she wondered what she'd done by agreeing to accompany Lalita and her relatives. She wondered if she'd fallen into a trap.

At the same time, she was aware that she might be insane—that all these terrors might be no more than illusions, like horrible faces that sprang out of a dream. And yet . . . who could blame her for being afraid? Her own parents had tried to sell her to the tigers. Then St. Maur had admitted he was looking for the ruby himself. And then . . . Lalita and these men she said were her cousins were acting in peculiar ways and were, almost certainly, hiding the ruby that everyone wanted.

And she couldn't swear that they, too, weren't weres. In fact, she remembered the concerned question about whether the powersticks were loaded for weres, which made no sense at all if the three of them were human. And if they were weres, then they were probably intending to sacrifice her.

Out of her racing thoughts, a single certainty emerged: she was not safe here. And when casting about in her mind for a place and a person she would be safe with, she came again and always to St. Maur. He had been cruel, yes, and he was a were. But he'd come back to warn Lalita. And it wasn't possible that he had the same fate in mind for Sofie as the tigers. If it were so, instead of refusing to see her, he would have kidnapped her and taken her to a place where she could be sacrificed for his own purposes.

No, more than that, had that been his plan, he'd have found out earlier that she was the ruby's heiress, and he'd have been planning to get hold of her whether or not he could get his hands on Soul of Fire.

So, St. Maur was the one person she knew for a fact she would be safe with. And she had sent him away, forever.

DUPLICITOUS INTENTIONS;
THE INNER MAN

"You'll have to tell Sahib General," Bhishma said. "You'll have to tell him that this city exists, and that its people are planning something horrible." He looked thoughtful. "You might want to tell him it's a were kingdom. Don't tell him about sepoys in the ranks, though. I'm afraid of how my comrades will react to the sight of Gold Coats in the encampment, but they should be fine if it's clear they're there to investigate the city of the tigers. Even the tiger sepoys will be fine. They've been getting nervous."

They were halfway back through the verdant tunnel of vegetation. William wasn't sure what he'd seen was as grave as Bhishma made it out to be. He wasn't sure what it all meant, but he could see that Bhishma was taking it seriously. He had no idea, though, what Bhishma thought William could tell the general, or why it would matter. And he couldn't understand the problem with Gold Coats in India. Oh, he'd heard it mentioned, but he didn't understand the native perspective on it. "Why would they revolt at the sight of Gold Coats?"

Bhishma shrugged. "Because we—weres are sacred to a lot of local religions. So many of the religions believe in some form of understanding, of spirit-union with an animal that is also part of the divine. And it is believed that if all the weres of India are exterminated, then India itself will die. That the land and the magic of the people will vanish." He sighed. "Look, the Muslims tried to eliminate all the weres in India, and they were almost overthrown before they decided to accept the ways of the land. And the British, when they first arrived, centuries ago, were intelligent enough to infringe on local customs as little as possible. If a were is not dangerous or if the natives don't mind it, they do nothing. The only weres that have been hunted in India are those who go on rampages and try to kill everyone."

"I know a were," William said, his words coming out through his unwilling lips, as though someone else were saying them. It was the whole thing with St. Maur. He must tell at least part of it to someone and explain why he wasn't seeking death for a dragon, that most dangerous of all weres. "And I have no intention of denouncing him or having him killed." It was the first time he'd said this aloud, the first time he'd admitted it. He smiled into Bhishma's shocked expression. "Perhaps I'm more Indian than I thought."

"Perhaps," Bhishma said, gravely. "But in all honesty, Sahib, what started my fears of a mutiny were rumors that there were Gold Coats landing in Calcutta, Delhi and Mumbai. If there are Gold Coats seen in this region, then all hell will break lose."

"Why this region most of all?" William asked.

"Because there are so many weres here," Bhishma

said, with a curiously shy look at William. Unlike most of the native sepoys, Bhishma wore his hair longish, pulled back and held in place by a tie. Now the tie had come loose, probably pulled off by one of the vines as they came through the tunnel. It left Bhishma's very straight, dark hair falling like a curtain in front of his face whenever he inclined his head. He inclined it now. "You have to understand, we are a remote region. The various lords of India largely have left us alone. It means that there is more of everything here that is truly Indian. Like weres."

"I see," William said, though in fact he didn't see at all. His mind persisted on following an uncontrollable course of its own, wondering how such a man, who looked so much like a bronze statue of antiquity—merciless and majestic—could by simply lowering of his head look very much like a young man, nervous and confused.

"I will tell the general about the city. Not about any weres in the garrison," he said, softly, wishing for nothing more than to reassure his companion, who suddenly looked so vulnerable. "I will tell him that the tigers are planning something, but I can't promise that he will take any action. He ignored me before." Internally, William was trying to think of what he could tell General Paitel about the whole plan—everything St. Maur had told him—without giving St. Maur away. He didn't know how to do it. And yet he must.

Bhishma looked at him while his hand went up to sweep his hair back, and suddenly he smiled disarmingly. "Sometimes the best we can do is try, isn't it? Sometimes all a man of honor can do is his best, and let go of all that is not in his purveyance."

William nodded. A good philosophy, if only he could implement it. He tried to explain. "It's just that, in the crystal, I saw . . . a massacre, people killed."

Bhishma shot him a concerned look. "I know. I've seen it in your eyes, the horror of it, long before you said anything."

"Is that why . . . ?" William hesitated. He had no real need to know, but he wanted to. Had he been going around the garrison looking like one pursued by demons? What about him had caused Bhishma to seek him out? He took a deep breath. "Look here, why did you come to me? Why did you choose me to tell about your fears? It might have been better if you'd gone to General Paitel directly and spoken to him. I have almost no power."

Bhishma chuckled. "The general? Listen to a sepoy?"

"Well, they call him There and Back Again Paitel. They say he's very devoted to his men and they to him. They say he's survived all these years thanks to the devotion of his native troops and how attentive he is to them."

Bhishma shrugged and looked away. "Perhaps he is attentive to his troops, to those who've served with him. Those close to his age, who've seen battle with him. But a young sepoy coming to him with a story involving were-tigers . . . Well, he's more likely to think I've gone mad."

"He might think I've gone mad, too," William said, ruefully.

Bhishma looked at him, and his face took on a slow, considering frown. "No. You're the son of his old friend. He will not do that."

"Yet I'm not the son of your old friend. There are several English officers here. So why did you come to me?"

Bhishma took a deep breath. Swallowed. "You looked... worried. You looked as though you cared, as though you gave a damn about... about everything. You looked..."

He turned fully to look at William and William turned, too, in response. They were almost at the end of the tunnel, where they could fully stand up. And, facing each other, they looked into each other's eyes. "I thought..." Bhishma said. He seemed to be having difficulty speaking. His breath came fast and hard, and William realized, somewhat surprised, that his own breath was echoing it. They were so close he could feel Bhishma's warm breath on his face. So close that they were breathing each other's breath.

It was like, William thought, feeling feverish, like when young boys cut their fingers and mingled their blood so that they would be blood brothers forever. They were sharing breath. The most ancient cultures in the world used to believe that breath was the essence of life. Were their lives becoming intermingled in some way? Yet what did they have in common, except their fear of a coming massacre. Their grandfathers had fought on opposite sides of the 1857 mutiny. Their grandfathers had both died as a result of that mutiny.

Bhishma's eyes were black—dark, impenetrable—and there was in them some plea that William couldn't quite understand. Something was happening, something passing between them, gaze to gaze, some language older than words, and quite alien to the waking mind. Something only understood by the deeper levels of the brain, where dreams played hide-and-seek with one's desire.

Not knowing what he did, but obeying an overpowering impulse that he could not have stopped any more than he could have stopped himself from breathing, William leaned forward toward the other man.

And Bhishma leaned forward, too, and tilted his face up. Their eyes met with a sudden shock, of jarring recognition and thundering surprise.

And then William understood.

WAKE NOT THE BEAST;
THE PATH OF THE DRAGON

Peter woke up in a cave and tried to remember how he'd got there. After he'd left Sofie and her escort behind, he'd flown away, more or less haphazardly. He'd eaten. He thought it was a buffalo, though there was a very good chance it had been some other sort of animal, even one of the sacred cows. All he could remember was a horned animal, in the dark.

And then he'd gone in search of a place to sleep. He hadn't been very conscious by then. Flying for almost two whole days, in dragon shape, had left him confused and stumbling. His progress had denuded trees of birds and fields of all sorts of creatures great and small. They'd run in front of him, in his human form, as they'd run from a forest fire.

He'd lain down in what appeared to be little more than a covered ledge, and had immediately fallen asleep. He had no idea how long he'd slept, nor where he was. It was nighttime, and he was cold, and the sky was a perfect, serene dark blue, pierced through with stars.

Dark blue like Sofie's eyes. He'd warned her maid.

And her maid had said she would take care of Sofie, that she would make sure that Sofie and the ruby wouldn't both fall into the tigers' hands, at least not at the same time.

And yet, Peter couldn't feel easy. It was all, he thought, very much like a disease. You caught it, and you weren't even aware of it. A scratch at the back of the throat, a confusion in the head, and you didn't think anything of it, except maybe that you were tired, that you needed more sleep.

And then suddenly you realized that you were ill, really ill. It had happened so gradually and by steps, you hadn't realized it until you were tossing in a bed, wet through with your own sweat, while grim doctors sent for the local clergyman in all haste. His feelings for Sofie were like that. They had come upon him so gradually that he hadn't even been aware of their approach. They'd snuck up on him like a thief in the night. But they were now completely unavoidable.

Slowly, he brought out his eye and invoked its seeing powers. He had to find where Sofie was. And he had to go to her.

HOPING FOR WINGS;
THE RUBY; SAVING IT ALL

"If you'll wash your face and hands, miss, I'll have your supper ready when you come out," Lalita said. Sofie nodded and said nothing in response.

She was sure that her surmise about Lalita had been right. The place they'd stopped for the night proved it. Somehow in the middle of nowhere Lalita had managed to commandeer a bungalow with all possible comfort. She'd told Sofie it was just a place that some friends of hers worked, and that, the owners being absent, it was free for them to occupy. But Sofie didn't believe it. For one, in India, places were rarely left completely empty and without even a servant to care for them. And yet, she and Lalita and the two men were the only occupants of this spacious bungalow.

Sofie didn't know if they'd broken into the place, or if Lalita had somehow commandeered it. Lalita was someone or something of great importance. *Princess.*

And why would a princess engage in this charade and pretend to be Sofie's loyal servant unless she intended on doing something to take advantage of the situation?

As she stood before the small basin set atop a
dresser of elegant English design, and washed her face
and hands with a bar of soap that smelled of lavender,
Sofie thought to herself that in her place, St. Maur
would have sliced them to bits till they confessed what
they wished to do. A rueful smile flitted across her face
because she knew it to be true, and she felt despicable
for wishing he were here to do it for her, to save her
from having to find a way out of this situation.

Lalita came in to check on her, and asked her down
to the kitchen to share their meal. Sofie ate a little of
the circular, flat bread, the kind cooked over a spirit
lamp, and less of what appeared to be some native
soup heavy on spices.

While she ate, she observed her companions. They
were all very subdued—even Hanuman, who was normally quite garrulous. After eating, Sofie pleaded
tiredness and went to bed. But she wasn't tired. She
was oddly excited and full of certainty. She had decided what to do.

She was going to steal the ruby, and then she was
going to find St. Maur. While it occurred to her that he
might be very far away indeed—on the other side of
the continent or the other side of the world—something in her whispered that he wasn't. Something in
her was as sure as she was of her own name, or of being alive, that he wouldn't go very far. Not until he was
sure—absolutely sure—the whole situation was safe
for her. She'd heard the worry in his voice when he'd
spoken to Lalita.

And that concern had made Sofie decide he would
be the safest possible guard for herself and the ruby.
He would not hurt her. In fact, she realized, with a

small shock, he was more likely to die defending her than to kill her.

A wave of longing for him flooded her, but the desire alone wasn't going to save her. She was sure she knew where the ruby was. Whether dressed, half-dressed or completely naked, Hanuman always kept a pouch around his middle. It was securely tied to him so that it wouldn't fall off. And it was never opened. Ever.

Sofie was certain the ruby was there, but the question was, how to get it without alarming him. Hanuman seemed strangely alert. All of them did. And they were certainly more on their element than she was. And then an idea occurred to her, as she fretfully washed her hands once more and thought of going to bed.

This bungalow, however procured, was clearly the habitation of an English family. The lavender soap, the embroidered hand towels, the clothes hanging in the heavy wardrobe in her bedroom—surmounted by a porcelain statuette of an elephant rearing—all of it proclaimed this the inhabitation of an English Family. And where the English were, they brought with them such modern conveniences of life as were common in England.

She thought of how, in England, she'd heard young ladies or matrons say they'd take a spoonful of laudanum for their headache or to conquer a sleepless night. So many of the young wives exiled to India had trouble sleeping: the strangeness of the land, the oppressiveness of the climate, the fear of the natives, all of it conspired to make them feel that they could not possibly sleep a wink. Of course, thee were also strong army wives and women who'd been raised in India and to whom all of the inconveniences others mentioned were no more than attractive features of the place. Sofie hoped that the lady of this house hadn't been one of the annoyingly sturdy types. She very much hoped that.

Carefully, methodically, opening and closing doors and drawers as quietly as possible to avoid Lalita's overhearing her, Sofie searched for laudanum. She found it at the back bottom of the wardrobe, under a mound of starched pillowcases. In earlier years, laudanum had been considered a blameless vice, but now it had come to be frowned upon. Obviously, whoever the lady of this house was, she was ashamed of her need. But fortunately, the need existed. Sofie slipped the small bottle filled with thick yellowish liquid into her apron pocket. She knew that Lalita took her tea full of sugar, so full that Sofie used to tease her about maybe desiring a little tea with her sugar. She didn't know about the men, but she hoped they would fall for her trick.

She bustled past a small parlor and down the stairs to the kitchen, where the three of them were sitting around the table. They'd been talking quietly, but they stopped at her entrance.

"Anything I can do for you, miss?" Lalita asked, looking faintly alarmed.

Sofie shook her head. "I'm not as tired as I thought I was," she said. "Perhaps it is the strange bed or . . . you know, the tigers pursuing us. I thought what I'd really like is a good cup of tea and to talk. Will you have a cup with me?"

While she spoke, she set a teakettle on the stove.

The stove was a rarity in India—a true, cast-iron English stove. She wondered if the nervy housewife who took laudanum had insisted on it, and she puzzled over how she managed to keep it in fuel. The landscape of India was such that wood and coal were often at a premium. And besides, the coal stove would be ridiculously hot during the summer. Most of the cooking in India was done on spirit lamps or piles of cow dung. But Sofie was glad the lady of the house had a stove, and that someone—probably Lalita, who was as ignorant of the Indian ways of living as Sofie herself, at least when it came to the practice of them—had stoked a fire in it. The embers were still going and the surface of the stove was still hot. The kettle was half-filled, and Sophie looked through the cupboard on the far end of the kitchen till she found tea.

Once the tea was made, Sofie insisted on serving it. Lalita had a puzzled expression on her face as she watched Sofie do so, but she said nothing, probably thinking that what Sofie was doing was a way to calm her nerves. Which it was. It would calm her nerves very much to get hold of the ruby and be on her way to St. Maur.

She served the tea, spooning sugar into each cup and, in the middle of her bright chatter, dropping in laudanum from the bottle she'd concealed in her sleeve. She'd read in some book that Lucrezia Borgia had used that method herself—at least, when she wasn't messing about with powder in rings.

Lalita watched Sofie with a bemused expression, as though she were trying to figure something out. The men acted completely oblivious to the idea that she might even plan something. After all, in their world, she supposed, women existed to serve men. Which made it all the stranger how much respect they showed Lalita, and that they called her princess. Unless she *was* a princess.

Sofie made herself a cup of tea, without laudanum. She hadn't known what dosage to apply for the three, but she'd used the five drops some woman had told her were ideal to send one to sleep.

It must have worked, because by the time she had finished her own tea, their heads were on the table, and they were snoring softly.

Sofie set down her cup. It was a nice cup—a really fine Sevres porcelain. She hoped it escaped unscathed the natives' surprise at finding themselves duped.

She forced herself to wait, and counted to fifty in her mind, to make sure they were asleep—and deeply, too—before she bent down, and with trembling fingers pulled out the pouch that Hanuman wore under his tunic. Then, just as carefully, she unfastened the bit of ribbon that tied it shut.

He didn't move. If it weren't for the slight movement of his chest, she'd have wondered if he was dead. But he was definitely breathing, so she pulled the flap of the pouch aside to reveal . . .

The ruby, in all its faulty glory. It flared as Sofie reached for it and held it in her hand. It was a wild light, reddish and faltering, but Sofie interpreted it as a flash of recognition.

"Shhh," she told the ruby, as though it was a living thing. It felt like a living thing, warm and pulsing in her hand.

She grabbed a sharp little silver-handled knife from the drawer—a knife that smelled like it mainly had been used to cut lemons. But it was sharp, and she felt better with it in her hand. If she was going out alone, she wouldn't go defenseless, she thought as she stepped out of the house and into the night outside, looking at the sky, hoping for the sound of wings.

A GENERAL'S MORNING ROUTINE; WHERE THE WHOLE STORY IS BETTER THAN PART; ENTIRELY THE WRONG DECISION

William was admitted to the general's chambers while the general was shaving. Most men of that rank had barbers do it for them, but the general—in his voluminous red silk robe—shaved himself in front of a small mirror in an elaborate frame atop the dresser. He'd just covered his face in white froth with a ratty looking brush, and now he was wielding an ivory-handled straight razor with gusto.

"What is wrong, my boy?" he asked William. "You look like you've been dragged through hell backwards."

William *felt* like he'd been dragged through hell backwards. His certainty that he could control himself and his desires had just been proved a lie. He didn't want to think of what he'd done. He didn't know how he could ever face Bhishma again. He didn't know how he could face himself again. He shut the images and feelings of his recent actions out of his mind and concentrated, instead, on the problem of the tigers and what would happen if they chose to mutiny.

"I've been . . ." He amended the sentence mentally before he could say *I've been out in the forest with one of the sepoys*. True and probably not incriminating, as far as that went, but he couldn't imagine saying it without blushing and stammering. "That is, one of the sepoys showed me to a place that the natives say is the kingdom of the were-tigers."

He half expected the general to poo-poo his evidence, and General Paitel might have, had he not at the moment been doing his moustache line, his lips pursed to one side and firmly closed.

"I know, sir, you said it was my imagination, but I believe I must tell you . . ." He swallowed as he realized what he would have to tell, how much he would have to explain—and how carefully he would have to avoid telling a good part of it. And not just the last few hours' occurrences. He thought it would be best if he didn't denounce St. Maur. The man had done nothing to him—even if he had, accidentally, revealed a flaw in William's makeup. "I must tell you that while I was in London, I was approached by members of the . . . of the magical secret service, sir."

The general lowered the razor. His eyes met William's in the mirror. His eyebrows rose.

"Oh, I wasn't quite recruited. Nothing as fancy as that, sir. But you see, I had recently become friendly with a young lady, Miss Sofie Warington. I was offered a sum to marry her, on the condition I would use my marriage to her to acquire a jewel that had been passed down through inheritance in her family."

"Eh?" the general said. "A jewel?"

"Yes, sir. I didn't know what it meant any more than you do just now, sir. And while I liked Miss Sofie, I did not love her, nor had I any intention of marrying her." Little had he known how unlikely it was he would ever love any woman. "I . . . thought we wouldn't suit."

The general nodded. "Demmed rum business, that, making a man marry for political reasons. Mind you, I know it's done and done quite often, but . . . demmed rum business."

"Yes, sir," William said, meekly. "When I declined, I was told that I would be sent to India, to . . . inquire here after the presence of that jewel."

"Eh?" the general said again. "They told me they were reinforcing the military presence here."

"They were, at that," William said. "Though part of it was to give coverage to their sending me to India."

"And did you find the jewel? And what does all this have to do with weres?"

William told him. He told him what the jewel was and why they had wanted Sofie with it, though William very much wanted to believe—and to judge from his short and forceful interpolation, so did the general—that the secret service would not sacrifice an innocent young woman. But they perhaps would use her in some other way to obtain the cleaning and recharging of the ruby. William explained it all, omitting only the fact that St. Maur was a dragon and the fact that he, himself, had just found his impulses very far from resistible when it came to handsome sepoys with chiseled features and boyish smiles.

I'm not the first one to do this, nor shall I be the last. Most people are not discovered. Who is going to

believe the word of a native over mine? And why
would the native bring the matter up?

He felt a cold, queasy sense that there were many
reasons the native could bring it up, among them if
William refused to repeat the experience. But he
would not think about that the experience, the experi-
ment, wouldn't happen again. He knew his susceptibil-
ities now. He would hold them at bay.

"And you say the tigers are after the jewel?" the
general said.

"I'm afraid so, sir, yes. I keep trying to think of
other ways to explain their being ready for a triumphant return of their rulers, but—"

"And this Miss Warington is a British subject,"
General Paitel said, not really to William, more to himself as he thought the matter through. "Besides, we
cannot allow the natives to get hold of such an artifact,
not one they can use to challenge British power." He
resumed shaving, removing the last bits of white
foam—and quite a bit of black hair—from his face very
rapidly. Then he wiped his face and turned to William.
"No, we can't allow that tomfoolery. The Indians
aren't ready to rule themselves, if indeed they will
ever be. If we let go, one cannot even imagine the conditions that will result. There will be wars of religion
and of caste, and wars arising out of long-term personal
grievances. Nepalese will fight the Bengalese and massacre them; Muhammadans and Hindus will be at
each others' throats. All the native rajs will wage war
against one another. The resulting anarchy would cost
the lives of millions. Every time I travel through
Nepal, I tell you, I find them sharpening long knives,
ready to fall upon the Bengalis, should we ever leave.

It's not to be thought of. For their own good, we must continue to govern them, and prevent their self-destruction."

So General Paitel, who had spent most of his life in India, thought the natives were all children, who must be watched every minute, lest they fall upon one another in a frenzy and break all their toys. William shook his head. Fortunately, the general was intent on his own thoughts and didn't notice, or he might well think that William was disputing his ideas.

And William didn't want to dispute anyone's ideas. First and foremost, he wanted to wash. He was very much afraid that he would never feel clean again. And he was terrified that the terrible craving would once more overtake him and drain him of both dignity and self-control.

A TERRIBLE WAKENING; THE
REGRETS OF HINDSIGHT;
A PANICKED DRAGON

"Lalita," a stranger's voice called. Lalita heard it, as if from a distance. By degrees, she came back from the deep sleep that had enveloped her, and became aware of her face resting on a hard surface. She was sitting in a chair, and she had been profoundly asleep.

She heard herself moan before she could open her eyes, and then fought for full control of her body. Her eyes opened, and then—

She started to full wakefulness. Before her stood the Englishman who was a dragon, naked as the day he'd first seen light.

"Lalita," he said, and she realized it was the second time he had called her. "Lalita, where is she? Where is Miss Warington?"

"Upstairs," Lalita said, her voice sounding pasty. Her mouth tasted like ashes, and her tongue felt as though it was made of cork. "First bedroom to your right. Though it might be a good idea if you were . . . a little more formally attired."

"No. She is not there. I looked already." He

sounded panicked. In fact, he sounded as though he was barely holding himself in check. He set his hand on the table—a strong brown hand, Lalita thought, very human, very British with its closely pared nails. "I tell you, she's gone."

A quick glance around told Lalita that her companions were gone, too. No Hanuman. No Maidan. Which meant . . . She didn't know what it meant, except that Sofie was gone, and perhaps Hanuman and Maidan had gone with her. But where would they go without Lalita? A wild panic set in—a fear that they, like the tigers, meant to kill Sofie, and thus restore the ruby.

Of course, it had to be nonsense. But all the same, what could it mean? Besides the obvious fact that she'd been duped—that, as she'd suspected, there had been something behind her uncle's insistence on her taking Hanuman with her. And that Maidan had come in at a very propitious time, just as she'd thought before.

"Hanuman!" she called. "Maidan."

Around the corner from the sitting room there came, tumbling, two monkeys. She didn't think they'd had the time to see St. Maur, or perhaps they didn't care. They tumbled from what must have been the servants' sitting area, and they changed as they entered the kitchen. They looked . . . disheveled and sleepy, just like Lalita herself felt, and . . . slightly off. As though they, too, felt the kind of hazy headache that plagued her.

She opened her mouth to ask them what they'd done with Sofie, but before she could, Hanuman said, "Miss Warington is gone, Princess. We've scoured all the countryside, as far as we could go, and she is gone."

Before Lalita could answer, St. Maur rounded on Hanuman with intense, immediate concentration. "How? I entrusted her to you."

Lalita could only send her companions a mute pleading look to remind them, lest high spirits should lead them to believe otherwise, that a dragon was not a creature they wanted to enrage. But to her surprise, Hanuman bowed very correctly and spoke with calculated calm, as though some instinct warned him that the best protection against an enraged Englishman was always impeccable manners. "As to that, sir, we talked to some naturals hereabouts—"

"Naturals?"

"Monkeys," Maidan said. "In a state of nature. We call them that. We can talk to them, a little. It is often possible between a were form and a natural."

"I wouldn't know," St. Maur said. "Not many natural dragons."

"No, sir," Hanuman said. "But we talked to them, and the young lady walked out of here, we were told, late last night. She took her bag with her, and she headed that way." He pointed vaguely westward.

"And none of you stopped her? None of you cared? What kind of protectors are you?"

"There's more," Hanuman said. He had the red pouch tied around his middle, as he'd had it since Calcutta, when they'd gotten hold of the ruby. Now, for the first time, it seemed to Lalita that the pouch looked . . . deflated.

Hanuman untied it from his middle and flung it on the table. The cloth collapsed in on itself. "That's why we were looking for her," he said. "The ruby is gone, and she took it." Glancing up at St. Maur—who was clutching his hair and looked as if he might be sick at any minute—he added, "I think she gave us syrup of poppies. I don't know how she got it, but I know syrup of poppies. I know its symptoms. I traveled in China when I was young."

"Syrup of poppies?" St. Maur said, as though the thing was totally unknown to him.

"The tea!" Lalita said, as her brain connected. "She insisted on making tea for all of us last night—I thought it very odd, because, you know, Miss Sofie is not like that. She's not stuck up or anything, but she never..." She shook her head as her thoughts coalesced. "She rarely offered even to make tea for her friends, though she would, of course, if someone were sick or in dire need. I thought..." She moaned as she realized the full extent of her stupidity. "I honestly thought it was just that she was so brokenhearted over you, and trying to do things to keep herself occupied. I never thought—who would think it!—she would try to poison us or... or put us to sleep."

"Heartbroken? Over me?" St. Maur asked, suddenly, his expression so surprised that he looked positively half-witted.

"Of course," Lalita said, looking at him. "What did you think?"

"I..." He shook his head. "That doesn't matter. I must find out where she's gone. If she has the ruby, she will be in the greatest of dangers."

Maidan, rummaging near the teapot, had found a small flask, which he held up. "Laudanum, it says," he said. "To take for headaches and insomnia."

"Laudanum!" St. Maur repeated, almost in the tone one would say a swear word. "Of course. This house is occupied by a British family, is it not? How did you get it?"

"They are absent from the area. On a visit to some distant friends, and took their people with them, except for those that live nearby. And those took a holiday with their families." Hanuman shrugged. "A window of the master's room was not quite closed enough."

"And of course Sofie would know how to find the laudanum, hidden in the mistress's room," St. Maur said. He looked—not scared, not worried, more... awake. Dry-eyed and terrified. "Which way," he said, turning to Hanuman, "did your *natural* cousins say Miss Warington went?"

"South-southeast," Hanuman said. "Down that path there." He pointed at the dusty road in front of the house. "Heads toward Meerut, I think."

St. Maur leapt out the door. There was a moment of disturbance, little more. A cough, a wrenching twist of the body—then the dragon flapped his wings and gained altitude.

And Lalita turned to Hanuman and asked, "Did you lie to him?"

THE ADVANTAGES OF ASSIDUOUS PERSONAL HYGIENE; PERFIDY AND SUSPICION; A DISASTER IN THE MAKING

William was in the bath. To his carrier's and his sweeper's chagrin, they'd both been commanded, three times now, to bring the water for fresh baths and then to empty the water again as he took yet another bath. It had started as an impulse, a feeling that he would like to be really clean—needed to be clean. And then it had...

He didn't know what it had. By the third bath, he was starting to wonder why he had bathed. He'd thought...he'd thought so many things about himself that didn't seem to be true. He'd thought he was a normal man, with normal wishes and normal intent, and that had vanished when the scales fell from his eyes on seeing the dragon.

He scrubbed his arms with the stiff-bristled bath brush, trying to figure out what exactly he was trying to wash away. His skin was wrinkled and waterlogged, and there could be no dirt remaining, no sweat—nothing that anyone could use to perceive what he'd been doing and thus recoil in horror from him. So what was he scrubbing?

It all revolved around his not being the man he'd thought he was. After he'd realized his fatal attention to his own sex, he'd thought he was strong enough to withstand it and that nothing in his external world—nothing outside his own mind and heart—would ever need give away what went on in his head and how he truly felt. But that had vanished in a moment, with Bhishma's look at him, and then the touch of Bhishma's hands. . . .

He rested his head on the edge of the tub and a dry sob tore through his throat, followed by just as dry a chuckle. It wasn't Bhishma's touch he was trying to wash from his skin. It wasn't, as his father would doubtless say, his sin in having allowed such actions, such . . . pleasures. No, what William had been trying to wash away was . . . himself.

At the back of his mind—in that unthinking place where strange impulses hid—he'd been trying to scrub away who he was, in the vain hope that under it all would hide the William he'd always thought was there: the uninteresting, self-effacing young man who'd been a typical student at Eton, a quiet scholar and an unenthusiastic companion in rides and parties and hunts.

What a fool he'd been. He stood up and reached for his towel, which hung haphazardly from a nail on the wall. And at that moment he heard the door of his room burst open, and his sweeper yell, "No come in! Sahib bathing!"

And in response, a man's voice, speaking with authority in an angry, irate tone, and in Indian. Fast

Indian. *The tigers,* William thought, and then, not very coherently, *They've come. The mutiny has started.* He started out of his bath, holding the towel around his middle.

The sword. He must go for his sword.

He ran into his room, and stopped. Bhishma stood there, yelling at the carrier, his face distorted by rage, and something very much like tears shining in his eyes. *What is he telling the man? What is he saying?* Like a man caught in a nightmare, he thought that his actions were about to be exposed—that what he'd thought to keep so secret would now burst forth before all the world. To Bhishma, he shouted, "A moment. Please, give me a moment." To his carrier, he ordered, full voice, "Go away, please. Leave us alone."

The carrier fixed him with a foreboding, baleful gaze and said, "You sure, Sahib? He dangerous man."

Oh, you have no idea how dangerous. William nodded, briskly, as he tied his towel around his middle and reached for his cigarette case and lighter. This was going to necessitate cigarettes. To be honest, this necessitated some brandy, but William hadn't been, up until now, the sort of man who carried a flask of spirits. *Perhaps I should change that.* Just an hour ago, he'd been wondering how he could ever face Bhishma again. That time had arrived far sooner than he'd expected. If he'd envisioned anything at all, it was seeing Bhishma out on parade, blushing to meet him. But instead he was meeting Bhishma here, in his room, in a state of undress.

In Bhishma's defense, the man seemed to be in some kind of distress. He was wildly running his hands through his hair, which had once more slipped free of the bonds that kept it tidy normally. William had to re-press a sudden desire to smooth that hair, and tamped it down firmly, even as he struggled with his lighter, trying to light the cigarette that trembled between his fingers.

Bhishma stared at him and let out a long exhalation, as though he'd been holding his breath all this time and had just now exhaled. "How could you?" he asked, in a tone of deep disbelief.

William dropped his lighter and stared. "How could I what?" he asked, with a total want of politeness. Through his mind, in a mad cavalcade, ran preposterous ideas. *What does he mean how could I? How could I what? Take a bath? Smoke? No. It can't be that. Perhaps he heard of my visit to the general and thinks ... But how can he think that? And even if he thinks it, how could he dare do something like this?*

In no particular order, stories he'd heard from old Anglo-Indians at the dinner table, at his grandmother's house, came dancing into his mind. Sepoys who found their wives with other men and shot both the guilty couple and all the children of the union, just in case. Sepoys who killed a girl who was betrothed to them because she smiled at another man. Indians who went on a rampage because of some perceived slight, some perceived betrayal.

But I'm not married to him. I'm not betrothed to him. Oh, he said things—things lost in the frenzy that had left in William's mind no more than a vague trail of promises and heated compliments. He'd said he'd wanted William from the first time he'd seen him. And he'd said words about their hearts and souls meeting, which sounded like lines cribbed from Sanskrit poetry.

And I wasn't even standing by a yellow rosebush,
William though, madly. *And now he'll make a scene—
one of those scenes that I've heard about so often, one
of those scenes Grandmama's friends referred to as
an evidence of the hot blood of people in these climes.
And then . . . I'll have to go away. Everyone will know.
I'll have to resign my commission. I'll have to desert.
I'll have to—* The image of his parents receiving dire
news in a letter, that he had seen in the crystal came
back to him with the force of a gut-punch.

Bhishma was still staring at him, mouth half-open in
surprise. "What do you mean, what? You don't know?"

*And now he'll knife me for being admitted to the
general's room while he was shaving and in his robe.*
Incongruously, William wanted to chuckle at the
thought that the general's splendid, silken dressing
gown could have inspired lust in anyone, even in someone of his dubious self-control. He looked toward his
sword, still propped up against the bedside. Could he
retrieve it in time? A fine thing if he went down in din-
nertime lore in English country houses for having been
knifed to death by his Indian lover.

"What have you been doing these last four hours?"
Bhishma asked.

"Bathing."

"For four hours?"

"I . . . Look, this is not about my bathing habits,
is it?"

Slowly, consideringly, Bhishma shook his head.
"No. It's about the Gold Coats."

"What?"

Bhishma surged forward so suddenly that William,
who held a cigarette in one hand and a lighter in the

other, didn't even have a chance to make a mock-dive for his sword. Which was just as well, because Bhishma wasn't wielding a knife. He just extended his hand and grabbed William about the forearm and dragged him to the window, where he used his other hand to tear the drapes apart, flooding the room with the blinding noonday sun of Meerut. William, too stunned to protest, looked out. And dropped his cigarette and lighter again, this time onto the desk.

"What?" he said, unable to think of another word. Downstairs in the courtyard, natives were lined up, as though on parade, while fifty or so Gold Coats circulated among them, stopping at each man, presumably interrogating him. Another fifty or so Gold Coats had powersticks at the ready. Ready to do what? Shoot?

"What can I have to do with it?" he asked. "I didn't know . . ." How could the Gold Coats be here? But his mind was working. In four hours the general could have sent for the Gold Coats from Bombay by fast carpetship.

William didn't know for a fact that there were Gold Coats in Bombay, but he knew Gold Coats had been sent to Calcutta, and so it stood to reason they'd been sent to other major cities.

Bhishma let go of William's arm. He made a sound that could be laughter—or a cry—intercut by a hiccup. "The general sent for them. Whatever you told him, what he understood was that there were were-tigers amid the sepoys here. He sent for the Gold Coats, to interrogate the sepoys. And to cage them for transport to execution."

"But . . . I didn't tell him that!" William said, indignantly. He thought of the general's look. Was it possible that was what he understood? Very possible. After all, William had mentioned the uprising of 1857, when most of the deaths had been caused by were-sepoys.

"But this is the worst thing he could have done!" William said.

"Oh, you've noticed that, too?" Bhishma asked, and gave another hiccup-laugh. "Now he's turning the sepoys against the English. The people who should guard you. He's pushing them into deciding whether they're loyal to the English, or loyal to their people and their religion. How do you think most of them will topple when they can no longer stand in the middle?"

"Are there . . . Are there weres amid the sepoys? Were-tigers?"

Bhishma looked confused for a moment, then shrugged. "What do you think?"

What do I think? Bhishma's grandfather was a sepoy, in a contingent where most of them turned into elephants during the mutiny. But the were gene doesn't work like that. At least, it doesn't work like that in Europe. But Bhishma says that here it works differently. There's more magic. And also, probably, a lot more were-children. Of course.

"Are you a were?" he asked, the words ripping out of his mouth before he could stop them.

Bhishma gave him a level look, as though trying to evaluate his ability to withstand an answer, then said, "Yes."

"I see. A tiger?"

Hiccup-laugh. "No."

"Oh." And desperately, reaching for some form of

sanity, some way out of this, "What did you think I could do now? Why did you come to me?"

Bhishma took in breath slowly, hissing between clenched teeth. "I didn't think. I just thought... I wanted to know why you'd done it... I thought..." He shrugged. "I know you have no power. Only I thought you had—"

"You thought I had deliberately denounced were sepoys to the general? Deliberately denounced you?"

Bhishma's sweaty hand ran back through his hair. "Something like that."

"Shouldn't you be outside, answering questions? Are they going to—"

"I'll go," Bhishma said, almost humbly. "I'll go to the line. I'll say... I didn't hear."

A sudden surge of fear seized William. "They'll ask you more probing questions for coming in late. They'll push you more."

Bhishma sent him a strange look of disbelief and said, "Don't worry, Sahib. I won't say anything about... you."

William shook his head forcefully, suddenly furious Bhishma could think that was his concern. "No, I don't mean that. I mean they will push you harder. They will try to get you to change."

"Oh, that." He flashed a sudden, wild smile. "I won't do that here."

And he went away, leaving William holding his towel around his waist and thinking that things were, after all, far more complicated than he'd thought.

THE TIGERS' FURY;
ALL LOST; WINGS AT LAST

Sofie was surrounded by tigers. She'd heard the tigers following her for the last hundred steps, at least. She'd stooped briefly to find a rock and held it in her hand. She knew it was insufficient protection. In her mind, she rehearsed the spells she'd learned at Lady Lodkin's, including the Spell for Repelling Daring Interlopers and Putting Off Would-Be Assaulters. It was said of that spell, faithfully told to all the young girls in London, that once a woman armed with no more than a conventional amount of power had kept the Napoleonic troops at bay and kept herself unmolested until rescued.

When Sofie had heard that story, she had snorted derisively. But now she must, desperately, hope it was not a lie, after all. Because as the little road she'd been following crested a small rise, she found it barred by six—six!—well-grown, well-fed tigers.

Sofie looked up at the sky, still distressingly empty of wings, and thought to herself that this was the end. She turned around and started walking the other way. She could go back to the house where they'd lodged.

Perhaps Lalita and the others intended to do to her the same thing the tigers intended, but it was highly unlikely that Lalita—even if she and the men were noblemen of some sort—intended on rending her limb from limb.

But padding along the plowed fields waiting only the end of the drought came more sleek, powerful tigers, the twins of those who barred her path the other way.

She could throw her rock, but there were more than a dozen of them now, and she had only one rock. The ground underneath was remarkably nonrocky. She supposed she could throw handfuls of dirt at them, which was as likely to do any good as throwing rocks, because Sofie had never had any kind of aim. Yet, despite her lack of aim, she wished she could have a powerstick, or even a considerable amount of power to throw at them. She didn't. Oh, she had magic power. She was, after all, as the ruby attested to, descended in a direct line from Charlemagne. But her power was not extraordinary and, of course, she hadn't learned any extraordinary spells with it.

She'd have to use the only self-defense spell they'd taught her. She muttered under her breath, then held up her hand, concentrating the power and then flinging it. A satisfying blast of light erupted—golden light, shimmering in a done all around her. It should hold intruders at bay.

But in the front row, one of the tigers twisted and writhed and stood on two legs, showing himself to be a young man. A familiar young man. The same young man whose torture had brought about her break with St. Maur.

He bowed to her, a smile on his handsome face. There were newly healed scars on his body, Sofie realized, and she thought of the legends about how fast a were healed.

"Miss Warington," he said, smiling at her, showing teeth that were just a little too white, a little too long, a little too sharp. He stepped forward into the dome of golden light, making only the smallest of dismissive gestures. The light vanished, leaving Sofie unprotected.

"There are two choices here, Miss Warington," the tiger-prince said, with his irritating, superior smile. "You can come with us quietly, in which case we will take you on that flying rug." He pointed earnestly to a rug set by the side of the road. "Or alternately, we can drag you. In which case you'll still go on the flying rug, but probably unconscious."

It was at this point that Sofie threw the rock. She threw it without thinking, threw it with the certainty that it would be futile. But the prince was very close, and the rock flew true, hitting the side of his well-shaped head and causing a shower of blood to erupt. The tigers leapt.

And at that same moment, a claw descended and grabbed Sofie, lifting her up in the air. Half unbelieving, feeling as though she were dreaming or crazy, she looked up and saw St. Maur's wings spread above her, the fire-flicker wings. And she wanted to cry. But instead she screamed, "Burn, them, burn them," her voice bitter and commanding.

St. Maur made a sound that, for some reason, seemed to her very much like draconic laughter. And then he spun and rolled, with her still firmly held in his claw. And while she let a little scream be torn from her lips, he flamed—a great torrent of fire sweeping the road.

He didn't get all of the tigers. Most of them had already fled. But the prince, caught mid-change, erupted like a great human torch.

And then they were flying away. What seemed like bare moments later, St. Maur put her down by a flowing river, and shifted. "You must stop," he said, still coughing as he recovered from his shift, "letting yourself be surrounded by tigers. This could get old."

She gave him a jaundiced look, from the top of his handsome head and down his bare body. How little modesty she had these days! Seeing St. Maur naked had become so normal that she didn't even blush. Instead, she looked for cuts, for scars, for some mark of what he'd been doing since he left her. He didn't even look tired. "Did you sleep?" she asked, sharply.

He gave a chuckle. "Yes, Nanny Warington, I slept," he said, as he dove under a tree and made a pass that revealed his luggage. "And I ate. Was it worry about my healthy regimen that caused you to drug your companions and leave?"

"No," Sofie said. "I left because I didn't feel safe. They call Lalita Princess, you know, and I don't believe they are joking, so I started thinking that perhaps she had been placed with me so she could gain my confidence and get the ruby. And I thought I didn't have any guarantee that they, too, didn't mean to sacrifice me to heal the ruby and get the power it brings. So I drugged them and left."

"Because walking alone down the roads of India seemed safer?"

"I didn't think I would be walking alone," she confessed. "You see . . . I'm a conceited person. I thought you'd be watching over me."

He wasn't dressing, as she'd half expected. Instead, he'd got a cigarette out of his luggage, lit it and was smoking. She noted his hand trembled slightly, even as he made neat smoke rings in the still, warm air. "Some strange idea of guardian angels you have, Miss Warington. Your parson should have told you that while angels have wings, they rarely have scales."

But his trembling hands gave away how shaken he was. Despite his detached, ironical words, he was in fact moved, and had been scared. And he had come for her. "But you came and rescued me anyway," she said, perhaps a little smugly.

He looked at her. He didn't exactly smile, but the corners of his eyes crinkled, just a little, and he took a puff on his cigarette. "I came for you. And I'd have done it sooner, if my body hadn't wholly collapsed under the exertions of the last two days." He appraised her coolly. "How much do you know of what I've been doing?"

"I heard you talking to Lalita," he said.

"I thought you might have, you sly baggage," he said. And the way he pronounced *baggage* was quite the highest compliment she'd ever been paid. Sofie smiled at him, ignoring the supposed insult of the word.

"And what did you think? Of what you heard?" He looked suddenly anxious. "Were you very heartbroken over Blacklock?"

She shook her head. "No. It . . . I've been thinking I was a great fool. You have to understand, all of them said they loved me. All of them said . . ." She shook her head again. "He just seemed the most credible of them, the most sincere. And I was a fool. I should have realized no man would marry me like that, out of hand, with no dowry, no connections, nothing to my name."

"Many men would," St. Maur said, firmly. And then, in a lower voice, as though addressing his remark to some distant divinity who wouldn't listen anyway, "And many more long to." He took a puff of his cigarette. "But William Blacklock is not one of them. Or else, he would marry you because he thinks it's his duty, and I don't think you—"

"No, I . . . Would you think me very foolish if I told you only the deepest of love could ever entice me into the married state?" Sofie asked. "I've never told anyone but . . . I've long been so resolved."

"Who am I to judge? I don't expect I will ever be married. People like me shouldn't be, you know. Not fair to some poor woman who'd find herself incinerated on our wedding bed."

"Oh, I don't think you'd do that," she said. She remembered the dragon leaning over her—the great dragon head, the slightly spicy smell that was noticeable about St. Maur even in human form, and far more noticeable in dragon form. Like the smell some snakes give off, she thought. She thought of the look in the dragon's eye—the gentle, almost protective look. The same look she saw, now and then, in St. Maur's eye.

"Perhaps not," St. Maur said. "But then, neither should people like me have children and pass on the curse. Even if . . . even if it doesn't follow to my children, it could be worse. It could appear later on, on some quite unsuspecting descendant. As it did with me."

Sofie felt a sudden impulse to ask him how he thought his ancestors had coped with it. Doubtless, not all weres were killed. Most weren't even discovered. And doubtless, they reproduced, else how would new weres keep being born? But she suspected it was a losing battle. St. Maur had made up his mind. He would have no children of his blood. A form of suicide, she thought. And perhaps a reflection of how much rage he'd turned on himself.

"I'm surprised you let me burn the prince, you know?" St. Maur said, in a teasing tone. "I thought he was a great favorite of yours."

"Oh, don't be horrible," she said. "It was only seeing him tortured . . ." She thought of the fast-healing scars. "Will he come back again? Will he come back again, now, as he did from the torture?"

St. Maur shook his head. "No. That's one of the ways to kill us. The best, of course, is to remove our heads. But the favored means of eliminating weres—back before blades were trustworthy enough to do the deed in a timely manner, and back before powersticks were developed to sap our strength long enough to allow the execution to take place—was to tie us as strongly as possible, in such a way that we would remain bound in both forms, and then pile a great deal of wood all around us, and set fire to it. If we are burned past a certain point, we cannot heal."

Sofie shivered. "You speak of it so calmly."

"It happened to people long ago, in Europe. Mostly in the time before Charlemagne. You can see it, still, you know, in history books—charming woodcuts of weres being burned."

When he got like this, it was as though he'd retreated behind a barrier of ice. Or perhaps it was an odd sort of wishful thinking, a reflection of that terrible rage at himself that she'd glimpsed. As though he hated himself for being a were.

"What are we doing now?" she asked. "You are not dressing?"

"As you see," he said. "I am not dressing. My original idea was to change and take you back to Lalita and her friends, though they might be a little upset with you—"

"No. I can't trust them. They are . . . royalty. I'm not sure how, but they are royalty."

"Were royalty," St. Maur said. "Monkeys."

"Monkeys?" she asked, shocked, her eyebrows rising. And in the next moment, she grinned. "How appropriate."

"Yes, I thought so, too. And, Miss Warington, I don't think they have any intention of sacrificing you."

"Perhaps not, but I don't feel safe with them. I decided, before I ran away, that you were the only person I feel truly safe with."

She saw the softening in his eye, before surprise replaced it. "You did? Why?"

"Because you had the opportunity to do what you would with me, when we were on the road alone, but you did not."

"I didn't know you had the ruby with you."

"I didn't have the ruby with me. Hanuman did. But you didn't even look for the ruby. That was not your priority."

He raised his eyebrows and looked at her, contemplatively. "Let's grant, then," he said, "that I am your great white knight, *sans peur et sans reproche*. Let us grant that my intentions are pure and all my thoughts are bent on good deeds. What do you think I can do for you?"

"For me?" she said, puzzled. "Nothing. I decided that the best thing we could do with the ruby . . ." She thought about it. "Well, you said that the ruby is not really mine. You said it belongs in the most ancient temple in mankind."

"That is one way to look at it," St. Maur said. "Though forgive me if I say I expected some possessiveness on your part toward a jewel that's been in your family for so long."

"No," she said. "The only thing the ruby was good for was my dowry. And I don't think I'll marry."

"I don't think you'll be able to avoid marrying."

"What do you mean?" she asked, her cheeks heating.

"Helen of Troy could not live a quiet life," he said, throwing his cigarette butt down and stepping on it. "And I don't think you can be an old maid."

"What great foolishness," she said, derisively. "Mind you, they didn't teach us the true classics in school. Lalita found some other copies of our books, in the library, and she said that the ones they taught us from had all the naughty parts pulled out. But all the same, I expect that Helen of Troy was really not so very pretty. She was just no better than she should be."

He laughed. "Very refreshing, Miss Warington. Then I will grant you that you don't intend to marry, and that you want to give me the ruby. What should we do with it?"

"Well, fly away from all these tigers and . . . things."

"Yes. And?"

"And use that ruby to find the other ruby. And then, you see, you can go. Because even if they find me, they won't find the ruby on me."

"Ah, I can go. And you?"

"I will find some mission and learn to make myself useful."

"In the salvation of souls?" he asked. She felt as though he was mocking her, but she saw nothing funny at all in her decision.

"If need be," she said, stoically.

ELEPHANTS ON PARADE GROUNDS; MAYHEM AND LOSS

He knew in his heart what the sound was, before his mind understood it. There were screams and the sound of ripping wood and falling masonry, and before William fully had time to think or make a decision, he was running, his feet carrying him toward the place of the disturbance.

He had been walking to the general's house slowly, trying to think of a way to tell him that the Gold Coats should concentrate less on weres in the ranks and more on the tigers outside the garrison. And he could imagine the general's counterargument—that one must be sure of those at one's back before facing the enemy. And William had not yet come up with a good response for that when he heard the sound.

Suddenly he was running to the disturbance, at the same time that others were, and his first thought was that elephants were not supposed to do this. Not elephants. He'd seen elephants in India. A lot of elephants. The army didn't use them, but Indian peasants did. The patient creatures were beasts of burden and transport, agricultural machinery and building aids. What they were not was war machines. Not until this moment.

He ran into the middle of the crowd, his brain beating a steady *Let it not be Bhishma who's changed shapes!* And then, suddenly, the crowd stopped, and started pushing backwards. William alone withstood the movement, and the crowd went around him, screaming. And what they were running from was... magnificent.

Two young male elephants were rampaging, with swaying trunks throwing people out of their way, stomping them to a bloody pulp on the parade ground. William thought of Polybius quoting Scipio, and the words escaped his lips unbidden: "The day shall be when holy Troy shall fall. And Priam, lord of spears, and Priam's folk."

And suddenly he realized that an elephant was right in front of him, raising its foot, and William rolled aside, and the elephant's foot came down where he used to be, and William ran. He turned just in time to see the Royal Were-Hunters shoot at the elephants, with multiple discharges of their weapons.

They weren't causing destruction on purpose, he thought, frantically. *They were scared.* Followed by an even more frantic, *Let neither of them be Bhishma!*

He pressed forward in the crowd, just in time to see the elephants topple. Their fall shook the ground. Their bodies writhed and twisted, and their shapes changed into two sepoys he remembered seeing, though he couldn't think of their names. They both looked very young and very scared, and he stared at them, feeling immense relief that neither of them was

Bhishma. He bit his lower lip to keep himself from screaming out. He wasn't sure what he would scream out. He wasn't sure what he should do or what they should do. Because on one hand, the sepoys hadn't gone mad on purpose. And on the other hand... On the other hand, they had killed people.

The Gold Coats were moving the two young sepoys, lifting them and binding them. William thought they would take them over to trial or court-martial. But, beside him, he heard an English officer say, "They're going to build the pyres. To burn them."

"They are?" William asked, unable to stop himself. "Burning them?"

The man looked at him, as though William had taken leave of his senses. "Of course. It's either that or behead them."

"But... They didn't trample anyone on purpose. They seemed loyal before. I never heard ill of them. I've... I've read that change is involuntary. And perhaps they were just scared?"

The other man continued to stare at William, with complete shock. "But... my dear fellow, don't you see? It's not what they did or didn't do. They are dangerous weres, and they can't be trusted. I know we can't kill every were in India, not with the way their culture protects them, but these are in the service of Her Majesty, and as such are on English soil. Them, we can burn."

STRANGE EVENTS AND STRANGE REASONS; WHERE LALITA ASKS FOR HANUMAN'S HELP

Lalita insisted they clean the house before they left. She felt strange doing it, and could imagine from Hanuman's strange look and Maidan's sudden rolling of eyes that this was not, in fact, what they would have done, if given a choice. But she had spent too much time in England. Or perhaps too much time among nonweres. She knew that it wasn't a natural thing to her kind, who had always taken what they could when they could from the edges of non-were society.

She didn't know whether to be pleased or shocked that Hanuman did not complain about cleaning up. He'd been behaving altogether oddly, as had Maidan. She'd never fully understood what Maidan meant to do or why he'd been sent. And she didn't understand his concession to Hanuman. And, worst of all, she couldn't be sure that Sofie and St. Maur hadn't been right in their suspicions of the monkeys' intentions. Had Maidan and Hanuman been sent by her uncle with the intent of capturing Sofie and sacrificing her to the ruby?

And at the bottom of it all was discomfiture that Sofie—Sofie, who had been as close to her as a sister, despite everything—hadn't come to her and told her of her doubts, had instead chosen to drug her along with the two men.

Her head was slow and aching, and she felt queasy and confused as if hungover, as she dressed herself for the day and wondered what they should do next. It finally occurred to her, as she drank yet another cup of tea, that where they went and what they did today depended, most of all, on what Hanuman and Maidan intended, and whether they wanted to sacrifice Sofie or not. Not that Lalita had any intention of allowing them to kill her friend. She wasn't even angry at Sofie—more put off and hurt.

But she needed to know what Hanuman and Maidan intended. Without that, she couldn't make a decision. She went in search of Hanuman, whom she found making Sofie's bed, with an intent expression on his face—and an utter lack of ability. He'd pull the sheet on one side and attempt to stuff the edges under, only to have to go to the other side and redo the part that had come loose. She didn't know whether it was because he, too, was suffering a hangover from the narcotic, or whether he was truly that inept, but the combination of his clumsiness and the long-suffering look on his face as he trudged around the bed again to put it in order made her cover her mouth with her hand—which was insufficient to stifle the giggle that rang forth like the pealing of a bell.

He noticed her for the first time, and looked up, blushing. "Princess," he said.

She grinned at him, disarmed by both his courtesy

and his ineptitude. Stepping into the room, she lifted a corner of the mattress, showed him how to fold the edge and then let the corner rest again, before going to the other side of the bed and repeating her actions. He looked as though he'd just been enlightened. "Ah. So there is a science to this!"

"Yes," she said, and observed while he did the remaining two corners aptly enough. "Why are you changing the bed?"

"Your friend slept in it," he said, and waved toward the pile of sheets in a corner of the room. "You said we were to make the house look untouched. I thought that one look at the bed and they'd realize it wasn't, so..."

"Won't they notice the pile of used sheets?"

He flashed her a wide grin. "I'll put it in the laundry when I'm done. Princess, trust me, no one in an English household will notice if there is an extra set of used sheets in the laundry. And none of the servants will judge it worthy of informing their masters."

A sudden enlightenment dawned on Lalita. "You were a servant once, in an English household."

He laughed, a sudden cackle. "My mother was," he said. "My father was an Englishman."

She looked at him, puzzled, taking in the straight, glossy black hair, the black eyes, the bronze skin. She'd taken him for an Indian of her caste, meaning that they were naturally lighter than most of the lower castes in India. But now she could see in the rise of his nose, the shape of his chin, something English, perhaps.

He was looking at her, his expression unreadable. She wondered if there was anger in it, or perhaps sadness. But no; there seemed to be only expectancy. He was waiting for her to do something, say something.

She said the first thing that came to her wandering mind. "You're a sport."

He bowed slightly, his features still tense. "I'm a throwback, at any rate. My mother was not a shifter. If her ancestors were, she did not know it." An impish smile broke through the gravity. "Then again, you know what men in our tribe are. Not exactly the most . . ."

"Careful in their love affairs?" Lalita asked, with a smile. "No." And then, because he still seemed to be waiting for her to say something. "How did you end up at court?"

"At twelve, my mother took me to a monkey of her acquaintance, and he took me to King Buhdev, who, for reasons of his own, took a shine to me. He said I was smart and accomplished and just what the monkey-people needed." He frowned slightly and said, in the tone of a school-child trying to repeat complete lessons, "I should say that, at the time, his reasons were a mystery, but not so later on. He taught me to use monkey magic, and the extent of my powers and abilities. And when I was fifteen, he sent me out on the first of my missions."

"Missions?"

"Your uncle has . . . things he wants done, such as delegations to other were tribes—things he could not entrust publicly to one of his courtiers."

"So you are his secret operative?" Lalita asked.

Again another small bow. "Something like that. I have traveled most of the globe, including China and Europe. I've seen something of the world, and learned a lot of languages. And now your uncle has called me home."

"Ah."

"You've probably guessed what his plans are?"

"Have I?"

He bowed to her. "You do know you are your uncle's heir, do you not?"

"No," Lalita said, in shock. "My uncle has sons. Maidan—"

Hanuman was shaking his head. "Your cousin Maidan has no more hope of getting the throne than I do. In fact, our hopes are exactly alike. They both depend on your choosing one of us as a husband."

Lalita felt faint. To her lips, unbidden, came a protest; "One of you two?" she asked. "And no other?"

Hanuman laughed—a show of spirit more like the monkey-man she'd first met and unlike the very quiet and subdued monkey of today. "Oh, I'm sure others, if you can find them and if they are monkey-men, Princess." Then his face sobered again. "But I will confess that your uncle, our king, thought you should choose from the two of us. Your cousin because he is of the royal family and of royal blood. By any understanding, his credentials are impeccable and he will be accepted by all the court."

"And yourself?" Lalita asked.

"Myself, because I'm not any of those things. Your uncle thinks the line has perhaps had...too many cousin marriages and not enough outside blood. He likes my abilities, and the way I think, which he's kind enough to term *unconventional*. And he thinks I would be a good...." He looked away from her. "Father of kings."

She felt her cheeks heat and said, to change subject as much as because she wished to know, "None of which tells me why my uncle would make me his heir, nor what all of it means."

"It is not a very common situation in the kingdom. You see, there are far more shifter men than shifter women. Women can and do carry the gene, but are rarely weres themselves. So normally the crown passes from father to the first son who is born with the power to shift forms."

She bobbled her head in acknowledgment. She knew all this.

"But when a were-woman is born anywhere in the royal family, that means that all her sons will be of exceptional ability, and all of them will be weres. So the woman is always the heir in those cases." He looked as if he was calculating mentally. "It's happened . . . five times in the recorded history of our people. And all their sons were those that history does not forget."

"Oh," Lalita said. "So my uncle sent you and Maidan . . ."

"Well, your uncle sent me first," he said, and grinned. "But then Maidan persuaded him to give him a chance also. And Maidan is his firstborn and favorite son."

"Then he was not in the temple at Benares," she said, and felt a considerable relief at the idea that her cousin had not been among those many monkeys scrabbling at her clothing.

"No," Hanuman said.

"Tell me, Hanuman, and tell me true, did my uncle also order you to secure my friend Miss Warington so that she could be sacrificed to heal the ruby?"

The answer was immediate. "No. I will not deny that we had an interest in acquiring the ruby. But your uncle never considered blood magics as a way of cleansing it, Princess!" His voice reproached her for even thinking it. "You know that is not the way of our people."

"Then what did you intend to do with the ruby?"

"Even flawed and broken as it is," Hanuman said, "your uncle believed it would show the direction of the other ruby. I'm not... perhaps..." he added, with a thoughtful look, "the greatest magician who ever lived. But I am undeniably one of the best witch-sniffers. Your uncle thought me capable of following the link of magic between the rubies even without Soul of Fire pointing at the other one. And so I would be. And then, in possession of the other ruby, the one that's whole..." He shrugged, as if to say it didn't matter.

"And have you now wholly given up any hope of getting the ruby?" Lalita asked.

He looked surprised. "Of course not."

"I see," she said. "You simply do not intend to do battle with the dragon for it?"

"No need to do battle with the dragon, Princess. In my experience, monkeys are best at pinching what's unguarded, and obtaining what's forgotten. The dragon won't always be vigilant, and I thought..."

It was her turn to laugh, remembering his performance as sweeper in the Waringtons' household, and the way he'd stolen the ruby from under their eyes. She wondered, for just a moment, if Hanuman was ever capable of gravity. If she married him, would he be serious in lovemaking? Or was everything a game with him?

"But I think," Hanuman said, suddenly pensive, as if he'd heard her thought, "the dragon might be truthful about the rubies. He says that he gave Heart of Light to his friend. And having had Heart of Light in his reach, why would he want Soul of Fire? Unless he was telling the truth?"

He gave a theatrical sigh. "I wonder if your uncle knew that. And if this was a test for me as well, to see how sharp I am. I think the ruby might be too dangerous a way to obtain freedom for our people. If your friend were not still in danger, I'd abandon the game now."

She pulled her mind forcibly away from some foolish questions and asked, "You think the dragon has found her?"

"If I read his look right, I think that particular dragon would move Earth and sky to find her," Hanuman said. "And not for the ruby, either."

"What would you know of his look?"

"I have seen it in my mirror."

She choked a little, but forged on. "So, we are to follow the dragon."

"If you say we are. You are in charge here."

"I see," Lalita said. "This is a test for me as well, is it? And if I fail, then my uncle will find a way to leave succession to Maidan or one of his other sons?"

"I did not say that."

"I am not stupid."

"No, Princess, you are not that."

"However, I do not know what to do. I came to you for help."

He looked so disappointed, she felt forced to add, "Oh, not with deciding what to do next. Hanuman, what happened to the other dragon?"

Hanuman blinked at her in surprise. "The other dragon?"

"Back in Calcutta, you said you smelled two dragons. Yet we found only one. And I started thinking..."

"I haven't smelled the other one since we...met this dragon. Do you think—do you think they travel together?"

"I don't know," Lalita said. "But I don't like it."

"And what do you wish me to do, Princess? I will warrant you that if there are two dragons with the ruby, rather than one, it will make it more difficult to obtain. But I do not believe you'd be less protective of your friend."

"No," Lalita said. "But all the same, I'd like to know what we're up against. You see, it is so unlike Sofie to drug us and leave."

"She thought we intended to sacrifice her to cleanse the ruby," Hanuman said. "The tigers have her scared, and Englishmen know next to nothing about weres. She would judge on the only weres she knows."

"Still, why would she not trust me? We've been friends since we were little."

"How can I solve that for you, Princess?"

"Did the other dragon come with the Englishman?"

"No. There is only one scent of dragon in the house, and that very faint, and coming from the kitchen, where the Englishman was. But there is another scent here. I am trying to identify it..."

His nose twitched again. It seemed odd to Lalita that a witch-sniffer who could smell a dragon all the way across the house, from the kitchen, was hesitating over this other scent, so close to him.

At last, Hanuman looked up. "Princess, your friend is spelled. I think—from the stink of it—the spell was put on by the tigers."

"Oh, I know that," Lalita said. "That is why she sleepwalked. Even in London. But...are you sure that the tether was put on her by the tigers? How would they do it?"

"How is easy," Hanuman said. "They would have cast about for the stone, and then their soothsayers would tell them the stone's redeemer was already born. It wouldn't tell them she was a child. From the strength of this, the way it entwines with her magic itself, I think it's been there since shortly after she was born."

I think they've been on to her existence...magically...since she was born. They just didn't know what age she was. Or that she'd been sent to England. They expected her to come to them....I think that explains her blind wandering."

"And why she went so very far. Of course she couldn't find members of the Kingdom of the Tigers in England, but—"

"But in her sleep she tried to," Hanuman said.

Lalita closed her eyes, letting the full implications of all of this sank in.

THE CAVE ABOVE
THE WORLD; THE
INADEQUACY OF DESIRE

"I could take you somewhere," Peter said, aware of speaking more from his heart than from his mind. "Somewhere where you could be safe."

Sofie—he couldn't actually think of her as Miss Warington, not while she was there with him, in this little rocky cave on the face of a sheer cliff—looked at him speculatively. She looked very much as though she were mentally fitting him for the insane asylum. There was that edge of disbelief to her gaze, as though she was afraid of what he might say next. She cleared her throat, and despite the soft curves of her face and body, managed to look thoroughly schoolmarmish as she said, "My dear St. Maur, you can't possibly be serious."

"Indeed, I am very serious," he said. "I could take you to Paris. Or London. Or somewhere away from all this."

"And do you think all this wouldn't follow me? The tigers and the monkey and doubtless another dozen or so powers all wanting the ruby and me? Please, milord, do not treat me as though I were a child."

"No," he said. "Not a child." He felt lost. He wanted, more than anything, to make her happy, to make her safe. And he did not know how to go about it. "I will do what I can. Anything I can."

Sofie reached into her pocket and pulled out the ruby, which still flickered with red light in irregular bursts. "Here, milord, take it. The fate of the world depends on it. My fate is but a small thing."

He took it, reverently. He'd seen Heart of Light in its proper setting, in the eye of the oldest avatar of mankind. Were it not for having seen it—not for having heard the voice of the goddess in his head—he would never have believed that he was worthy of touching it.

But the strange thing was that as he touched it, nothing answered him. It was all . . . dead and silent. There was no echo, no voice from it. The flames flickered within the ruby, and magic bursts erupted from it, but there was no mind, no intelligence left.

It was, Peter thought, much like a very old person's mind when the animating principle has fled. Memories remain and impulses, but the brain no longer remembers the dreams and aspirations that once animated it. He reached for the ruby with all the magic he had.

His answer was a babble of voices, in all the languages of mankind. He thought of Nigel's last letter, telling him that he should use Soul of Fire to find Heart of Light and Nigel himself, since Nigel was traveling the world, trying to escape *some very suspicious characters on my trail.*

Peter sat down, heavily, on the moss-carpeted cave floor. "It is no use," he said, dispiritedly. "The ruby is broken beyond repair." He knew as he said it that this wasn't true. There was a way to heal the ruby. Her blood. Her sacrifice. It wasn't a price he was willing to pay. Let the world be damned. Let the world continue existing in its present disharmony. Let the universes continue to fracture till none of them contained any magic at all. But let Sofie live.

Perhaps a better man—a real man, and therefore surely better—than him would at some future time find the courage he lacked to do the unspeakable.

She blinked at him in confusion. He realized, with a longing that almost wrung a groan from him, that he would give a king's ransom to be able to kiss those eyelids fringed by long black lashes. He would gladly trade the rest of his days for the opportunity to cup her soft cheek in his hand. He would go naked and hungry and beg—like those poor creatures that beg on the streets of India—to just once follow the curve of her chin as it flowed into her soft neck, and to kiss the hollow of her throat where it met the lace of her collar.

"But . . . you said you were sent to find the jewel," Sofie said, those lashes fluttering, her eyes showing a hint of tears. "You said you were sent by the oldest avatar of mankind to reclaim the ruby and take it back to her. How can you tell me it's dead now?"

"Perhaps the avatar doesn't know," he said, looking away from her. "It is possible. It is . . . very old, you know, and . . . it is not in touch with the ruby. Hasn't been for centuries now. Perhaps it's like when a person's limb is amputated. I used to hear . . . My father had a friend who was a war veteran. And he told us that he could still feel the leg that had been amputated. He said that the worst thing was when the weather was humid and his long-missing knee hurt him horribly, and there was nothing he could do. Perhaps . . ." he said, as his voice lost force. "Perhaps it is thus with the avatar as well."

"No," Sofie said. Her features were animated in a sort of rage. "No. It cannot be. I refuse to believe . . . I refuse to think that something that old, with that much power, could not or would not know what to do. You don't know how to activate it? You never asked? You don't know of any method that doesn't involve . . . my death?" Her voice grew increasingly more agitated. "How like a man not to ask something like that! Any woman on being told to recover a magically raped ruby would have asked. They would have asked how to waken it. And if the answer was that they had to kill an innocent maiden, they would . . . any woman would resist it. Find another way. But you thought you knew it all. All gentlemen think they know it all."

Like that, she turned her back on him and walked to the mouth of the cave. He jumped after her, to ensure she did not jump from the mouth of the cave. But she turned slightly, then rested her forehead on the stone. She stayed like that—and Peter, behind her, with hand stretched to her shoulder, didn't know what to do. She was very angry at him. And some part of him thought she was right to be mad. He had made rather a muddle of it all.

And then her shoulders shook, and a sob escaped her, dry and desperate.

Her pain resounded through him, tearing at his heart and soul. Without thinking, he pulled her to him.

Her face was wet with tears as she raised a desperate gaze. "I'm sorry," she said. "I didn't mean any of those horrible things. It's just—"

"Shh," he said. She was warm and real in his arms. He felt whole and started. He'd never thought of himself as broken before. It was as though when his father had sent him away from home and land, he'd fallen down a hole. Fallen into a world of irreality, where he had only himself to look after, and only he mattered. It wasn't just that no man should live alone, he thought. It was that having no one that mattered but oneself, no life to preserve but one's own, made a man less than a man—just a creature of the fields, seeking a safe burrow to while away its existence. "Shh," he said, holding her close, feeling her heartbeat against his own. He'd forgotten he was naked. He'd forgotten everything. His lips, with a mind of their own, kissed her forehead, her eyes, her cheeks, tasting the salt of her tears like an exquisite liquor. She was so warm, her skin so soft, her breath intoxicating, and the little gasps she gave at his touch were a sound that he couldn't help but crave once he heard it. He could write a poem about the curve of her ear and the delicate feel of her neck, where her hair tapered off into a few very soft, short locks. He looked at her face, and their gazes met, and then their lips. Her mouth opened to invite his tongue. She tasted, somehow, of apples and honey and the flavors of forgotten spring back in Summercourt.

St. Maur had gone insane, and he didn't care. But color rose to her cheeks in a flood and her hands went to his shoulders and she pushed him ever so slightly away. "Milord," she said, still against his lips. "Milord."

With an effort, Peter controlled himself, pulled himself away. What a fool he was! How could he have let himself get so carried away? Good thing one of them had retained their sanity. "I'm heartily sorry," he said. "I don't know what came over me."

"Oh, never mind that," Sofie said. She had somehow got turned in their embrace, and she was facing the mouth of the cave, and pointing at the clear skies beyond.

On the far horizon, half a dozen flying rugs approached.

"Are those the tigers?" Sofie asked.

"They might be," he said. "We can't risk it." He pushed the ruby into her pocket. And then he started to change into a dragon again.

A FOOL'S ERRAND; ACROSS CULTURES AND TIME

William stopped. He'd come on a fool's errand. If he were caught, he could very easily be dishonored, turned out of the army, perhaps killed. He had heard of Gold Coats killing those that tried to free or assist imprisoned weres.

And William didn't want to do it. All his life, he'd trusted the histories and those who knew better. He'd heard how dangerous weres were. He'd *seen* how dangerous weres were. Those rampaging sepoy-elephants had killed . . . fifteen people. But as William had lain on his bed, what haunted him was the fact that the sepoys hadn't tried to follow him when he'd rolled away. The elephants hadn't set out to kill him.

He didn't know what it was like to be a were, but he had seen the native sepoys being interrogated by the Gold Coats. He'd seen their expressions as they stood under the guns, trying to answer questions that he was sure felt very strange to them.

William couldn't know—couldn't even guess—at the processes that would cause someone to change shape into an animal. But he'd seen the shock and despair in those young men's eyes when they had shifted back to human. And so they would be killed. Killed for the sin of being what they had been born.

And William knew only too well how much the inner man could not be denied by the outer one. And while he could understand—even accept—that the sepoys could be dangerous, he very much doubted they would have changed were it not for the unusual pressure that had been brought to bear. What had been done to them was the equivalent of tormenting a dog into attacking, then shooting him because he had attacked.

William had turned in his bed, tangling himself in his sheets, unable to sleep. He couldn't help feeling they were committing a great injustice in killing these young men. And it was the sort of injustice that could lead to more death.

There was a new tension in the camp; William had felt it. There were looks from the sepoys and looks from all the Indian servants. There was a feeling of anger, of resentment. A feeling of . . . of something impending, like the feeling in the air before a thunderstorm.

Well, William was not going to allow it. And so he had armed himself with the necessary spells, and he'd come through the sleeping camp. There weren't many people on guard at the barracks where the young men were confined. Only two Gold Coats, their resplendent livery shining by the light of the moon as they talked together. William had approached them from the side of the camp, wearing a dark cloak, which hid his clothes. Knit with the shadow of the building, he was all but invisible.

He wondered if the guards would spot his trick, then shook his head. No. They were expecting—if anything—a native attack. Perhaps a native magical attack. But they wouldn't expect British magics, much less British schoolboy magics, of the type used to play pranks on masters and prefects throughout the breadth of the isles.

William closed his eyes and thought a prayer. Let him succeed in this. Let him free these men. He knew that he was damned, but he couldn't allow injustice to go forward.

Removing a vial from within his sleeve, he hoped he hadn't lost his knack of preparing this spell—the same spell he'd used as a young man when he wanted to leave the dorm after lights out, or when he simply didn't want to be in a class and wanted his masters to think he was still there.

He pointed the vial at the corner of the barracks opposite the men, and uncorked it. He felt the force he'd imprisoned there earlier escape, and he gave it shape with his mind. In the corner appeared three swarthy, intimidating-looking natives—the sort of natives that every Gold Coat newly arrived in the region would fear.

"Hey," one of the guards shouted, as he saw them. "Hey."

The natives—really just an air elemental given shape by his wishes and thoughts—continued attempting to force their way through a boarded-up window. One of the guards fired, but the natives seemed not to notice.

"They're protected by some spell," one of the guards said. His comrade nodded. And just as William had expected, they rushed toward the elemental, leaving the barracks door unguarded.

William threw a spell of unlocking at it and then ran, full tilt, to the door.

As he reached it, he became aware of someone else coming in with him, at the same time, shoulder to shoulder.

Bhishma! he thought, as he closed the door and looked toward the native, who smiled at him and put his finger to his lips. Turning, he did something to the door—closing it, William could tell, in a way that no one would be able to perceive it had ever been unlocked. It would look and feel locked, and no trace of the spell would be found.

William, meanwhile, turned toward the young men, who were just wakening in their cages. They looked at William in fear, but he put his finger to his lips, commanding them to silence, then used the unlocking spell on the cages. Both cages were locked tight with British magic, so no one on the inside could open them, and especially no Indian magic could touch them. They were, however, vulnerable to being opened from the outside. By an Englishman.

Leaving the cages unlocked, William turned toward the windows, which were barred on the outside and also spelled to prevent their being opened by magic. As he expected, though, they were not secured from the inside—and again, they didn't bar against English magic. After all, why should an Englishman let the sepoys go free?

William smiled without mirth. He exerted his magical force on the windows, forcing the one that was on the other side of the building from where the guards were out, then down, smoothly and without noise. There was only one very small space between the building and the wall. Bhishma was already helping the young men out through the window, and William went after them, out into the warm night air.

He threw a spell of confusion over the whole thing, though it wouldn't last long once the Gold Coats started probing it. It was a schoolboy's spell, designed to hide the origin and intent of the magical work done. It would never resist expert forensics.

But that didn't matter. He'd done what he thought he should do. When the authorities discovered his involvement and came for him, he would go quietly.

William had started along the narrow dark passage between the barracks and the wall of the encampment, when a hand shot out of the shadows and held his arm. "Wait," a voice said, almost soundlessly.

William turned. In the shadows, he could just barely make out Bhishma's face.

"Why?" Bhishma asked, still in that almost soundless whisper.

"I . . . couldn't allow the injustice."

The hand on his arm let go. "Thank you," Bhishma said. And then he was gone.

TOWERS OF SILENCE;
TWO BAD CHOICES

"Look. There," *Sofie said, sinking her hands into the* dragon's neck ruffle, trying to get his attention. For hours they'd been flying—first in one direction, then the other—trying to evade the rugs.

Now there was only one in pursuit, and as it got too close, St. Maur turned and burned it. Rug and rider went up in flames.

Sofie knew, because it had happened before, that another rug would appear to take up the chase. She'd come to the conclusion that they were tracing them through witch-sniffers. She didn't know how they were managing to call up rugs, but it didn't matter. They'd done it again and again for hours.

They'd been flying all day. She could feel the tiredness in the great body beneath her, the weariness with which the great big wings lifted and flapped. He couldn't fly much longer—certainly not without either food or sleep. She must find them shelter. She saw the towers rising ahead of her.

From the towers came a feeling—something she couldn't quite identify, except for saying she'd felt it before, around the temples in Benares. It was the feeling of divine power. It would be enough to mask them from any witch-sniffer. For a while, at least.

She pointed at the towers and the dragon went toward them. The towers stood on a hill rising almost straight up from the sea, and she was surprised to see the sea—surprised they'd got so close to it, somehow. How long had St. Maur been flying? They must stop somewhere as soon as possible.

The area around the towers was built into a beautiful garden and shaded by tropical trees. The roads leading up to the area were well kept. Perhaps here she and St. Maur could evade ambush for a while.

The towers were twenty-five feet or so in height and ninety feet in diameter, and the vultures that flew over them in circles squawked in fear and winged away as St. Maur flew near.

"The tower," she yelled, indicating that he should land. But instead he moved away from it, flying down to its base instead. She started to open her mouth to reproach him, but he shifted, and in the shape of a very pale man, collapsed to the ground, dropping their bags.

"The tower," she said, almost in a whisper. "You were supposed to fly up to the tower."

He shook his head. He was taking long, gasping breaths. "No. These are the towers of the Parsees. The Towers of Silence. They follow the dictates of Zoroaster, who thought not only fire but also earth and water, too, were too sacred to be polluted with dead bodies. They expose the corpses atop the towers, to the vultures."

"Oh," Sofie said, thinking she understood. "You thought it best not to defile the rites of another religion?"

He flashed teeth at her, in something far less than a smile. "No. I just can't trust myself right now. Not as hungry as I am."

"Oh," she said again, not knowing what else to say. Hard to speak to this urbane man and know that part of him, deep inside, was the beast, and that the beast was seeking to get out. Hard to understand. She had spent all this time with him, and she was not sure where the division lay, nor how much control St. Maur had over the dragon.

He rose, tottering on his feet. "I must eat," he said.

She looked in horror from him to what looked like a great city nearby. "Here?"

Another flash of teeth, not quite a smile. "I hear vulture is quite tasty," he said, and she felt her face set in horror. Then he grinned more genuinely. "Fish. There are fish in the sea. Dragons are always at least half aquatic. You sit here, in the shadow of the divine power. I'll go fish."

Instead, she followed him to the edge of the cliff and looking out of the sea. The sun had set, and the dragon's wings were quite visible—shining with their own fire—as he flew and dipped over the sea. There were boats of native fishermen, with torches, but no one seemed to take notice of the dragon.

He dipped into the sea now and then, and she presumed he caught something for his trouble, but when she saw him dip toward one of the fishermen's boats, she stood up in alarm. Only, St. Maur didn't touch the fisherman. He only dipped momentarily, then flew toward her. He changed as he tumbled onto the cliff, so he landed as a man, holding something in his hand.

As he extended the something toward her, she saw

it was a fish, between two slices of bread. A smoked fish, she determined, as she accepted it. "Why, milord," she said, "how clever of you. Getting fish already smoked."

"Isn't it?" he asked. He sat holding his knees.

"Are we going to sleep here?" Sofie asked. "In the shadow of the divine influence from the towers?"

He sighed. "I don't know. I don't think it's enough to shelter us for long. They will find us."

"But then . . ."

"I don't know, Miss Warington. I don't know what to do."

Sitting on the ground near towers used to dispose of the dead, eating a smoked fish and thin, circular bread while a completely naked man sat beside her, Sofie felt suddenly very confident. Her whole life, people had decided things for her and told her what to do. She'd rebelled against marrying the repulsive raj, but since then she'd done nothing but follow St. Maur's lead and allow him to protect her. Now it was time for her to think.

There were only two ways to stop her from being a target for the tigers. One, there was a chance they could wake the ruby with the blood sacrifice, but the last thing that Sofie wanted was to give power to creatures who would use blood sacrifice to obtain it.

And two . . . She looked slyly at St. Maur, out the corner of her eye. "You could deflower me," she said.

He made a sound between a choke and a splutter and turned to look at her. "I beg your pardon?"

"Wait, please, listen. If I . . . then the tigers wouldn't be able to perform their ghastly sacrifice, would they?"

"You must . . . truly, you must pardon me." His face

was aflame. "I don't think I could. Not . . . like that. If the world were different, if we were different, I could maybe be the right man for you. I'm as well born as you could hope for, and I'm not, I hope, of a boorish frame of mind, nor wholly terrible to look at. But what I am and what I do . . . What happens to me when I change shape is not something that you could wish for in any husband. Or that you deserve in your husband."

"I wasn't asking you to be my husband," she said, tiredly. "Just—"

"No," he said. It was almost a scream. "No. If I were to . . . No. Your entire life would be blighted. Forever. I can no more do that than I could kill you."

"I see," she said. "And you're quite sure you can't activate the ruby?"

"It's dead," he said in a faraway voice. "There is no soul there."

"I see," she said again. "So there's nothing for it, but . . . to go on."

He was silent. Silence stretched between them. Sofie thought of how hot it was, how muggy. All these days, with them together, it had been hot, and everything around them parched. The sun of India. How she'd missed it all the time she'd been in England. And now, how she longed for the monsoons' cool rains. The rains she'd never see. "Milord, I am still hungry I don't suppose those fishermen . . ."

He looked at her, amused and just faintly surprised. He smiled a little. "I suppose you didn't eat much," he said. "What with running away from your friends and all. And even if you don't change . . . yes, I could see you'd get hungry."

He stood. He allowed his body to become a dragon.

She watched him fly away over the sea, toward the little boats with their lights. She hated to see him risk himself so, on a ruse of hers. But she didn't know what else to do. The fate of the world depended on this one jewel. And the only way to make the jewel live was for her to die—or for one of her descendants to die. Her death, alone, would heal the world's magic and restore it to its normal pattern. Her death or that of her daughter . . . or her granddaughter.

How could she live knowing that by living she was probably condemning a descendant to sure death?

She got the ruby from its wrapping and held it in her hand, its broken light dazzling madly. She thought she saw the dragon turn toward her. No. She must do it quickly. He wanted to spare her. He didn't understand there were fates worse than death—such as living knowing you have blighted the life and ended the mission of the man you loved. Such as living always looking over your shoulder for the enemy trying to harm you or seize the jewel. Such as knowing if you had a daughter you'd be raising her for the same fate. Probably spelled and followed by tigers before the cradle.

The dragon was flying back. Sofie pulled her small knife from the pouch inside her sleeve, where she'd hid it, and unwrapped it from her handkerchief.

Now, now, now, her mind urged, as Peter flew back. It occurred to her she didn't even know how to do this. All she knew was what she'd seen in the one play she'd watched in London. *Romeo and Juliet.* She held the ruby to her chest. And she drove the dagger into what she hoped was her heart.

Brilliant ruby light exploded all around her.

LOVE AND MADNESS;
WHEN A HEART BREAKS;
THE LAST POSSIBLE CHOICE

Peter saw the light of the ruby as he flew out to sea. It made him turn his head in surprise. What was Sofie doing? Trying some spell to heal the ruby? He wished against all odds that she'd succeed. He knew it was impossible, wishful thinking. A fairy tale, such as people told themselves when all hope was gone.

A man in the boat was offering him fish and bread and Peter took it, lifting it gently from the man's hand, so as not to hurt him. Then he turned back, toward the cliff.

Suddenly, the air dazzled with brilliant reddish light. He looked, in astonished terror, as too many words ran through his mind, too many words to put into sentences or even into coherent thoughts.

He flew desperately to her, and seemingly without transition—without remembering changing—he was in human form, kneeling beside her prone form on the cliff. He registered faint surprise that with all this, the dragon had not thought to eat her. But the dragon-mind rose in him, complaining that this was Sofie, not food.

Sofie should have looked grotesque or repulsive. She did not. She'd fallen back from her sitting position, with the ruby clasped to her chest. She looked like a little girl holding a favorite toy to her heart, while around her someone had splattered some particularly red dye in great profusion.

The red light escaping from between her fingers told him the ruby was now healed. A mad thought crossed his mind, of grabbing the cursed thing and flinging it out to sea. But he couldn't. Nigel was waiting—somewhere—with Heart of Light, his life an endless race against enemies in whose hands the ruby would destroy the world. And now that Soul of Fire was activated, it, too, would bring immense power, power that the wrong people were probably tracking right now.

No, he couldn't throw the ruby away. He couldn't negate Sofie's great sacrifice. He felt hot tears run down his cheeks, and lifted his hand to wipe them, only to find he was still holding the smoked fish. He let it fall and looked at Sofie. "My love," he said, softly, pulling hair away from her face. "My love." Now that she was dead, he could call her that. Her memory could belong to him as she never had. And yet, he'd rather have her alive. "I wish . . ."

He couldn't say what he wished—that he were the one lying dead, exchange his worthless life for her dear one; that the world were sane and fate less cruel . . .

Instead, he reached gently for the jewel and pulled it from between her fingers—which tried to clutch it tighter! For a second he thought it was the stiffness of a corpse, but . . .

But Sofie couldn't possibly have cooled that fast. She couldn't be clutching the jewel with a dead hand.

He reached for her chest, blindly. An inappropriate image of how outraged she'd be at his reach crossed his mind, and he chuckled mirthlessly, even as he felt her chest and the very faint—but real, he was sure of it—beating of her heart. He frowned at the silver dagger embedded in her chest and suddenly, in a flood of warm relief, he realized that she had no idea where her heart was. She'd put the dagger a good deal too far toward her shoulder.

But then . . . why had it worked? Why was the jewel healed? Could it be that when the legend said blood was needed, it was just that, blood, and not her death? Or could it be her intention to sacrifice herself that had done it? So much of magic was intention. . . .

It didn't matter to him. What mattered was that she was alive. For some reason, this brought a new spate of tears. He watched them fall upon her face. She was still not for him. He was still a cursed thing who could never have her. But she would live.

He smiled through his tears.

Slowly, it was born upon his mind that his love, alive though she might be, was still wounded. Very wounded. A life-threatening wound, if not immediately fatal. He must take her . . . somewhere. But he must perforce also take the ruby with him. . . .

The thought of flying into Delhi made his blood run cold. In the city there surely would be weres and half-baked magicians, all struggling to follow the ruby. Wherever he left her there, someone would know she was important to whomever commanded the power of the primeval ruby. They might not know the ruby's name, or its legend, or even its history, but they would know it was power.

He could well imagine people hungry for that power taking Sofie hostage. Demanding he give them the ruby, somehow.

No. Not a big city.

And then the image of the cantonment in Meerut rose in his mind. There was William, and in a garrison, surely they would have surgeons used to incisive wounds. They would save her. Surely.

Of course, there were the tigers, but Peter would only be stopping for a very brief moment. William— even if he inexplicably did not wish to marry Sofie— had impressed him as an honorable man. Peter could entrust Sofie to his care. And then he would have to go find Nigel. Surely Sofie would be chaperoned by garrison wives. She wouldn't have to marry William. And with Soul of Fire removed from the area, there would be no reason for the tigers to worry Sofie. The marahaj would not want her at all. And she could go back to her parents' home. Back to her ordinary existence.

He felt a small pang at that, but it was foolish. Her happiest life would be one away from him.

He allowed his body to become the dragon, and then he picked her up with infinite care. Clutching the ruby—which had stopped shining madly—and the far more precious cargo of Sofie's body, he set off to Meerut. After he dropped her off, he'd touch down to briefly attract the tigers' attention. All would be well.

Holding their luggage and the ruby in one paw, her lifeless body held like a baby against his immense, scaley chest, he lifted off, soaring above the Towers of Silence.

SUMMONS; WHEN
EVERYTHING GOES MAD

"General Paitel would be very grateful," the Gold
Coat said, with absolute correctness, "if you would
give him the pleasure of an interview, Captain
Blacklock."

It has come, William thought. He knew that he
would never leave that interview a free man. And in a
way, there was a sense of relief in that. He'd done what
he could. He'd known the laws he was violating, the
crimes he was committing when he'd let the sepoys out
of their confinement. He'd known, too, that his attempts at confusing the evidence were inadequate.
This was not Eton, and his crime was not stealing jam
from the kitchens.

Strangely, after returning to his room, he'd fallen
asleep, deeply, dreamlessly. And in the morning, he'd
prepared for his arrest. He was wearing his best uniform and had taken particular care over his toiletry
and the combing of his hair. He didn't know how he
would be confined, or if he would still be considered an
officer and a gentleman till his court-martial, and his
inevitable hanging. It didn't matter. He had made his

peace with the fact that his career was over, and probably his life with it.

The only thing he hadn't been able to do was eat breakfast. He'd been toying with it for the last half hour, and now he pushed the plate of braised kidneys away with a great sense of relief.

"Very well," he said. Reaching for his gloves, he put them on and prepared to follow. The Gold Coat looked mildly surprised. Had he been expecting William to fight? No such thing. He'd go, as he knew he must in the end, quietly.

They walked out through the main door of the bungalow where William Blacklock was housed, and into a world that exploded in pandemonium.

William had heard the expression before, but never seen it. All of a sudden there were shouts—screams of elephants, roars of tigers, cries of men. Powersticks erupted. Spells were cast. Counterspells were flung. Fire, smoke and movement covered the whole yard. The well-packed dirt of the parade ground was flung up by the magical force released.

Ahead of William, the Gold Coat hesitated. But William didn't hesitate. He didn't know what had caused this, he wasn't sure what was happening, but he had seen this scene before, with changed sepoys and normal sepoys and even servants, all fighting the Englishmen, and the Englishmen fighting back. It was battle and madness and violence.

William looked across the parade ground, to where he knew he would find her—the young blond matron he'd seen dead in the crystal, sheltering her son. He didn't know how she had died and he didn't care. He just knew this one thing wasn't going to be the same.

He flung himself across the fraught expanse, flung himself in front of her.

A blast from a powerstick hit him in the chest.

Odd, he thought. *So this is how it ends.* And then he thought no more.

BATTLE LINES

Below Peter, the garrison quarters, the parade grounds, the whole area of the cantonment boiled in a fight, so that he couldn't tell friend from foe. If there were either friends or foes in that confusion.

And Peter, locked in the dragon's body, wondered where exactly he could land. Tigers were suddenly on his heels on flying carpets. He hadn't even noticed them. He supposed they'd just now caught up with him, called by the jewel's power.

He couldn't safely flame them while cradling Sofie. And he couldn't land outside the garrison. They would be on him in no time. But if he landed inside the garrison proper, he would become caught in the mayhem.

He couldn't see any way around it. At least if he landed in the maelstrom, there was a chance, amidst all the fighting, that the tigers would miss him. A chance he would find someone with whom to entrust Sofie.

He made for a clear spot, away from the elephants—he would not and could not risk being trampled by an enraged elephant—and landed.

He set Sofie down and cradled her, casting madly

about for someone, anyone, who would be sane and aware and trustworthy enough to take charge of Sofie's unconscious body. He *must* do it, and he *must* leave before the tigers came for him. He didn't dare change. He hunched over Sofie, clutching the ruby in his hand, still cradling her in his arms.

A group of Gold Coats formed, just out of reach of Peter's flaming, and clearly having decided that he was the main menace here, pointed were-loaded power-sticks at him. Peter could have flamed them. But it could be argued this once that they thought they were attacking him in self-defense. And in this close a melee, he stood a good chance of hitting even more innocent people.

In the mayhem, all Peter could understand of the surrounding confusion was that an elephant had William Blacklock by the middle of the body, holding him aloft with his trunk. The two disappeared in the melee a moment later, and Peter was glad. He didn't want to see anyone he knew beat to pieces. Even if the chap already looked dead.

Such senseless death. And if they didn't stop it soon, his Sofie would die, too. He couldn't allow that. He wished with all his heart and mind that they would stop fighting, that the evil ones would die and everyone else spared. And that there would be peace.

THE MANY KINDS
OF SACRIFICE

Suddenly, in his closed talon, the ruby erupted in light and heat. Peter should have dropped it, but instead he held it tighter—as if to protect the world from its power.

He registered somewhere in his consciousness that the sudden flash of blinding red light had made the Gold Coats drop their powersticks as though they were red-hot. He saw that several tigers fell dead in their tracks and writhed as their corpses returned to human form. He noticed people looking confused. But he thought only of Sofie.

In his mind, a voice spoke—a voice that was made of light and music, more beautiful than all the sunrises in the world, more enthralling than the melodies of angels. It spoke in words he didn't understand, in words that didn't belong to any language he knew or had ever heard—and yet in words that communicated light, love, caring.

Several of the would-be combatants had fallen to their knees, crying. It was all of the benedictions and absolutions in the world rolled into one.

He noticed that elephants and the remaining tigers were shifting back to human form, naked and crying. The Gold Coats were weeping, too.

But Peter thought only of Sofie.

Aloud he called, "Does anyone know healing? Anyone? We must stop her bleeding. Please, we must stop her bleeding."

A woman came running, carrying a two-year-old boy. A blond, small slip of a woman, who said, softly, "I've nursed my husband and his comrades on encampments wherever the empire sent us. There is no wound, short of fatal, that I cannot treat."

She handed the child to Peter and, undaunted by the light radiating from the ruby, she took hold of the big knife and pulled it out slowly, all the while uttering hasty spells. And the blood stopped, so that when the knife was wholly out, there was only a little trickle of blood, and Sofie was still breathing.

"Is she healed?" he asked her.

"Oh, no, sir. I closed the wound, but it's still frail. It will reopen with too much exertion. And she lost a lot of blood. It will be over a month, or more, before she's back to normal. You can't take her anywhere till then."

"But . . ." A month. He would be gone long before then. He had to be gone. He must get the ruby to Nigel. Now activated, it would be a beacon to all forms of greed in the world. If he didn't get it to its twin. He could not defend the ruby alone for a month, stopped in one place. But beyond that, he thought it was best if he was removed from Sofie and if Sofie was removed from him. He'd become fond of her, and she of him. And the gods would *not* annihilate time and space to make two lovers happy.

"I will look after her, sir," the lady said. "Someone saved me and my little boy, the least I can do is look after someone else. And she is very beautiful, isn't she?"

"Yes, she is." One last, longing look, to assure himself of how divinely beautiful Sofie was. Then, while the woman looked around for someone to help carry Sofie, Peter stooped and grabbed the ruby. Before the lady had turned back, he'd shifted forms and taken to the sky.

He could feel the link pulling between Soul of Fire and Heart of Light. He would follow it, to find Nigel. And then they would return to Africa and to the temple, where they would restore the ruby to the avatar.

And then...and then Peter would finally send his letter out, renouncing Summercourt. And he would lose himself in the world, trying to mend his broken heart.

There was a thunderclap above, and as though something had rent the heavens, the streaming rain of the monsoons started pouring down, drenching the world.

VENICE

Peter flew and flew and flew, till his wings ached with it. And yet the voice in the ruby whispered to him and gave him power and strength.

One morning he found himself in Venice and back in human form, in a well-cut suit, every inch the English lord. He'd been in Venice before, in his days as a young revolutionary, and the place beckoned to him with its old palaces, its narrow waterways.

At first, he'd been shocked that Nigel would be here, in this very populous city. And then he realized that, like Benares, Venice was so old and full of magic and power, it masked almost everything. Oh, not the ruby itself. Nothing could mask the ruby. But it confused things and made the place of the jewel and its exact possessor harder to pinpoint.

Unfortunately, this meant it made his task more difficult, too. Following the pull of the jewel in his breast pocket, Peter wandered about the gilded expanses of St. Mark's Cathedral. He went to the palace of the Doges, in which the Venetian council once sat, when, centuries ago, Venice had been an independent republic.

From the second story of that palace, it was possible to cross the canal to the prison, via the Bridge of Sighs, a covered stone passageway through which criminals had once been led to trial.

Someone within the cool stone confines of the bridge was reading Byron's poem addressed to the city: " 'I stood in Venice, on the Bridge of Sighs; A palace and a prison on each hand; I saw from out the wave ... ' "

"Such rot, isn't it?" a voice said, lightly from Peter's elbow, and he turned around, to glance at its source.

He noticed the gentleman was tall and pale-haired and that his face had that curious tanned-red color of very fair people who spent a lot of time outside in exotic climes. It was only as his eyes met the gaze from a pair of eyes that burned like well-cut sapphires that Peter recognized the man.

"Nigel, by Jove. Nigel Oldhall." His call started as a loud cry, but it changed rapidly to a whisper as he remembered that other people might be looking for his friend.

Nigel must have remembered it, too. With a quickness of movement and mind that Peter hardly recognized in his old schoolmate—Peter always having been the more commanding of the two—Nigel did something with his hand and Peter felt as though a veil of disguise had fallen over both of them.

"Come," Nigel said. And Peter went, following him, watching the way his old friend cut through the crowds, without pushing, without seeming to shoulder through them. Nigel made it look like effortless sailing through masses of tourists and locals.

Down on the side of the canal, men were singing. Nigel called a gondola with a gesture. He gave directions in what sounded like a fair approximation of Italian, and smiled at Peter's astonished look. "I've always been good with languages, you know, old chap. Always."

He must have given the right directions, because in no time they were ensconced into a snug booth of a coffeehouse, sitting upon dyed leather sofas, while a massive gilded eagle seemed to extend its wings paternally over the both of them. The coffee shop was called The Golden Eagle, and the waiter brought them cups of excellent Turkish coffee and little congealed cakes that seemed to be made mostly of wax and coloring.

Peter nibbled a cake indifferently and peered across the table at his friend, who appeared exactly like a more tanned version of the old Nigel, but whose eyes and look and demeanor were all very different. He looked, Peter thought, like an adult. A commanding adult, at that.

"Where have you been?" Peter asked at last.

Nigel shrugged. "A bit everywhere. That letter I sent you, the one from Peru, did you ever get it?"

Peter allowed his eyes to widen. "Peru? The last letter received was from St. Petersburg."

Nigel shrugged. "I had some odd idea," he said, "of going by degrees toward India. I came in through Russia, and . . . I just caught a carpetship—working as flight magician—to the most distant point possible. So . . . Peru. But then I found myself followed there, too, and I caught the first carpetship flight, which as it happened brought me here." He shrugged. "Would you think me insane if I told you that in Peru, something else joined in pursuit of me? A dragon? But not a dragon like you at all. It had no wings. It flew like swimming on air."

Peter nodded. "I fought the creature," he said. "At least if it was a blue one."

"Have you now?" Nigel said with interest. He looked weary, but also ... energized. It was difficult to tell why or how. "And do you have Soul of Fire?"

Peter reached in his pocket and took out the jewel. It was the last thing he had from Sofie. The last thing. And he missed her horribly. He realized somewhat in surprise that he'd been missing her presence these many days. He wanted to tell her about the horrible congealed cakes. He wanted to show her the eagle with its wings extended. He wanted ...

Nigel took the jewel.

"So you'll be returning it to Africa now," Peter said. And, as a thought occurred to him, "Should I give you a ride, old man?"

Nigel frowned at him. "You sound very reluctant, even as you offer."

"No, I—" Peter said, and stopped. He realized he'd sounded reluctant indeed. The thought that Nigel would be going to Africa and there meeting his ex-wife, Emily, and Kitwana, her new husband, intruded out of his confused emotions. And such was his state of mind, he couldn't help blurting, "Are you afraid to see her again? Emily?"

"Who?" Nigel said, then smiled, to show he'd been joking. "No," he said. "At least I don't think I am. I mean ..." He shrugged. "I might have been in love with her once. At least, I thought it was love at the time, and so did she, else she'd never have married me. But you know . . . I don't think it was love. I think true love is something else very different altogether.

"Mind you, if our adventure hadn't happened, if we hadn't been forced to quest for Heart of Light, Emily and I were close enough to each other, and suited well enough, that we might have rubbed along together very tolerably for forty or so years. Raised a few brats. Yes, I daresay it would have been fine."

"And yet you don't resent Kitwana?"

"No. Because even if we'd lived together in friendship and charity for forty years, Emily and I would never have had what she has with Kitwana. What we'd have had was habit. What they have is true love—an insane emotion that constrains one to take up the oddest sacrifices for his loved one and which will stop at nothing but happiness . . . for the one you love.

"I think it must be very rare for people to love so. And since Emily and Kitwana did, I couldn't stand between them."

"But then . . ." Peter said. And realized he was speaking to himself more than to Nigel. But then, that was how he had felt for Sofie. And how did she feel toward him? He remembered her sacrifice. Had she done it to cleanse the stone that he might fulfill his mission. Or had she done it for the world? Was there a chance she *loved* him? Love. How rare was it. And if she loved him—however unlikely, however ill-advised—would she be happy without him?

He should take Nigel to Africa, then go back to India as soon as possible. He *must* find out how Sofie was. Her wound, though healed, might have reopened. The thought that she was ill and suffering and longing for him made him twitch.

"There was someone," he said, entirely without meaning to. "In India."

"Someone?" Nigel said. Then, with sudden comprehension, "A woman?"

"The most wonderful woman in the world, Nigel. Full of such courage..." He sighed. "I left her wounded, and I wonder how she's doing." He shook his head. "Right, we shall take you to Africa, and by then perhaps I'll have gotten over my need to find out."

But Nigel grinned at him, his eyes sparkling with mischief. "Farewell, you are a great fool. What do you mean have gotten over it? If you love her and if she is, as you say, the most wonderful woman in the world, shouldn't you give in to your wish to see her?"

"I am," Peter said, sternly, feeling the need to remind Nigel, "a dragon."

Nigel picked up a tasteless pink oval cake and nibbled it with every appearance of enjoyment. "So you are. And what does that mean?"

"Nigel! I wouldn't inflict on any woman my—"

"Oh, there's worse things you could inflict," his friend said. "Remember my brother, Carew, and how much delight he took in abusing us when we were young and in boarding school? Imagine a woman being given a choice between you and him? Which one do you think would make her the better husband?"

"Neither."

"Yes, but—"

"Oh, all right, myself. I've suspected lately that if I truly loved the woman, I wouldn't ... you know, flame her in the heat of passion."

Nigel grinned. "I'm sure your ladylove will appreciate that. What is her name, by the way?"

"Sofie," Peter said, and he put all of his longing into the name, which came back all whisper and half sigh.

"I see," Nigel said, standing up and straightening his coat and his tie. "Then I would advise you to go to her now. Go to her as soon as may be. You're not so far from India here as you'll be deep in Africa. Just go now. Take the shorter route. Don't make her wait."

"But . . . I can help you. Restoring the ruby is our joint mission."

"No. Finding it was our joint mission. As long as the rubies get back, I don't think they care how. And there is a carpetship leaving in a couple of hours that will take me to southwestern Africa. From which a very few days will see me to our destination."

"But . . ." Peter said, miserably, "I can wait a few days. . . ."

"I don't think you can. Not if you're that worried about her. Not if there's any chance at all she'll slip through your fingers. I see from your narrowed eyes there is. Go to her, Peter. Accept your own desires for once. Not all impulses are bad impulses. Learn to find out which aren't."

THE GARDEN AGAIN

William had taken months to recover. He'd wakened in this paradise among verdant trees, with the first rains of the monsoon washing down the leaf-and-branch roof of a rustic cabin. He was laying on a pile of leaves, roughly covered with what appeared to be an old sari. Moving hurt. Thinking hurt. And when he saw Bhishma come in the door of the cabin, he knew he was dreaming.

But it turned out he wasn't. "I couldn't stay behind, you see," Bhishma had told him. "The sepoys we freed suspected you and I were ... that you and I were involved."

"But I thought ..." William had protested. "Your culture is not as ... disapproving of ... of love between men as mine is, is it?"

And Bhishma had looked at him puzzled for a moment, then his eyes had danced with secret amusement. "Oh, not for that, but ... But you see, it was not *what* I did, it was *with whom*. You are a no-caste." His smile made him suddenly look very young. "I am defiled."

It wasn't a very good joke—now, months later,

William wondered if it had been a joke at all—but they'd laughed until they cried.

William had nothing to go back for, any more than Bhishma did. By then the letter would've been sent, and his parents had gotten it, saying their son had died heroically in a quickly thwarted uprising. They had grieved, he was sure, but nothing could be served by his coming back from the dead now. He suspected if he did, there would be the matter of the freed sepoys. Treason. Betrayal of Queen and Country. No, better not come back to life just so that his parents could watch him die, dishonored in the gallows.

So he, who had never been very sure of paradise, embraced his afterlife in its fullness. It wasn't a bad life. As soon as he was fully healed—which should be any day now—he would be able to hunt with Gyan. They had long since become Gyan and William—here, away from the world, being called Bhishma and Sahib seemed like foolishness—and until then he could fish and trap. He was fishing, at that moment, leaning against a tree, by a stream, using an improvised rod and a line Gyan had procured from who knew where.

William was thinking how convenient it was that villagers hereabouts near-worshipped weres, or at least respected them enough not to think too much of what was going on here, between these two men. You never knew with primitive cultures, and these people in the wilds of the Himalayas were very primitive in-deed. Gyan swore some were even cannibals. But none bothered them. Instead, they were respectful, and even traded with Gyan and William—cloth and pottery and simple furniture, in exchange for the fish and meat they caught.

He heard Gyan coming through the trees, whistling tunelessly as he did when he had been lucky at his hunt.

And it was as close to paradise as William wanted to get.

BRIDE'S VISIT

Mrs. McCleod had left Sofie alone with Lalita, happy that Sofie had a visitor. She was a gentle soul, Aimee McCleod, and it would never occur to her to question the friendship between a maid and her former mistress, or to think it strange the two of them should sit there, smiling in the still-bearable sunlight of spring.

"So you're married," Sofie said. "Which of them?"

"Oh, Hanuman," Lalita said, smiling. "It was always Hanuman. And you? When will you be married?"

Sofie sighed, feeling again the cold emptiness she'd first experienced when she'd awakened and he was gone. Aimee was sure he would come back, but Sofie knew better. He would think he was defiling her, and he would die rather than return.

"I don't think I'm going to be. At least, there is no one who wants to marry me. And I once told ... I once told St. Maur that I would only marry for the greatest love. And, you see ... that can't happen, because ... he doesn't wish to marry me. And I can't stay with Aimee much longer, though she's been good to me. But I don't want to go back to my mother and father, either. So, well ... Perhaps I will join a mission. Or find work as nanny or something. And then ... well ... maybe someday I'll find someone to love. Or maybe when I'm very old, like ... like forty or something, I won't mind so much not loving, and I will marry for companionship."

She was aware her voice sounded thin and pathetic, but she didn't expect the shock in Lalita's eyes. "You must have been hurt very badly, indeed," Lalita said. "The Sofie I knew would never have just let him leave. Not if she loved him. The Sofie I knew would get a flying rug and make him realize what he was throwing away."

"I would, but ... I don't have the slightest idea where he might be."

"Your friend Mrs. McCleod says he left his luggage behind. Did he?"

"Yes, he was gone immediately, with just the ruby. He didn't want me to wake while he was still nearby."

"But that means you've got his eye, haven't you? The eye of the dragon? The scrying device?"

"Oh," Sofie said, blushing a little, because she had gone through his luggage several times, in search of a hint, a clue to his location.

"Use the eye, Sofie. Find out where he is."

"But the eye isn't mine."

"Nonsense. Those get traded and passed on from generation to generation. Besides, it is his eye and he loves you. I'm sure it will obey you."

"Oh," Sofie said, unwilling to admit that the words, like the rain after the drought, fell upon her parched heart and revived her.

She got the device. In Aimee's darkened little

parlor, she unwrapped it. It looked like an eye and yet not, and she stared into its green depths, transfixed, trying to see Peter.

And suddenly she heard the sound of wings, from the balcony outside the parlor.

DRAGON SEEKING MAIDEN

Peter landed on the balcony, only slightly worried the dragon might have been seen. But the cottage where he'd glimpsed—from a distance—someone who looked like the woman who'd healed Sofie was on the outskirts of the cantonment, facing the parade grounds— which were, right then, deserted under heavy rain. Gold Coats were nowhere to be seen. In fact, the rumor Peter had heard said that after suffering heavy losses in the new rebellion, they'd been sent back to England. All of them.

On the balcony, Peter changed back to himself, and dressed, very quickly, in the clothes he'd been carrying in his claw, and which were, therefore, completely soaked from the rain.

When he'd finished dressing, he glanced up, and found the woman who'd healed Sofie standing by the door, facing him. She looked amused and she was smiling, and this gave him hope that Sofie was well.

"Where is Miss Warington?" he asked. And with worry, "And is she well?"

And he heard Sofie Warington's voice say, "Milord

St. Maur!" and she stood by the balcony door, staring at him.

"Well, well, we'll be gone," the blond woman said. And though Peter had no idea who *we* was, he had not the slightest curiosity.

"If you'll come into the parlor," the woman said, and led them into a semi-dark room with two sofas and several of the collapsible tables used in this climate. Sofie was pale, Peter thought. And her dress looked like the one she'd worn on the travel . . . and as if it had been imperfectly darned.

But to him she looked better than a duchess in satin and brocade. He was overcome. He stared at her like a man might stare at food when he is starving. Under his breath he said, *"Baggage."* His voice came out tender and catching.

She didn't seem offended. "Rogue," she said.

Then she more or less pulled him, and more or less was pulled by him, onto one of the nearby sofas. Peter realized, to his shock, that they were alone.

He wanted to tell her it wouldn't work and that she was making the worst mistake of her life. He had not counted on the way she looked, however, which made his breath catch in his throat. He had not counted on the way she smelled, like forest primeval or fecund land. He had not counted on the silken feeling of her hair against his fingers, or the way his mouth craved the taste of her skin.

In the cool darkness, he kissed her face all over, and held her close, and felt her heart beating against his. His lips met hers, and they feasted on each other's mouths, their tongues meeting, their embrace growing tighter. She'd had her hair atop her head, in a becoming coiffure he supposed she'd seen in London. His seeking fingers undid it, and reveled in her hair's satiny feel.

"I came," he said, pulling back a little, "to say good-bye. To tell you you'd be happier without me."

She fixed him with a stern look from her steady blue eyes. "You can't leave at all," she said. And before he could protest, added, "You can't. And don't say foolish things. I know you think you're under a curse and that staying with me will destroy my life, but I beg you to believe me, it won't destroy it nearly as much as if you leave. I love you, Peter Farewell, Earl of St. Maur. And if you leave me..." The stern eyes became implacable. "If you leave me, I shall follow. I will follow you while I have feet, St. Maur. And when my feet are worn through, I shall follow you on my knees."

"No," he said, in faint protest.

"Yes," she said. "These weeks without you have been like death, and I would rather be alive. Do you think that others haven't had the problem you do? You're not a child now. You can control yourself. And I'll be there to help you."

"But... if we have children..."

"They might be like you," she said. "And they might not. Likely they won't. It's not that common, is it? People inherit it from very distant ancestors, usually. But if they are like you, we won't be so foolish as to send them wandering the world. You'll teach them how to control themselves instead of expelling them from your sight."

"Yes," he said, half-convinced. He'd never thought of it that way. Surely were people must be able to hide their nature and lead normal lives. Otherwise they would never have children. And he'd never have been born.

He was so taken by the idea, he was quite unable to resist it when she pressed herself close to him. And he let his lips do what they had for such a time longed to do, gently kiss their way down her velvety throat, to the place where it receded in a hollow and the lace of the collar came up to hide it.

BRIDE'S PRICE

Outside the parlor, Aimee looked at Lalita, her eyes dancing with secret mirth. "You did say they were engaged, did you not? So there can be nothing wrong with their being alone."

"Nothing at all. I'd swear to it," Lalita said, as she shamelessly listened to the voices within the parlor.

But at that moment the voices subsided into silence, and there was a long time of silence, from which a single word emerged. "Baggage!"

Then the silence resumed, punctuated now and then by odd sighs and exclamations that weren't words.

A louder sigh broke the silence, and Miss Warington's voice said, "Why, Lord St ... Peter! I thought you didn't eat people."

"For you, my dear, I will make an exception."

Lalita felt her color rise. "This is likely to take some time."

"Is this how it's normally done?" came Miss Warington's voice.

"I don't know. I never ... You see, I was afraid I would change and incinerate my lover."

"Oh, milord, you're not *that* hot."

A gurgle of laughter from St. Maur. "Shut up, baggage. I'm trying to romance you."

Lalita rolled her eyes. If St. Maur was besotted enough to laugh at such jokes, she would stay away until they'd come down to Earth.

She reached to her waistband and brought out a pouch. She had bespelled it so that only Sofie could open it. To Aimee, she said, "For them. When they emerge."

"Er . . ." Aimee said.

"My uncle says it is by rights theirs. For what they did to save the ruby."

"The jewel that stopped the fight?" Aimee asked.

"The very same."

"Then I hope that pouch is full of jewels, too, and precious stones. Because they saved my husband and all our friends."

Lalita considered for a moment. But the jewels were charmed. No one else could even open the pouch. Only Sofie and St. Maur. And besides, she felt no duplicity from Aimee.

Smiling, she admitted, "That is exactly what it is full of."

OVER EUROPE

We are married. Sofie thought, *as she leaned close to* the dragon's back and sank her hands into its neck ruffle, which felt, startlingly, as Peter's loose curls at the nape of his neck did, when she pushed her fingers into them while he was in human form. *We are truly married.*

And despite her having told him she would like nothing better than to be married out of hand, somewhere, after eloping he'd insisted on doing the proper thing. "So many things are wrong with this union," he said, "I want to make everything else as right that I can."

She had no idea what he meant about things being wrong. He'd gone to her parents and asked their consent. She didn't know what he'd told them, but the consent had been immediately granted. Perhaps because Peter had parted with one of the diamonds in that pouch that Lalita had given them, through Aimee McCleod.

So that was well, though Sofie had absolutely no intention of keeping up too close a connection with her parents. It was hard to forget they'd almost sold her for blood sacrifice. She could forgive, but not forget.

They were going to live on St.... no, Peter's estate—she must remember to call him Peter; he'd asked her most fervently, telling her St. Maur always made him feel she was talking to his father—for which he had very grand plans. "It is just a large rambling house," he said. "And some half a dozen farms, including the home farm. And a whole lot of flocks. But with the money we have, we can make the estate as lovely as it was in my great-grandfather's day. Or at least as wealthy. We'll repair the house, but we won't really *change* it. It and the gardens around it have a wild beauty all their own. Just like you."

She thought he was very silly, but she was looking forward to the house anyway. It was his house, and it was clear that he loved it. As she loved him. And as he loved her.

On one thing only had her new husband stuck, and could not be moved. "I will not take a carpetship," he'd said. "No matter how much I can control myself, I will not be confined that long, in such a small space with so many strangers. Something would go very wrong."

She didn't care. She leaned forward over his neck, while beneath her Europe stretched, as dark and mysterious as any of the unexplored continents. Lights shone here and there, the mirrors of the constellations in the sky. Soon, they would fly across the ocean, and then, at long last, into England. Peter had told her that he knew a place to land where no one would see them. And how from there they could rent horses or another conveyance to the nearest town, and eventually make their way to his beloved Summercourt. "Where I will make my land manager happy," he had said, "by assuming all my responsibilities, and then some."

A thought of the rubies, to which they owed all their happiness, intruded. Peter said his friend Nigel would be taking them back to their temple in Africa, even now.

She said a little prayer for the rubies'—and Nigel's—safety, then leaned forward, resting her head on the warm, soft neck of the dragon, and whispered in the general direction of his ears, "I love you, Peter Farewell, Lord St. Maur."

He flapped his wings, once, twice, gaining altitude. Below them, Europe was a small thing, of little importance. And around her, his wings sparkled like captive fire.

ABOUT THE AUTHOR

Sarah A. Hoyt was born in Portugal more years ago than she's comfortable admitting. She currently lives in Colorado with her husband, teen sons and a clowder of various-size cats. She hasn't been to Africa in twenty-some years, but she would like to visit again. Around four dozen—at last count—of her short stories have been published in magazines such as *Weird Tales, Analog, Asimov's* and *Amazing,* as well as various anthologies. *Ill Met by Moonlight,* the first book of her Shakespearean fantasy trilogy, was a finalist for the Mythopoeic Award. Sarah is also working on a contemporary fantasy series starting with *Draw One in the Dark,* and—as Sarah D'Almeida—is in the midst of a Musketeers' Mystery series starting with *Death of a Musketeer.* Her website is http://sarahahoyt.com/.

If you loved *Heart of Light* and *Soul of Fire,*

be sure not to miss the riveting conclusion

to this series, as Nigel's tale is finally told in:

HEART *and* SOUL

by

Sarah A. Hoyt

On sale November 2008
Here's a special preview:

On sale November 2008

Red Jade held her breath as her brother prepared to set fire to the paper boats and the hordes of carefully detailed paper dragons. She wanted to close her eyes and shut out the scene, but her will alone kept them open. Through the screen of her eyelashes, she saw Wen approach the altar upon which the funerary gifts of their father had been set. Above that, another altar held the tablets of their ancestors.

Red Jade had supervised and arranged it all. She had made her father's women cut and glue and color and gild for days, so that on the lower jade table there stood a palace in paper—the palace her family hadn't possessed in millennia. To the right of it stood row upon row of paper boats, minutely detailed, like the barges upon which Red Jade had spent her whole life. In the middle stood representations of the court—men and women meant to be her father's servants in the afterlife: a coterie of pretty paper dolls for a harem, and a group of broad-shouldered male dolls for the hard tasks her father's spirit might want done, and to protect him from whatever evil he might encounter. On the left, in massed confusion, were perfect, miniature paper dragons. Herself, in dark red. Red Jade. And Wen in Blue. For some reason, seeing them there, before the palace that would never be theirs, made the tears she refused to let fall join in obscuring her sight.

Her brother, whom she must now think of as the True Emperor of All Under Heaven—though her family had been in exile for many centuries and she doubted the present usurpers even knew of their existence— held the burning joss stick in his hand and dropped slowly to his knees.

Let him not fall, Red Jade prayed, and she wasn't sure to whom, though it might have been to her father's spirit. Only she didn't know if her father cared, and she wished there was someone else she could appeal to. *Let Wen not fall,* she told herself, sternly, and felt a little more confident. It was insane to think she could keep Wen upright and within bounds of proper behavior through the sheer power of her mind, but then . . . she always had, hadn't she? And she had hidden his addiction from her father, as well.

When had she ever had anyone else to ask for help? So when she saw Wen's head start to bob forward, like the head of one overcome with sleep, she willed him to stay up, on his knees, facing forward.

Wen straightened. The joss stick swept left and right, setting all the pretty paper images aflame. And Red Jade fought against the sob climbing into her throat even as the sound of her father's concubines erupting into ritualistic screams deafened her mind. She would miss her father. She was afraid for Wen and her own future. But, in this moment, all had been done well, and Wen was behaving as he should.

She finally allowed her eyes to shut as Wen's voice mechanically recited the prayers that should set their father's soul free and make it secure in the ever after.

Their father was dead. He'd been the Dragon

King, the True Emperor of All Under Heaven, the descendant of the ancient kings of China. Wen, his only son, must inherit the throne. Because only Wen could protect his half-sister, the daughter of the long-dead, foreign-devil concubine.

She followed him to his room after the ceremony. It was her father's old room, in the main barge of their flotilla. Servants and courtiers prostrated themselves as Wen passed by, knocking their foreheads against the dusty floor, but he didn't seem to notice. Wen was tired and anxious. His eyes kept darting here and there, as though he had trouble focusing both sight and mind.

The men surrounding him—his father's advisers—probably knew as well as she did that he longed for his fix of opium, but they gave no indication of it. It was all "Excellency" this and "Milord" that as each competed with the other, asking boons on this, his first day in power. Repairs to this barge and additions to that one, and a promotion in the precedence of yet another.

All of them Wen ignored, walking just ahead, his eyes blindly seeking. But as the entourage prepared to follow him into his quarters, he spun around and clapped his dismissal. At the back of the group of followers, Red Jade stood waiting, not quite daring enter her newly powerful brother's room without his permission. For years she'd protected him and helped him, but now he was Emperor and her ascendance over him was gone.

But seeing her at the back, he smiled and motioned for her to approach, which she did, closing the door behind her.

"We're done now, Red Jade," he told her, his man's tones distorted into a child's whine. It was a voice that had only developed after he started smoking opium. "I've done what you wanted, and now I'm tired."

Part of Red Jade felt sorry for him. They were of an age, she and Wen, though Wen was the son of the First Lady, her father's official wife. Red Jade was only the daughter of a concubine with red hair and blue eyes who had been stolen off a foreign carpetship.

And though Red Jade looked Chinese, with her long, smooth dark hair and black eyes, she knew her eyes had a blue sheen, and there was something to her features that wasn't quite right. She was also too tall.

Her father had teased her about it, telling her they'd never get her a husband. No man would want to look up at his lady.

The recollection that Zhan would be out there, prowling and planning to make her his, sent a shiver of fear up her spine, and made her catch her breath. "Not yet, Older Brother," she said. "We must be able to lift and move the dragon boats. I—"

He gave her one of the startlingly cunning looks that he could give—a sudden expression of knowledge that belied the normal dreamlike tone of his days. "You mean *you* must lift them."

His look was so like her father's that she bowed deeply and whispered, "I do not mean to take over your ..."

"No," Wen said, and shook his head. "No, of course, not. But let's not play games, Younger Sister. Not with each other. We both know that the opium interferes with flying the boats. I would not risk my people." He turned abruptly towards a table that was set at the foot of his bed. Bed and table both were gilded, and inlaid heavily with semi-precious stones. They were very old and had come—centuries ago—

from their ancestors' palace. Now they stood in un-easy contrast with the rest of the furniture, which ranged from heavy, foreign, mahogany furniture scavenged from carpetships to improvised pieces put together from flotsam and tatters.

The boxes, like the table, were made of fragrant woods and covered in gold leaf and jewels. Jade had seen them open before, when her father had been searching for something. So she knew what they contained—papers and jewels, most of them magical and bequeathed to them by long-lost generations. Wen rummaged through the boxes as if he knew what he was looking for, and Jade held her tongue while he did so.

"Ah," he said at last. He held aloft a heavy signet ring, with a bright red stone, upon which were chiseled the characters for Power and Following. Jade, who'd never seen that ring, blinked at Wen.

"Father showed me all these boxes before he died," Wen said. "And he told me what each jewel and paper did—magically, as well as symbolically. This ring was worn by our father when his own father was incapable of ruling the Dragon Boats, in his final years of life. So our father wore the ring, and with it could command the Dragon Boats with the magic of the Emperor. He could also command all of the Imperial power."

"But..." Red Jade said, stricken. "I am only a woman. And my mother—"

"Was a foreign devil, yes," Wen said, with unaccustomed dryness. "But Jade, you've been doing half of Father's work for years—everything that didn't require Imperial magic. And, now..." He shrugged. "I can be the Emperor, or I can dream." He gestured towards his hookah on the small, rickety pine table near the gilded bed. "I'd prefer to dream."

Their eyes met for a moment. Jade had never truly discussed his addiction with him, because Wen would get defensive and change the subject. So he'd never before admitted the power his dreams held over him, and never so bluntly confessed that he cared for nothing else.

What did he mean to do? Did he mean to leave her in charge of the Dragon Boats when he left? Did he think that the Dragon Boats would accept the rulings of a woman, and a woman with foreign blood in her veins?

Zhan would take over. Zhan would . . . She felt her throat close. She couldn't tell her brother the disgust she felt for his second-in-command—once her father's second-in-command. Though he was of an old dragon dynasty, and powerful in magic and might, she didn't trust him. And she did not wish to be his wife.

But Wen was reclining upon his cushions and looked at her, mildly surprised, as though she had stayed much longer than he expected. He waved his hand. "Go, sister. I am tired. I've had too much reality."

Jade bowed and walked backward—as she'd once done in her father's presence—till she was at the doors. These she opened, without turning back, and left, still bowing—making sure that everyone saw her bow, so they knew she respected her brother and valued his authority.

While the guards at the door of her brother's chambers closed the doors, she turned and walked away, linking her hands together as she did so. Her right hand covered her left, and she felt the red jewel on her finger. The jewel with the power to make the boats fly.

But the jewel only worked if the Emperor had

power. Had Wen's opium dreams grounded the boats forever?

Red Jade saw Zhan before she lifted her eyes. Or rather, she sensed him, his hulking, broad-shouldered presence barring her way. Amid the various milling courtiers, only he stood squarely in her path.

He was a tall man, and though he was close to her father's age, he could still be said to be handsome. His dark hair showed very few white threads, and though he wore his beard closely shaven—unlike most men in the Dragon Boats—he let his moustaches grow long, framing his broad, sensuous lips. Jade had heard his father's women talk and giggle about him, claiming his dark eyes glowed like banked fires, but Jade could not see anything attractive in him.

She could not remember a time when she had not been afraid of Zhan. She remembered being very small—maybe two or three—and coming out of her mother's quarters to find Zhan in the hallway. She had instantly run back to the safety of her mother's arms, though she couldn't say what she'd thought Zhan might do to her. Surely even Zhan, arrogant as he was, wouldn't have dared hurt the daughter of the True Emperor.

Since adolescence, Jade had found other reasons to dread the man. He looked at her with a covetous sort of hunger—the type of look she imagined a ravening tiger might bestow upon a juicy buffalo. It made her shiver and blush and look away. And, more often than not, this caused him to chuckle drily.

This danger, she knew, was more real than any she might have imagined as a toddler. Zhan was her father's second-in-command, because he was the most noble of the Dragon Barge leaders. His family was descended from Jade's own family, many generations back. As such, he had royal blood in his veins, and was entitled to almost as much respect as Wen and Jade. If Wen's father were to marry her off, whom else would he choose for a husband? Few of the land-bound nobility even knew that Jade was their equal, let alone their superior, and most of them were descended from the interlopers and not proper noblemen of China at all.

But Jade didn't want to marry Zhan, and now she made sure the look she gave him was full of a haughty chill. "Ah, Prince of the High Mountain," she said, addressing him by the title that his family had worn many centuries before.

"My lady," he said, bowing in the most correct way possible. But he didn't get out of her way and he straightened almost immediately, his eyes challenging her.

"Is there something you require of me?"

"Only to know when his majesty, the true Emperor, intends to make the Dragon Boats fly. By tradition, he won't be fully in power till he does. Until then, it leaves things . . . in dispute."

Did Zhan intend to challenge Wen? Steeling herself, she said briskly, "His Majesty is tired. He's given me the ring and the power to fly the boats myself."

"You?" Zhan looked at Jade as though she had suddenly grown a second head.

"As his nearest in blood, I will be able to channel his power whenever he doesn't feel like exerting it."

"But . . ." Zhan looked like a man who had just had a rug pulled out from under him.

"Yes?"

"But . . . I'd talked to his majesty your father, and I've . . . I meant to talk to your brother too, but . . . I don't know if you . . ."

Surprised that Zhan could be so discomposed—Jade had never seen him in less than perfect control—she lifted her left hand with the oversized ring on it. "I hold the power of the True Emperor," she said, simply, even as her heart thumped hard in her chest and she wondered if Wen was in fact the true Emperor. If his magic, damaged as it would be from opium, would be able to lift the Dragon Boats.

Zhan looked . . . worried. Which was odd, because if she and Wen couldn't make the boats fly, then Zhan would kill them both, and the power would devolve, naturally, upon him.

So what was worrying Zhan?

Looking up, she signaled, wordlessly, that she was willing to listen to his words in private.

"It is about the jewels of power," he said, as soon as they were isolated enough that no one else would hear them. "The twin jewels." He spoke the words with reverence and so close to her face that his hot breath tickled her cheek. He smelled of ginger and garlic.

"What twin jewels?"

He sighed. "This is why I'd prefer to speak to His Majesty. Women are not told these things, nor are they supposed to enmesh themselves in the affairs of men."

Jade thought of Wen, who by now would be well lost in his opium dreams. He might have heard of the jewels—or not, considering that their father had never been very fond of Wen. If he'd told anyone secrets of state, he was far more likely to tell them to Jade. So instead of speaking, she simply raised her hand, with the ring on it.

Zhan made a sound like a pricked balloon. "There are two rubies of great power, upon which the whole power of the world rests. The whole magical power."

"Impossible," Jade said. "For if that were true, then none of us would have magic or the ability to use it."

Zhan made a sound that might have been a cough or a hastily swallowed put down on the mental power of women. Having heard him deliver such opinions before, Jade suspected it was the latter. "I mean," he said in the tone of a master who is barely holding back from caning a disobedient pupil, "that the jewels anchor the power of the world. That without them, no one in our world would be able to hold magic. Beyond that..." He shrugged. "Many centuries ago, it is said the king of the foreign devils stole one of them and made the magic in it his own, so that magic would pass only to him and his descendants. Which is why the magic in Europe goes only to a few families, and why European mages are much stronger than those in other lands— the Dragon Boat people excepted, of course."

"Ah, *a legend*," Jade said, managing to convey in those words the disdain she felt for Zhan.

He recoiled as though slapped. And for a moment, as he looked up at her, his dark eyes burned with unmistakable hatred so strong that it shocked even her. But almost immediately he smoothed over his expression into the vague, deferential gaze he usually gave her.

"It is a legend with a lot of truth," he snapped. "The queen of the foreign devils, Queen Victoria"—he pronounced the name as an imprecation—"thought so too. She sent envoys of her own to find the remaining jewel. I found out about it, with my foreseeing magic, and I have followed their exploits ever since. Even though they found the other jewel, they didn't give it to the queen. Instead, one of them took the new jewel and the other went in search of the old spent jewel ... which he found and healed somehow. Now one of the envoys has both jewels, and I know where he is headed. I had a vision that told me which carpetship he will be traveling on." Zhan's eyes burned with light, as if he were feverish. "We can intercept the ship. We can take the jewels."

"Why should we?" Jade asked, taken aback by the naked lust in the man's voice.

Zhan looked at her as if she had taken leave of her senses. "They are the most powerful jewels in the world. They contain power over all the magic on Earth. Whoever holds them can deny magic to everyone else by means of a simple ritual. Whoever holds them could rule the world."

Jade couldn't think of anything that Wen would want less. And if the rule of the world were to devolve upon her shoulders by default, then it was more burden than she needed.

"Your brother would truly be Emperor of All Under Heaven," Zhan said.

"He *is* Emperor of All Under Heaven," Jade snapped.

"In name, at least. But with this ..." Zhan's voice dropped and slid, caressing like velvet. "With this, he could rule like your distant ancestors. He could take over the palace, and eject the interlopers."

At this, Jade paused. Getting back their proper place was something altogether different. Since the invaders had taken over the land of her ancestors, they'd lived like pariahs aboard the Dragon Boats. Most people thought them pirates, vagabonds, people of no account. To be able to recover their position and power was something that Jade could not turn down. In fact, it it would be a sin against her ancestors to refuse.

And a secret, almost unheard, thought whispered: If she were to recover the throne of her ancestors, then she could find someone else to take over looking after Wen, and she, herself, could choose a husband from all the noblemen in the kingdom. Not many would aspire to marry the daughter of a Dragon Boat pirate, but how many would vie for the sister of the Dragon King?

"Ah," he said. "I see that you know your duty."

"Perhaps," she said, unwilling to concede anything. "But how are we to accomplish this daring feat? Yes, we've attacked carpetships before, but surely if this carpetship is carrying such a treasure as you describe, then it will have an armed escort. Are you suggesting that our Dragon Boats are enough to face the wrath of the devil-queen's army?"

"No escort," he said, making a dismissive gesture with his hand. "No armed men. This man who carries the jewels is no longer working for his queen, nor is he traveling with her permission. He is attempting to return the jewels to Africa."

"To Africa?" Jade said, in dismay, thinking of the distances they would have to fly to intercept such a carpetship. Not only that, but they would fly over many peopled lands, many places where others were bound to see them. And with her magic being bound to the Kingdom, she wasn't sure at all if it would work over foreign lands.

"Are you afraid that you can't fly the boats that far?" Zhan asked. "Perhaps we should ask His Majesty—"

"No," Jade said. His Majesty would probably not be of much more use than an infant now. She thought hard. Her mother had told her, far back in childhood, that a good part of her magic was from the foreign devil side of Jade's ancestry. Surely that would be enough to allow her to fly the Dragon Boats wherever she needed.

"Very well, then. How do we go about this?"

"I have drawn a map from my vision." From his sleeve, Zhan pulled a scroll which he opened, showing Jade where they were and where the carpetship would be when they reached it.

Jade looked at the vast expanse of undulating lines which she supposed signified the ocean in between and bit her lip, but said nothing.

"So, milady, do you think you can make the boats fly?"

"I'm sure I can. By the power of my brother, the Emperor." She glared at Zhan and swept past him, to the place where the Emperor stood while making the prayer that caused the boats to fly. It was a place on the deck, just outside the Emperor's quarters, looking out over the entire flotilla. "If you're sure we can take the carpetship?"

"That I am sure of. This ship is no stronger than the *Light of the Orient*. And your father and I took that easily just last month."

Jade did not dignify that with an answer. Instead, she stepped out onto the flat, polished deck. She could feel the courtiers assemble in a rough circle behind her, as they waited for her to make the boats fly.

She heard the conversations diminish from normal voices to whispers, and finally from whispers to a heavy silence. The news must have spread that she was using her brother's power. She could sense the doubt and confusion in all their minds. Those who knew of Wen's problem would doubt Wen's ability to wield any power, and those who didn't know of it would, of course, question Jade's ability to borrow that power.

Their doubt pricked at Jade's consciousness like thorns. In her mind, she said the prayer she'd heard her father say hundreds of times before, but nothing happened.

She folded her hands, her right hand covering the ring. Was she imagining it, or was the stone warm to her touch? She took a deep breath. Her father always said the prayer aloud. Perhaps she must do the same. But what if the prayer failed?

Jade choked back a laugh. It didn't matter. If Wen's power failed her, then neither of them would last long enough to worry about anything ever again. And the Dragon Boats would be Zhan's problem.

Taking a deep breath, she started reciting the prayer to the gods of wind and air, and to her ancestors. She begged them to take the Dragon Boats and bear them aloft, bend them to her commands.

After she finished, there was a long, expectant silence, then the whispers started again, behind her, in various tones of worry. Then, suddenly, the jewel caught fire. Warmth and light shone from it, displaying the bones of her fingers through her skin. She made a sound of surprise and removed her hand, and the red light of the jewel shone over the Dragon Boats. And then the boat rocked beneath her feet, rising slowly, like a bird taking wing.

With her ringed left hand, she pointed above and to the east, in the direction the boats were to take. And, as one, they rose, bright and tattered under the sun— Dragon Boats with their elaborately carved prows, their multicolored sails, their shabby decks, their multitudes of gaudily dressed dragon lords.

Jade cast a triumphant look at Zhan. Was she mistaken, or did he look a little disappointed?

But he also looked excited. And greedy. They would raid at his command, but if he thought Jade would be confined to the women's quarters as she normally was when everything started, he was out of his mind.

The twin jewels, with their power, were too rich a prize for the ambitious Zhan. No, this was one raid Jade herself would take part in. Her father had taught her to fight as well as the men her age. And though he hadn't encouraged her to go to battle, she was as capable as most. More capable then Wen. She would put on men's clothes and join the fray.

Zhan could not be trusted out of her sight. And she had no intention of letting the dragon throne be stolen.

SF 2008